Last Men
in London

Last Men in London

Olaf Stapledon

Bibliographical Note

This Dover edition, first published in 2011, is an unabridged republication of the work originally published by Methuen & Co., Ltd., London, in 1932.

Library of Congress Cataloging-in-Publication Data

Stapledon, Olaf, 1886–1950.
  Last men in London / Olaf Stapledon.
    p. cm.
  Unabridged republication of the work originally published by Methuen & Co. Ltd., London, in 1932.
  ISBN-13: 978-0-486-47601-8
  ISBN-10: 0-486-47601-1
  1. London (England)—Fiction. I. Title.
  PR6037.T18L37 2011
  823'.912—dc22
                                                                  2010050643

Dover Publications, Inc.
Mineola, New York

Bibliographical Note

This Dover edition, first published in 2011, is an unabridged republication of
the work originally published by Methuen & Co., Ltd., London, in 1932.

Library of Congress Cataloging-in-Publication Data

Stapledon, Olaf, 1886–1950.
    Last men in London / Olaf Stapledon.
        p. cm.
    "Unabridged republication of the work originally published by Methuen &
Co., Ltd., London, in 1932"—T.p. verso.
    ISBN-13: 978-0-486-47601-8
    ISBN-10: 0-486-47601-4
    1. London (England)—Fiction. I. Title.

PR6037.T18L38 2011
823'.912—dc22

2010050348

Manufactured in the United States by Courier Corporation
47601401
www.doverpublications.com

Contents

Contents

Preface

THOUGH this is a work of fiction, it does not pretend to be a novel. It has no hero but Man. Since its purpose is not the characterization of individual human beings, no effort has been made to endow its few persons with distinctive personalities. There is no plot, except the theme of man's struggle in this awkward age to master himself and to come to terms with the universe. This theme I seek to present by imagining that a member of a much more developed human species, living on Neptune two thousand million years hence, enters into our minds to observe the Terrestrial field through our eyes but with his own intelligence. Using one of us as a mouthpiece, he contrives to tell us something of his findings. The shortcomings of his report must be attributed to the limitations of his Terrestrial instrument.

This book is intelligible without reference to another fantasy, which I produced two years ago, and called *Last and First Men*. But readers of that earlier book will find that *Last Men in London* is complementary to it. In both, the same Neptunian being speaks, formerly to tell the story of man's career between our day and his, now to describe the spiritual drama which, he tells us, underlies the whole confused history of our species, and comes to its crisis today. The present book is supposed to be communicated from a date in Neptunian history later than the body of the earlier book, but before its epilogue.

The last section of the chapter on the War, though it makes use to some extent of personal experience, is none the less fiction.

It will be obvious to many readers that I have been influenced by the very suggestive work of Mr Gerald Heard. I hope he will forgive me for distorting some of his ideas for my own purpose.

My thanks are due once more to Mr E. V. Rieu for many valuable criticisms and suggestions; and to Professor and Mrs L. C. Martin (who read the untidy manuscript) for condemnation and encouragement without which the book would have been much worse than it is. Finally I would thank my wife both for hard labour, and for other help which she is apparently incapable of appreciating.

Let me remind the reader that henceforth and up to the opening of the Epilogue the speaker is a Neptunian man of the very remote future.

September 1932   W. O. S.

Introduction

The Future's Concern with the Past

MEN and women of Earth! Brief Terrestrials, of that moment when the First Human Species hung in the crest of its attainment, wavelike, poised for downfall, I a member of the last Human Species, address you for a second time from an age two thousand million years after your day, from an age as remotely future to you as the Earth's beginning is remotely past.

In my earlier communication I told of the huge flux of events between your day and mine. I told of the rise and fall of many mankinds, of the spirit's long desolations and brief splendours. I told how, again and again, after age-long sleep, man woke to see dimly what he should be doing with himself; how he strove accordingly to master his world and his own nature; and how, each time, circumstances or his own ignorance and impotence flung him back into darkness. I told how he struggled with invaders, and how he was driven from planet to planet, refashioning himself for each new world. I told, not only of his great vicissitudes, but also of the many and diverse modes of mind which he assumed in different epochs. I told how at length, through good fortune and skilled control, there was fashioned a more glorious mankind, the Eighteenth Human Species, my own. I hinted as best I might at the great richness and subtlety, the perfect harmony and felicity, of this last expression of the human spirit. I told of our discovery that our own fair planet must soon be destroyed with all the sun's offspring; and of our exultant acceptance even of this doom. I told of the final endeavours which the coming end imposes on us.

In this my second communication I shall say little of my own world, and less of the ages that lie between us. Instead I shall speak mostly of your world and of yourselves. I shall try to show you yourselves through the eyes of the Last Men. Of myself and my fellow-workers, I shall speak, but chiefly as the link between your world and mine, as pioneering explorers in your world, and secret dwellers in your minds. I shall tell of the difficulties and dangers of our strange exploration of ages that to us are past, and of our still stranger influence upon past minds. But mostly I shall speak of men and women living in Europe in your twentieth Christian century, and of a great crisis that we observe in

1

your world, a great opportunity which you tragically fail to grasp.

In relation to the long drama which I unfolded in my earlier communication it might well seem that even the most urgent and the most far-reaching events of your little sphere are utterly trivial. The rise and fall of your world-moving individuals, the flowering and withering of your nations, and all their blind, plant-like struggle for existence, the slow changes and sudden upheavals of your society, the archaic passions of your religious sects, and quick-changes of your fashionable thought, all seem, in relation to those aeons of history, no more than the ineffective gyrations of flotsam of the great river of humanity, whose direction is determined, not by any such superficial movements, but by the thrust of its own mass and the configuration of the terrain.

In the light of the stars what significance is there in such minute events as the defeat of an army, the issue of a political controversy, the success or failure of a book, the result of a football match? In that cold light even the downfall of a species is a matter of little importance. And the final extinction of man, after his two thousand million years of precarious blundering, is but the cessation of one brief tremulous theme in the great music of the cosmos.

Yet minute events have sometimes remarkable consequences. Again and again this was evident in the great story that I told. And now I am to describe events some of which, though momentary and minute in relation to the whole career of man, are yet in relation to yourselves long-drawn-out and big with destiny. In consequence of these momentary happenings, so near you, yet so obscure, man's career is fated to be the weary succession of disasters and incomplete victories which I described on an earlier occasion.

But the account of these events, though it is in some sense the main theme of this book, is not its sole, not even its chief purpose. I shall say much of your baseness, much of your futility. But all that I say, if I say it well, and if the mind that I have chosen for my mouthpiece serves me adequately, shall be kindled with a sense of that beauty which, in spite of all your follies and treasons, is yours uniquely. For though the whole career of your species is so confused and barren, and though, against the background of the rise and fall of species after species and the destruction of world after world, the life of any individual among you, even the most glorious, seems so completely ineffective and insignificant, yet, in the least member of your or any other species, there lies for the discerning eye a beauty peculiar not only to that one species but to that one individual.

To us the human dawn is precious for its own sake. And it is as creatures of the dawn that we regard you, even in your highest achievement. To us the early human natures and every primitive human individual have a beauty which we ourselves, in spite of all our triumphs, have not; the beauty namely of life's first bewildered venturing upon the wings of the spirit, the beauty of the child with all its innocent brutishness and cruelty. We understand the past better than it can understand itself, and love it better than it can love itself. Seeing it in relation to all things, we see it as it is; and so we can observe even its follies and treasons with reverence, knowing that we ourselves would have behaved so, had we been so placed and so fashioned. The achievements of the past, however precarious and evanescent, we salute with respect, knowing well that to achieve anything at all in such circumstances and with such a nature entailed a faith and fortitude which in those days were miracles. We are therefore moved by filial piety to observe all the past races of men, and if possible every single individual life, with careful precision, so that, before we are destroyed, we may crown those races our equals in glory though not in achievement. Thus we shall contribute to the cosmos a beauty which it would otherwise lack, namely the critical yet admiring love which we bear toward you.

But it is not only as observers that we, who are of man's evening, are concerned with you, children of the dawn. In my earlier message I told how the future might actually influence the past, how beings such as my contemporaries, who have in some degree the freedom of eternity, may from their footing in eternity, reach into past minds and contribute to their experience. For whatever is truly eternal is present equally in all times; and so we, in so far as we are capable of eternity, are influences present in your age. I said that we seek out all those points in past history where our help is entailed for the fulfilment of the past's own nature, and that this work of inspiration has become one of our main tasks. How this can be, I shall explain more fully later. Strange it is indeed that we, who are so closely occupied with the great adventure of racial experience, so closely also with preparations to face the impending ruin of our world, and with research for dissemination of a seed of life in remote regions of the galaxy, should yet also find ourselves under obligation toward the vanished and unalterable past.

No influence of ours can save your species from destruction. Nothing could save it but a profound change in your own nature; and that cannot be. Wandering among you, we move always with fore-knowledge of the doom which your own imperfection imposes on you. Even if we could, we would not change it; for it is a theme required in the strange music of the spheres.

I *The World of the Last Men*

1. HOLIDAY ON NEPTUNE

WHEN I am in your world and your epoch I remember often a certain lonely place in my own world, and in the time that I call present. It is a corner where the land juts out into the sea as a confusion of split rocks, like a herd of monsters crowding into the water. Subterranean forces acting at this point once buckled the planet's crust into a mountain; but it was immediately torn and shattered by gravity, that implacable djin of all great worlds. Nothing is now left of it but these rocks. On Neptune we have no mountains, and the oceans are waveless. The stout sphere holds its watery cloak so tightly to it that even the most violent hurricanes fail to raise more than a ripple.

Scattered among these rocks lies a network of tiny fjords, whose walls and floors are embossed with variegated life. There you may see beneath the crystal water all manner of blobs and knobs and brilliant whorls, all manner of gaudy flowers, that search with their petals, or rhythmically smack their lips, all manner of clotted sea-weeds, green, brown, purple or crimson, from whose depths sometimes a claw reaches after a drowsing sprat, while here and there a worm, fringed with legs, emerges to explore the sandy sunlit bottom.

Among these rocks and fjords I spent my last day of leisure before setting out on one of those lengthy explorations of the past which have made me almost as familiar with your world as with my own. It is my task to tell you of your own race as it appears through the eyes of the far future; but first I must help you to reconstruct in imagination something of the future itself, and of the world from which we regard you. This I can best achieve by describing, first that day of delight, spent where the broken mountain sprawls into the sea, and then a more august event, namely the brief awakening of the Racial Mind, which was appointed for the exaltation of the explorers upon the eve of their departure into the obscure recesses of past aeons. Finally I shall tell you something of my own upbringing and career.

Almost the first moments of that day of recreation afforded me one of those pictures which haunt the memory ever after. The sun had risen over a burning ocean. He was not, as you might expect in our remote world, a small and feeble sun; for between your age and ours a collision had increased his bulk and splendour to a magnitude somewhat greater than that with which you are familiar.

Overhead the sky was blue. But for Neptunian eyes its deep azure was infused with another unique primary colour, which your vision could not have detected. Toward the sunrise, this tincture of the zenith gave place to green, gold, fire-red, purple, and yet another of the hues which elude the primitive eye. Opposite there lay darkness. But low in the darkness gleamed something which you would have taken for a very distant snowy horn, whose base was lost in night, though its crest glowed orange in the morning. A second glance would have revealed it as too precipitous and too geometrical for any mountain. It was in fact one of our great public buildings, many scores of miles distant, and nearly one score in height. In a world where mountains are crushed by their own weight these towering edifices could not stand, were it not for their incredibly rigid materials, wherein artificial atoms play the chief part. The huge crag of masonry now visible was relatively new, but it could compare in age with the younger of your terrestrial mountains.

The shadowed sides of its buttresses and gables, and also the shadowed faces of the near rocks and of every stone, glowed with a purple bloom, the light from a blinding violet star. This portent we call the Mad Star. It is a unique heavenly body, whose energies are being squandered with inconceivable haste, so that it will soon be burnt out. Meanwhile it is already infecting its neighbours with its plague. In a few thousand years our own sun will inevitably run amok in the same manner, and turn all his planets to white-hot gas. But at present, I mean in the age which I call present, the Mad Star is only a brilliant feature of our night sky.

On the morning of which I am speaking there lay full length on

6

the brink of a little cliff, and gazing into the pool beneath her, a woman of my world. To me she is lovely, exquisite, the very embodiment of beauty; to you she would seem a strange half-human monster. To me, as she lay there with her breasts against the rock and one arm reaching down into the water, her whole form expressed the lightness and suppleness of a panther. To you she would have seemed unwieldy, elephantine, and grotesque in every feature. Yet if you were to see her moving in her own world, you would know, I think, why her name in our speech is the equivalent of Panther in yours.

If you or any of your kind were to visit our world, and if by miracle you were to survive for a few moments in our alien atmosphere, gravity would make it almost impossible for you to support yourselves at all. But we, since our bones, like our buildings, are formed largely of artificial atoms, and are far more rigid than steel, since moreover our muscle cells have been most cunningly designed, can run and jump with ease. It is true, however, that in spite of our splendid tissues we have to be more solidly built than the Terrestrials, whose limbs remind us unpleasantly of insects.

The woman on the rock would certainly have surprised you, for she is a member of one of our most recent generations, whose skin and flesh are darkly translucent. Seeing her there, with the sunlight drenching her limbs, you might have taken her for a statue, cut from some wine-dark alabaster, or from carbuncle; save that, with every movement of her arm, sunken gleams of crimson, topaz, and gold-brown rippled the inner night of her shoulder and flank. Her whole substance, within its lovely curves and planes, looked scarcely solid, but rather a volume of obscure flame and smoke poised on the rock. On her head a mass of hair, flame-like, smoke-like, was a reversion to the primitive in respect of which she could never decide whether it was a thing for shame or complacency. It was this pre-historic decoration which first drew me toward her. In a closer view you would have noticed that on her back and the outer sides of her limbs the skin's translucency was complicated by a very faint leopard-like mottling. I also bear that mottling; but I am of the sort whose flesh is opaque, and my bronze-green skin is of a texture somewhat harsher than I should choose. In her, how well I know it, the skin is soft and rich to the exploring hand.

While I watched her, she raised her face from studying the water-dwellers, and looked at me, laughing. It was that look which gave me the brief but strangely significant experience the memory of which was to refresh me so often in your uncouth world. It was not only that her face was lit up with merriment and tenderness; but in that fleeting expression the very spirit of humanity seemed to regard me. I cannot make you realize the potency of that glance, for the faces of your own kind afford almost no hint of such illumination. I can only assert that in our species, facial expression is more developed than in yours. The facial muscles respond to every changing flicker of experience and emotion, as pools respond to every breath of wind with a thousand criss-cross rippling tremors.

The face that now looked at me was unlike terrestrial countenances both in its subtly alien contours and in its dark translucency, which half-revealed the underlying paleness of bone. It was like a stirred and dancing pool of dark but warm-tinted wine, in which the sunlight revelled. But the eyes were bright jewels capable of many phases from sapphire to emerald.

Like others of our kind, this girl bore two additional bright eyes in the back of her head. They sparkled quaintly in the archaic glory of her hair. Like the rest of us, she had on her crown yet another and more important organ of vision which we call the astronomical eye. Normally sunken level with her hair, it could at will be projected upwards like a squat telescope. The exquisite development of this organ in her had determined her career. All of us are in a manner astronomers; but she is an astronomer by profession.

Her whole face, though so brilliantly alive, was unlike any human type known to readers of this book, since it was so much more animal. Her nose was broad and feline, but delicately moulded. Her full lips were subtle at the corners. Her ears moved among her locks like the ears of a lion.

Grotesque, you say, inhuman! No! Beside this the opaque and sluggish faces of your proudest beauties are little better than lumps of clay, or the masks of insects.

But indeed it is impossible for you to see her as I saw her then.

For in that look there seemed to find expression the whole achievement of our race, and the full knowledge of its impending tragedy. At the same time there was in it a half-mischievous piety toward the little simple creatures that she had been watching, and equally, it seemed, toward the stars and man himself.

Smiling, she now spoke to me; if I may call 'speech' the telepathic influence which invaded my brain from hers.

That you may understand the significance of her words, I must explain that in our Neptunian rock-pools there are living things of three very different stocks. The first is rare. One may encounter in some sheltered cranny a vague greenish slime. This is the only relic of primeval Neptunian life, long since outclassed by invaders. The second stock is by far the commonest throughout our world. Nearly all our living types are triumphant descendants of the few animals and plants which men brought, deliberately or by accident, to Neptune from Venus, nearly a thousand million years before my day, and almost as long after the age that you call present. Third, there are also, even in these little fjords, a few descendants of those ancient men themselves. These very remote cousins of my own human species are, of course, fantastically degenerate. Most have long ago ceased to be recognizably human; but in one, whose name in our language you might translate 'Homunculus', nature has achieved a minute and exquisite caricature of humanity. Two splay feet glue him to the rock. From these rises an erect and bulbous belly, wearing on its summit an upturned face. The unpleasantly human mouth keeps opening and shutting. The eyes are mere wrinkles, the nose a wide double trumpet. The ears, deaf but mobile, have become two broad waving fans, that direct a current of water toward the mouth. Beneath each ear is a little wart-like excrescence, all that is left of the human arm and hand.

One of these degenerate human beings, one of these fallen descendants of your own kind, had attracted my companion's attention. Laughing, she said, 'Little Homunculus has got wind of his mate, and he can't unstick his feet to go after her. What a pilgrimage it will be for him after a whole month of standing still!'

She looked down again and cried, 'Quick! Come and see! He's loose, he's moved an inch. He's waddling at breakneck speed.

Now he's got her, and she's willing.' After a pause she exclaimed, 'What a world this pond is! Like the world that you are to plunge into so soon.'

Then she looked up at the fierce star, and the light in her face changed and chilled. She became like your Egyptian Sphinx, which looks across the desert and waits, for something unknown and terrible, but the appointed end.

Suddenly she laughed, sprang to her feet, ran down the rock-edge to the sea, and dived. I followed; and the rest of the morning we spent swimming, either far out in the bay or among the islets and fjords, chasing each other sometimes through submarine rock-arches, or clinging to a sunken tussock of weed to watch some drama of the sea-bottom.

At last, when the sun was high, we returned to the grassy place where we had slept, and took from the pockets of our flying-suits our meal of rich sun-products. Of these, some had been prepared in the photo-synthesis stations on Jupiter, others came from the colonies on Uranus; but we ourselves had gathered the delicacies in our own orchards and gardens.

Having eaten, we lay back on the grass and talked of matters great and small.

I challenged her: 'This has been the best of all our matings.' 'Yes,' she answered, 'because the shortest? Because after the richest experience in separation. And perhaps because of the Star.'

'In spite of all your lovers,' I exulted, 'you come back to me. In spite of your tigers, your bulls, and all your lap-dog lovers, where you squander yourself.'

'Yes, old python, I come back to you, the richer for that squandering. And you in spite of all the primroses and violets and blowsy roses and over-scented lilies that you have plucked and dropped, you come back to me, after your thousand years of roaming.'

'Again and again I shall come back, if I escape from the Terrestrials, and if the Star permits.'

Our conversation, let me repeat, was telepathic. If I were to report all that passed from mind to mind as we lay in the sun that afternoon, I should fill a book; for telepathic communication is incomparably swifter and more subtle than vocal speech. We ranged over all manner of subjects, from the difference between her eyes and mine, which are crimson, to the awakening of the Racial Mind, which we had experienced some thousands of years earlier, and were so soon to experience again. We talked also about the marriage groups to which we severally belonged, and of our own strange irregular yet seemingly permanent union outside our respective groups. We talked about the perplexing but lovely nature of our son, whom she had been allowed to conceive at our last meeting. We spoke also of her work in one of the great observatories. With other astronomers she was trying to discover in some distant region of our galaxy a possible home for the human seed which, it was hoped, would be scattered among the stars before man's destruction. We spoke also of the work on which I am engaged as one of the million specialists who are trying to complete the exploration of the human past by direct participation in it. Inevitably we spoke also of the Star, and of the coming destruction of our world; and of how, if we were both alive in that age we would cling together.

Before sundown we clambered over the rocks and ran inland over the flower-strewn turf. But at last we returned to our grassy nest; and after supper, when darkness had fallen, we were moved to sing, together or each in turn. Sometimes our choice fell upon the latest, wildest, scintillations of rhythm and melody, sometimes on the old songs of her nation or mine, sometimes on the crude chants which we explorers had discovered among the ancient peoples and in extinct worlds. In particular I taught her a Terrestrial song which I myself had found. With difficulty we formed the uncouth syllables and caught the lilt. With difficulty we called up in imagination the dark confusion that gave it birth, the harshness of man to man, and the yearning for a better world. Readers of this book may know the song. *Old Man River* is its name.

While we were still striving with this archaic melody, the colours of the sunset gave place to the profound azure which the Neptunian sky assumes by night for Neptunian eyes. Stars began to appear, first singly and faintly, then in companies and brightly patterned constellations. The wide heaven flashed with them. The Milky Way, flung from horizon to horizon, revealed itself to us, not as a pale cloud-zone, but as an incredibly multitudinous host of lights. Here and there our astronomical eyes could detect even those misty points which are in fact the remote universes. Our singing was now hushed into a murmuring and wordless chant; for this comparatively simple yet overwhelmingly significant percept of the night sky commands us all with a power which might seem to you extravagant. It is, as it were, the visible epitome of our whole thought and feeling. It has for us more than the potency of your most venerated religious symbols. It stirs not only the surface of our being but the ancestral depths, and yet it is relevant to the most modern ventures of our intellect.

While we were still saluting with our voices and our spirits this august and never-too-familiar presentation, the Mad Star rose once more, and scattered its cold steel across the sea. We fell silent, watching. Its dread effulgence extinguished the constellations.

Whether it was the influence of those barbarian melodies that we had been savouring, or a mere flaw in my nature, I know not; but suddenly I heard myself cry out, 'Hideous! That such a world as ours should be burnt, wasted such a world of spirit and sweet flesh!'

She looked quickly in my eyes, with amazed laughter thrusting down dismay. But before she could speak I saw rightly again. 'No!' I said, 'not hideous, but terrible. Strange, how our thoughts can slip back for a moment into the bad old ways, as though we were to lose sight of the great beauty, and be like the blind spirits of the past.'

And she, 'When the end begins, shall we still see the great beauty? Shall we see it even in the fire?'

And I, 'Who knows? But we see it now.'

Silently we watched the Star climb with increasing splendour of violet and ultra-violet illumination. But at last we lay down together in our sheltered grassy nest, and took intimate delight in one another.

At dawn we rose. After a short swim, we put on our flying-suits, those overalls studded with minute sources of sub-atomic energy on the soles of the feet, the palms of the hands, and the whole front surface of the body. It is with these that all lesser flights are performed in our world; and as the action entails much skill and some muscular exertion, it is a delight in itself. Side by side we climbed the air, until the coast was like a map beneath us. We headed inland, first over a wide tract of rock and prairie, marsh and scrub, then over corn and orchard, sprinkled with innumerable homes. Once we passed near a great building, whose crystal precipices towered over us with snow on their cornices. A white cloud covered its upper parts, save for one slender pinnacle, which tiptoed into the sunlight. Sometimes a flying-boat would detach itself from the walls or emerge from the cloud. As we travelled over more densely inhabited regions, sprinkled somewhat more closely with private houses and cottages, a more numerous swarm of these flying-boats continually passed over our heads in all directions from horizon to horizon at so great a speed that they seemed darting insects. We encountered also many fliers like ourselves. Many we saw beneath us, moving from house to house across the intervening tillage. At one point an arm of the sea lay across our route; and there we saw, entering dock, a five-mile long ether-ship, lately returned from Jupiter or Uranus with a cargo of foodstuffs. She was a great fish of stainless metal, studded with windows over her back and flanks. Hidden under water also there would be windows; for this seemingly marine monster could rise like a cormorant, with a great churning of the ocean, to find herself within a few minutes surrounded above and below by stars.

At noon we reached another wild district, and took our meal near a warren of creatures which I can best describe as Neptunian rabbits. The form of these furry descendants of an extinct human species was chiefly determined, as so often with our fauna, by gravity. For support they use, not only their short thick legs, but also their leathern bellies and tails. No sooner had we sat down to eat than these mammalian lizards crowded round us in the hope of titbits. One of them actually made off with a loaf; but before he could reach his earth I captured him, and administered such punishment that henceforth the whole tribe treated us with more respect.

When our meal was over, we took leave of one another. It was a gay, grave parting; for we knew that we might not meet again for thousands of years, perhaps not before the sun, infected by the Mad Star, should already have begun the destruction of our beloved

13

world. When we had looked in one another's eyes for a long moment, we buckled on our flying-suits once more; then, in opposite directions, we climbed the air. By dawn next day we had to be at our appointed stations, far asunder on the great planet's surface, to participate in the Racial Awakening, the sublime event to which every adult person on the planet must needs contribute.

2. MEN AND MAN

When an attempt is to be made to call the Race Mind into being, all adult persons on the planet seek their allotted places near one or other of a number of great towers which are scattered throughout the continents. After a preparatory phase, in which much telepathic intercourse occurs between individuals and between the group minds of various orders which now begin to emerge, there comes a supreme moment, when, if all goes well, every man and woman in the world-wide multitude of multitudes awakes, as it were, to become the single Mind of the Race, possessing the million bodies of all men and women as a man's mind possesses the multitude of his body's cells.

Had you been privileged to watch from the summit of the great needle of masonry round which I and so many others had gathered on that morning, you would have seen far below, at the foot of the twenty-mile high architectural precipice, and stretching to the horizon in every direction, a featureless grey plain, apparently a desert. Had you then used a powerful field-glass, you would have discovered that the plain was in fact minutely stippled with microscopic dots of brown, separated by almost invisible traces of green. Had you then availed yourself of a much more powerful telescope, you would have found, with amazement, that each of these brown dots was in fact a group of persons. The whole plain would have been revealed as no mere desert, but a prodigious host of men and women, gathered into little companies between which the green grass showed. The whole texture of the earth would have appeared almost like some vegetable tissue seen through the microscope, or the cellular flesh of Leviathan. Within each cell you might have counted ninety-

14

six granules, ninety-six minute sub-cellular organs, in fact ninety-six faces of men and women. Of these small marriage groups which are the basis of our society, I have spoken elsewhere, and shall say no more now. Suffice it that you would have found each dot to be not a face, but a group of faces. Everywhere you would have seen faces turned towards the tower, and motionless as grains of sand. Yet this host was one of thousands such, scattered over all the continents.

A still more powerful telescope would have shown that we were all standing, each with a doffed flying-suit hanging over an arm or shoulder. As you moved the telescope hither and thither you would have discovered our great diversity. For though we are all of one species, it is a species far more variable even than your domestic dog; and our minds are no less diverse than our bodies. Nearly all of us, you would have noted, were unclad; but a few were covered with their own velvet fur. The great majority of the Last Men, however, are hairless, their skins brown, or gold, or black, or grey, or striped, or mottled. Though you would recognize our bodies as definitely human, you would at the same time be startled by the diversity of their forms, and by their manifold aberrations from what you regard as the true human type. You would notice in our faces and in the moulding of our limbs a strong suggestion of animal forms; as though here a horse, there a tiger, and there some ancient reptile, had been inspired with a human mind in such a manner that, though now definitely man or woman, it remained reminiscent of its animal past. You would be revolted by this animal character of ours. But we, who are so securely human, need not shrink from being animal too. In you, humanity is precarious; and so, in dread and in shame, you kill the animal in you. And its slaughter poisons you.

Your wandering telescope would have revealed us as one and all in the late spring or full summer of life. Infants had been left behind for the day in the automatic crêches; children were at large in their own houses; the youths and girls were living their wild romantic lives in the Land of the Young. And though the average age of the host gathered below you was many thousands of years, not one of its members would have appeared to you aged. Senility is unknown among us.

15

Regarding us in the mass, you would have found it hard to believe that each human atom beneath you was in reality a unique and highly developed person, who would judge the immature personality of your own species as you judge your half-human progenitors. Careful use of the telescope, however, would have revealed the light of intense and unique consciousness in every face. For every member of this great host had his peculiar and subtle character, his rich memories, his loves and aims, and his special contribution to our incredibly complex society. Farmers and gardeners, engineers and architects, chemists and sub-atomic physicists, biologists, psychologists and eugenists, stood together with creative artists of many kinds, with astronomers, philosophers, historians, explorers of the past, teachers, professional mothers, and many more whose work has no counterpart in your world. There would be also, beside the more permanent denizens of Neptune, a sprinkling of ethereal navigators, whose vessels happened to be on the home-planet, and even a few pioneers from the settlements on Uranus and Pluto. The ethereal navigators who ply between the planets are our only transport-workers. Passenger traffic on the home-planet takes place entirely in private air-boats or flying-suits. Freight travels automatically in subterranean tubes, some of which, suitably refrigerated, take direct routes almost through the heart of the planet. Industry and commerce, such as you know, have no representatives among us, for in our world there is nothing like your industrial system. Our industry has neither operatives nor magnates. In so far as manufacture is a routine process, it is performed by machinery which needs no human influence but the pressing of a button. In so far as it involves innovation, it is the work of scientists and engineers. In so far as it involves organization, it is controlled by the professional organizers. As for commerce, we have no such thing, because we have no buying and no selling. Both production and distribution are regulated by the organizers, working under the Supreme College of Unity. This is in no sense a governing body, since its work is purely advisory; but owing to our constant telepathic intercourse, its recommendations are always sane, and always persuasive. Consequently, though it has no powers of compulsion, it is the great co-ordinator of our whole communal life. In the crowd

16

beneath you many members of this Supreme College would be present; but nothing would distinguish them from members of the other and equally honourable professions.

If you had watched us for long enough, you would have noticed, after some hours of stillness, a shimmering change in the grey plain, a universal stirring, which occurred at the moment of the awakening of the Racial Mind throughout the whole population of the planet. The telescope would have revealed that all the faces, formerly placid, were suddenly illuminated with an expression of tense concentration and triumph. For now at last each one of us was in the act of emerging into the higher self-hood, to find himself the single and all-embracing mind of a world.

At that moment, I, Man, perceived, not merely the multitudinous several perceptions of all men and women on the face of the planet, but the single significance of all those perceptions. Through the feet of all individuals I grasped my planet, as a man may hold a ball in his hand. Possessing all the memories of all men and women, not merely as memory but as direct experience of the present, I perceived the whole biography of my generation, nay, of my species, as you perceive a melody, in flux yet all of it 'now'. I perceived the planets whirling round the sun, and even the fixed stars creeping about the sky like insects. But also at will I perceived movements within the atoms, and counted the pulsations of light waves. I possessed also all the emotions and desires of all men and women. I observed them inwardly, as a man may introspect his own delighting and grieving; but I observed them dispassionately. I was present in the loving of all lovers, and the adventuring of all who dare. I savoured all victories and defeats, all imaginings and reasonings. But from all these teeming experiences of my tiny members I held myself in detachment, turning my attention to a sphere remote from these, where I, Man, experienced my own grave desires and fears, and pursued my own high reasoning and contemplation. Of what it was that then occupied me, the Mind of the Race, it is impossible for me, the little individual who is now communicating with you, to say anything definite. For these experiences lie beyond the understanding of any individual. But this at least may be said. Waking into this lofty experience, and looking down upon my individual members as a man may regard the

17

cells of his flesh, I was impressed far more by my littleness than by my greatness. For in relation to the whole of things I saw myself to be a very minute, simple, and helpless being, doomed to swift destruction by the operation of a stellar event whose meaning remained unintelligible to me, even upon my new and lofty plain of understanding. But even the little individual who is now communicating with you can remember that, when I, Man, faced this doom, I was in no manner dismayed by it. I accepted it with exultation, as an evident beauty within the great beauty of the whole. For my whole experience was transfused and glorified by the perception of that all-embracing and terrible beauty. Even on that loftier plane of my being I did but glimpse it; but what I glimpsed I contemplated with an insight and a rapture impossible in my lowlier mode of being.

Had you remained upon the tower until the following morning, you would have seen, shortly after sunrise, the whole plain stir again. We were preparing to go. Presently it would have seemed to you that the surface of the planet was detaching itself and rising, like dust on a wind-swept road, or steam from hot water, or like a valley cloud seen from a mountain-top, and visibly boiling upwards. Higher and higher it would have risen toward you, presently to resolve itself even for the naked eye into a vast smoke of individual men and women. Soon you would have seen them all around you and above you, swimming in the air with outspread arms, circling, soaring, darkening the sky. After a brief spell of random and ecstatic flight, they would have been observed streaming away in all directions to become a mere haze along the horizon. Looking down, you would now have seen that the grey plain had turned to green, fading in the distance into blues and purples.

The dispersal of the gatherings does not put an end to the racial experience. For an indefinite period of months or years each individual, though he goes his own way, living his own life and fulfilling his special function in the community, remains none the less possessed by the race mind. Each perceives, thinks, strives as an individual; but also he is Man, perceiving racially, and thinking in manners wholly impossible in the humbler mode of being. As each cell in a brain lives its own life, yet participates in the experience of the whole brain, so we. But after a while the great being sleeps again.

After the awakening which I have just described the racial mentality endured for many years; but one class of individuals had perforce to refrain from any further participation in it, namely those who were to engage upon exploration of the past. For this work it is necessary, for reasons which I shall explain later, to cut off all telepathic communication with one's fellows, and consequently to leave the telepathic system in which the Race Mind inheres. Yet it was expressly to further our work that this particular awakening had been ordained. It was to strengthen us for our adventures. For my part, as I hastened first to my home and thence through the upper air in my flying-boat toward the Arctic, I felt that I had been kindled with an inextinguishable flame; and that though I must henceforth be exiled from the lofty experience of the Race Mind, I had acquired a new fervour and clarity of vision, which would enable me to observe your world with finer insight than on my earlier visits.

3. BIOGRAPHICAL NOTE

At this point it seems desirable to say a few words about myself, so that you may have some idea of the kind of being who is communicating with you, and the angle from which he is regarding you.

I am at present twenty thousand years old according to your Terrestrial reckoning, and therefore I am still in the spring-time of my life. My parents were chosen for me. They had long been intimate with one another, but the call to have a child arose from the knowledge that there was need of such a being as they together could produce. Recent improvements in man's powers of entering into past minds, together with the new urgency for completing the exploration of the past before our own world should be destroyed, had increased the call for past-explorers. For such a career I was destined even before I was conceived; and while I was still in the womb, the eugenists were still influencing me so as to give me novel powers.

During infancy I remained with my mother. Throughout my life I have retained a closer intimacy with her than is common in my world; for with her tenderness and strange innocent ruthlessness she embodies for me the very spirit of the past and the primitive. And these have enthralled me always. Not that in your eyes she would have seemed primitive; but underlying all her reasonableness and sophistication I detect that savage temperament which, perhaps partly because of my own extreme sophistication, I so enjoy in others.

I spent my thousand years of childhood in the manner characteristic of my race. Mostly I lived in a children's residential club. We managed it with more dash than efficiency; but in intervals between domestic duties, games, quarrels and sentimental attachments, we managed to lay the foundations of our education. Even at this early stage my predisposition toward the primitive and the past was beginning to wake. While others were making toy etherships and model planetary systems, I was digging for fossils, haunting museums, brooding on ancient folklore, and writing histories of imaginary past worlds. In all my recreations and in all my studies this interest was ever apt to insinuate itself.

My second thousand years was spent, as is customary with us, in the reserved continent called the Land of the Young. There our young people sow their wild oats by living as savages and barbarians. During this phase they are definitely juvenile in disposition. They appreciate only such barbarian virtues as were admired even by the most primitive human species. They are capable of loyalty, but only by an uneasy and heroic victory over self-regard. Their loyalties are never easeful, for they have not yet developed the self-detachment of the adult. Further, they care only for the beauties of triumphant individual life. The supernal beauties of the cosmos, which form the main preoccupation of grown men and women, are hidden from these young things. Consequently our adult world lies very largely beyond their comprehension.

For some centuries I gave myself wholly to a 'Red Indian' life, becoming a master of the bow and arrow, and a really brilliant tracker. I remember too that I fell in love with a dangerous young Amazon with golden hair. My first encounter with her was warlike. She escaped, but left her javelin in my shoulder, and her presence in my heart. Long afterwards, when we were both in the adult world, I met her again. She had by now entered upon her career, having been chosen as one of our professional mothers.

Later still, she volunteered to submit to a very dangerous maternity experiment, and was so shattered by it, that the eugenists had finally to put her to death.

I had not been many centuries in the Land of the Young before my master passion began to assert itself. I set about collecting material for a complete history of that juvenile world. For this end I sampled every kind of life in every corner of the continent. I also sharpened my perception, or so I persuaded myself, by intimacy with many resplendent young women. But long before I had completed my history, the work began to be interrupted by visits to the adult world.

There is a party in the Land of the Young who preach that the juvenile world is happier and nobler than the world of the adults. They send missionaries among those whom they know to be turning from the primitive, and seek to persuade them to join a small and pathetic band called the Old Young, who elect to remain in the Land of the Young for ever. These poor arrested beings become the guardians of tradition and morality among the nations of the Young. Like the village idiot, they are despised even while at the same time their sayings are supposed to be pregnant with mysterious truth. I myself, with my taste for the past and the primitive, was persuaded to take the vow of this order. But when I was introduced to one of these bright old things, I was so depressed that I recanted. It came as a revelation to me that my task was not actually to become primitive, but to study the primitive. It was borne in on me that even the past and the primitive can be understood and loved better by the full-grown mind than by the primitive itself.

During their last century in the Land of the Young our boys and girls normally develop beyond the larval stage very rapidly, though not without severe mental agony. For during this period the mind is in bitter conflict with itself. It clings to the primitive, but is at the same time nauseated; it yearns toward the mature, but is at the same time fearful and reluctant. This profound metamorphosis of body and mind continues for some centuries even after the young person has entered the adult world. The simple male or female sexual characters specialize themselves into one or other of the ninety-six sub-sexes. Intelligence soars into a new order of proficiency. New centres of the brain integrate the nervous system so

21

perfectly that henceforth behaviour will be, without exception, and without serious struggle, rational; or, as you would say, moral. At the same time the faculty of telepathic communication appears; and, through the cumulative effect of constant telepathic intercourse, the mind comes into such exact understanding and vivid sympathy with other minds, that the diversity of all serves but to enhance the mental richness of each.

This radical change of nature, which raises the individual in a few centuries to a new plane of experience, was for me the more torturing because of my innate hunger for the primitive. This same characteristic made it difficult for me to reconcile myself to the highly complex adult sexual life of my species, which is based on the marriage group of the ninety-six sub-sexes. My group formed itself with unusual difficulty; but, once constituted, it was maintained without undue emphasis. Only once in a century or so are we moved to come together, and live together, and love together; and then only for about a year. During these periods we take delicate joy in one another, and in ourselves. And though we remain self-conscious individuals, a single group-self emerges in us. We spend much of our time rapt in the perceptions and thoughts which are possible only to the minds of the sexual groups; brooding especially on the subtleties of personality and super-personality, and preparing the ground for the recurrent phases of that far more complex mode of consciousness, the Mind of the Race. Apart from these occasional periods of group-mentality, each of us lives an independent life, and is only obscurely conscious of his group-membership. Nevertheless, much as, after swimming, a freshness may vaguely cheer the body for the rest of the day, or after sun-bathing a tingling beatitude, so for each of us participation in the group affords an enhanced vitality which may endure for many decades.

When I had settled into my sexual group, I was about three thousand years old. My body had attained that youthful maturity which with us is perennial, and my mind had shed all the follies of the Land of the Young. I was apprenticed to work which was perfectly suited to my nature. It was exacting work, for the novel powers with which I was endowed were as yet imperfectly understood. But my working hours would have seemed ridiculously short even in your most ardent trade-unionists. Only for a few years in every century was my mind actually absent from the contemporary world. Only for a decade or two would I devote my mornings to formulating the results of my research. Though inevitably the past, and my study of the past, would be nearly always in my thoughts, the great bulk of my time was occupied with other activities. For decade after decade I would merely watch the manifold operations of our great community, wandering into all countries, seeking intimacy with all sorts of persons, peering through microscopes and astronomical instruments, watching the birth of inventions in other minds, studying the eugenists' plans for new generations, or the latest improvements in etherial navigation. Much of my time was spent in ether-ships, much in the Uranian colonies, much in the interior of the mine-honeycombed Pluto. Sometimes I would go as a guest into the Land of the Young to spend years in comparing our own young things with the primitive races of the past. Occasionally I have been chiefly concerned for a decade at a time with the appreciation or practice of some creative art, most often with our supreme art, which I must reluctantly call 'telepathic verse'. Somewhat as auditory verse uses sound, this most subtle of all arts uses our direct sensitivity to ethereal vibrations for the evocation of rhythms and patterns of sensory images and ideas. Sometimes, on the other hand, I have been absorbed in some special problem of natural science, and have done little but follow the experiments of scientific workers. Much of my time, of course, has been given to cosmology, and much to metaphysics; for in my world these subjects compel the attention of every man and woman. Sometimes for a year or so I would do little but rebuild my house or cultivate my garden; or I would become wholly absorbed in the invention or construction of some toy for a child friend. Sometimes my main preoccupation for several years has been intimacy with some woman, of my own nation or another. It must be confessed that I am more disposed to this kind of refreshment than most of my fellows. But I do not regret it. In these many brief lyrical matings of body and mind I seem to experience in a very special manner that which unites the developed and the primitive. Now and then, like most of my fellows, I spend a decade or so in lonely wandering, giving myself wholly to the sensuous and instinctive life. It was on one of these occasions that I first met the translucent woman whom I have called Panther. Many have I loved; but with her, whom I meet only in the wilderness, I have a very special relation. For whereas my spirit turns ever to the past, hers turns to the future; and each without the other is an empty thing.

This great freedom and variety of life, and this preponderance of leisure over work, are characteristic of my world. The engineer, the chemist, even the agriculturist and the ethereal navigator, spend less time at their own special tasks than in watching the lives of others. Indeed it is only by means of this system of mutual observation, augmented by our constant telepathic intercourse, that we can preserve that understanding of one another which is the life-blood of our community. In your world this perfect accord of minds is impossible. Yet your differences of racial temperament and of acquired bias are as nothing beside the vast diversity of innate disposition which is at once our constant danger and our chief strength.

From the time when I had reached full maturity of mind, and had become expert in my special calling, up to my present age of twenty thousand years, my life has been even, though eventful. I have of course had my difficulties and anxieties, my griefs and my triumphs. I lost my two closest friends in an ether-ship disaster. Another friend, younger than myself, has developed in such a strange manner that, though I do my best to understand him telepathically, I cannot but feel that he is seriously abnormal, and will sooner or later either come to grief or achieve some novel splendour. This has been my most serious anxiety apart from my work.

Work has been by far the most important factor in my life. Peculiarly gifted by inheritance, I have co-operated with the equally gifted fellow-workers of my generation to raise the art of past-exploration to a new range of power. My novitiate was spent in studying one of the earlier Neptunian civilizations. Since then I have acquired considerable first-hand knowledge of every one of the eighteen human species. In addition I have specialized in some detail on the Venetian Flying Men and the Last Terrestrials. But the great bulk of my work has been done among the First Men, and upon the particular crisis which you call present.

Apart from the exigencies of my work, two events have produced profound changes in my life; but they were events of public rather than private significance, and have affected the whole race with equal urgency. One was the first occasion on which we awakened into the racial mentality. The other was the discovery of the Mad Star, and of the doom of our world. For all of us these two great happenings have changed a life of serenely victorious enterprise into something more mysterious, more pregnant, and more tragic.

II *Exploring The Past*

1. THE PORTAL TO THE PAST

IT was with an overwhelming sense of the mystery and formidable
beauty of existence that I hastened, after the racial awakening,
toward that Arctic settlement which we call the Portal to the Past.
Travelling now by flying-boat, I soon reached the icefields; and by
noon the great towers which marked my destination stood like
bristles on the horizon. Already I encountered many other boats
and boatless flyers, bound for the same goal. Presently I arrived,
docked my little vessel in her appointed garage, and entered the
great white gate of the particular tower which concerned me. Greeting some of my colleagues, I passed through the entrance hall and
stepped into one of the many lifts. In a few moments I had sunk
a thousand feet below the ground. I then proceeded along a lofty
and well-lit passage, in the walls of which were doors, at intervals
of a hundred yards. One of these I opened. Within was a comfortable room, in which were chairs, a table, cupboards, and a bed.
At the far side of the room was a window, opening from ceiling to
ground, and beyond it a delightful sunny garden. How could this
be, you wonder, a thousand feet below ground? Had you walked
out into the garden, you would have seen that in the luminous blue
ceiling there blazed an artificial sun, and you would have felt a
refreshing breeze, which issued from among the bushes.

Behind every one of the doors in the many underground passages you would have found similar rooms and gardens, varying
only in detail according to the tastes of their occupiers. Such are
the apartments where we explorers of the past undertake our
strange adventures. You ask, why in the Arctic, why underground?
Our work demands that the mind shall be isolated from the contemporary human world; only in a remote land, and beneath its
surface, can we escape the telepathic influence of the world-
population. Our telepathic intercourse is based on the transmission and reception of ethereal vibrations from brain to brain.

Normally our powers of reception are kept under strict control, so that we receive messages only when we will. But, in the peculiar trance which is our medium for exploring the past, this control fails; so that, unless the explorer is isolated, his mind is lashed like a pond in which torrential rain is falling.

When I had entered my room and shut my door, I went out into my garden and walked up and down for a while, preparing my mind for its adventure. I then brought out from the room a drawer full of rolls of microscopically figured tape, which in my world take the place of books. In normal circumstances these little rolls work by systematically interrupting the radiation of a special instrument. This radiation penetrates the brain of the 'reader', and is interpreted telepathically by the telepathic organ of his brain. But since in the catacombs no radiation other than the normal solar wave-lengths is permitted, we explorers have to learn actually to read the rolls, with the aid of a microscope.

I now spent many hours lying on the turf in the sunshine, reading about the epoch which I was to visit. After a while I re-entered the room and pressed a button in the wall. A tray appeared, bearing an appetizing meal. When I had finished this, and dismissed the tray, I returned to the garden and my studies. For a period equivalent to about ten days I lived in this manner, studying, meditating, eating occasionally, but sleeping not at all. Sometimes I would break off my studies to tend my garden. Frequently I would swim about in the pond among the bushes. But for the most part I merely browsed on my books or on my own records of the past. Toward the end of this period of preparation, I grew desperately sleepy. To keep myself awake, I had to walk up and down more and more, and my dips in the pond became more frequent. It was almost time to be gone. I drew my little bed out into the garden and made it ready to receive me. I pressed another button, which would make day slowly become night. I took a final dip and a final walk, then staggered to my bed and lay down in the twilight.

But even yet I must not sleep. Instead, I concentrated my attention on the recurrent rise and fall of my own breathing, and on the nature of time. This process I had to maintain for about thirty hours, without food or sleep or any respite. Toward the end of this period, had you seen me, you would have said that I was at last falling asleep, and finally you would have declared me to be in a very profound slumber. And so in a manner I was, save that a single organ in my brain, usually dormant, was now intensively active, and preparing to take possession of my whole body as soon as my brain should have been refreshed by its deep sleep. After a couple of days of unconsciousness I did indeed wake, but not to the familiar surroundings.

For months, even years or decades, my body might now remain inert upon its bed, save for periodic risings to perform its natural functions of eating, drinking and excretion. Frequently also it would walk for hours at a time in the garden or bathe in the pond. But these activities would be carried out in complete abstraction, and had any one spoken to me at these times, I should have been unaware. For the higher centres of my brain were wholly possessed by the past. To any one watching me during these routine activities, I should have appeared as a sleep-walker. At these times, no less than during the long periods of quiescence on my bed, the observer would have seen that my face, and sometimes my whole body, was constantly influenced by emotion and thought. For during the whole trance, of course, my brain would be experiencing sequences of events in the remote past, and my whole body would respond to these experiences with my normal emotional reactions. Thus to the observer I should appear to be asleep and dreaming, save that my expressions would be far more definite and systematic than those of a dreamer.

Here I will mention one point of philosophical interest. The duration of the trance has no relation to the duration of the past events observed. Thus I might lie in my comfortable prison for a year, and in that time I might observe many years of past events, or many thousands of years, or even the whole span of man's history. The length of the trance depends only on the complexity of the matter observed. I might for instance spend a year in observing an immense number of simultaneous events which took only a few minutes to occur. Or I might cover the whole life of one individual in far more detail than was afforded by his own consciousness of his life story. Or I might sweep through whole epochs, tracing out only some one simple thread of change. In fact the length of the trance depends simply on the brain's capacity to assimilate, not upon the actual duration of the events observed.

When as much material has been gathered as can be conveniently grasped, the explorer gradually withdraws his attention from the past. He then sinks into an undisturbed sleep which may last for several weeks. During this phase his body shows none of that ceaseless emotional expression which is characteristic of the main trance. It lies inert, as though stunned. Finally the explorer's attention begins to concentrate itself again, and to revert once more to his own body and its surroundings. He wakes, and lies for a while passively accepting the new visual impressions. He then lives in his apartments for months or years recording his experiences in rough notes, to be organized at a later date. Sometimes, when this process is finished, he chooses to return at once, without respite, to the past for further data. Sometimes he leaves his room to confer with other workers. Sometimes he decides to drop his work and return to the contemporary world for refreshment.

2. DIFFICULTIES AND DANGERS

How it comes that at the moment of the onset of the trance the explorer is freed from the limitations of his own date and place I cannot tell you. Suffice it that the process involves both a special organ in the brain and a special technique, which has to be learned through a long apprenticeship. In that moment of awakening the worker has seemingly a confused experience of all the great successive epochal phases of the human spirit, up to his own date. But as the content of that supreme moment almost wholly escapes his memory as soon as it is past, it is impossible to say anything definite about it. He seems, indeed, to see in a flash, as though from another dimension of time, the whole historical order of events. Of course, he sees them only schematically. Their vast complexity of detail cannot be grasped in an instantaneous view. What he experiences can only be described (unintelligibly I fear) as a summation of all happening, of all physical, mental and spiritual flux. One is tempted to say also that he is aware of the human aspect of this flux as a vast slumber of the spirit, punctuated with moments of watchfulness, a vast stagnation troubled here and there with tremors of tense activity. Though all this is seen in an instant, it does not appear static, but alive with real passage and change.

This sublime moment must not be permitted to endure, for it is lethal. Immediately the explorer must begin to select that part of the historical order which he desires to study. To do this he must adopt the fundamental attitude of mind, or temperamental flavour, which he knows to be distinctive of the desired period. This process demands very great skill, and involves a host of uncouth and nerve-racking experiences. As soon as he begins to succeed in assuming the appropriate mental attitude, all the periods save that which he has chosen fade out of his consciousness, and the chosen period becomes increasingly detailed. He has then to specialize his mental attitude still further, so as to select a particular phase or group-culture within his period. And this specialization he may carry further again, till he has brought himself into the mind of some particular individual at a particular moment. Having once gained a footing in the individual mind, he can henceforth follow all its experiences from within; or, if he prefers, he can remain in one moment of that mind, and study its microscopic detail.

Such is the essence of our method. First we have to attain the momentary glimpse of eternity, or, more precisely, to take up for one instant the point of view of eternity. Then by imagination and sympathy we have to re-enter the stream of time by assuming the fundamental form of the minds or the mind that we wish to observe. In this process we have to work by means of a very delicate 'selectivity', not wholly unlike that physical selectivity which you exercise when you pick up ethereal messages on a particular wave-length. But this process of picking up past minds is far more delicate, since the system of basic mental patterns is very much more complex than the one-dimensional series of wave-frequencies.

When our ancestors first acquired the power of 'entering into the point of view of eternity' they suffered many disasters through ignorance of its principles. Very many of the earliest explorers succumbed simply by failing to keep their bodies alive during the trance. Their sleep turned into death. Others fell into such violent convulsions that they damaged themselves irreparably, and were mercifully killed by the superintendents. In other cases the normal trance lasted indefinitely, the body remaining alive but unresponsive for millions of years. A section of the catacombs was until recently filled with these persons, who were looked after by the attendants in the hope that some day they might wake. But a few thousand years ago it was decided to do away with some, and use others for experimental purposes.

Of the early explorers who successfully emerged from 'the point of view of eternity' into some past epoch, many returned insane. Others, though sane when they woke, kept falling into the trance again and again. Others were so embittered by their experiences that they became plague-spots in the community, and had to be requested to stop their hearts. Of these, some few refused, and remained at large, doing so much damage that finally they were put to death. One or two of the pioneers, and one or two of my contemporaries also, have returned from the trance with a peculiar kind of insanity, which suggested that they had actually found their way into the future, and that they still regarded our contemporary world as an episode in the remote past. Unfortunately they could give no account of their experiences; but in one of the earliest cases the recorded ravings seem to refer to the Mad Star, which did not earn its name until long afterwards.

In the early stages of the work few persons were engaged on it, and all that they could do was to collect random incidents from the very recent past. Gradually, however, the technique was greatly improved. It became possible to inspect almost any sequence of events in the history of our own species. This could only be done because the basic mental patterns of all the races of our own species had already been fairly well worked out by our psychologists and historians. Later, however, the psychologists began to formulate a vast theoretical system of possible basic mental patterns; and after some barren experimenting the explorers finally learned to assume certain of these patterns in the trance. The result was startling. Not only did they, as was expected, gain access to many primitive cultures upon Neptune, but also they began to find themselves sometimes in alien worlds, apparently much smaller than their familiar planet. The proportions of common things were all altered. The seas rose into great waves; the lands were often buckled into huge mountain ranges. The native organisms, though unfortified by artificial atoms, were able to attain great size and yet

31

remain slender and agile. And these facts were observed through the medium of human types the existence of which had never been guessed. The very planets which these races inhabited could not be identified. No wonder, since all traces of Earth and Venus had long ago been wiped out by the solar collision that had driven man to Neptune.

This discovery of past worlds was even more exciting to us than the discovery of America to your own ancestors; for it entailed incidentally the overthrow of a well-grounded theory, which traced the evolution of the human race to a primitive Neptunian organism. Interest in the exploration of the past now greatly increased. The technique was developed far beyond the dreams of the early explorers. Little by little the outline of man's whole history on Earth and Venus was plotted, and tract after tract of it was elaborated in some detail.

In observing these extinct species, the explorers found traces of experience very different from their own. Although, of course, the basic mental pattern or temperamental ground-plan was in every case one which the explorer himself had been able to conceive, and even in a manner assume, in order to make contact with these primitive beings at all, yet when the contact had been made, he seemed to enter into a new mental world. For instance, he had to deal with minds whose sensory powers were much more limited than his own. Looking through those primitive eyes, he saw things in much less detail than through his own eyes, so that, though he observed everything with all the precision that his host's crude vision could afford, yet everything seemed to him blurred, and out of focus. The colours of objects, too, were diluted and simplified; for several colours familiar to us are hidden from more primitive eyes. Consequently the world as seen through those eyes appears to us at first strangely drab, almost monochromatic, as though the observer himself had become partially colour-blind. The other senses also are impoverished. For instance, all touched shapes and textures seem curiously vague and muffled. The sensations of sexual intercourse, too, which with us are richly variegated and expressive, are reduced in the primitive to a nauseating sameness and formlessness. It is impossible for you to realize the jarring, maddening effects of this coarseness and emptiness of all the sensory fields, especially to the inexperienced explorer, who has not yet learned to submit his spirit generously to the primitive.

In the sphere of thought, we find all the primitive species of man, however different from one another, equally remote from ourselves. Even the most advanced members of the most advanced primitive species inhabit worlds of thought which to us seem naïve and grotesque. The explorer finds himself condemned to cramp the wings of his mind within the caging of some gimcrack theory or myth, which, if he willed, he could easily shatter. Even in those rare cases in which the ground-plan of some edifice of primitive thought happens to be true to the simplest basic facts of the cosmos, as in your own theory of relativity, the superstructure which it ought to support is wholly absent. The explorer thus has the impression that the cosmos, with himself in it, has been flattened into a two-dimensional map.

In the sphere of desire the explorer has to deal with very unfamiliar and very jarring kinds of experience. In all human species, of course, the most fundamental animal desires are much the same, the desires for safety, food, a mate, and companionship; but the kind of food, the kind of companionship, and so on, which the primitive human mind seeks, are often very foreign and distasteful to us. Take the case of food. Of course the explorer's body, lying in the catacombs on Neptune, does not, if perchance he is inhabiting some primitive glutton of the past, suffer dyspepsia; save occasionally, through the influence of suggestion. But none the less he may experience acute distress, for his brain is forced to accept sensory complexes of overeating which in normal life would disgust him. And they disgust him now. Even when overeating does not occur, the food percepts are often repulsive to our centres of taste and odour. In the matter of personal beauty, too, the explorer is at first repelled by the grotesque caricature of humanity which among primitive species passes for perfection, much as you yourselves may be repelled by the too-human animality of apes. Often, when he is following the growth of some primitive love-sentiment in your epoch, he is nauseated by the adored object, and by the intimacy in which he is reluctantly entangled. It is much as though a part of the mind were to watch the other part entrapped into romantic adoration of a female ape; as if with infinite disgust one were to find himself pressing against those hairy thighs. But indeed in this matter, as in others, since it is not mere animality that disgusts, but the failure to be human, the explorer is far more outraged than if he were compelled to cohabit with an ape. With familiarity, however, these repulsions can be surmounted. Just as your disgust of the ape's approximation to the human is a weakness in you, due to lack of vision and sympathy, so our tendency to a disgust of your own crude approximation to the human is a weakness in us, which we have to learn to transform into a reverent, though often ironical, sympathy. Just as the surgeon may become accustomed to delving among viscera, and may even find beauty in them, so the explorer may and must accustom himself to all these primitive forms, and find beauty in them too. Of course the beauty which he discovers in the adored yet repulsive apewoman is never simply identical with the beauty which delights the adoring ape-man; for it is a beauty which includes within itself both that which delights the primitive and that which disgusts the developed mind.

To all the preoccupations then, and to all the ways of life, and all the ideals, of the early races, the explorer must react with that delight which triumphs over contempt and disgust. Of course there is very much in this sphere which he can whole-heartedly enjoy, since much in primitive life is the unspoiled behaviour of the animal, and much also improves upon the animal. But at a very early stage primitive man begins to torture his own nature into grotesque forms, inadvertently or by intent; much as, inadvertently, he tortures his domestic animals, and by intent he turns his pets into freaks and caricatures. This violation of his own nature increases as he gains power, and reaches its height in primitive industrial communities such as your own. In such phases the individual body and spirit become more and more distorted, impoverished, noisome. The early explorer, studying these phases, was hard put to it to prevent his overwhelming indignation and nausea from spoiling his study. He had, of course, to observe it all as though it were happening to himself, since he observed it through the suffering minds of its victims. And so he was almost in the position of a sick doctor, whose spirit must triumph by delighting in the study of his own disease.

Grotesque sentiments such as the lust of business success or economic power of any kind, and indeed every purely self-regarding passion, from that of the social climber to that of the salvation-seeking ascetic, are experienced by the explorer with something of that shame which the child, emerging into adolescence, may feel toward the still-clinging fascination of his outgrown toys, or with such disgust as the youth may feel when he wakes from some unworthy sexual infatuation. But this shame and disgust the explorer must learn to transcend as the surgeon the disgust of blood. Even the passions of hate and gratuitous cruelty, so widespread in your own and all other primitive species, he must learn to accept with sympathy, in spite of his spontaneous revulsion from them and his well-justified moral condemnation of them.

One great difference between ourselves and most primitive minds is that, while in us all motives are fully conscious, fully open to introspection, in them scarcely any of their more complex motives are ever brought fully to light. Thus when the explorer is following some train of action in a primitive mind, he very often observes an immense discrepancy between the mind's own view of its motives and the real motives which he himself sees to be in fact the source of the activity. To experience all the daily and hourly perversities of a life-long complex, to experience them not merely through clinical observation but in the most intimate manner, puts him to an extremely severe strain. At every turn his own mind is wrenched by the conflict in the mind that he is observing. And in him the conflict is wholly conscious and shattering. Not a few of our early observers became infected by the disorder which they had been studying, so that when they returned to their native world they could no longer behave with perfect sanity, and had to be destroyed.

To sum up, then, the earlier explorers were often desperately fatigued by the monotony of primitive existence and the sameness of primitive minds; and also they fell into disgust, an agony of disgust, with the crudity, insensitivity and folly of the primitive. From the one point of view it might be said that the Neptunian found himself condemned to sift the almost identical sand-grains of a desert, and even to record the minute distinctive features of each grain. From the other point of view, it was as though he had been banished from the adult world to the nursery or the jungle,

35

and was actually imprisoned in the mind of babe or beast. For, once settled in the mind which he has chosen to study, the explorer is indeed a captive until study calls him elsewhere. Though he thinks his own thoughts, he perceives only what the other perceives, and is forced to endure every least sensation, thought, desire and emotion of the other, be it never so banal. Like one who feels within his own mind the beginnings of some mania or obsession which, though he recognizes that it is irrational or base, he cannot control, so the explorer is doomed to experience sympathetically all his subject's thinking and desiring, even while he is nauseated by it. No wonder, then, that many early explorers were tortured by disgust or ennui.

Long before my time, most of these dangers and irks of exploration had been greatly reduced. One serious trouble, however, remains, and has even increased. A great army of workers was of course bred with special aptitudes for supra-temporal experience, and with special insight into the primitive types of mind. These new workers were given also a special enthusiasm and sympathy in respect of the past; and herein lay their danger. In my day every member of the race has something of this enthusiasm and sympathy; and we explorers have them in an extreme degree. So enthralling do we find the past, even in all its monotony and squalor, that many have succumbed to its spell, and lost all footing in the present world. Rapt in some great movement of history, or in some individual life-story, the explorer may lose, little by little, all memory of the future world of which he is a native, may in fact cease to be a future mind inspecting a past mind, and become instead a mere undertone or freakish propensity in the past mind itself, or in many past minds. In time even this may vanish, so that the explorer becomes identical with the explored. If this occurs, his own body, situated in the future and in Neptune, gradually disintegrates and dies.

Certain other troubles hamper even the most modern explorers, in spite of improved technique. The method by which we enter a past epoch is, as I have said, this process of shaping our minds to the basic pattern or ground tone of the epoch to be studied. But when the explorer desires to enter a particular individual, he must try to assume the complex form or temperament which is distinctive of that individual; or else he must seize on one unique desire or thought, which he supposes to be peculiar to that individual at a certain date of his life. Now this process of mental infection or association does not necessarily work in his favour. Often, when he is trying to establish himself in some mind, or even when he has long been established, some chance association in his own thought-process may suddenly snatch him away from the object of his study and fling him into some other mind. Sometimes this other is a contemporary of the recent object of study; but often it is a mind in some different epoch or world. When this happens, not only is the study broken short, but also the explorer may be very seriously damaged. His brain, on Neptune, suffers such a fundamental and rapid readjustment that it is grievously jarred and strained, and may never recover. Even if he does not actually succumb, he may have to take a long holiday for recuperation. Fortunately, however, it is only the more extravagant dislocations that are really dangerous. Occasional jolts into minds of the same basic pattern as the original object of study are more exasperating than harmful.

Often when the explorer is resident in a particular individual he encounters through that individual's perception another individual, who, he thinks, would repay immediate study. He has then to observe this other carefully through the perceptions of the first, so as to discover, if possible, some entry into his mind. This may be very difficult, since one primitive mind's awareness of another is often so erroneous and biased that the perceptions which would make for true understanding of the other fail to occur. Moreover there is always the danger that, when the explorer attempts this 'change of mounts' he may fall between them, and be flung violently once more into his native location in time and space. Or again, he may at the critical moment be snatched by some chance association into some other epoch or world. Such accidents are of course very damaging, and may prove fatal.

Here I may mention that some minds, scattered up and down the ages, defeat all attempts to enter them. They are very rare, only one in millions of millions; but they are such as we should most desire to enter. Each one of these rare beings has caused the ruin of a great company of our most able explorers. They must be in some vital respect alien to us, so that we cannot assume their nature accurately enough to enter them. Possibly they are themselves subject to an influence future even to us. Possibly they are possessed and subtly transformed by minds native to some world in a remote stellar system. Possibly, even, they are under the direct influence of the cosmical mind, which, we hope, will awaken in the most remote of all futures.

Explorers of the past incur one other danger which I may mention. Sometimes the past individual under observation dies suddenly, before the explorer can foresee the death, and free himself. In many cases, of course, he knows the date at which the other's death will occur, and can therefore, having prepared himself for a normal departure, observe the course of events right up to the moment of death, and yet escape before it is too late. But sometimes, especially in pioneering in some unexplored region of history, the explorer is as ignorant of the immediate future as the observed mind itself. In such cases a dagger, a bullet, a flash of lightning, even an unforeseen heart-failure, may fling him back to his own world with a shattering jerk, which may irreparably damage his brain, or even kill him outright. Many of the early observers of your recent European War were caught in this manner. Resident in the mind of some soldier in action, the observer himself was annihilated by the shell that destroyed the observed. If burial were one of our practices, we, like you, might have our war graves of 1914 to 1918, though they would not have been dug till two thousand million years later. Nor would they be decorated by national emblems. Nor would they bear the cross.

3. INFLUENCING PAST MINDS

Our power of taking effect on past minds is much more restricted than our power of passively observing their processes. It is also a much more recent acquisition. To you it seems impossible; for future events, you suppose, have no being whatever until their predecessors have already ceased to exist. I can only repeat that, though future events have indeed no temporal being until their predecessors have ceased to exist with temporal being, all events have also eternal being. This does not mean that time is unreal, but that evanescence is not the whole truth about the passing of events. Now some minds, such as ours, which are to some extent capable of taking up the point of view of eternity, and of experiencing the eternal aspects of past events in other minds, can also to some extent contribute to the experience of those minds in the past. Thus when I am observing your mental processes, my activity of observing is, in one sense, located in the past. Although it is carried out from the point of view of my own experience in the future, it enters the past through the eternal side of past events in your minds. When I act upon your minds, as for instance in inculcating thoughts and images in the writer of this book, that activity of mine is located in your age. Yet it is done, so to speak, from my purchase in the future, and with all my Neptunian experience in view.

From this rare but important action of the future on the past it follows that past events, which themselves cause future events, are in part the product of future events. This may seen unintelligible. But in fact there is no more mystery in it than in the reciprocal interaction of two minds that know one another. The one, which owes its form partly to the other, is itself one factor determining the other's form.

As I said before, the only way in which we can influence a past mind is by suggesting in that mind some idea or desire, or other mental event, which is intelligible to a mind of that particular order, and is capable of being formulated in terms of its own experience. Some minds are much more receptive than others. The great majority are wholly impervious to our influence; and, even among those who are not insensitive, very many are so strictly dominated by their own desires and prejudices that any thought or valuation which we consider worth suggesting to them is at once violently rejected.

There are many complications and difficulties in this strange work. In the first place we may chance to do serious damage to the past mind by unwise influence, for instance by presenting it with ideas which are too disturbing to its nature. For though some ideas are so foreign to a mind that they are simply rejected, others, though alien to the superficial part of its nature, may be incendiary to the submerged part, as sparks falling upon tinder. Thus an idea which to the explorer seems straightforward and harmless may produce in the past mind a self-discrepant experience both of revelation and of horror; and the resulting conflict throughout the mind may lead to catastrophe. Or the idea may so captivate and exalt the unfortunate person that he loses all sense of proportion, is instigated to some fantastic course of action, and finally comes into serious collision with his society.

Another difficulty lies in the fact that our influence is not always voluntary. Thoughts and desires of our own, which we have no intention of transmitting, may sometimes find their way into the mind under observation; and their effect may be disastrous. For instance, a sudden surge of contempt or indignation on the part of an inexperienced explorer, when he observes his 'host' commit some egregious folly or meanness, may flood a hitherto complacent mind with bewildering self-contempt. And this novel experience, coming thus without preparation, may shatter the whole flimsy structure of the mind by destroying its carapace of self-pride. Or again, the explorer's own clear-eyed and ecstatic view of the cosmos, as both tragic and worshipful, may sear the optimistic faith of a primitive religious mind, without being able to raise it to the loftier worship.

Our influence, then, upon the past is a very much more precarious and restricted power than our past-exploration. All that we can do is to offer to a very small minority of minds some vague hint of a truth or of a beauty which would otherwise be missed, or some special precept, or seminal idea, relevant to the mind's particular circumstances. This may be done either by a constant 'tilting' of the mind in a certain general direction, or, much more rarely, by occasional impregnation of the mind with some precise idea or valuation. In very exceptional cases, which number no more than one in many thousands of millions, we can subject the individual to a constant stream of detailed suggestion which he himself can embody in a more or less faithful report. But here we find ourselves on the horns of a dilemma. To undergo this detailed suggestion, the individual must be extremely receptive; but in the main those that are extremely receptive lack originality, so that, in spite of their detailed receptivity, they either entirely miss the true spirit of the communication, or fail to embody it in a manner capable of stirring their fellows. On the other hand the highly original minds, even when they are also very receptive, tend deliberately to ignore the detail of the suggestion. Thus they produce works which, though true to the spirit of the suggestion, are embodied in manners expressive of their own genius.

4. HOVERING OVER TIME

I must now give you a more precise idea of the strange experiences which befall the explorer when he is trying to get a footing in some particular moment of some particular past mind. Each explorer has his own technique, and each adventure its own vicissitudes; but I shall tell simply of my own approach to your world and epoch on that occasion which I have already begun to describe.

Emerging presently from that ineffable moment in which I participated in the eternal view, I was at the outset conscious of a vague restlessness, a most poignant yet indefinite yearning, and along with this a violent and confused agitation of all my senses. Even though this was not my first excursion into these realms, I was overwhelmed with the pathos of man's ever-unsatisfied and blindly fumbling desire, and equally by the tyranny of his rare joys and the torture of his distresses. At the outset this yearning and this sensory tumult were, so to speak, all that there was of me; but with an effort I woke to something more precise. I held the obscure thing away from me, and looked at it calmly. As I did so, it developed under my very eyes, the eyes of my mind, into a surge of specific primitive cravings and passions, which, though I lived them as my own, I also regarded, as it were, from a great height of aloofness. I was now experiencing the summed and confused experiences of all mankind. They came to me with the vagueness of a composite photograph, but also with that sense of multitude, of innumerable individual uniquenesses, which one may sometimes catch in listening to the murmur of a great crowd. Yet all these multitudinous experiences were in a manner mine, and combined into one experience, like the single deliverance of a man's two eyes. I was terrified and longed for safety, hungry and lusted for food. I was enraged against some obscure adversary. I tasted the joy of murder, and equally the final despair of the victim. I was solitary, and my flesh burned with sexual potency; outcast, and my mind hungered for companionship.

Against this vast enduring background of primitive craving I experienced also momentary gleams of loftier desire, rare and faint as voices heard above the storm. I felt the longing and the delight of spiritual intimacy with another mind, the longing and the delight of truth, the longing and the delight and glory of participation in a great community, the longing and the delight of faith. I felt also the terror, the despair, the peace and final ecstasy, which is the way of true worship. But all these illuminations of the spirit were no more than stars piercing for a moment the storm-cloud of the primitive.

While I was undergoing all these obscure impulses, tumultuous messages were also pouring in through all my senses. At first indeed I received such a medley of impressions that I was aware only of a nondescript and distressing commotion. But, as I attended to this, the matter of the various senses began to differentiate itself. Thus at first I seemed to be subjected to a general pressure all over my body; but under scrutiny this developed into a profusion of hardnesses and softnesses, roughnesses and smoothnesses, rotundities and angularities. I felt the pressure of earth under my feet. I felt myself lying on hard ground, and then on a kindly bed. With my hands I felt a multitude of textures, as of stone, treetrunks, fur, and the incomparable touch of human flesh, in all its repellent and its enticing modes. I felt also a vague warmth and chill, which, by attending to them, I could develop into violent heat and cold, or the bite of fire and frost. Innumerable pains invaded me. At first they seemed to struggle against a sense of physical well-being, a tingling healthiness; but soon pain triumphed; for it had at the outset a compelling poignancy which increased alarmingly under attention. The whole surface of my body, it seemed, was tortured; and my internal organs were all gripped in agony. My brain throbbed and burned, and was stabbed through and through in all directions. But in truth the brain that was thus tormented was not mine, nor the bowels mine, nor the skin. The source of my torture lay in the innumerable bodies of my predecessors. Wrenching my attention from this horror, I noticed a confusion of tastes, fragrances and stenches. And along with these there came sounds. A muffled roar, as of the sea or a distant bombardment, grew as I listened to it into a crashing and shrieking, which reverberated through my whole body. By a special act of attention, a straining of the mind's ear, I could penetrate beyond this uproar, and hear an obscure vocal sound, which, as I listened, became inarticulate lamentation, flecked here and there with laughter.

In the field of vision I experienced at first nothing but a vague brightness above and obscurity below. This was due to the fact that in most minds of all periods, save those in which indoor life predominates over outdoor life, daytime-experience contains in the main a light sky and a darker ground. As soon as I began to attend to the matter of this vision, it revealed itself as being after all rich with detail. First, both in the light and in the dark field, there moved unrecognizable shadowy forms and occasional colours. Then aloft I began to see white clouds sailing in blue sky, then widespread rain-cloud, then thunder-cloud, and then in a moment the broad unbroken blue; then night, obscure, starry, moonlit, and again obscure. Below, I saw sometimes hills, crags, tree-tops, meadows, bright flowers and plumage, sometimes breakers on the shore, sometimes huts, mansions in many styles, or congested towns, sometimes interiors of splendour or comfortable homeliness or squalor. All these forms kept appearing, vanishing, reappearing, invading one another and exterminating one another, like the visions that haunt us between waking and sleeping. I saw also forms of beasts, and human forms of all the species, from hairy pithecanthropus, and your own fantastically clothed half-human kind, to those large and noble beings who were the last Terrestrials, and the bat-like fliers of Venus, and my own immediate ancestors on Neptune. I saw limbs writhing in agony, limbs dancing, limbs straining in toil and sport, fair limbs embracing, limbs grotesque and crippled. Faces also appeared and vanished, singly or in crowds, faces eager and disillusioned, faces twisted by pain, or by rapacity, faces expressionless as pebbles, faces of terror, hate, meanness, faces of peace and of exultation; child faces, faces of maturity all aglow with life, faces grey, wrinkled, sagging, old; and faces of the dead, impassive, sealed against experience.

Along with these visions of humanity, would sometimes come faint sexual sensations, which, when I attended to them, opened out into a whole world of amorous experience, of lyrical first matings and desolate repetitions, of violations, thwarted crises, lonely make-shifts, of the bland unions of long-tried lovers, of senile failures, and the whole gamut of perversions.

Intermingled with these purely perceptual visions, there came to me all manner of experiences of personal relationships. I was flooded with the lovings and hatings, of all men and women, by their co-operations and rivalries, by all the modes of leadership, by all fealties and servitudes. I became a mother toiling for a son whose thought was not of her; I became a son held within the soft, strong meshes of his home. I had a glimpse, as it were both from without and from within their minds, of myriads of the boys and girls of all the species, opening their eyes in amazement upon life, knowing neither what they ought to be doing with it nor even how to wrest from it the simple joys they so vaguely ·conceived. I glimpsed likewise the myriads of grown men and women, with all their hopes thwarted, and their minds desperately concerned only to keep their bodies alive, or at most their heads above their fellows. And the old I glimpsed also, with their lives written indelibly into the great story of worlds. Through their eyes I watched the young things rising up all around them and beyond them, like birds that rise and leave their wounded on the ground. It seemed too that I entered into the minds of the innumerable toilers of all the aeons. I felt the ache and the leaden weight of their limbs, the sick ache of their eye-balls, and the hopelessness of their crippled souls. I felt also the calm of spirit, the strenuous peacefulness, of those few who are wholly and gladly possessed by their work.

There poured in upon me also all the thoughts and fantasies and ideals of all men and women in all ages. My mind reeled and staggered in the tide of them, and was swept to and fro upon the great ocean of whimsies and dreams, doctrines and theories. With the pre-human beings, I fashioned imaginatively, step by step, the whole world of perceptual common sense, that tissue of theories and images, so true and so false, which to most human beings of all species appears to be the unquestionable real. I observed, as in my own mind, the flashes of primeval genius that had gone to the making of that great medley of fact and fiction. With the ape-men, too, I projected souls into trees and mountains, storms and stars. And with them also I felt the first painful birth-throes of true intellect. To trap my prey, to beguile my mate, or build my shelter, I reasoned, I put two and two together. But every motion of this reason I distorted with fantasies born of mere desire, and when this hybrid failed me I blamed reason.

All manner of laborious reasonings and intricate bright myths flashed across my mind and vanished. In the twinkling of an eye I savoured cosmology after cosmology, I saw Shiva, Odin, Zeus, Jaweh and his fair offspring Jesus, and innumerable other god-heads, of wrath and righteousness, of wisdom, of power, of love, emanations from the minds of all the races, all the species of man. And with these I tried out a million sciences and philosophies, amongst which, as yet ever so faint and remote, like the voices of two bright confident quarrelling children, that 'materialism' and that 'spiritism' which resound throughout your little play-room world. Theories, theories, myriads upon myriads of them, streamed over me like wind-borne leaves, like the contents of some titanic paper-factory flung aloft by the storm, like dust-clouds in the hurricane advance of the mind. Gasping in this vast whirling aridity, I almost forgot that in every mote of it lay some few spores of the organic truth, most often parched and dead, but sometimes living, pregnant, significant.

5. DESCENT AMONG THE FIRST MEN

During the whole of this early stage of my adventure I was already trying to select from the confusion of experiences something which might serve to bring me nearer to your own particular phase of the human process. My chief method of directing myself toward your age is, as I have already said, to assume imaginatively, and as precisely as possible, first the basic temperamental pattern of your species, and then the particular form of it which is characteristic of your period, and of that unique point and moment of individuality which I desire to study. This work I was already attempting; but it was hampered on this occasion, and on most others, by the prodigious influx of perceptions, thoughts and emotions which I have attempted to describe. I was like a swimmer swept hither and thither by great waves, and scarcely able to make the particular rocky creek which is his haven.

I had first to conceive, and emotionally assume, the general form of all primitive human mentality, so as to exclude from my view the whole of my own species, and also that other, abortive, phase of spiritual maturity, which took place just before man left the earth. I had to become in imagination a bewildered limited being, ignorant of its own nature, ever racked by inner conflicts which eluded its apprehension, ever yearning to be whole, yet ever carried away by momentary cravings which were ludicrous even in its own estimation. With patience I was able to achieve this piece of inner play-acting with such success that I began to have definite but fleeting glimpses of individuals and incidents among the primitive kinds of men, now a winged Venerian, skimming his wild ocean, now a woman of the Third Men, ruddy and lithe, feeding her beasts, now a scarcely human early inhabitant of Neptune. These individuals I perceived, of course, through the eyes of some contemporary; and if ever I troubled to look at 'my own' body during these experiences, I perceived it to be not my familiar body at all, but of the same species as the observed individual. Perceiving through the eyes of past beings, I perceived their bodies as though they were each in turn my own body.

I had now to select that mode of the primitive which is distinctive of your own species, a mode characterized by repressed sexuality, excessive self-regard, and an intelligence which is both rudimentary and in bondage to unruly cravings. Now though all the races of your species in all its stages manifest, in spite of their differences, one unique blend of these factors, yet the process of imaginatively assuming this mode of mentality is dangerous; for there is another species, one of our fore-runners on Neptune, which is strangely like you in this respect. I now found myself, as often before, oscillating painfully between these two phases of man's career. I saw now the hills and tall trees of Earth, now the plains and bushes of Neptune. I assumed now the spidery limbs and jaunty gait of a Terrestrial, now the elephantine legs, kangaroo arms and grave demeanour of an early Neptunian. I listened for a moment to Attic disputation, then suddenly to primitive Neptunian grunts and clicks. It was as though I were listening-in with a radio set of bad selectivity. Or, to change the image, I was a storm-tossed buzzard among the hills, beneath me a dividing range, on either side of it a valley. Into one of these valleys I purposed to descend, but the wind kept thrusting me back over the ridge into the other. At one moment I saw beneath me the desired valley; then, after a vain struggle, the other. At length, however, by a violent effort of attention I succeeded in concentrating upon your species and avoiding the other. Gradually the imagery and thought which flooded in on me came to be entirely derived from the First Men, in one or other of their phases.

But my experience was still chaotic. I had indeed a strong but vague apprehension of your species as a historic whole, of its many long phases of somnolence and its few brief effulgences. And after careful inspection I detected that sense of cosmical tragedy which overwhelmed, or, from your point of view, will overwhelm, the more intelligent of your descendants, when they realize that their species is setting inevitably into decline. But for the most part I had merely a sickening confusion of random samples from all your ages. Thus, at one moment I was an Aurignacian, engraving his cave wall with vivid shapes of deer and bison, while my fellow-hunters peered with admiration through the smoke. Now I was a Chinese citizen of that Americanized world-state which lies future to you; and I was speaking in worn and polluted English to my Soudanese wife. Now I was an Elizabethan dame, tight-laced and plastered with jewellery. Suddenly I flashed many thousands of years ahead into that Patagonian civilization which is the last weary effort of your species. I was a prematurely aged boy, prostrate in a temple before the grotesque image of Power. Not until many more of these visions had appeared, and been dismissed, did I find myself approximately in your age. I was an Indian confronting a topeed, bare-kneed Englishman. Rage was in my heart, fear, contempt and subterfuge, and as little understanding of the other as he had of me.

Fatigued but now more hopeful, I forced myself rigorously into the mentality which is common to most members of a primitive industrialistic community. To you this curious mode of experience

47

is so familiar that you do not suspect its rarity and oddity, though
many of you feel that it is neither wholesome nor inevitable. That
you may realize the violent effort of imagination and emotional
control that was now incumbent on me, I will set down the main
features which render the primitive industrial mentality so difficult
for the explorer. To revert to the image which I have already used,
it is as though the buzzard, having successfully descended into the
valley of his choice, were now to enter the ventilation shaft of an
old disused mine, and were to sink downwards in the dark through
fetid air, with scarcely room to keep his wings outspread. No wonder that he suffers considerable distress and incurs serious dangers,
before he finally alights amongst the pale and eyeless fauna of the
pit. No wonder that his own eyes take time to accustom themselves
to the dim phosphorescence which is the sole illumination of that
world. When the explorer seeks to establish himself in your society,
he has first to assume that jarred and restless mood which is common to all those whose habitual environment is alien to their
native capacities. In particular he must imaginatively produce in
himself the lifelong strain of perceiving streets, traffic, and stuffy
interiors, instead of the landscapes which originally moulded his
capacities. He must also reconstruct in himself the unconscious
obsession with matter, or rather with the control of matter by
machinery and chemical manipulation. He must conceive also the
mind's unwitting obeisance and self-distrust before its robot offspring. Further, he must subject his own free-roaming spirit to the
hideous effects of a narrow specialism, both of body and mind.
He must conceive the almost inconceivable ignorance and groping
hate of the being whose life is moulded to one narrow round of
duties and perceptions. Equally he must conceive the profound
unwitting guiltiness of the primitive industrial master, and also of
that idle scum that floats on the surface of all primitive industrial
societies.

Little by little I reproduced in myself this cramped and ungener-
ous mode of the mind; and, as I did so, visions of your world came
crowding in upon me with increasing vividness. I became a half-
naked woman in a coal-mine of your Industrial Revolution. I crept
on hands and knees along a low gallery. Tugging at the collar like
a beast, I dragged a truck. The trace passed between my legs. I was

48

whimpering, not from any present discomfort, but because I had lost a keepsake. This incident was obviously a century or more too early, but others followed, and more and more of them were of your period. I had now to seek out a particular individual among you, and a particular moment of his life. But in doing so, I nearly suffered catastrophe. On Venus there was once, or rather from your point of view there will be, an industrial phase much like your own in certain respects, although the species which produced it was very different from yours. Into that epoch I was suddenly flung by I know not what detail of identity. A face which was obviously not of the First Men, a pale and blinking frog-like face, with a running sore beneath the left eye and a fantastic hat cocked backwards, slowly grimaced at me. For one anxious moment I feared that I should be trapped in that Venerian phase of man, with my mind still moulded to the mentality of the First Men. But by a desperate effort of concentration upon the Terrestrial mode of experience I managed to disengage myself from this dangerous irrelevance. And with one leap I found myself back again at the desired point of your history.

6. IN THE STREETS OF LONDON

I was in a town. A great red vehicle, roaring and trumpeting, was in the act of swooping upon me. Leaping out of its track, I ran to the pavement where two contrary streams of pedestrians brushed past one another. As the archaic chariot left me, I saw on its flank the English word 'General', in letters of gold. I had already become familiar with this device on my previous visit to your world, and I now knew that I must be in London somewhere between the invention of the motor-omnibus and the socialization of all such vehicles under a metropolitan authority. The clothes of the women pedestrians were of the style worn in 1914. Skirts left the ankle exposed, waists were confined within broad belts of ribbon, hats were large, and poised high on the crown. Clearly I had struck the right period, but who was I, or rather who was my host? I noted with satisfaction that his basic mental pattern fitted very precisely the mood which I had already myself assumed to take me to my chosen object of study. Surely this must be the young man whom I sought. I shall not reveal his name, since with its aid he or his relatives might recognize the portrait, or the setting, which I must give in some detail. I shall therefore refer to him simply as Paul. I had already observed him on an earlier visit, but now I proposed to follow him through the most critical moment of the career of his species.

Paul was gravely agitated. I noticed a visual image looming in the recesses of his mind, an image not open to his own introspection. It was the face of his pet enemy of childhood days, and it was streaming with tears and blood. The child Paul had just put an end to this lad's bullying by defending himself with a table-fork. He now consciously felt once more (though he knew not why) the horror and guilt that he had suffered long ago at the sight of his enemy's damaged cheek. The experience was now accompanied by confused images of khaki, bayonets, and the theme of a patriotic song. Paul was experiencing, and I experienced through him, a distressing conflict of blood-loathing and martial fervour. Evidently I had come upon Paul in the midst of his great crisis. Like so many of his contemporaries, he was faced with the necessity of deciding whether he would or would not fight for king and country and gallant little Belgium. But with Paul the situation was complicated by the fact that ever since his childhood I had been tampering with his mind so as to make him more sensitive to the momentous issues which were at stake.

Had I needed further confirmation that my host was indeed Paul, it was available. He was now passing a shop which bore a panel of mirror between its windows. Such mirrors I had often noticed in your cities, cunning devices for attracting the attention of your amusingly and fatally self-gratulatory species. My host slackened his pace and gazed into the mirror. Indeed he actually halted for a moment. I at once recognized the youthful and anxious face that I had perforce so often observed in the shaving-glass. But I noticed that its habitual expression of watchful self-reserve was now intensified with some kind of suppressed but haunting terror. Neptunian vision detected also, contrasting with this callow distress, a gleam of contemptuous irony, new in Paul.

Only for a moment did Paul regard himself. With a blush and an impatient jerk he turned away, and looked anxiously to see if any one had been watching him. Immediately, with a deeper blush, he faced the mirror again, and pretended to be searching for grit in his eye. Amongst the crowd of passers-by, two figures were approaching, and almost upon us. The young man was in khaki. The girl clung to his arm with demure possessiveness. He did not notice Paul, but she caught Paul's eyes as he was turning toward the mirror. In the fraction of a second that elapsed before his eyes could free themselves, he saw that she dismissed him as no true male, that she thanked God her man was a soldier, and that she was ready to do her bit by yielding herself unconditionally to him. Real tears welled in Paul's eyes to wash out the imaginary grit. I took a hasty glance at the most recent memories of my host, and saw that while he had been walking along the Strand after his lunch he had been subject to several encounters of this sort, real or imaginary. By now he was badly shaken. He turned down a side-street, and wandered along the Embankment. Presently he was calmed by the quietly flowing water, still more, perhaps, by the Obelisk, that proud ancient captive among Lilliputians. To Paul it seemed refreshingly indifferent to their ant-wars. Suddenly his peace was shattered. Half a dozen urchins approached in military formation, accompanied by martial rhythms on an old tin can. As they passed him, one of them struck up on a mouth-organ an excruciating but recognizable version of a catchy song already in vogue among the troops. I felt Paul's mind rear and plunge beneath me like a startled horse. Many times he had heard that tune; many columns of troops he had seen, with full equipment, marching toward the great railway terminus for entrainment toward the coast. But this commonplace little incident stirred him more deeply. It filled him with a desperate longing to be at one with the herd, to forget himself in the herd's emotions. to sacrifice himself heroically to the herd's gods.

A visual image now flashed into his view, a shop-front converted into a recruiting office. The window displayed posters to incite the laggard, 'Your king and country need you', and so on. This image Paul now greeted with a violent assent. On the heels of that swift mental gesture there followed a fleeting tactual image of a hand's pressure on his hand, as though the whole nation were congratulating him on his decision.

Paul hurried away from the river with an almost swaggering gait. He took a short cut by back-streets to the recruiting office that he had so often passed, and as often circumvented so as to avoid its blatant reproaches. Street after street he threaded, and in each succeeding street his resolution was less secure and his swagger less evident. The only clear conviction in his mind, was that, whichever course he finally took, he would regret it, and feel ashamed that he had not taken the other. His perplexity was the outcome not only of the objective moral problem as to what course was in fact the right course, but also of a subjective psychological problem, namely what would his motives really be if he took this course, and what if he took that.

I myself, observing his mind as he hurried along in dangerous abstraction among pedestrians and vehicles, was able to detect in him many motives hidden from his own observation. There is no need to give a complete inventory of the tangled impulses that were pulling him hither and thither in his perplexity, but one point must be made clear because of its significance. Paul's indecision was in fact only superficial, was indeed illusory. To me, though not to Paul himself, it was evident that he had resolved on his course a good month earlier, and that however much he might seem to himself to be vacillating, his will was already fixed. This curious state of affairs was due to the fact that his deciding motive was not clearly apprehended; while at the same time he was very poignantly aware of a conflict between other motives which were not strictly relevant to the problem at all. Thus, he dared not enlist, lest his motive should be merely moral cowardice; he dared not refuse to enlist, lest his motive should be merely physical cowardice or moral pride. Whatever course he chose would almost certainly spring from purely selfish motives. In fact although the decision had indeed really been made long ago, he had ever since been chafing within his illusory cage of morality and selfishness, like a captive beast that rubs itself painfully against its bars without hope of escape.

The same forlorn task was occupying him when at last the recruiting office leapt into view. It was a corner house, diagonally opposite him. He stepped off the pavement, dodged the traffic, and was already half-way across, when his resolution finally vanished.

At the door stood a sergeant with a red, white and blue cockade. He had already sighted Paul, and was preparing to greet him with acquisitive geniality. Paul's legs continued to carry him toward the door, though weakly; but Paul's mind now woke to a surprisingly clear conviction that, whatever the reason, this thing must not be done. He reached the pavement. The sergeant stood aside to let him pass. Paul was almost in the doorway when he suddenly veered and scuttled away. His conviction vanished, but he continued to hurry along the pavement. Tears came to his eyes, and he whimpered to himself, 'Coward, Coward'; with which verdict the sergeant doubtless agreed.

But to me, the detached observer, it was evident that though Paul was on the whole more of a coward than the average, and would have made a very bad soldier, it was not cowardice that had put him to flight. It is difficult to describe the determining though deeply hidden motive which, on this occasion as on others, snatched him away from the recruiting office. It was a motive present also in the majority of his contemporaries, though in few was it able to disturb the operation of more familiar motives. The real determinant of Paul's behaviour was an obscure intuition, which your psychologists mostly fail to recognize as a basic and unanalysable factor in your nature. They fail to recognize it, because in you it is so precarious and so blind. You have no satisfactory name for it, since few of you are at all clearly aware of it. Call it, if you will, loyalty to the enterprise of Life on your planet and among the stars; but realize that, though it is a natural product of age-long events, and though it cannot express itself at all unless it is evoked by education, it becomes, at a certain stage of evolution, a bias as strong and unreasoned as the bias in favour of food or offspring. Indeed these propensities are but gropings toward this more general but equally non-rational bias. This it was that in Paul, partly through my earlier influence, partly through his own constitution, was strong enough to turn him aside on the threshold of the recruiting office. This it was that in the majority of Paul's contemporaries caused, indeed, grave agony of mind, but could not bring them to refuse war.

III *The Child Paul*

1. PAUL AND HIS NEPTUNIAN PARASITE

WHY do I choose Paul for study? Why do I propose to tell you more
of him than of any one else in my collection? I have examined in
detail at one time and another an immense number of specimens of
your kind, not only your contemporaries but many others whose
date is earlier than yours, and many who in your day are still to live.
I have made myself familiar with every trait and whim, every minute episode in the minds of selected individuals from among the
Greeks, the Indians, the early Teutons, the ancient Egyptians, the
Chinese of all China's phases, and also the still unborn Americans
and Patagonians. In fact, there is no race of the First Men that has
not yielded me samples; which, as I have grown intimate with them,
have so captivated me with their fantastic personalities that I have
come to regard them not merely as specimens but, in a manner, as
friends. For these beings have yielded me the secrets of their nature
to an extent impossible in normal intercourse; and yet they have
never communicated with me, and for the most part have never
suspected my existence.

If I chose, I could tell you many strange secrets about your
famous characters, for instance about your Queen Elizabeth, who
is among my collection. Through her eyes I have looked not only
on the fair face of Essex, but also on that abnormal formation of
her own body which caused her to be so lonely, so insistent on her
womanhood, and withal so kingly. And I have tasted her bitter
rage against fate, her greedy self-love, her love of England.
Leonardo da Vinci also I have inhabited. It was I that tormented
him with a thousand ideas in advance of his age. It was the enigma
of my influence in him that he embodied in pigment as a smile.
Aknahton also I swayed, and in his wife's face my influence
conjured another smile. There are moments in my life on Neptune
when my beloved specimens crowd in upon my memory and overwhelm me with the infinity of their uniquenesses; when, forgetful

of my own Neptunian personality, I seem to be nothing but the theatre in which these many play their parts.

If it is incredible to you that I should have millions of these intimates, remember, not only that the minds of the Last Men are far more agile and far more capacious than your minds, but also that I have spent many thousands of years upon the work, and that in most cases a whole terrestrial lifetime occupies me for no more than a day of my life on Neptune. Of course even my millions of specimens can afford only partial knowledge of your kind. But those of my colleagues who have been working in the same field have worked with no less industry. No doubt all of us together have studied only a minute fraction of your species; but at least we have by now sampled every culture, every local strain, every generation. And your own age, since it is the turning-point of your history, we have sifted again and again with special care.

Why then out of all this collection do I choose Paul as the text and the epitome of what I have to say to you? I choose him because he does epitomize in his character, his circumstances, and his reaction to my influence, the spiritual crisis of your age, and indeed the doom of your species. It would not be true to say that he was an exceptionally average member of his race. Far from it. Though in a sense typical and significant, Paul was not average. Indeed both in character and in circumstance he was rather unusual. Yet he is typical in that he illustrates very clearly the confused nature of his species, and the disorder of its world. In Paul's life there appear with an almost naïve simplicity of outline certain phases of spiritual growth, distorted by the all-pervading blight of his age, nay of his species. In all of you, from the earliest flint-worker, even to the last survivors of Patagonia, the conflict between the primitive simian nature and the genuinely human (or from your point of view the super-human) is present as a fundamental condition of life. In Paul the old simian nature was undisguised and insistent, while the new human nature had defined itself with precision and emphasis. The conflict therefore was clear.

I pride myself somewhat on the discovery of Paul. My crowning research upon the mentality of the First Men and on the crisis of their career demanded a specimen such as I knew would be hard to find. I cannot tell you at all clearly what was necessary, since you are ignorant of the principles of my work. But, to repeat, I had to select an individual both typical and unique, a being of average intelligence, average abilities, average strength of will, but one in whom the simian and the distinctively human were both well developed and delicately balanced. Further, he must be one capable of a degree of self-consciousness abnormal in your species. Many other more subtle requirements I must leave unmentioned. In order to discover this unique creature I had to explore not only your own age but many earlier generations in search of genetic strains favourable to my requirements.

In the Seventeenth Century there was a German family which promised what I wanted; but in them the desirable features were complicated by a musical sensitivity which in many individuals afforded escape from the conflict. I noticed, however, that those members of the clan who most nearly fulfilled my requirements had a subtly characteristic laugh; or rather that, though they laughed in many different styles, the laughter of each had a curious fleeting tremor of bewilderment. Armed with this clue, and certain others more introspective, I continued my search, until in the England of King Alfred I found a similar and even more promising strain. This I followed through the generations hither and thither. One branch of it, the most promising, was exterminated by the Black Death, another became hopelessly contaminated by interbreeding with a strain of defectives, a third produced witches in the Sixteenth Century and mystics in the Seventeenth. Early in the Eighteenth Century a member of this line married into another stock which I had already marked out, and produced a number of more scientifically-minded folk. Throughout the Eighteenth and early Nineteenth Centuries this line suffered social decline, and proliferated in a swarm of poverty-stricken households scattered over the industrial north of England. From one of these sprang Paul's grandmother, who by good fortune married into yet another of my chosen lines. Paul's father also was of a stock that had already interested me.

Having now discovered my unique specimen, I first took a hasty glance at his career, and found to my delight that circumstance was destined to intensify and clarify in him the characteristics which I proposed to study. In that first hasty glance I saw also the quite

unmistakable effects of a Neptunian influence, doubtless my own
influence which I had not yet exerted. I then proceeded to make a
thorough investigation of every line of Paul's ancestry, in order
that I might know his nature through and through. Many volumes
could be filled with the results of this inquiry, but here I need not
elaborate. Incidentally I traced the evolution of Paul's physical
appearance, of his nose, eye-brows, hands, and so on. A curious
twist of the hair of his left eyebrow, which was a recessive character, and had not appeared in any of his more recent ancestors, came
in with a French strain in the Fourteenth Century. A certain
scarcely noticeable prominence of the cheek-bones I traced to a
Danish invader of the Eighth Century, and beyond him through
Swedes and Finns into Central Asia. Another remarkable line of
his ancestry, in part responsible for his intellectual curiosity and
certain features of his thumb-print, took me via a Dutch merchant
of the Seventeenth Century, a Rhenish baron of the Thirteenth,
various Swiss herdsmen and Italian farmers to Syracuse, and so
to ancient Greece, where one of Paul's ancestors once handed a
cup to Socrates. But apart from a dozen or so curious threads of
this type, which of course occur in many family trees, Paul's
ancestry was the usual tangle of intercrossing lines, stretching back
in manifold complexity among the Norse, the Low Germans, the
Ancient British, and the Neolithic, and beyond these to the common forefathers of all your races. It would have been useless to
trace Paul's ancestry any further in detail, since nothing more that
was distinctive of Paul himself remained to be discovered. In the
more remote past the genes that were to produce Paul were ancestral also to the mass of his contemporaries. This story was already known to me.

I must now tell you what it was that I intended to do with
Paul, and how I carried out my plan. I wished to perform certain
delicate experiments on him and observe his reactions. To
some of the readers of this book the mental vivisection which I
had to practise upon Paul may seem merely brutal. I would remind them first that it was a necessary part of a very lofty task;
second, that Paul himself in his best moments would have gladly
accepted all and more of my torturing manipulation for the sake
of that high enterprise; and lastly that the final result upon

Paul, the individual human being, was a very great spiritual enrichment.

It is difficult to give you any clear idea of my aim beyond saying that, having found this uniquely typical yet also exceptionally self-conscious being, I intended to influence him periodically in such a manner that he should see his world as far as possible from the Neptunian point of view. I should then be able to observe in detail the effect of this vision on his primitive nature. Had he been of the heroic type, this policy would have turned him into some kind of prophet or crank. But he was made of milder stuff, and would never spoil my experiment in that style. Indeed, one effect of my intermittent manipulation of his experience was to inspire him with a dread of showing himself to be different from others. Just because he possessed a whole secret world of his own, and was prone to see the actual world turn farcical or hideous in the light cast by that other world, he became increasingly anxious to maintain a secure footing in the actual world and conform to all the customary modes of behaviour. For in spite of his Neptunian vision he remained essentially a product of his own world. But as my influence extended, he was forced to admit that there was something in him profoundly alien to his environment, something alien even to himself. At times he feared he was going mad; at other times he would persuade himself with immense complacency that he was 'inspired', and that he must indeed be a prophet; but as he was incapable of any such heroism, this delusion was soon shattered. There were moments when he threatened to break into two personalities, one the natural Paul, the other a violent and spasmodic idealist. But I had chosen him carefully; he was too well integrated actually to succumb to this easy solution of his conflict. Instead of disintegrating, he remained one mind, though torn and perplexed.

But as time passed a change came over him. At first he had regarded his native terrestrial mentality as himself, and the Neptunian influence as alien, disturbing, irrational, insane. He was fascinated by it, but he wished to keep it thoroughly suppressed and ineffective. Later, however, it came to seem a divine enlightenment, sane and joyous, still alien to himself but most precious. Then at last he began to try to live according to my influence, and incurred at once the ridicule and hostility of his own world. With horror he now foreswore his 'inner light' which had so misled him. He earnestly tried to become blind to it, and to be like his fellows. But my influence left him no peace. It found something responsive in him, which, as he matured, was emboldened to identify itself wholly with the Neptunian point of view. Little by little he came to think of this Neptunian factor in his mind as truly 'himself', and the normal Terrestrial as 'other', something like an unruly horse which his true self must somehow break in and ride. There followed a period of struggle, which ended in despair; for it became clear that he could not master his Terrestrial nature. Indeed, it seemed to him that he himself was bound and helpless upon the back of this uncontrolled animal; or that while his body and his mundane intelligence went about the world performing all manner of aimless antics, his essential spirit was imprisoned somewhere in his head watching all, but almost wholly impotent. This essential spirit which he regarded as 'himself' was not, of course, merely my influence in him; it was his own best and most human nature, on which my influence was able to work. But this best of his was only the rudimentary best which was characteristic of his species; and though my influence had endowed it with an immense treasure of imagination, it remained almost wholly ineffective, as is usual with your kind. Yet there were times in his life when Paul did succeed in acting in a manner that was really human, and on these occasions my influence played a part. Of these crises I shall presently tell.

2. THE CHILD PAUL

I know Paul perhaps better than I know myself. I have *been* Paul. I have been Paul throughout his life, and watched him to the very moment of his death. The more important passages of his life I have experienced again and again. I know little intimate facts about him, like the feel of the inside of his mouth. I know the feel of Paul slightly drunk, Paul sexually excited, and Paul with one of his bad colds. I know, far better than Paul himself knew it, the obscure tone of his whole body, when through eating too many muffins, he seemed to see the world itself turn foul. I know also, and can hold together for comparison, the feel of Paul the child, Paul the boy, Paul the young man, stiffening into middle age, and Paul awaiting death in helpless senility.

Fortunately there is no need for me to tell you all the details that I know about Paul. I have only to make you realize the main mental themes or motifs of his life. I need not, for instance, tell you much about his birth. It was a normal birth. Several times I have examined the obscure experiences which harassed him during that earliest of his adventures. For it seemed possible that even then something might have occurred to contribute to his idiosyncrasies. But neither in his passage into the outer world nor in his fungoid pre-natal experience (so difficult for the explorer to penetrate) did I find anything significant, save what is common to all his kind. In Paul, whose nature was more sensitive than the average, the shock of exchanging the elysium of the womb for an alien world was serious, and was accentuated somewhat by the clumsiness of the physician. But it caused no unusual damage to his mind, nothing but the common yearning toward a warmer, cosier, less noxious world, which, in so many of you, favours legends of a golden age in the past, or of a golden heaven in the future.

One feature of Paul's experience of birth was indeed significant, and served to confirm my choice of him as a subject of experiment. Like many others, he did not breathe till a smack made him take breath to bellow. I experienced, of course, his bewildered fury at the chastisement. I also experienced his awareness of the cold air that flooded his lungs, and the shock of glee that came with it. In that instant a connexion was registered in Paul's mind for ever after, a connexion between what I may call fate's smiting and the breath of life. In after years Paul was to know himself a coward, yet in spite of his cowardice, he was ever to seek in the harshness of fate for the breath of a new life. Even though, in all his ages, he yearned to creep back into the warm close peace of the womb, he craved also to absorb into his blood the atmosphere of a wider world.

I need not describe Paul's arduous self-education in the cot, the nursery and the garden. Like all organisms he had to learn to cope with his world. Like all animals he had to grapple with the problems of perceiving and acting in a world of space and time. Little by little he learned to observe and to respond to all manner of objects, such as the rotund and fragrant dairy of his mother's breast, and the less delectable bottle. He learned the geography of his own body, mapping it out patiently, unwittingly, day by day, in a surprisingly intricate system of explorations, discovering that all these complex findings fell together beautifully in a three-dimensional system of touch and sight. Many great arts he acquired, first the art of sucking, and of shifting about in bed, then the art of the rattle. Presently he learned how to use his whole body as a vehicle to transport him to and fro in a wider sphere. He mastered the more dangerous arts of crawling and walking, the art of the bouncing ball, and so on. Meanwhile he had distinguished the soothing and indignant tones of the human voice. Also, the intermittent human breasts and arms and laps and voices had fallen into order to make more or less constant systems, each of which might be expected to behave in a distinctive manner. Then at last he discovered that human voices had meanings, and that he himself could use these noises so as to make the great grown-up creatures do his bidding.

This power of controlling the movements of adults was one of Paul's most exciting early triumphs. It was a limited and erratic power. All too often the great creature refused to obey, or actually turned the tables and compelled him to do what he did not want to do. Altogether these adults were a very perplexing fact in Paul's early life. In some ways they were so necessary and reliable, in others so inconsequent and even noxious. Of course, Paul did not consciously make these generalizations, but they were implied in his behaviour. Thus in certain respects, such as physical care and protection, he trusted the adult absolutely, but in others he learned to expect nothing but misunderstanding and ridicule. In yet other respects he himself was so influenced by the prestige suggestion which these mighty beings brought to bear on him, that many of their unintelligible admirations and taboos gradually took root in his own nature. For instance, he slavishly accepted their views about sex. Very early in his childhood he had begun to take an interest in those parts of his body which adults pointedly ignored. He had discovered that a vague pleasure occurred when these

61

organs were touched. But long before he was told that it was wicked and dangerous to take any notice of them, he already profoundly felt that it was so, merely through the awkwardness that beset adults whenever he referred to them. Had Paul been born a young baboon or chimpanzee he would at least have escaped the agony of mind and waste of energy which, as I shall tell later, he, like so many of his kind, incurred through this too ready acceptance of adult standards. Meanwhile it was inevitable that, before sex became an imperious need, Paul should adjust himself to adult standards in this as in so many other respects. Adults were objects which one had to learn to cope with, just as one had to learn to cope with dogs and chairs and fire. Sometimes one failed and suffered for it, but on the whole one succeeded.

I must not, however, dwell on the process by which Paul gradually mastered these earliest problems. In all his adventures, I, his parasite, tasted his success and failure. I suffered all his bumps, scratches and scaldings. I saw beforehand what was impending. I saw both that it was inevitable and that with a little more skill it might have been avoided. Had I chosen, I might have played the mother to him and saved him from many a disaster, but it was better to let him learn. During his earliest years I refrained from any kind of influence, since it was important that he should develop normally up to a certain stage.

Little by little Paul's world crystallized into extensive patterns. No longer a meagre and obscure flux of dream-like forms, it became a more or less reliable world of 'common sense', a house and garden, with surrounding continents made up of other houses and gardens, streets and fields. Gradually also he was able to look backwards not merely into a confused cloud of pastness but along a brief but orderly vista of nights and days.

But with this gradual increase of order in his daylight world, Paul became more and more distressed by that other chaotic world which swallowed him at night. When the light was put out and he was left alone in bed, the whole reliable order vanished. Even if he kept his eyes shut, terrifying shades confronted him with their vague and shifty forms. He saw animal heads and shoulders, and stealthily moving gorilla arms. They kept changing from one thing into another thing. They were unintelligible and therefore terrible.

Still worse, sometimes the seething confusion of shadows would be dominated by a single staring eye. Paul could not escape it. Wherever he looked, there it was, watching him. Perhaps it was God's eye, seeing right through him, coldly noting all his most secret wickedness. Perhaps God had done away with the world of day because Paul had been so naughty in it. Perhaps there was nothing now but Paul and God and the close dark, with one streak of light pretending to be under the door, to keep up appearances. Somehow the Eye seemed to him both very wise and very stupid, a vindictive clever thing, that intended to kill him just by gazing at him, for no reason but that he did not please the Eye. Sometimes Paul was so terrified that he screamed. Then an exasperated grown-up would appear and ask what on earth was the matter. He could never tell, for grown-ups were somehow blind to the night world, and would think him silly. But to me, Paul's trouble was very real, and also intelligible. To Paul, though he knew it not, the night was the womb. When he was very sleepy, it promised rest and peace; but when he was not sleepy, he regarded it as a well of blackness, stuffiness, formlessness, negation. It threatened to swallow him back from the bright orderly extra-uterine world of day, with its complicated geography, its reliable persons, and its winds that came with obscure messages from still wider spheres.

Throughout Paul's life this contrast of the day world and the night world lay at the back of his thinking and feeling, influencing it, perplexing it. As he grew older, however, the two worlds seemed to interpenetrate more and more, until at last he found that there was a day view of everything and a night view also. But which was the true view? Perhaps the night view of things was in fact just nightmare, a bad dream. But then perhaps it was the other way round. Perhaps the whole day universe was just a foolish dream of the eternal foetus imprisoned in the eternal womb. In early days, of course, Paul never thought of the problem in this way, but I myself could see how the obscure movements of his mind were related to the forgotten experience of birth.

There was one aspect of the night which seemed even to the child Paul very different from the night which imprisoned him in bed, namely the starry sky. He seldom saw it, but even a brief glimpse of it would have lasting effect on him. It gave him a sort of calm elation which fortified him against the terrors of darkness, and would sometimes even last into the next day, soothing his troubles and tempering his joys. This experience, which played an important part in Paul's life, was not simply a spontaneous outcome of his own nature. It was in part due to my presence in his mind, though in part also to his native disposition. Throughout his life, these occasions on which he was able to regard the night sky had a very considerable effect on me, the imprisoned and often fatigued observer of all his experience. They afforded me refreshing glimpses of something common to his world and my own. When I had become too deeply immersed in the minutiae of Paul's behaviour, and was beginning to feel your world more real than mine, the sight of the stars, even through the inefficient eyes of a member of your species, would recall to me with great vividness the Neptunian plains and dwarf jungles, the sky-piercing towers and bland inhabitants of my own far-future world. This vivid recollection would rekindle in me the still, flame-like ardour which is the spirit of our doomed but unperturbed community. And the serene emotion which then surged through me would infect Paul also, lending a tone to his experience, which, though he could never properly account for it, he came in time to recognize as in some manner a gift from a source beyond his mundane nature. I well remember the hush of surprise and gurgle of delight with which the child Paul first greeted the stars. He was in his mother's arms. He stretched out his own fat arms and turned his head slowly from side to side, surveying the heaven. On another occasion, much later, when he was being brought home from a Christmas party, so tired that he could hardly walk, a brilliant night sky overpowered him so that he burst into tears of uncomprehending joy.

As the years advanced, Paul's sense that the starry night was present even by day became an increasing influence in his life. This was partly my doing; for I soon found that by giving him visual images of the night sky in the midst of mundane situations I could help him to regard the affairs of himself and his companions with Uranian detachment. There was an early stage in his development when, through this action of mine, he came to think of the universe as a sandwich made of the upper and nether night, with, between them, the meat of day. Below was the horrible darkness and confusion and closeness which he encountered in his stuffy bedroom. Above was the high mystery of the stars. Between was the world of familiar things.

This middle world had already spread outwards to become a vague expanse of countries, embracing somewhere beyond the familiar streets all kinds of wonders, which were nevertheless definitely day-time wonders. Somewhere there was India, full of tigers, elephants, jewelled princes, and jugglers. Elsewhere lay Iceland, all solid ice, with rivers of fire running down the crystal volcanoes. Then there was France, where they ate frogs and snails and were terribly polite; Germany, where they made cheap copies of English toys, and fought duels; Greece, where they wore no clothes except helmets with clothes-brushes on them; Egypt, all mummies and crocodiles; Fairyland, where magic happened more easily than in England. Yet even in England, magic was not unknown. There was Santa Claus, and dozens of lucky and unlucky things to be sought and avoided.

Over the whole world of countries hung the sky, a blue or cloudy ceiling. Here a discrepancy entered into Paul's universe. If you thought about it from the day-time point of view, you believed that beyond the sky and the stars there was heaven, full of winged angels in nightgowns, their eyes always turned upwards. And above them again was God, whom Paul had somehow come to think of as a huge grown-up, sprawling from horizon to horizon, and looking down precisely at Paul, with eyes that saw even his thoughts. Somehow those eyes were the same as the Eye that stared at him in the nether darkness of his bedroom. When Paul remembered the Eye by day, he would repeat rapidly, 'Oh God, I love you, I love you, I love you.'

But if you thought of things from the point of view of the starry night, God and the angels did not seem to fit in very well. Paul half believed that they were pictures painted on the ceiling of the day world.

In time, of course, Paul's day world ceased to be flat, and became a huge ball. At this stage the universe was more like a dumpling than a sandwich. Vaguely Paul still conceived the three levels of existence. The nether night was deep down within the ball of the

day world. The starry night was all around it. On the ball were all
the countries except Fairyland, which was nowhere. Many of the
countries were British Possessions, and red. At school he learned
much about England and the Empire, and became a patriot. The
English were – well, English. They had the greatest empire in the
world. They were the only people who played fair in games, and
were kind to animals, and could govern black people, and fight a
losing battle to the end, and rule the seas. And because they were
such fine people, God had hidden a lot of coal and iron under their
country, so that they could use it for ships and engines and for
making thousands of things that other countries were not clever
enough to make for themselves. God had also written the Bible in
English, because it was the best language, and the angels talked it.

Paul's patriotism was largely an affectation. At this time he had
a great longing to be like his fellows, and his fellows made it very
obvious that they were patriotic. Also he found in patriotism a
source of self-gratulation. Somehow or other, through patriotism,
the worm that was the ordinary Paul became one of the lords of the
earth. But there was also another factor at work. He had already
begun to feel an obscure impulse to devote himself to ends beyond
private gratification. Much of this sadly misconceived yearning
for lofty ends was expressed in bragging about his school and vilify-
ing other schools; but the Empire afforded it a more imposing
object.

3. EARLY EXPERIMENTS ON PAUL

Not until Paul was already at school did I begin to exercise a
deliberate influence over him. My aim was to prepare him to attain
in early maturity as complete an insight as possible into the Neptunian view of Terrestrial affairs. In his early years I seldom influenced him, but the rare occasions on which I did so had a deep
effect on him. They were designed to intensify his consciousness
beyond the normal limitations of his species. By goading and
delicately controlling his attention I contrived to make him start-
lingly aware, now and again, of data which commonly lie beyond
the apprehension of the First Men. The scope of my early work

upon him might be described by saying that I forced him to a more vivid sense of the reality and uniqueness of perceptual objects, of himself, of others as selves, and also of his own underlying unity with others, and of his own participation in the cosmos.

For instance, to deal with the simplest matter first, Paul once found a curious green pebble. He picked it up and examined it intently, noting with delight its veining, its smooth curvature, its rigidity. He turned it about, fingered it, tapped it. Then suddenly I flooded him with a spate of relevant imagery, visual and tactual, so that he seemed to encounter in this one pebble the whole splendour of sight, the whole poignancy of touch. The thing suddenly leapt at him with its unveiled reality. The change in his experience was as impressive as the change from imagery to actual perception, from picturing a friend's face to actually seeing it. It was as though the earlier experience, which at the time seemed normally vivid, had been after all but a shadowy imagination of a pebble, compared with the later experience, which was an actual apprehension of an objective reality. It was over in a moment. Paul dropped the pebble and collapsed on the grass, holding his head in his hands. For a moment he thought some one had thrown a pebble at him and that it had gone right through his head. He opened his eyes. Everything seemed ordinary again. Then he caught sight of the pebble, half-hidden under a dandelion leaf. It was just a little round green thing, but it seemed to look at him meaningly. As they regarded one another, Paul and the pebble, Paul felt the pebble rushing at him again. He covered his eyes and sat for a long while thinking of nothing but his splitting head. He had been rather badly hurt, but also he was intrigued. The effect was something like his forgotten experience of birth, a confusion of shock, pain, brilliant novelty, fear of the unknown, and exhilaration.

Paul spent the next two days in bed with a 'bilious headache'. When he was recovered, he went in search of his pebble. He picked it up almost as though it were a live bomb, but though it raised a vivid memory of the adventure, it gave him no fresh experience.

I repeated this experiment on Paul at rare intervals and in relation to very diverse objects, such as his precious knife, the tolling of a bell, a flying hawk, and his own hand. The last entailed a whole week in bed, for not only had he perceived his hand externally as he had perceived the pebble, he had also perceived it from within; and moreover he had been fascinated by his volitional control of it. It was a little grubby brown hand with black-rimmed nails and many scratches. He turned it about, bending and straightening the fingers, confidently willing it to perform various antics, intensely aware of his own fiat, yet not at all self-conscious in any deeper sense.

Through my influence Paul continued to suffer these experiences throughout his childhood. He became accustomed to them, and to look forward to them with mingled dread and zest. At length I judged him ripe for a different kind of experiment. He had been coveting a minute bronze dog which belonged to one of his companions. He tried to persuade the owner to 'swop' it, but in vain. Paul became more and more obsessed, and finally stole the dog. While he was guiltily playing with it in his own house I played a trick on him. I gave him an intense and detailed visual image of his friend rummaging frantically among his toys for the lost dog. So aggressive did this image become that it blotted out Paul's actual environment. It had, moreover, the intensified reality that he had first encountered in the pebble. Paul's reaction was strange. For a moment he stared at the hallucination, while hatred welled within him. Then, as soon as the vision had faded, he rushed into the street and dropped the little bronze figure down a grid. Henceforth he treated his former friend with shocking spite, mingled with terror.

I did not attempt to influence Paul's slowly dawning awareness of self till he was already well advanced in boyhood. One day, after he had been bathing with his favourite schoolfellow, the two boys, naked, wet, gleaming in the sunlight, had a friendly wrangle over a towel. They tugged in opposite directions, shouting and panting. For a moment they stood still, staring into one another's eyes. Suddenly I re-kindled in Paul all his past groping realizations of the difference between himself and the other, all his past obscure awareness of 'me' and 'you'. I focused, so to speak, the whole vague illumination of this mass of experience upon the present moment. As formerly the pebble and his hand, so now his friend and his own being, impinged upon him with overwhelming reality. It was a reality not alone of visual and tactual form but also of experiencing. Through my manipulation of his imagery he seemed to enter imaginatively into the mind of the other, to have the feel of a different being, in a different body. A fly settled on the other's neck. Paul felt it tickle, and felt the quick contortion that sent it away. Through the other's eyes he seemed to see his own intent face, and his own arms lightly pulling at the towel. He began murmuring to himself, 'I, Paul; you, Dick; I, Dick; you, Paul.' And through Dick's eyes he seemed to see his own lips moving. Through Dick's ears and through his own ears also he heard his own voice. Dick, meanwhile, had seen the sudden intensity of Paul's expression, and was alarmed. Paul saw, and vividly experienced, Dick's alarm. They dropped the towel. Paul reached out a hand and felt Dick's shoulder, as formerly he had felt the pebble. 'Odd!' he said, 'I've waked up. I do sometimes. But never quite this way before.' Dick began to question, but Paul went on, 'I sort-of woke to be really *me*. Then I was *you*. And both of us at once. Did it happen to you too?' Dick shook his head, very perplexed. Then came the headache. Paul dropped, and lay whimpering, with his hands over his eyes.

My next experiment was performed during a violent quarrel between Paul and Dick. Paul had spent a free afternoon making a boat. He was hollowing it with a gouge borrowed from Dick. Dick arrived to demand the gouge, which was long overdue, and was needed for hollowing his own boat. Paul, intent on his work and eager to finish it before tea, refused to surrender the tool. They wrangled, while Paul carried on his work. Dick tried to stop him. At this moment I forced on Paul a vivid apprehension of the other boy, and of his craving to have his tool, and of his rage against Paul. Paul stopped working. Once more he seemed for a moment to *be* Dick, and to see his own ugly scowl through Dick's eyes. For a moment Paul hung paralysed in a mental conflict. Then suddenly he jabbed Dick's hand with the gouge. Both boys screamed with Dick's pain. Paul rushed toward the door, crying, 'Beast, get out of me, you taste horrid.' Before he reached the door he vomited. Then he fled, yelling. He carried off the gouge.

This reaction of Paul's was very typical of his species. His brief insight into the other's point of view merely filled him with resentment. Typical also was his subsequent remorse, which tortured

69

him during his period of illness after this experiment. Dick had been
thoroughly frightened. It seemed to him that Paul had gone mad.
In time, however, the friendship was restored, and even deepened;
for Paul now treated Dick with a gentleness and understanding
beyond his years. Occasionally I induced in him the more vivid
apprehension of his friend and himself, but I carefully refrained
from doing so when their interests were violently opposed.

In this way I produced in Paul a self-insight and insight into
others which is very unusual in your species. His rare abnormal
experiences now coloured his whole life, and sowed in him the
seed of a lifelong conflict between the behaviour natural to his
kind and the behaviour which his enhanced insight demanded.
When he found himself forced to choose between the two, he almost
always acted in the baser way, though afterwards he was bitterly
remorseful. Once or twice, however, things turned out differently.
I will give one example.

Paul was one of those timid boys who is a constant temptation
to the bully. When any bullying was afoot in which Paul himself
was not involved, he always took care not to interfere. Sometimes
he would actually try to ingratiate himself with the stronger party.
One winter day at school, when Paul and a few others of his form
were supposed to be doing their 'preparation', the arch bully of
the form began tormenting a little Jew whom Paul intensely disliked. The smaller boys, with Paul among them, looked on,
applauding now and then with anxious giggles. I chose this moment for an experiment. With dismay Paul felt his cursed imagination beginning to work. He tried to bury himself in his French
exercise, but vainly. Do what he would, he could not help entering
imaginatively into 'that beastly little Jew'. Then he started being
not only the Jew but the bully also. He imagined the big lout feeling
the helpless self-disgust which he himself had felt in his one experiment in the art of bullying. I worked up this imagination till he
really apprehended the mind of the bully far better than the bully
himself. He realized vividly the drowsy, fumbling, vaguely distressed and frightened life that was going on in that hulk of flesh,
and was disguised even from itself by the pose of braggartism.
Suddenly Paul said aloud in a clear but dreamy voice, 'Chuck it,
Williams, you're hurting yourself.' There was a sudden silence of

amazement. Paul, terrified at his own voice, bowed over his French book. The bully remarked, 'Your turn next', and then applied himself once more to his victim, who squealed. Paul rose, crossed the floor, laid a hand on the bully's shoulder, and was sent crashing into the hearth. He sat for a moment among the cinders listening to the general laugh. Then slowly he rose, and slowly surveyed his grinning fellow-mortals. Williams gave an extra twist to the Jew's arm, and there followed a yell. Paul, saying quietly, 'Williams, you've got to stop', put his own left hand into the fire and picked out a large completely redhot coal. Ignoring the pain and the smell of his burning flesh, he went over to Williams and said, 'Now, clear out or I'll brand you.' Someone tried to seize Paul's arm. He used his coal with effect, so that the other retired. Then he rushed at Williams. The bully fled. I felt Paul's eyebrows rise and his lips twist in a whimsical smile. He stood dreaming for a moment, then restored the still faintly glowing coal to its place in the fire. Suddenly he caught sight of the charred and smoking mess that was his hand. All along he had been aware of the pain, but he had calmly ignored it. But now that the incident was completed, ignoring was impossible. His strange exaltation vanished. He gave one sharp scream, half for pain, half for surprise, and then fainted.

Paul's hand recovered within a few weeks, though of course it remained scarred for ever. Paul's mind was more deeply affected. He was terrified about himself. He felt that he had been possessed, and he dreaded being let in for even worse scrapes in the future. All the same, he was rather proud of himself, and half-wished he could be like that always.

4. PAUL'S CHANGING WORLD

During his schooldays Paul suffered more than the normal growing pains, for his mind was shooting upward in response not only to normal but to abnormal influences. He was outgrowing not only toys and childish interests; he was outgrowing the world which school life imposed upon him. Like a crab that has become too big for its shell and must struggle out of it, Paul was now too big for his world. It had cracked under the stress of his vital movement, and he was in the act of issuing from it in a soft vulnerable, but flexible and expansible covering, which some day would harden into a new and ampler dwelling-place.

Two conflicting influences dominated him at school, the impulse to assume the stereotyped 'schoolboy' nature and live comfortably in the schoolboy world, and in opposition to this the impulse to find himself and to find reality. He strove to live according to the schoolboy ethic, partly because he genuinely admired it, partly so as to assume the protective colouring of his surroundings. But he could never succeed. The forces at work within him were too strong for him. In his early schooldays Paul never clearly understood that he was trying to live two inconsistent lives at once. He did not know that, while he was so earnestly trying to adjust himself to the school universe, he was also trying to burst that universe apart and grow an entirely new universe to suit the expanding tissues of his mind.

This growth, or rather this profound metamorphosis, was controlled by certain experiences which had an enduring effect on him. They were, so to speak, the centres of reorganization which, little by little, changed the larval Paul into the adult imago. These seminal experiences were of two kinds, though he did not clearly distinguish between them. His attention was arrested, and he was stung into excited admiration by two widespread facts: by the intricacy and relentlessness of physical happenings, and also by biological perfection, or at least functional perfection of every sort.

Paul's sense of the austerity of the physical universe awoke early. Even in the nursery he had conceived an uncomprehending respect for the mechanism of natural events. This spontaneous movement of piety toward 'nature' developed not only into a strong scientific interest, but also into a strangely exultant awe, for which there seemed to be no rational justification.

It was his father who first pointed out to him the crossing wave-trains of a mountain tarn, and by eloquent description made him feel that the whole physical world was in some manner a lake rippled by myriads of such crossing waves, great and small, swift and slow. This little significant experience took place during a holiday spent on the Welsh moors. They were standing on a crag overlooking the grey 'llyn'. They counted five distinct systems of waves, some small and sharp, some broad and faint. There were also occasional brief 'cat's paws' complicating the pattern. Father and son went down to the sheltered side of the lake and contemplated its more peaceful undulations. With a sense almost of sacrilege, Paul stirred the water with his stick, and sent ripple after ripple in widening circles. The father said, 'That is what you are yourself, a stirring up of the water, so that waves spread across the world. When the stirring stops, there will be no more ripples.' As they walked away, they discussed light and sound and the rippled sky, and the sun, great source of ripples. Thus did an imaginative amateur anticipate in a happy guess the 'wave mechanics' which was to prove the crowning achievement of the physics of the First Men. Paul was given to understand that even his own body, whatever else it was, was certainly a turmoil of waves, inconceivably complex but no less orderly than the waves on the tarn. His apprehension of this novel information was confused but dramatic. It gave him a sense of the extreme subtlety and inevitability of existence. That even his own body should be of this nature seemed to him very strange but also very beautiful. Almost at the outset, however, he said, 'If my body is all waves, where do *I* come in? Do I make the waves, or do the waves make me?' To this the father answered, with more confidence than lucidity, 'You are the waves. What stirs is God.'

This experience remained with Paul for ever. It became for him the paradigm of all physical sciences, and at the same time an epitome of the mystery of life. In his maturity he would often, when he came upon still water, pause to disturb its serenity. The little act would seem to him darkly impious yet also creative. He would mutter to himself, 'God stirs the waters.' Sometimes he would take a handful of little stones and throw them into the pond, one after the other in different directions. Then he would stand motionless, watching the intersecting circles spread and fade and die, till at last peace was wholly restored.

Paul's first view of the moon through his father's modest telescope was another memorable experience. He had already seen a ship disappearing below the horizon, and had been told that the earth and the moon were round. But actually to see the rotund

73

moon, no longer as a flat white shilling, but as a distant world covered with mountains, was an experience whose fascination he never outgrew. Throughout his life he was ready to gaze for ten minutes at a time through telescope or field-glass at the bright summits and black valleys along the line between lunar night and day. This vision had a startling power over him which he himself could not rationally justify. It would flash mysteriously upon him with bewildering and even devastating effect in the midst of some schoolboy activity, in the midst of a Latin lesson, or morning prayers, or a game of cricket, or a smutty story. Under the influence of this experience he began to devour popular astronomy books. He looked with new eyes at the first page of the school atlas, which had hitherto meant nothing to him. Rapidly the schoolboy universe ceased to be the whole real universe, and was reduced to a very faulty picture of a tiny corner of a universe which teemed with suns and inhabited worlds. For at this stage he imagined that every star was attended by a dozen or so populous planets.

He was perplexed to find that most adults, though many of them fully believed in some such universe, did nothing with the knowledge. That which to him was so significant was to them either tiresome or terrifying. Even his father, who had helped him to discover the new world, did not seem to appreciate it as it deserved. To the father it did indeed seem wonderful. He called it 'sublime'. But for him it remained merely a sublime irrelevance. It compelled his attention, and in a manner his admiration also; but the tone of his voice, when he was talking of it, suggested a veiled reluctance, almost resentment. He seemed, in spite of all his scientific interest, to be happier and more at home in the world of the Iliad or of the 'Faerie Queene'. The son, on the other hand, though he did his best to appreciate these dream worlds, was never moved by them. But the stars gave him an intense exhilaration, which, when he tried to justify it to his father, turned out to be, or to seem, wholly irrational.

Another overwhelming fact that gradually emerged into the child Paul's ken, partly through the help of his father, partly through his own unaided apprehension, was what he came later to call 'the aliveness of all living things'. His boon companion of early days had been a terrier, with whom he used surreptitiously to share his bread and butter, bite by bite. Of course he believed that this creature had a mind much more like his own mind than was actually the case; but also, by long experience of this animal, he learned to enter into imaginative sympathy with a mind that was not human. This canine friendship drove deep into his own mind and heart both a sense of the kinship of all living things and a sense of their differences. Though Jack could enter into a romp, he could never be induced to play trains. Nor could he be persuaded that rabbits were beings like himself, whose lives should be respected. Paul himself, of course, had to make that discovery; but even in his earliest fly-tormenting and beetle-crushing phase he was already making it. Later there came a stage when this mystery of alien lives was his chief absorption and his chief perplexity. He would watch ants toiling through the grass-jungle with food for the public store, or 'talking' to one another as they met on one of their highways, or fighting to the death in organized battle. Always, of course, he imputed far too much of human intelligence to these strange beings. But even when at a much later date he discovered this error, he remained firm in his sense of their fundamental community with himself. Even worms, exploring the soil with their blind noses, seemed to him infinitely more like himself than the soil they devoured. And when one of them was snapped up by a thrush, Paul suffered an agony of indecision, debating whether to save the worm or let the bird have its dinner in peace. When he saw a cat with a mouse, he rushed indignantly to the rescue; yet somehow, after the event, he fell to wondering if he had merely been meddlesome.

In short, during this phase of his growth he was overwhelmed with what some would call a mystical apprehension of the inner being of all living things, and shocked by their insensitivity to one another, their essential harmfulness to one another. He was troubled by the fact that he himself ate meat and wore leather boots, and amazed that even kind-hearted persons, who doted on their own pets, did likewise without any hesitation. He was still more distressed by a streak of real sadism which survived in himself. At one time he used to catch wasps and cut them in two, so as to observe the strange behaviour of the parts. Worse still was his reaction to stag-hunting. His rare excursions into the world of sport did not occur until he was in his last year at school. They ceased while he was at the University. A well-to-do and much respected friend of his father sometimes invited Paul to spend part of the summer holidays at his house in Devon. He taught Paul to ride, and was determined to make a sportsman of him. When the lad was considered proficient, he was taken out to follow the hounds. With a sickening guiltiness, a sickening sense of his own bad horsemanship, with a sickening blend of adulation and contempt for the rest of the field, he let himself be bumped over moors and through covers, down lanes and through villages, till surprisingly he found himself in at the death. There at last was the stag, chin-deep in a river, or slithering on the roof of some outhouse in a village street, or more majestically at bay in the angle of two hedges. Then Paul exulted, even while he sickened with shame and pity. Why did he do it? he wondered. Why did he stand there watching the great weary beast mauled by the hounds, while the huntsmen tried to grab one of its antlers from behind? And when the knife went home, why did he feel, just for a fraction of a second, a sudden glee and triumph? Why was he so anxiously self-complacent as he stood at his horse's head chewing cake and apples, while the stag was disembowelled and the hounds clamoured for their share? Why did he so desire to be taken for one of these sporting gentry, these overgrown schoolboys? These questions remained for Paul unanswered. Clearly his larval nature was making a desperate effort to reject the more developed mentality that I was forcing on him. In spite of his incompetence, he felt toward the sporting English gentleman not merely respect and envy but a deep kinship. In his revulsion against the primeval hunter and fighter, and aristocrat, he was divided against himself. Essentially the same conflict racked him a few years later when the war forced him to choose once and for all between the two allegiances. But of course in his war-perplexity, the primitive motive was reinforced by much that was by no means primitive.

IV *Paul Comes of Age*

1. PAUL AND SEX

I HAVE now to describe Paul's advance from boyhood to early
manhood, which he reached just before the outbreak of the European War. In order to do this I must tell chiefly of his changing
reactions to three facts in his experience, namely to sex, to personality, and to the immense impersonal.

As I have already said, Paul discovered early in his childhood
that a very special and delectable experience could be obtained
from that part of his body on which his elders had conferred a most
intriguing mystery. Their dropped voices, their hesitations, their
veiled suggestions and warnings, had long ago roused his curiosity
and prepared him to feel guilt in his new pleasure. Later, during
adolescence, the natural development of his body, combined with
the influence of stories and drawings circulated at school, increased
his itch of experimentation in this field. His own sensitivity, which
had been exaggerated by my influence, made him peculiarly
susceptible.

In this new experience Paul found something unique, arresting,
mysteriously significant, yet significant of he knew not what. I
myself, the observer of these disturbing events, can only describe
the character which he seemed to himself to find in them, by calling
it an impression of almost mystical fulfilment, or of communion
with some presence, or being, or power, wholly beyond the grasp of
his intellect. It was as though he had unexpectedly discovered how
to reach down and touch the deep, living heart of reality, and as
though this contact were to quicken him through and through with
an exquisite, though deadly thrill. The experience was all too
brief, and after it came a vague fear. In the very act it seemed to be
promising more than it could ever give. That fleeting contact with
the heart of things was but an earnest, seemingly, of some more
profound and lasting penetration, not yet to be achieved.

Now this attainment and this promise were not wholly illusory.

77

To minds that have passed far beyond your stage of growth, every sensory experience whatever may afford this exquisite, inebriating sense of contact with objective reality. More primitive minds, however, seldom attain this insight. For them it is only when the sensuous has the added glamour of rarity, or of sin and sanctity, that it can deliver its full content. And so the amazed spirit falsely assumes that only through this one particular sensory window can it reach out and touch reality. Among you the sexual experience alone has universally this unique significance and power. For in you, as in the apes, almost alone among mammals, reproductive potency is constant and excessive. And in nearly all your cultures the consequent excessive interest in sex has been thwarted, in most cases very clumsily.

In Paul's case it soon became clear that, unless I intervened, the mystery and horror with which sex was treated would cause in him an obsessive fascination. His plight is well enough expressed in a poem which he wrote at this time, but showed to no one. I should explain that henceforth he was frequently to indulge in what he regarded as poetical expression. I shall occasionally quote from his writings to illustrate his spiritual progress. Note that even at this early stage he was deserting the forms of verse that were still orthodox. Here is the poem.

SIN

I have touched filth.
Only with the finger tip I touched it,
  inquisitive of the taste of it.
But it creeps.
It has spread over my body a slime,
and into my soul a stupor.
It is a film over the eyes,
blurring the delicate figuring and ethereal hue of things.
It clogs the ears.
The finer tones of truth are muffled from me.
Beauty has turned her back on me.
I have shamed her, I am desolate.
There is no escape from myself.
And in my loneliness, –
It was because of my mad loneliness, –

I touched again,
I dabbled for a moment in the sweet filth,
and fled back shuddering in the silence.
Presently I shall slink down again and wallow,
for solace in my mad loneliness.

One of the most difficult facts for the Neptunian explorer to grasp about primitive minds is their obsession and their abject guilt and disgust in respect of bodily appetites. In the constitution of the last human species the excess energy of these appetites is very largely sublimated, innately, into the spiritual and intellectual life. On the other hand, whenever they do demand direct satisfaction, they are frankly and zestfully gratified. In Paul's species it was the sexual appetite that caused trouble. Now it did not suit me that Paul should become tangled inextricably in sex. His whole generation, I knew, was going to develop along the lines of sex mania, in revulsion from the prudery of its predecessors. But it was necessary that Paul should maintain a true balance, so that his spirit's energies should be free to direct themselves elsewhere.

The method by which I brought peace to Paul's troubled mind was easy to me, though disturbing to him. Whenever he began to worry himself with guilty fears, I would force upon his imagination scenes from another world, in which not sex but nutrition was the deed of supreme uncleanness and sanctity. Little by little I pieced together in his mind a considerable knowledge of an early Neptunian species whose fantastic culture has many points in common with your own. Let me here tell you briefly of that culture.

On Neptune, then, there once lived, or from your point of view, there will live, a race of human beings which attained a certain affluence and social complexity, but was ever hampered by its morbid interest in nutrition. By what freakish turns of fortune this state of affairs was brought about, I need not pause to describe. Suffice it that physiological changes had produced in this human species an exaggerated mechanism of hunger. This abnormality saddled all its members with a craving for food much in excess of biological need; and from the blundering social repression of this craving there arose a number of strange taboos and perversions. By the time this Neptunian species had attained civil life, the function of nutrition had become as perverse and malignant as the function of reproduction in your own society. No reference might be made to it in public, save to its excretory side, which was regarded as a rite of purification. Eating became a private and vaguely obscene act. While in many social situations sexual intercourse was a recognized means of expression and diversion, and even drinking was permitted in the less puritanical circles so long as it was performed through the nose, eating in the presence of another person was not tolerated. In every home a special privy was set aside for eating. This was stocked during the night by the public food carriers, who constituted the lowest caste of society. In place of your chastity ideal there arose a fiction that to refrain from eating was virtuous, and that the most holy persons could live without eating at all. Even ordinary folk, though pardoned for occasional indulgence, were supposed to refrain from the filthy act as far as possible. Repressed nutrition had by now coloured the whole life of the race. The mouth occupied in its culture much the same position as the phallus with you. A vast and subtle symbolism, like that which in your culture is associated with the sacred and obscene reproductive act, was generated in this case by the sacred and obscene nutritive act. Eating became at once a sin and an epitome of the divine power; for in eating does not the living body gather into itself lifeless matter to organize it, vitalize it ? The mouth was, of course, never exposed to view. The awful member was concealed behind a little modesty apron, which was worn below the nose. In prehistoric times the lips had formed the chief visual stimulus to sexual interest, and like the rump of the baboon had developed lavish coloration and turgescence. But very early in the cultural development of the species the modesty apron became universal. Even when the rest of the body was unclad, this garment was retained. And just as in your culture the notorious fig-leaf is vaguely suggestive of that which it conceals, so, in this Neptunian culture, the conventionally decorated covering of the mouth came to mimic furtively the dread orifice itself. Owing to the fact that in polite society no sound might be made which betrayed movement of the lips, speech became distorted and debased. One curious consequence of this obscenity of the mouth was the peculiar status of kissing. Though sexual promiscuity was almost universal, kissing was a deadly sin, except between man and wife. A kiss, bestowed in privacy and darkness, was the true consummation of marriage, and was something infinitely more desirable and more disturbing than the procreative act itself. All lovers longed to be united in a kiss; or, if they were innocents, they looked for some unknown fulfilment, which they vaguely and guiltily felt must be somehow connected with the mouth. Coitus they regarded merely as an innocent and peculiarly delightful caress; but the kiss was the dark, exquisite, sacred, mystically significant, forbidden fruit of all their loving. It was a mutual devouring, the act in which, symbolically, the lover took the substance of the other within his or her own system. Through this connexion with romantic love the kiss gathered to itself all that obscure significance of tender personal relations, of spiritual communion between highly developed personalities, which in your world the same romantic love may confer on coitus. Further, since, like your Trobriand Islanders, the less sophisticated races of this species were often ignorant of the connexion between the sexual act and conception, and since, as with those islanders, sexual intercourse outside the marriage bond often failed to produce offspring, it was commonly believed in the more primitive of these Neptunian societies that the true reproductive act was the kiss. Consequently conception and child-birth came to be endowed with the same mystery, sanctity, and obscenity as nutrition. Sex, on the other hand, remained delightfully uncontaminated. These traditions maintained their power even in civilized societies, which had long ago realized the truth about parenthood. Children were carefully instructed in the hygiene of sex, and encouraged to have blithe sexual relations as soon as they needed that form of expression. But in respect of nutrition they were left in disastrous ignorance. As infants they were suckled, but in strict seclusion. Later they were taken to the food-privy and fed; but they were trained never to mention food in public and of course never to expose their mouths. Obscure and terrifying hints were let fall about the disastrous effects of gustatory self-indulgence. They were told not to go to the privy more than once a day, and not to stay longer than necessary. From their companions they gathered much distorted information about eating; and they were likely to contract diverse kinds of nutritive perversion, such as

81

chewing stones and earth, biting one another or themselves for the taste of blood. Often they contracted such a prurient mania of thumb-sucking, that mouth and thumb would fester. If they escaped these perversions, it was by means of ignorant licentiousness in the food-privy. In consequence of this they were prone to contract serious digestive disorders, which moreover, if discovered, inevitably brought them into contempt. In either case they incurred a shattering sense of guilt, and contracted by auto-suggestion many of the symptoms which rumour attributed to their vice. In maturity they were likely to become either secret gourmets or puritans.

The effect of introducing Paul to this remote world was beneficial in more ways than one. Not only did it lead him gradually to regard his own sexual nature with a new tolerance and a new detachment, so that his mind was no longer tethered to the stake of sex; it also gave him a considerable insight into the mentality of his elders, and opened his eyes precociously to the farcical aspect of his species. Of course, he did not seriously believe his visions. Or rather, as the alien world embodied itself with increasing detail in his mind, he could not entirely disbelieve it, but came to regard it as 'over there', instead of 'here' like his own world. I had, of course, made him picture the Neptunian species. He glimpsed its squat stone cities, thronged with nude and bulky caricatures of his own race. He saw their mouth-aprons, and their secret vices of nutrition. He saw also their frank sexual behaviour, and actually from the study of sex in that remote age and world he learned much about sex in his own race. Not only so, but he learned his first lesson in that general detachment from the purely Terrestrial values, which I needed to produce in him. He learned, too, to scrutinize all prized and all condemned things to discover whether they were prized or condemned for their own sakes or for some other reason. For instance, comparing his fantasy world with the normal world, he saw that sexual activity and nutritive activity were both valued in both worlds, but that in each world one of these activities had gathered a purely accidental and farcical significance. On the other hand, in both worlds, love, the passionate admiration of spirit for spirit, was a genuine experience which lent something of its glory here to sex, there to nutrition.

Paul's mysterious life of imagination gave him an understanding of human nature far beyond his years. Combining with his enhanced self-consciousness, it made him strangely sympathetic yet strangely cynical. His companions regarded him as 'queer'. At most times he behaved as a rather selfish and rather cowardly boy, and he was not incapable of spite. Yet at any moment, it seemed, he might blaze up with what to his companions seemed an almost insane generosity and an entirely self-oblivious courage. At other times he displayed a disconcerting indifference and remoteness. In the middle of some wild game he would suddenly 'fade out', play his part perfunctorily or not at all, and presently be seen watching the action with an interest that was somehow not the interest of a boy.

During his schooldays Paul was generally in love with some other boy or with a girl. His erratic temperament prevented the course of true love from running even as smoothly as it does with normal young human animals. One day he would be terrifyingly earnest, next day entirely uninterested, or, worse, interested in the manner of a scientific observer. One day he would be possessive, touchy, spiteful, the next day devoted and self-oblivious. Consequently his loves were uneasy, brief, and in retrospect bitter. The more he was defeated, the more he longed for a lasting intimacy. The more he longed, the more 'impossible' he became. During the latter part of his school career he grew increasingly aware of and absorbed in human personality. It came to seem to him that the only thing of any account in life was the intimacy of one person with another, in fact with a perfect mate. His whole attention was given to the task of finding for himself the perfect mate. Gradually he began to realize that he would never succeed, and indeed that success was almost impossible. It seemed to him that human beings were doomed to miss for ever the only goal worth seeking, and that in their fated striving for it they must ever lacerate one another.

It was with this conviction that Paul ended his much-prolonged school career and embarked upon an arts course at the University of London. He was very unlike the ordinary 'freshman'. Some years older than the average, cripplingly self-conscious, scholastically backward and erratic, but equipped with a very unusual stock of random knowledge, and of insight into human nature, he seemed to his fellows an amiable but rather tiresome freak.

While he was still at the university Paul met a young woman some years older than himself, whose image was destined to be a permanent influence in his mind. From the Terrestrial point of view she was no doubt a delightful creature, though not a paragon of classical or any other recognized kind of beauty. Even to the Neptunian eye, sufficiently fortified by long Terrestrial experience, she was not without charm. Of course, very little of her was visible. Save for the face and hands, her whole body was covered and insulted by the peculiarly grotesque clothing of her period. But in her face there was something more than the prettiness which attracted the males of her own species and was a source of a certain winsome complacency in herself. There was a vitality in it which to me was elusively reminiscent of the full-blown and fully conscious beauty of women of my own species. In fact, there was a hint of the more fully human and more frankly animal spirit, which the Last Men look for in woman and the Last Woman in man. But in the eyes of her contemporaries, and in her own eyes too, this pervading characteristic of her face, of her slow free gait, and, as I was later to discover, of her body also (about which there was something of the young cart-horse), was but an oddity, a blemish. Now Paul believed that he was attracted only by her conventional prettiness. He did not know that my influence had inadvertently brought him under the spell of a beauty beyond his usual ken. He prided himself on being able, in spite of his adoration, to point out and ridicule her imperfections, and even delight in them. He did not know that these very 'imperfections' of body and mind were the source of her strange spell over him. He recognized, almost apologetically, that they made her for him lovelier, more individual, more real, more peculiarly herself. He did not recognize, though in fact he obscurely felt, that her peculiarity was not a falling short from, but a transcending of, Terrestrial beauty. Mentally she was, he felt, exquisitely complementary to himself, yet basically at one with him. She was able to appreciate and enrich his inner life of fantasy, which hitherto he had never revealed to anyone. She flattered him by regarding him as a 'genius'. He was well content that she should treat him also as a dear simpleton whose dreams were impracticable. Above all, he was strengthened by the knowledge that each had become to the other a most necessary playmate and helpmeet, and that each had already been spiritually enriched by the other for ever after.

This girl, whom I will call Katherine, took delight in ' bringing Paul out of his shell', in helping him to hold his own in social intercourse. She taught him to dance; and, though the physical contact made his head swim, he did her credit. They went to many dances, but the custom of the period forbade them to dance together more than two or three times in an evening. Dancing was at first their only opportunity of close contact; for a strange reason. This fundamentally downright and generous creature had unfortunately been educated in a puritanical tradition. Through loyalty to her father, for whom, as I later discovered, she felt a deep affection, she corseted her nature within the limits of a strict social and moral etiquette. By native constitution strong both in animal zest and in maternal tenderness, by upbringing severely conscientious, she had tried to solve the inevitable conflict between her generous vitality and her moral severity by kindliness toward others and strictness toward herself. Maintaining her own puritan conduct, she took vicarious delight in the peccadilloes of others. It was partly her combination of romantically puritanical idealism with imaginative sympathy that won Paul's respect. Her relation with Paul was at first extremely correct. It had to compensate for the restriction of its physical side by a romantic efflorescence on the mental side. They found many intellectual and aesthetic enthusiasms in common. They also inculcated in one another a common zeal for social service. He swore that in the great cause of making a better world he would 'wear always the armour of her love' so that nothing should strike him down. His own love for her would be his lance. Her beauty would be his inspiration, her sense of beauty his guiding star. Theirs was a union, they told one another, primarily of spirit and spirit. The body should fulfil its minor function, in due season.

It was extremely interesting to see how Paul acted his part during the first weeks of this intimacy. The detachment from Terrestrial values which I had been teaching him, at first enabled him to ridicule and damp down his cravings for a more sexual relationship. Neptunian fantasies helped him here. But soon they began to work on the other side also. He came to see the folly and futility of his romance. Externally he remained for long the tame squire of his beloved; but inwardly, though often he was a selfless admirer of this lovely human animal that had confided in him, sometimes he was sheer greedy sex, chafing within the bonds of decency. At other times, behind his caresses he was ice-cold, or even disgusted, or just an ironical observer, correlating events Terrestrial with events Neptunian. But for long these great inner fluctuations appeared to the beloved only as slight whimsical changes of mood, to which with maternal tact she gladly adjusted herself.

As time passed, however, Paul became more 'difficult'. Hitherto, in spite of his moods, he had seemed to the young woman absolutely safe, absolutely devoted to their common code of decency. His occasional respectful importunity flattered her without seriously disturbing her. But now his normal mood began to be penetrated with rather terrifying moments in which his personality seemed to change to something at once more cynical and more violent, more remote and more animal. Most terrifying was the fact that, to her own amazement, she could not feel disgusted, but only conscientious.

The crisis occurred on a summer evening after a dance. Paul and his beloved, flushed with exertion and mutual delight and exalted by a sense of their own daring unconventionality, escaped through the garden to the bare down that fringed their suburb. Arm in arm they walked, then seated themselves on the grass to watch the rising moon. After the usual discreet caresses, Paul extended a reverent hand and stroked her throat. His finger-tips ventured down to the white expanse of bosom, revealed by her low-cut evening dress. Surprised less by his boldness than by her own sudden delight, she caressed the caressing fingers. He ventured further, feeling his way toward her breasts. Paralysed between desire and anxiety, she allowed him to explore those warm, secret, holy excrescences.

This little tactual event, this marvellous, ecstatic new experience, affected both somewhat violently. For Paul it seemed to constitute an important new stage in that quest which had so long tormented him, the quest for reality. It seemed to fulfil, or almost fulfil, at once his hunger for sexual contact and his yearning for spiritual intimacy. It had about it a quality of home-coming after long absence, as though he had been there before in some forgotten existence. It was indeed as though the starved exile, who had for so long been nourished only on phantoms, and had lost even the memory of his motherland, were to find himself back once more in the bosom of reality, bewildered yet fundamentally at home. In her it roused both sexual warmth and also a poignant tenderness almost as of mother for babe. She was torn between a sudden longing to give herself wholly and a sudden alarm at this unprecedented invasion.

How distressed these two innocents would have been had they known that a third person was witness of this shocking deed, that another human being, a man older than Paul by some thousands of years (though not to be born till long after the earth's destruction) was noting through Paul's eyes the moonlit eyes and features of the girl, was himself caressing, though through Paul's hand, the thrilled Terrestrial breasts, and comparing them with corresponding objects upon Neptune! All these data, and also Paul's own guilty swooning ecstasy, I observed with sympathy born of the most intimate acquaintance, but also with amusement and some impatience, in spite of the detachment and remoteness of two thousand million years.

Even Paul himself was in a manner a detached spectator of his own behaviour. He himself was in a manner standing outside himself and observing these two young courting mammals. This detachment I myself had induced in him. For already at this time of his life I had trained him to be the calm spectator of his own reactions in every fervent experience. In the present case it seemed good to emphasize certain aspects of the matter for him. I therefore began to influence the course of his thoughts. As he savoured the experience, he became increasingly aware of a disturbing and fantastic under-current to his delicious perceptions. He saw with the mind's eye an early Neptunian couple engaged upon an act which to them was one of shocking licentiousness and excruciating delight, but to the Terrestrial eye was merely ridiculous. This guilty pair stood facing one another, their mouth-aprons removed. From mouth to crimson mouth there stretched a curious fruit, not unlike a much-elongated banana. With mobile lips both he and she were drawing this object into the mouth, and eating it progressively. They gazed into one another's kindled eyes, their cheeks aflame.

Clearly they were both enrapt in that exquisite sweet horror which is afforded only by the fruit that is forbidden. Paul watched the banana shrinking, the faces approaching one another. His own hand, feeling the responsive breasts, paused, lay inert. The fruit had vanished. The faces made contact in a long mumbling kiss. The vision faded. Paul was left with an agonized conflict of the sublime and the ridiculous, for it was evident to him that in this farcical scene he had witnessed the exquisite union of two impassioned spirits.

For a moment Paul stayed motionless, wondering whether to an alien eye he and Katherine would seem any less comic. Almost he decided to withdraw his hand. But now that I had forced him in the very act of single-minded zest to take an unsympathetic view, I was able to give him an exaltation which was secure against ridicule because it included ridicule. First I let him suffer in a single flash of insight the stabbing pleasure of those two Neptunians. I then flooded his mind with a spate of visions, such that he seemed to himself to be witnessing in a few seconds the whole pageant of amorous adventure. He seemed to see the earliest mutual devourings of microscopic jellies in the sea, the far-flung pollination of great trees, slow reptilian embraces, the aerial copulations of swallows, the rutting of stags, the apes' more conscious amorousness. He saw human forms, brown, yellow, black or white, in their first adventurous fondlings, or clipped together. He saw them now in caves, now in jungle lairs, now in snow huts, blubber-lit, now in lake dwellings, the water lapping the piles, now in curtained Tudor four-posters, now in jangling iron bedsteads in slums, now between fine linen sheets, now among the bushes of public gardens, furtive, struggling with clothes, now beside moorland tarns, the untrammelled limbs sun-darkened, glossy. Throughout this experience Paul retained a flavour of the earlier ludicrous scene over the forbidden fruit; but he gathered also a new sense of the deep, groping earnestness of sex. And this jerked him into one of his rare moods of heightened consciousness. The little breast and nipple beneath his hand suddenly revealed itself to him in a most poignant vision, and at the same time the individual spirit of the girl (so it seemed) was laid bare dazzlingly to his own spirit's gaze. He saw, moreover, that she wanted what he also wanted.

But now the girl, sensing a change in his mood, and feeling that something ought to be done, first pressed his hand upon her yielding breast, and then tried to extricate it. Paul felt the soft flesh crushed between his fingers. Exulting, he gripped, so vigorously that she gave a little scream. Then suddenly she found herself caught in an embrace that was altogether too frankly sexual to be tolerated. Yet, to her own surprise, she yielded to it for a moment, savouring the new experience. Then it became clear that if she was to preserve any longer that which a virtuous young lady is supposed to cherish more than life itself, she must take immediate action. She struggled, expostulated, then suddenly, greedily, seized Paul's lip between her teeth. The pain shot through him like lightning. His grip relaxed. They separated. While he mopped his bleeding mouth, she arranged her clothing, swore she would never see him again, and then retreated toward the house with all the dignity she could muster.

But they continued to meet, for each had by now become necessary to the other. The intimacy deepened. They became 'engaged', though for financial reasons they had no prospect of marriage. They saw one another every day. The solid basis of their friendship, their mental insight into one another and joy in each other's natures, compelled them to seek one another. But their love was becoming warped by the longing for that final bodily intimacy which both craved, but she dared not permit. To the Neptunian observer it was obvious that for both their sakes she ought to have cut herself away from him once and for all, or else to have yielded fully to her own desire and his. For the former course she had no will. The initial feminine reluctance, the desire to preserve herself intact, had long since given place to the no less feminine hunger to give herself and be merged with her chosen male. But an irregular union would have been intolerable to her self-respect. She was a child of her age, and her age was still in spirit, though not in date, 'nineteenth century'. Though under Paul's influence she had recently begun to modify her puritanism, and now liked to think of herself as 'modern' and unconventional, there was a point beyond which she dared not go.

The months passed. Paul became more and more obsessed. He thought of nothing but love-making and his own unhappy situation. It became neecssary that he should stagnate no longer; for the year 1914 was approaching, in which he must be fully recovered from all the fevers of adolescence. I therefore decided to interfere. Two courses were open to me. Either I could make the girl give herself, or I could remove her. From the Neptunian point of view the obvious course was to let Paul have his way, and gain the little treasure of experience that would thus be added to him. In many ways they would both have benefited. They would have found new health and vigour of body, and for a while new peace and vitality of mind. But I knew that, harmless and invigorating as this culmination would have been for other individuals and in another society, for these two young Terrestrials it would have brought disaster. In the first place, they might have inadvertently produced a new individual of their species; and then both mother and child, and the young father also, would have been persecuted by the barbarian society in which they lived. I judged that such an experience would render Paul unfit for my experiment. It would have tethered his attention for too long to the personal. Secondly, they would have suffered a spiritual disaster, for they themselves both accepted the code which they would have infringed. Had I driven them on to taste their innocuous, pretty, forbidden fruit, they would soon have become a burden to one another. With the inevitable cooling of ardour they would have assumed a false obligation each to the other, and at the same time they would have lapsed into guilty disgust, recriminations and moral degradation. This would have side-tracked Paul's attention for too long a period.

I therefore decided to remove the girl. To do this I had first to enter her mind and discover how I might conveniently effect my purpose. Poor child, she would indeed have been overwhelmed with shame and horror had she known that for several weeks all her most private acts and secret thoughts were observed by a hidden, an indwelling and a male spectator. I was, for instance, present one Saturday night while she lowered her still coltish body into a hot bath, tingling and gasping as the heat devoured her. I detected her mind's quick backward glance at Paul's devouring but unfulfilled embraces. I noted also that she let the hot water flow and the temperature of the bath rise till she was on the verge of agony, before she finally sat up and turned off the tap. I was present also at her dreams, in which so often she let Paul have his way, before she woke and was regretfully thankful it had only been a dream.

A brief study of her personality sufficed to show just which of the young men in her environment would best suit her nature. I turned her attention in his direction; rather roughly, I fear, for I noticed that she began to have doubts of her sanity. In self-pride and in compassion for Paul she clung for a while to the old love, but in vain. She struggled desperately against her fate, bitterly ashamed of her impotence and fickleness. But by a kind of inner hypnotism I forced her to receive into her heart the image of the new love that I had chosen for her. I made her dwell on his admirable and charming qualities, and I blinded her to his somewhat grotesque appearance. Very soon I had made her undertake a vigorous, almost shameless campaign upon him. Much to his surprise and delight, much to the bewilderment of their mutual friends, this unassuming but prosperous young merchant found himself the adored adorer of one who hitherto had treated him merely with calm kindness. I now filled the bemused young woman with immodest haste for the wedding. Within a few weeks the pair did actually enter into a union which, owing to my careful selection, was quite the most successful marriage of their generation. I bore in mind, however, that it would later become desirable to bring her once more into relation with Paul.

While these events were proceeding I was in a sense resident in two minds at once; for when I had done my work upon the girl, I returned to Paul at the very instant in which I had left him. Thus I was able to watch his reactions to the whole drama, and to help him triumph in his defeat.

When first he had begun to suspect that she was turning away from him, he plunged into a more determined suit. But I was now very constantly treating him with visions and meditations of an impersonal kind, which so drenched his wooing that it became less persuasive than disturbing. In fact, by philosophical and poetical extravagances he frightened Katherine into the arms of his rival. When at last he learned of the marriage, he passed, of course, through a phase of self-pitying despair; but within a fortnight he was already, through my influence, no less than through native resilience, beginning to explore a very different field of experience.

91

2. PAUL DEVOUT

When Paul had recovered from the first shock of his misfortune, he emerged to find himself painfully oscillating between two moods. In the one he strove to protect his wounded soul under a bright new armour of cynicism. She was just an animal, and her behaviour was the expression of obscure physiological events. And so, after all, was his own. The love that he so prized had no intrinsic virtue whatever. In the other mood, however, he clung to the faith that though this love of his had foundered, nevertheless love, the mutual insight and worship of one human person for another, was good in itself, and indeed the supreme good of life. All other goods, it seemed, were either negligible, or instrumental to this greatest good. He had recently lived for many weeks on a plane that was formerly beyond him. Now in his loneliness he began to go over again and again the treasure that he had acquired, namely his new and overwhelmingly vivid and delightful apprehension of a particular human being, called Katherine. Bitter as was his loneliness, this treasure could never be taken from him. And the more he pored over it, the more he asked himself whether it was exceptional, or whether it was a fair sample of existence. Hitherto he had increasingly thought of the universe in terms of mechanical intricacies and the huge star-sprinkled darkness, or at best in terms of a vital but impersonal trend of all things toward some goal inconceivable to man. But now he began to regard all this as mere aridity in which there was no abiding place for the one superlative excellence, human personality, love-inspired. It was borne in upon him at last with new significance that love was 'divine'. He began to find a new and lucid meaning for the brave statement, 'God is Love'. It meant, surely, that this best of all things known to man was also present in spheres beyond man's sphere; that human personality and love were not the only nor the highest forms of personality and love; that Love, with a capital L, Love which was not merely a relation between persons but somehow itself a Person, an all-pervading and divine Person, was after all the governing power of the universe. If this were indeed so, as many professed to believe, then all human loves must, in spite of temporary frustration, be secure of eternal fulfilment. Even his love for Katherine and her no less divine, though now distracted, love for him must somehow, 'in eternity', have its fruition.

I must not here describe the struggle that took place in Paul's mind between his cynical and his devotional impulses. It was a fluctuating battle. Wandering along Gower Street, with his hands in the pockets of his grey flannel trousers, and half a dozen books under his arm, he would breathe in cheerfulness with the dilute spring air of London, till, as he pursued his course round Bedford Square, God was once more in his heaven. In Charing Cross Road he would stray into the 'Bomb Shop', and be confronted with new doubts. Walking over the spot where subsequently Nurse Cavell's monument was to proclaim her courage and her countrymen's vulgarity, the poor boy would sometimes be infected by a momentary and unintelligible horror, derived from my own foreseeing mind. Soon the placid bustle of the great railway station would bring comfort once more; but on the journey to his southern suburb he would be flung again into despair by the faces of sheep, cattle, pigs and monkeys that masked the spirits of his fellow-travellers. Then at last, walking bare-headed on the suburban down that overhung his home, Paul might once more, though rather wearily, believe in God.

It seemed to Paul that in his cynical mood he was definitely smaller, meaner and more abject than when he was once more unfurling on the battlements of his own heart the banner of his faith in the God of Love. In many of his contemporaries also much the same fluctuation of mood was occurring, and to them as to Paul it seemed that the issue lay between the old faith, however modernized, and the complete abnegation of human dignity. Yet Paul and his contemporaries were mistaken. It was not in faith but in utter disillusionment and disgust that the human spirit had to triumph, if ever it was to triumph at all.

While he was absorbed in his religious perplexity, Paul was intrigued by a group of fellow-students whose aim it was to solve the troubles of the modern world by making modern men and women into sincere Christians. They introduced him to a young priest, whom the whole group regarded as their spiritual leader. At first this young man's emphatic hand-grip and earnest gaze roused in Paul nothing but a new variant of the disgust and suspicion which, long ago, he had felt toward the ghastly heartiness of the family doctor. He was also repelled by the fact that the elect secretly referred to their master as the Archangel. But as he became better acquainted with the priest, he, like the others, began to fall under his spell. To Paul in his new phase of reverence for human personality, his new revulsion from 'materialism', this man appeared as a spiritual aristocrat, as one who could move about the world without being swallowed up by the world, without so much as dirtying his feet. He was 'other-worldly', not in the sense that he sought to escape from this world, but that he carried round with him an atmosphere which was not this world's atmosphere. Like those water-insects which take down with them into the deep places a bubble of air for breathing, he took down with him into this world a celestial ether to maintain his spiritual life.

So it seemed to Paul. But to his Neptunian guest the matter did not appear in the same light. During Paul's love affair I had of course to put up with much that was tedious and banal, but I had been constantly refreshed by the underlying simplicity and sincerity of the amorous couple. In the new incident, however, I had to watch Paul indulging in a very tiresome self-deception. He allowed his admiration for the person of this young priest to obscure his view of the universe. This aberration was indeed a necessary phase in his growth, a necessary process in the preparation of the experimental culture upon which I was to operate. But it was none the less a tiresome phase for the observer. Not that Paul's new enthusiasm was wholly misguided. Far from it. Even from the Neptunian point of view, this 'Archangel' was indeed in a limited sense a spiritual aristocrat, for undoubtedly he was gifted with a vision and a moral heroism impossible to most of his fellows. But he was an aristocrat debased by circumstance. He had not been able to resist an environment which was spiritually plebeian. Though in his life he faithfully expressed what he called the superhuman humanity of his God, he almost wholly failed to do justice to another and more austere feature of his own vision, a feature which indeed he never dared fully to acknowledge, even to himself, since in terms of his own religious dogma it appeared starkly as a vision of superhuman inhumanity.

Paul saw the Archangel often and in many circumstances, in

public meetings, at the homes of his followers, and at the boys' club which the priest had organized for the young 'rough diamonds' of his dockland parish. He saw him also at his church services. These impressed Paul in a perplexing manner. He noted, at first with some misgiving, the setting in which they took place, the scant and rather smelly congregation, so uncomprehending, but so obviously devoted to the person of the priest; the debased Gothic architecture and strident coloured windows; the music, so historic, so trite, yet to Paul so moving, the surpliced urchins of the choir, furtively sucking sweets, the paraphernalia of the altar, brass and velvet; the muffled noise of traffic in the great thoroughfare outside; and the occasional interruptions by some ship's steam-whistle as she nosed her way through the Thames fog toward China or the Argentine. In the midst of all this stood the tall, white-robed, fair-haired Archangel, intoning with that restrained yet kindling voice of his, which to Paul in his more devout mood made the hackneyed words of the service novel, urgent, significant with a piercing, blinding lucidity. In his rarer cynical mood, however, the same performance seemed no more meaningful than the ritual phrases of a parrot.

The Archangel's influence on Paul was partly physical. The younger man was attracted by the still athletic figure, the delicate firm lips, the finely cut aquiline nose. They seemed to him to embody ages of righteousness. In the priest's manner, too, he found a strong attraction. It soothed him, like a cool hand on the brow. Yet also it gripped him and shook him into life. But chiefly Paul was impressed by the man's sublime confidence, almost arrogance, in his own religious faith and practice, and by his lively bantering affection for the straying sheep of his flock. Paul's faith was weak. His love of his fellow-men was more theoretical than practical. But the Archangel, seemingly, was a real Christian. He practised what he preached. He really did love his fellows, not merely as savable souls but as unique individuals. He really did see something peculiar and beautiful in each person. He accepted others as he found them, and served them with the same spontaneity as a man serves his own needs. Through him Paul began at last to feel a real warmth toward his fellow human animals, and in doing so he felt exultantly that he was definitely rising to an ampler and more generous life. Because of this he became extremely ready to receive the metaphysical implications of the Archangel's religion, which also had been the religion of his own childhood, seldom seriously contemplated but always absent-mindedly believed.

Paul fancied that he now saw at last, with almost the intuitive certainty of elementary mathematics, not only that the governing principle of the universe was love, but that the actual embodiment of that love was Jesus. Moreover, under the influence of the Archangel, who had been stimulated by Paul's searching questions to make statements of doubtful orthodoxy, Paul now affirmed that the universe was celestial through and through, that all things in it, including Satan, worked together for the perfect expression of love, the perfect expression of the nature of Jesus. And the nature of Jesus, Paul learned not from the Bible but from contemplation of the Archangel. For the Archangel was very obviously sustained from morning till evening by a sense of the presence of his divine master. All who came near him were infected with something of this sense. He radiated a conviction of the ultimate rightness of all things, and at the same time he fired men with a zeal for putting the apparently wrong things right. Not that he was a mere stained-glass saint. Paul was proudly, lovingly conscious of the Archangel's vivid humanity, even of his little weaknesses, which served greatly to endear him to his admirers. He had, for instance, a quaint passion for raisins. After a trying day he would eat them by the handful, almost defiantly. They seemed to have for him the double attraction of the grape's sacred and profane significance.

Little by little Paul became an earnest Christian. Deep down in his breast, rather than in his mind, he argued thus, 'Can such a perfect being as the Archangel be mistaken about God? He is too wise. Can he be deceiving me? He is too sincere, too loving. If this man says that God is Love, it is so.' If ever his doubts returned, he would run to the Archangel to gain strength to abolish them. Once when this had happened, and the two were talking in the priest's sitting-room, before a fire that radiated optimism, while the landlady's cat lay asleep on the hearth-rug, Paul had what he considered a real religious experience. The Archangel had been patiently throttling Paul's doubts. 'Hang on to this, Paul,' he said,

'Love alone matters. And whatever is needed in the world for the existence of love is justified. What kind of a world is it that we actually find around us? I don't mean your beloved stars and nebulae and your pettifogging laws of nature. No doubt they are marvellous, and all part of God's house. But they are only the floor-boards. I mean the human world. What do you find there? You find Satan still at large. He always was, and always will be, till time is finished. And why? Because love that has not got to be for ever fighting is no more love than the unborn babe is a man. And so, Paul, we must thank God that, of his great love for us, he made Satan to torment us.' He paused, then continued: 'That's heresy! You see what happens if one thinks too much about these old problems. Think of Christ only. *Feel* his god-head. Can't you feel his presence in this room now?'

The Archangel raised his hand and looked at Paul as though listening to angel choirs. For some moments both remained silent. Gradually it came to seem to Paul that the room was all alive, all aglow, all a-murmur with a presence. Was it the presence of this man? Yes, but surely also it was the presence of Jesus. The room? Nay, the universe. The whole universe, it seemed, was somehow gathered into that room, and the whole of it was manifestly infused with the divine love. Everything was warm and bright, tender and true, or else heroically triumphant over an Evil that was not merely defeated but somehow shown never to have been really evil at all. To the adoring Paul it seemed that the very stars and outer universes came flocking into that little room, like lambs, to be comforted by this Shepherd, this supreme Archangel Jesus. They brought with them their little troubles, their sore feet and their stomachaches, and he, with the magic of his love, cured these little troubles so miraculously that they never had existed at all, save as occasions for his love. Paul and the universes nestled together like little white lambs in the bosom of this Love. Once more it seemed to him that he had made contact with reality, that he had penetrated this time surely to the very heart of the universe. The experience was very wonderful, very strange, yet also mysteriously familiar, with the familiarity of some forgotten existence, an existence so remote that it seemed entirely outside time. It seemed to Paul that an immense energy flooded in upon him. He felt in himself the ancient, the longed-for strength of faith. At last, after all his barren years, he was tense with a new vitality, fully charged, ready to spend himself in a new effulgent life.

The smiling, transfigured Archangel laid a hand on Paul's knee. Paul said, 'At last I feel Jesus.'

Now while Paul and the Archangel were yielding themselves to this glamorous experience, there was indeed a 'presence' with them in the room, though one of a very different nature from that which these two Terrestrial animals themselves had conjured in their imaginations. It was the presence of a man who had seen human species after human species wrest for itself out of chaos some slight amenity and some precarious faith, only to collapse into misery, into despair, often into agony. It was the presence of one who himself looked forward to the impending extinction of Man; who found in this event, and in all existence, overmastering beauty indeed, but for the love-sick human individual no consolation. Strange that it was my presence in Paul's mind, my coldly scrutinizing presence, that had lent actuality to his sense of union with the God of Love! The exhortation of the priest had made him notice in himself an obscure feeling which had already on earlier occasions fleetingly disturbed him with a sense that in some way he was 'possessed'. I now found him peering, as it were, into the recesses of his being in search of the source of this feeling, believing that what he would see would be the love-gaze of Jesus. Had he discovered what it was that actually 'possessed' him, had he come, so to speak, face to face with his Neptunian parasite, his vision would have been shattered, and no doubt he would have taken me for the Devil. But I was at pains to elude detection. Mentally I held my breath, as it were, lest any slight movement of my mind should reveal more of me than that vague 'presence' which he had so fantastically misinterpreted.

It was not easy for me to maintain my immobility, for the spectacle of Paul's fervour stirred me deeply, both toward pity and toward laughter. For what was it that was happening to him? Apart from the complication of my 'presence', which lent a spurious actuality to his vision, his experience was an epitome of the religious history of the First Human Species, a pitiable confusion of factors irrelevant to one another. In the first place Paul, partly through the wealth of cosmic imagery with which I had already drenched him, had indeed come face to face with the majesty of the universe. In the second place he had with Katherine experienced very vividly the great excellence which is called love. But the Christian tradition, working on him through his revered priest, had combined with his own desire so as to persuade him to attribute love to the pitiless universe itself. This confusion was caused partly by a trick played upon him by his own remote past. For the strange familiarity and the delicious consolation and peace which Paul had savoured in this religious moment were after all but an echo of his own obscure yearning for the tenderness of the breast and the elysium of the womb.

Henceforth Paul thought of himself as a soldier of Christ. He undertook a campaign of asceticism and general discipline. For instance, he made rules to limit his eating. When he succeeded in keeping them, the only result was that he rose from every meal with a wolfish craving, and thoughts of food haunted him throughout the day. He tried sleeping on his bedroom floor, but always before the night was over he crept guiltily into bed. His self-discipline was always half-hearted and ineffective, for he had no real faith in its spiritual efficacy. He did it, not with the earnestness of the God-hungry soul, but because earnestly religious persons were supposed to do so, and he wanted to be one of them.

Paul found great satisfaction in doing odd jobs for the Archangel. He took up work at the boys' club. Unfortunately he soon found that he was not much good with boys, having few of the attributes which they admired. He was useless at boxing and billiards, useless at back-chat. And he had no authority, for in his heart he was frightened of the boys. But for the Archangel's sake, and also for self-discipline, he stuck to the club. Finally he took charge of the canteen. He was cheated over halfpence, and at the end of the evening he basely made up the losses out of his own pocket. In intervals of selling coffee and buns he sat behind the counter reading. But this furtive practice caused him much heart-searching; and when the Archangel was about, he put his book away and tried to be genial with the boys.

Paul succeeded in persuading himself that nearly all his actions were expressions of his master-motive, to be a soldier of Christ

in the modern world. But as a matter of fact he had many quite
independent interests. He lived a varied and often hilarious life
with the little band of the Archangel's student admirers. He had
also several tentative amorous passages. He worked industriously
and with some success. He read much contemporary literature and
some popular science. But all his scientific thought he censored
rigorously for religion's sake.

Paul's religious fervour expressed itself chiefly not in action but
in writing free verse of a quasi-biblical character. He persuaded
himself that he had an 'urge' to produce verbal formulations of his
spiritual experience, that he was 'inspired'. But to his parasite it
was clear that what he produced in this phase was not wrung from
him by the intensity of experience. These poems were but literary
exercises, imitative in technique, and seldom vitalized by any
original imagination. The Archangel applauded these effusions
because they were correct in sentiment, but he regarded them as
merely play, not as a man's work for God. He could not perceive
that though they failed they meant much to Paul. It is worth while
to give one example for the light which it throws on Paul's mind at
this time.

MEN

Behold the sons of men,
who sin,
whose hearts are divine!
In selfishness they heap misery on one another;
yet for love they die.
They are blown about like dead leaves;
yet for love they stand firm.
For bread they trample one another,
yet for a dream they die.
Scatter gold among them, and they are beasts;
show them God, and they are sons of God.

3. PAUL FACES THE FACTS

Without my help it might have taken Paul some years to outgrow
his phase of mental obedience and spiritual confusion. But time was

pressing. I needed him to be well-advanced in his next phase at the close of his university career, so that he might be prepared to meet the crisis of 1914 in a significant manner. Therefore, when I had allowed him some months of play in his little Christian nursery, I began once more to exercise my influence upon him. I infiltrated him with images of cosmical majesty and horror, with apprehensions of human weakness and meanness and agony, with doubts and questions intolerable to his religion.

During the previous two years Paul had come across a number of distressing facts about the world, but he had contrived to see them in the rosy light of his religion. These experiences now, through my influence, began to haunt him. At all times of the day and night he was now liable to sinister visual and auditory images, either taken intact from his own past, or reconstructed in still more repugnant forms. It was as though hitherto he had been wandering in a luxuriant but volcanic land in which only now and again he had encountered the blow-holes and sulphurous jets of nether chaos; but now, it seemed, the whole terrain was heaving, cracking, belching under his feet. Over his books in his own comfortable suburban home he would be distressed by visions of the slum-tenement homes that he had visited when he was working for an 'after-care' committee. And somehow they seemed more sordid and overcrowded in imagination than in reality. While he was walking on the down, he would remember with abnormal distinctiveness a brawl that he had once witnessed in the East End. Bottles were thrown. A man's face was cut. A woman was knocked over. Her head came against the kerbstone with an audible crack, like the collision of bowls on a green. While he was reading or eating or walking, and especially while he was lying in bed and not yet asleep, faces would confront him; faces which, when he had encountered them in actuality, had seemed but opaque masks, grey, pinched, flabby, or purplish and bloated, but now in imagination revealed their underlying personalities to him with harrowing expressiveness. For I permitted him to see them as they would have appeared to a Neptunian fresh from the world of the Last Men. He had once been shown over a lunatic asylum. The faces that now haunted him were, he recognized, faces of sane men and women, yet they reminded him distressingly of those imbecile faces. Faces

101

of all kinds they were, young and old, business men, fashionable women, unshaven labourers, clerks, young bloods, lawyers; all pushing themselves forward at him, leering, smirking, whimpering, impressing, imploring, all so intent, so self-important, so blind. Somehow they reminded him of cheap ornate lamps, rusty, shop-soiled, and never lit. The queer phrase 'blind lamps' reiterated itself to him on these occasions. Another image haunted him in connexion with these faces, and seemed to him to summarize them all and symbolize the condition of his species. It was an image which I constructed in his mind in detail and with verisimilitude, and endowed with a sense of familiarity, though in fact it was not derived from his past but from his future experience during the war. He seemed to see, lying in mud, a dead mare, already decaying. From its hindquarters, which were turned towards him, there projected the hideously comical face of its unborn foal. The first time he encountered this apparition Paul was at a political meeting. Before him on the platform sat a company of politicians, city worthies and their wives. A cabinet minister was perorating. Suddenly Paul saw the foal, and in a flash recognized its expression in the speaker, in the ladies and gentlemen on the platform, in the audience. His gorge rose, he thought he was going to vomit. Stumbling over his neighbour's feet, he fled out of the hall. Henceforth he was very prone to see the foal, at lectures, at dances, in church. Even in the Archangel's smile he sometimes recognized with horror that foetal grin.

Another type of imagery and of thought I also forced on Paul at this time. I first impelled him to read works of contemporary literature and science which were discountenanced by the Archangel. Furtively he began to return to the interests that had been roused in him before he came to the university, interests in the intricacy of the physical world, in the types of living things, in the theory of evolution, in the astronomical immensities. But whereas formerly these things delighted him, now they terrified him, even while they fascinated. I took care that they should haunt him with imagery. He had curious sensations as of sweeping with increasing speed through space, while the stars streamed past him like harbour lights. Sometimes it seemed to him that he was dropping into the tumultuous and incandescent vapours of the sun. Sometimes he glimpsed spinning worlds, parched and airless, uninhabited, meaningless.

When Paul had been subjected to this violent influence for some weeks, he began, like many of his contemporaries, to find a kind of consolation in the theory of evolution, romantically interpreted. It made worm and ant and man fellow-workers in a great cause. Exactly what they were all working for, he did not know; nor could he justify his strong conviction that, though all had achieved something, man was doing far more than the others, and might yet do infinitely better. Those thrusting imbecile faces that haunted him, and were the faces of his fellow-men and himself, those foal faces, were really not men at all, not what men should be and might be, any more than the grinning and putrefying foal was a horse. Gallantly Paul now began to convince himself that the whole universe was striving toward some supreme expression of life, though blindly in conflict with itself, torturing itself. He wrote a poem in which man appeared as 'the germ of the cosmic egg'. Later he tore it up and wrote another in which the cosmic egg was said to consist entirely of germs, each of which was trying to devour the others and include their substance in its own expanding form. In another he declared that God was 'the Soul of the World, striving to wake'. He put great pains into the making of these verses, and had a sense of vision and achievement such as he had never known before. One short poem I quote, as it shows clearly the rebirth of my influence in him and the quickening of his own imagination.

EVANESCENCE

As a cloud changes,
so changes the earth.
Coasts and valley,
and the deep-rooted hills
fade.
They last but for a little while;
as cloud-tresses among the rocks,
they vanish.
And as a smile gleams and fades.
so for a very little while,
Life rejoices the earth.

> From the beginning fire,
> then frost, endless.
> And between, the swift smile, Life.
> From the beginning fire,
> then frost, endless,
> and between,
> Mind.

Paul ventured to show these poems to the Archangel. The young author was diffident about them, and did not expect them to be taken very seriously; but the manner in which the Archangel received them was something of a shock to him. Gently but also emphatically the priest told him that he was in danger of serious heresy. God could not be the soul of the world, since he had created the world and would survive the world. As for the cosmic egg, still more the 'evanescence of life in the [universe, Paul ought to realize that such bizarre ideas were dangerous, since they obscured the central fact of religion, namely the direct and eternal intercourse between God and man. Surely that amazing fact was far more interesting than these grotesque fancies. Paul was so upset that he turned actually dizzy and faint. No wonder, for here was the being whom he respected above all others and even took to be in some manner divine, condemning ideas which to Paul himself seemed to have very far-reaching and very beautiful significance.

This experience was the beginning of a long period of heart-searching in which Paul became increasingly aware of being torn in two directions, namely, toward the Archangel and toward something which he could not yet at all clearly see. He began to oscillate between two moods. One was a mood of interest in personality and the personal God whom man had rightly or wrongly conceived in his own image. The other was a mood of revulsion from man and his God, and of interest in all that vastness within which man is but a tremulous candle-flame, very soon to be extinguished. He could not integrate these moods in one. Yet whichever was the mood of the day, he felt obscurely but strangely that it was incomplete, that somehow the other was just as necessary, though at the moment he could not feel it. On the one hand was the Archangel, and Jesus, and all the humbler beauties of human persons. On the other was the rippled lake, the stars, the whole vast intricacy of nature. On the one hand was Love, and on the other the more mysteriously beautiful thing, Fate. And Life, how did Life relate itself to this profound dichotomy of the spirit? When he was in what he called the Archangel mood, he could without difficulty extend his interest so as to regard the story of evolution as the story of a great crusade of myriads of spirits freely striving to achieve some glorious end in praise of God, and sacrificing themselves by the way in myriads of casualties. When he was in the mood of the stars, he regarded the same great story as one somewhat intricate system of wave-trains spreading its innumerable undulations in ever-widening, ever-fading circles on the surface of existence, presently to vanish. Strange that, so long as he remained in the mood of the stars, this thought did not outrage him. He accepted it, not with reluctance, but with joy.

It was while he was still only beginning to discover the existence of these two moods in himself that Paul had to decide once and for all what he would do in the world. The Archangel said, 'If your faith is secure, prepare to become a priest of the one God. If it is not secure, find some solid practical work to do in the service of man.' Paul's faith was not secure. On the other hand, he dreaded the thought of being caught up in the mills of business or industry. And he did seriously desire to play some part in the great work of salvation. If it was not for him to turn men's attention to Jesus, at least he might turn the attention of the young to the many lovely features of existence. After much agonized hesitation he finally decided that he must become a teacher. He therefore persuaded his family to let him take a diploma, hoping that a thorough preparation would do away with his proved incompetence with boys. At the outbreak of the European War he was about to take up his first post, in one of the large suburban secondary schools of the Metropolis.

For some months Paul was engaged on what seemed to him a life and death struggle in two entirely different spheres. While he was desperately trying to acquire the art of teaching, he was at the same time, and increasingly, concerned with an unprecedented fact in his world, namely, the European War. Presently this fact gave rise to a new and bewildering personal problem, namely, the problem of his own conduct in a war-racked world.

At the school he had set out to inspire his pupils with the love of 'culture'. In fact he took the work very seriously. He spent many hours in preparation and correction, but was always behindhand, and therefore in class always uncertain. The boys soon found him out, and took delight in tripping him. He became more and more insecure. On the side of discipline also he came to grief, though he had excellent theories on this subject. Discipline, he argued, should be self-imposed, not imposed by others. Unfortunately such discipline is the most difficult to inculcate, especially amongst rebellious young animals who have been brought up on something different. Paul himself had none of that native and unconscious authority which alone could have ensured success in such circumstances. The boys soon found that good sport was to be had by baiting him. He changed his method, and tried to impose order, but could achieve no more than a partial suppression of disorder. The more tyrannous his control, the more gleefully did rebellion raise her hydra heads. Things came to such a pass that one afternoon when the last class was over, and the boys had stampeded away along the corridor, Paul, seated upon his dais, dropped his head forward on his chalk-dusty hands. I felt tears trickle through his fingers on to the desk. The syllables of a desperate prayer formed themselves in his throat and on his lips. 'Oh, God, oh, God,' he cried, 'make me different from what I am.' It seemed to him that he had reached the very rock-bottom of despair. For this despair was more acutely conscious, more precisely formulated than any of his earlier despairs. He was a grown man (so he imagined), and completely incompetent to deal with life. In adolescence his dread had been that he himself would miss fulfilment, that he would 'get stuck', stranded, and never explore the promised lands of life. But now he dreaded far more (so he persuaded himself) that he would never be able to do anything even of the humblest order 'to the glory of God'. This was now his master motive, to pull his weight, to do a man's work, to be able to look his fellows in the eyes and say, 'Of course I am nothing out of the common, but you can see that I am pulling my weight.' He longed to cut adrift and start all over again at something else. But at what? Outside his little prison there was nothing but the war. The boys were already skilfully torturing him about the war. Then why did he not go? He would make a wretched soldier, but the Government said that every one was needed. Even if he merely got himself shot, he would have 'done his bit'. And he would be quit of all this misery.

For some while he continued to lie with his head in one hand, while the other crumpled the harsh black folds of his gown. To go and be a soldier. What did it really mean? Military discipline. Doing stupid things just because you were told to. Pushing bayonets into straw dummies, and later into live bellies. Feeling those jagged shell splinters tear through your own flesh and bones. It was all inconceivably horrible. But apparently it had to be, since Civilization was in danger. Then surely he *must* go. And how good to be out of all this fiasco of teaching. Anything was better than that. How good to surrender one's conscience into the keeping of the army. That way surely lay peace of mind. Like surrendering your conscience to the Church. Give it to a general to look after. Yes, he must not stand aside any longer from the great spiritual purification and revival that the Archangel said was coming out of the war. It had begun already. The war was helping people to get out of themselves, helping them to see Jesus. The Archangel said so. Yes, he would enlist. Then there would be nothing to do but to obey, be courageous, relentless. Then all his troubles would be escaped. Just set your teeth and be a hero. So easy, compared with this work that was simply beyond him. He looked at his watch. Late! And he wanted to get his hair cut before catching the train home. Hurriedly he began to gather up his books.

Then he paused. Once more he bowed over the desk. Must he really help in their stupid war, their filthy, mad, backward-looking war, that was wrecking the civilization it was meant to save. It was like saving a man from death by an operation that was bound to be fatal. People said war was better than dishonour. But from the world point of view war *was* dishonour. Nothing was so base as war. Better far that the Germans should overrun Belgium, France, England. But no. The Archangel said this was all wrong. He said Jesus was definitely on our side. What was the truth about it all, what was the truth? 'Jesus, Jesus, help me, if you ever help any one. Why am I alive? What is it all for? Why is there this terrible world? Why are we all so horrible?' Jesus did not answer. Paul lay still, his mind almost blank; then he yawned, raised his head, and rested his chin on his hand. He had no further thoughts. He gazed vacantly at the chalk-grains on the desk.

At this point I undertook a serious intervention in Paul's mind. As he gazed at the minute white points of the chalk, I induced him to regard them as stars in the Milky Way. I then made him blow upon the desk. The whole galaxy shifted, spread outwards, streamed down the sloping board; thousands of stars tumbled into the abyss. Paul watched, fascinated. Then he shuddered and covered his face with his hands. I now flooded his astonished mind with images and ideas. In imagination he still saw the star-dust streaming, whirling. But I made him seize, with miraculous vision, one out of all the myriad suns, round which circled infinitesimal planets. One of these planets his piercing eye regarded minutely. He watched its surface boiling, seething, settling into oceans and continents. Then with supernaturally penetrative eyes, he saw in the tidal waters of the ever-fluctuating, drifting continents the living Scum, our ancestor. He saw it propagate, spread, assume a thousand forms, invade the oceans and the lands. He saw forests creep over the plains; and with his magically piercing vision he detected among the greenery a sparse dust of beasts. Reptiles clambered, ran, took wing, or reached up to crunch the tree-tops. In a twinkling they vanished. Then beneath his eyes a finer and more vital dust, the mammals, was blown into every land. Now the tempo of his vision slowed, slowed. Man, super-simian, sprinkled the valleys with his hovels, the lake-shallows with his huts, the hill-tops with his megaliths. He set fire to the forests, tilled the plains, built cities, temples, palaces, Nilotic pyramids, Acropolis. Along thread-like imperial roads the legionaries percolated, like blood corpuscles. Upon a minute hill, beside a city wall, a minute crowd existed and vanished. Presently there was a rash of churches, then little smoke-clouds of wars and revolutions, then a sudden tissue of steel tracks and murky blotches. And now to Paul's straining eyes there appeared for an instant a little crooked line stretching across Europe. On either side of this line wave-trains drifted, infinitely faint, confused, but unmistakable. Wave-trains of grey, blue, khaki, were seen to advance upon the line from East and West,

recoiling in feebler undulation athwart their own advancing
successors. They vanished. The tempo of the vision accelerated.
Aeons rushed headlong into pastness. The minute continents
deformed themselves. The little sun shrank, faded to a red spark;
and as it did so the little planet became snowy white, a simple
chalk-grain, which presently was lost in obscurity. The sun-
spark was snuffed out. Paul's gaze seized upon another sun. This
also was snuffed out. One by one, thousand by thousand, all the
stars were extinguished, till the whole galaxy had vanished. There
was nothing left but darkness. It seemed to Paul that the dark
flooded into his mind, wave upon wave. In vain he battled against
it. The spirit of night had triumphed. His mind reeled, sickened,
sank into unconsciousness. He lay still, with open eyes unseeing.
But though he was now profoundly tranced, I, who had worked
this change in him, still perceived through all his sense organs. I felt
the slight indigestion that had been aggravating his despond. I felt
the constriction of his collar, which was rather too small for him.
Presently I felt a fly walk across his eyeball. He took no notice. But
I, fearing that his trance might break too soon, caused his hand to
drive away the intruder, and soothe the irritation. Once more he
lay still.

When at length Paul emerged from this swoon, he found himself
recalling with strange distinctness the tarn where long ago he had
first watched the intersecting waves. In imagination he watched
them now, progressing, interlacing, fading, reappearing in varying
patterns on every quarter of the lake. On the actual occasion, they
had roused in him little more than intellectual curiosity; but now
they had acquired such grave significance that every briefest flurry,
every ripple, seemed to imprint its form upon his own being. At
first he resisted, though vainly. But soon the insistent rhythms
calmed him to acquiescence. He let them mould him, re-form him,
as they willed; and in this passivity he found peace. Presently he
raised his head, sat up, looked round at the desks, the maps, the
grey fields of the windows, his chalky hands, the clumsy writing
of some 'exercises' awaiting correction. All was as before, yet all
was now acceptable, strangely right, even beautiful. Under his
breath he whispered 'God! What a fool I was not to see it long ago!'

He looked at his watch, gathered up his things, and hurried

109

away. In his step I felt a new buoyancy, in the stream of his thoughts a new and bracing freshness. Soon, no doubt, he would return to his former despair, but the memory of this experience would never wholly desert him.

At this point I left Paul, and returned to my own world. My first task was to work up the material which I had gathered from Paul and others, and to make it known to my colleagues. Next I took that holiday which was described at the outset of this book. I also participated in the awakening of the Racial Mind. Then at last I came back to Paul, re-discovering him, not precisely at the date where I had left him, but a few days later. The good that I had worked in him seemed already to have disappeared. I found him, as I have already reported, in an agony of indecision, tortured by little incidents in the streets of London.

It will be necessary to tell how Paul finally tackled his war problem. But for the present we must leave him. My concern with him is incidental to my main theme. He is but an instrument through which I chose to observe your world, and through which I choose to exhibit your world to you. He is also a sample of that world. I have shown the instrument in some detail, and I have displayed the sample; warning you that, though peculiarly significant, it is not an average sample. You have seen that Paul, when he came face to face with the war, was already at grips with certain problems which are in fact the supreme problems of your age. Let me close this chapter by enumerating them. There was the problem of 'the flesh' and 'the spirit', the problem of human personality and evolving Life, the problem of the divinity of love and the austerity of fate. It was with these problems already troubling consciousness or stirring in regions deeper than consciousness, that all the more developed members of your species faced the war.

I now pass on to tell you how your war and your reactions to your war appear to the Last Men.

V *Origins Of The European War*

1. THE NEPTUNIAN ATTITUDE TO THE WAR

IN your Homeric saga the human conflict is observed and swayed by invisible but mighty presences. The achievement of each hero is the issue not simply of his own virtue but of the inspiration and machination of some favouring divinity. The gods and goddesses take sides, some with the Greeks, others with the Trojans.

In the war which I am to describe, the European War, the War to End War, which played so great a part in setting your species toward decline, every turn of events was noted by invisible presences, but these unseen observers were neither divine nor partisan. As on the Trojan plains, so on the plains of Flanders, the hills of Picardy and Champagne and Argonne, Tyrol's wild heights, the bogs and steppes of Russia, so equally in Arabia, Mesopotamia and Salonika, on the sea and in the upper air, in fact, wherever war was present or indirectly felt, there watched invisible and unsuspected presences. These were not gods and goddesses mentally inferior to the humanity that had created them, interested in men only to use them for their own petty though celestial strife; they were actual human minds. They strove not to give victory to one side or the other; they were concerned only to record and relish the ineluctable course of events, and to kindle in such of you as were open to their influence some glimpse of their own high zest.

When first we examined your war, it was not uncommon for us to observe in that epoch features which, inexplicable at the time, suggested that some still future influence of our own must be at work upon them, influences which we had not yet, from the Neptunian point of view, been able to exert. Thus to take the most striking example, in our earliest study we had been perplexed by the fact that the Salonika episode did not develop on the scale that might have been expected. Later in Neptunian time, we discovered that we ourselves were responsible. For it now turned out that certain persons in high military and naval posts were open to our

111

influence. We accordingly swayed them toward inertia, and thus deliberately prevented a sequence of events which would have been far more repugnant to us than those which actually occurred. But such large-scale influence is very seldom possible. Moreover we have become extremely chary of indulging in it; for not infrequently we have come later to regret our meddling.

In our world, as I have said elsewhere, the mature individual has wholly escaped the snares of private egoism. His will is for the racial good. But his heart may still be torn asunder in respect of conflicts between loyalty to the spirit of man and piety toward the actual issue of fate. Even as individuals, but far more clearly as the race mind, we pass beyond the human loyalty which is the spring of all our action, and see in the form of the cosmos a beauty superior to any human triumph.

Now although we regard events in your epoch with complete detachment from your many archaic aims, we do feel with you in your racial struggle to become more fully human. When you fail, or when we fail to help you, we grieve. When we take action in your world, we are often torn by doubt as to whether we shall in fact improve or mar the fortune of the race. But in us pity and doubt are tempered by our intuition that in the highest view the whole, although severe, is excellent. Even as individuals, we have this conviction of the superlative beauty of the cosmos. But in the unique racial experience this insight is far more developed, and has a very curious and beatific effect upon us as individuals. For, if our memory is to be trusted, the race mind, when it looks back on the texture of events accomplished in the past, finds each one of them to be a needed feature in the cosmical beauty. In that supreme experience, seemingly, man looks upon the cosmos with a new discerning vision, and would not have any past event to be other than in fact it is. Thus it seems that, in so far as we ourselves have influenced the course of events, our influence has indeed contributed to the cosmical beauty; yet in so far as we have refrained or failed to achieve what we planned, that inaction and that failure were also for the best, were contributory to that supernal excellence which is clearly seen only by the racial mind.

But do not suppose that, since apparently whatever has occurred is cosmically right, therefore human endeavour is unnecessary.

Only by means of endeavour can the great theme of the cosmos proceed. But also, by some influence which is not revealed to us, the issue of all human endeavour is seemingly controlled so that in its failures no less than in its triumphs it does in fact contribute to the excellent and perfect form of the Whole. I say 'seemingly'; for even to us it is not clear that it *must* be so; although hitherto, the more we have increased in spiritual stature, the more often and the more clearly have we experienced instances of its being in fact so.

Let us now revert to your war. It is perhaps needless to say that, on those rare occasions when we have influenced the course of events in your war, we have never been concerned merely to give victory to one side, or to the other; save when, as has sometimes befallen, an unhappy observer has become so infected by the terrestrial mentality that he has lost completely his Neptunian integrity and understanding. Such disasters are rare. For the most part our observers maintain their sanity and their detachment perfectly.

You may be tempted to suppose that the great concentration of our observers in and around the period of your first world war implies that we are interested in your war for the same reasons as you yourselves are normally interested in it. In this you would be mistaken. We do indeed enter into your feelings in regard to the war. No less fully than you yourselves have felt them, we feel your agony and despair, your glory and shame; for we have participated in them directly. But throughout, we have normally preserved our own detachment. Events which through your minds we have savoured as world-shattering and God-condemning we have seen also in their wider relations, and recognized as but microscopic features in the great whole. And so we have been able to regard your agony and passion with that blend of sympathy and irony which, upon a lowlier plane, the adult feels towards the ardours of children in their games, or the grief of children in their nursery troubles.

The strategy of your generals, for instance, has for us only the kind of interest which your own psychologists have found in watching apes baffled by the simplest problems of intelligence. As chimpanzees, tantalized by fruit which lies beyond their reach, may achieve or miss insight into the potentialities of sticks, packing-cases or ropes, so your commanders painfully achieved, or more often missed, insight into military potentialities which lay all the while patent to every Neptunian intelligence. Time after time we saw these gilt-edged commanders frustrated by problems which even your own brighter minds might well have surmounted. Again and again we saw thousands of lives destroyed, and hard-won military gains abandoned, through the stupidity, or even the mere personal conceit, of some single strategist or tactician. And though this kind of betrayal was the very stuff that we had come to study, and normally we could regard it with equanimity, there have been, for all of us, occasions when such lapses have kindled a certain amused exasperation, or, if we have been too long subjected to the terrestrial mentality, even a momentary rage.

Your war-time politicians, perhaps more clearly than your generals, displayed for us the essential weakness of your kind. We are not greatly interested in the political aspects of your war, save as expressions of factors in your nature much deeper than politics. In the antics of your political leaders, even more clearly than in humbler lives, we saw the insidious, devastating struggle between private interest, patriotism, and that newer, more difficult allegiance which serves before all else the race, or the essential spirit that is man. In the commonalty, public and private interest stood in less dramatic and less momentous conflict than in those who framed national and military policy. It might have been expected that those upon whose acts great issues hung would hold their self-regarding propensity the more firmly under control, that the vast public import of their conduct would induce them constantly to scrutinize their motives with relentless penetration. But no. Decisions which were ostensibly concerned only with the national good were determined in fact by envy, jealousy, or pride. Yet in most cases the agent himself, we discovered, never doubted his own honesty. Similarly, as you yourselves later came to recognize, policies which were expressed in the language of cosmopolitan idealism or of religion, were in fact inspired by nothing but national aggressiveness or fear, or by some even more disreputable private motive. This being so, the diplomatic history of your war period interests us not at all as a record of high policy, but solely as a tangle of psychological data.

With yourselves, interest in your war is often the mere lust of horror, the fascination of bloodshed and destruction. To us, your horrors are unimpressive; for, ranging up and down the aeons of human history, we have observed many more complete and harrowing devastations. We have seen races, civilized beyond your dreams, completely annihilated in swift, or again in long-drawn-out, disaster. We have seen whole populations writhing and shrieking in physical agony. Your restricted and aseptic mutual slaughter, almost homely and kindly in comparison with that which lies a few decades ahead of you, has therefore no horrific interest for us. It has of course the appeal of every human tragedy; but neither in magnitude nor in intensity of suffering is it at all remarkable. Through your minds and your flesh we do, indeed, experience it as unique, world-shattering and world-condemning. We savour very thoroughly the agony of despair which oppressed so many of you in the years of war. Imaginatively we contract our vision within the limits of your war-bound vision, and enter fully into your consequent world-disgust. Indeed, having entered there, we are sometimes shocked that you do not feel more deeply. For even the most sensitive of you is protected from suffering the full agony appropriate to your own short-sighted world-disgust by the mere crudity of his nervous organization, and the consequent obtuseness and callousness of his mentality.

If it was not horror nor yet political or military interest that caused us to flock in thousands to observe your war, what was it? Was it perhaps your acts of individual heroism, your self-transcendence in devotion to a cause? Or was it your rare impulses of generosity toward the enemy, your groping efforts to escape the obsession of nationalism, and to feel the unity of man? We have indeed watched respectfully whatever in your war was truly heroic, devoted. Even when we have been forced to smile at the ends upon which that heroism was squandered, we have recognized that in its degree it was indeed heroism, a virtue which to beings of your stature is precious and difficult. We have also recorded faithfully every occasion on which any of you has transcended nationalism. But we cannot agree with you in regarding your heroism as the very flower of human achievement, or your generosity and your timid cosmopolitanism as sublime triumphs of the spirit. In our world we are accustomed to a

completely relentless self-abnegation in all situations which demand
it. Any failure in this respect we attribute to insanity. And as for
cosmopolitanism, to put the interest of one nation before that of
another seems to any member of any of our thousand Neptunian
nations no less preposterous than for a man to favour his left eye
against his right.

If even your heroism is commonplace to us, seeming no more
remarkable than nursery pluck, what is it that we find in your war
to attract our interest? The answer can be simply stated, but its full
significance needs some further development. We came to see your
species face a situation such as it had never hitherto needed to face.
We came to see it fail to grapple with that situation in any manner
which could have saved it from a fatal spiritual poison, or auto-
intoxication. We knew that this failure was inevitable. We had
watched your nature evolve and your world situation develop.
We had watched these two factors cooperate to produce at a certain date a violent acceleration of world-change, and subsequently
a tangle of problems with which you could not cope. We had observed a neck-and-neck race between your developing nature and
the developing world, which your nature itself kept stimulating into
constant advance. The world won. We had seen far back in your
history the first stirrings of a new capacity in you, which, given time,
might well have so matured as to master even the kind of world in
which you now find yourselves. But your 'modern' world came
too soon. In the century before the war it developed with increasing
acceleration. You had neither the intelligence nor the moral
integrity to cope with your brave new world. When at last in 1914
accident posed you with a crucial choice, you chose wrongly. It was
inevitable that you should do so. Being such as you were, you would
most certainly choose as you did. But you have only yourselves to
blame, for your choice was a considered expression of your own
essential nature. The newer kind of behaviour, which alone was
really appropriate to the new world-situation, did indeed make
here and there a tentative appearance, and no doubt in very many
persons there was at least some leaning toward that behaviour; but
everywhere a rigorous suppression, both by governmental authority and by the primitive disposition within each individual mind,
prevented the more courageous and the only sane behaviour from

116

occurring; save here and there, spasmodically and ineffectively. And so inevitably you took the first step toward disaster.

This was the drama which we came to watch, and not your horrors or your heroics or your strategic prowess or your policies. The actors were the millions of Europeans and Americans. The dramatic conflict took place at first within each mind. It then became a struggle between those many in whom the archaic disposition was victorious, and those few in whom it was defeated. The immediate upshot of your choice was war; but in that choice you set in motion a sequence of causes and effects destined to develop throughout your future. During the war itself we saw your more percipient minds tortured and warped, not only by physical pain and fear, but by the growing though unacknowledged conviction that they had acquiesced in a great and irrevocable treason against the still-slumbering spirit of man; that through blindness or cowardice or both, they had betrayed that which was the only hope of the future. Very often, of course, this betrayal was at the same time itself an heroic transcendence of mere self-regard for the supposed good of a nation; but it was none the less betrayal of that half-formed and nobler nature upon which alone depended man's future well-being. During the war itself the working of this poison, this profound and almost unrecognized shame, was obscured by the urgency of the military situation. But after the war it acted with ever-increasing effect. This effect we have observed in detail, and I shall describe it. When I have told you of the war itself as it appears to us through your eyes, I shall tell how, after the war, a subtle paralysis and despair fastened upon your best minds, and percolated throughout your social organism. I shall tell how both in theory and in affairs you produced a spate of symptoms which your psychologists would call 'defence-mechanisms', designed unwittingly to conceal from yourselves the full realization of your treason and the clear perception of its effects.

That you may appreciate this drama in all its poignancy, I must first report briefly our findings in respect of the nature and the past career of your species, and of the delicate balance of forces which issued inevitably in this betrayal.

2. THE PHILOSOPHICAL LEMURS

Your historians, when they seek to trace the origin of your war, refer only to events which took place within the previous century. They single out such accidents as the murder of an archduke, the ambition of an emperor, the vendetta of two jealous nations, the thrusting growth of a new empire and the resistance of an old, the incompatibility of racial cultures, the debasing effects of materialism, or the inevitable clash of rival economic systems. Each of these factors was in some sense a cause of your war; but to assert that any of them or all of them together constituted the essential cause would be scarcely more profound than to say that the war was brought about by the movement of the pen that signed the first mobilization order. The Neptunian observer, though he duly notes these facts, seeks behind them all for the more general and more profound cause, by virtue of which these lesser causes were able to take effect. He looks further even than the birth of the nations of Europe many centuries before the war. He finds the explanation of your mutual slaughter by regarding it as a crucial incident in the long-drawn-out spiritual drama of your species.

Our observers have traced by direct inspection all the stages in the awakening of man out of his ape-like forerunner. Indeed, as our technique advances we are able to press back our exploration even along the generations of man's pre-simian ancestors. Our most brilliant workers have actually succeeded in entering a few isolated individuals of a much more remote past, when the mammal had not yet emerged from the reptile. They have savoured the sluggish and hide-bound mentality that alone was possible to the cold-blooded forefathers of all men and beasts. They have also savoured by contrast the new warmth and lambent flicker of experience which was kindled when the first tentative mammal began living in a chronic fever. But for the understanding of your war it is unnecessary to go further into the past than the emergence of the ape from the pre-simian.

Even at that early age we observe two themes of mental growth which together constitute the vital motif of the career of the first human species, and the key to your present plight. These themes are the increasing awareness of the external world, and the more tardily increasing insight into the nature of the human spirit itself. The first theme is one of fluctuating but triumphant progress, since it was but the mental aspect of the intelligent mastery of physical nature which brought your species to dominance. The second theme depended on the application of intelligence to another sphere, namely the inner world of desires and fears. Unlike apprehension of the external, it had no survival value, and so its progress was halting. Because this inner wisdom had long ago been outstripped by the outer knowledge, there came at last your war and all its consequences.

Our observers have studied minutely all the crucial events of this age-long drama. Searching even among the dark pre-simian minds, we have singled out in every generation every individual that has been in advance of his kind in respect either of outward prowess and apprehension or of inward self-knowledge. As one may extract any fragments of iron from a heap of rubbish by passing a magnet over its surface, so we, with our minds set to a slightly higher degree of practical intelligence or of self-consciousness than that of the generation under study, have been able to single out from the mass those rare individuals whose minds were definitely in advance of their contemporaries. We find, of course, that of these geniuses some few have succeeded in handing on their achievement to the future, while many more have been defeated by adverse circumstance.

Roaming among the pre-simian minds, we discovered one surprising efflorescence of mentality whose tragic story is significant for the understanding of your own very different fate. Long before the apes appeared, there was a little great-eyed lemur, more developed than the minute tarsier which was ultimately to produce ape and man. Like the tarsier, it was arboreal, and its behaviour was dominated by its stereoscopic and analytic vision. Like the tarsier also, it was gifted with a fund of restless curiosity. But unlike the tarsier, it was prone to spells of quiescence and introversion. Fortune favoured this race. As the years passed in tens of thousands and hundreds of thousands it produced large individuals with much larger brains. It passed rapidly to the anthropoid level of intelligence, and then beyond. Among this race there was once born an individual who was a genius of his kind, remarkable both for practical intelligence and for introspection.

When he reached maturity, he discovered how to use a stick to beat down fruit that was beyond his reach. So delighted was he with this innovation, that often, when he had performed the feat, and his less intelligent fellows were scrambling for the spoils, he would continue to wave his stick for very joy of the art. He savoured both the physical event and his own delight in it. Sometimes he would pinch himself, to get the sharp contrast between his new joy and a familiar pain. Then he would fall into a profound and excited meditation, if such I may call his untheorized tasting of his new mental processes. One evening, while he was thus absorbed, a tree-cat got him. Fortunately this early philosopher left descendants; and from them arose, in due course and by means of a series of happy mutations, a race of large-brained and non-simian creatures whose scanty remains your geologists have yet to unearth, and catalogue as an offshoot of the main line of evolution.

These beings have intrigued our explorers more than anything else in the whole terrestrial field. Their capacity for self-knowledge and mutual insight sprang from the vagaries of mutation, and was at first biologically useless. Yet, merely because in this species it was genetically linked to the practical intelligence which had such great survival value, it developed; until at last it justified itself in an event which from the human point of view seems almost miraculous. At an early stage the new race threatened to break up into a confusion of warring tribes, each jealously preserving its own fruit groves and raiding its neighbours. There was wholesale destruction of fruit. Starvation and mutual slaughter began to tell upon the nerves of this highly strung race. Population declined. Then it was that the miracle occurred. A certain remarkable female, the supreme genius of her race, organized a truce, and a concourse of all the tribes in the trees around a forest glade. Here, with the help of confederates and a heap of fruit, she performed an amazing pantomime, which might be called the forerunner of all sermons and of all propaganda plays. First, by means of dance and ululation, she put the spectators into an hypnoidal state of tense observation. She then evoked in them, by mere gesture and emotive sounds, a fury of tribal passion. At the moment when the companies in the tree-tops seemed about to fling themselves upon one another in battle, she suddenly changed the tone of her pantomime. By sheer histrionic ability she revealed to her bewildered but comprehending fellows her own agony of revulsion from hate, her own heart-searching and self-analysis, her own discovery of profound cravings which had hitherto been ignored. With no medium but the language of gesture and tone which she had in part to improvise, she praised love and beauty, she praised pure cognizance and spiritual peace. The enthralled spectators followed her every movement with unconscious mimicry. Each one of them recognized in his own heart that deeper nature which she was expressing. The result was something like a revivalist meeting, though shorn of the supernatural. In the midst of it the exhausted prophetess, overwhelmed by the emotional strain, succumbed to heart-failure, and thus sealed her gospel with death. The whole incident was miraculous enough, but still more amazing was the issue. Seemingly at one stride, the race passed to a level of self-knowledge and mutual loyalty which the first human species was to seek in vain, and which therefore it is not possible for me to describe to you.

At their height these amiable lemurs attained also a crude material culture. They had wattle dwellings, set in the forks of trees. They used rough wooden tools, and earthenware vessels, which hung from the branches like fruit. They even learned to plant trees so as to extend their forest. They dried their fruits, and stored them in clay-lined baskets. But to our observers this practical ability was less interesting than the precocious inner life with which it was linked. Nature had favoured these animals by setting them in a great luxuriant island. Their sole enemies, the great cats, they trapped to extinction. Unlike their cousins on the mainland, the ancestors of ape and man, these lemurs were neither over-sexed nor over-aggressive. Consequently their population remained limited in numbers, and united in sentiment. They rivalled the ants in sociality; but theirs was an intelligent, self-conscious sociality; whose basis was not blind gregariousness but mutual insight. When they had attained a very modest standard of amenity and a stationary social order, their native genius for self-knowledge and mutual insight combined with their truly aesthetic relish of acrobatics and of visual perception to open up a whole world of refined adventures. They developed song and articulate speech,

121

arboreal dance, and an abstract art based on wicker-work and clay. The flowers of personality and personal intercourse bloomed throughout the race. They began to generalize and speculate, in a naïve but promising manner. By meditation and self-discipline they cultivated mystical experience. It was with amazement, almost with awe, that our earliest observers felt the minds of these tailed, soft-furred arboreals grope toward and even surpass the intuitions of your Socrates and your Jesus. It might be said that these, who flourished millions of years before the Christian era, were the only truly Christian race that ever existed. They were in fact a race of spiritual geniuses, a race which, if only it could have been preserved against the stresses of a savage world, might well have attained a far lovelier mentality than was ever to be attained by the First Men.

This could not be. Nothing but rare good fortune had saved them from extinction throughout the million years of their career. It was by practical intelligence alone that they had won their position, not by self-knowledge, which in the early stages of evolution is indeed rather a hindrance than a help to the battling species. With security and a stereotyped social condition, their practical versatility declined. When at last a submarine upheaval turned their island into a peninsula, the gentle lemurs met their doom. A swarm of the still half-simian ancestors of man invaded the little paradise. Far less percipient than the natives, and less truly intelligent, but larger, more powerful, quarrelsome, and entirely ruthless, these fanged and hirsute brutes overpowered the lemurs by numbers and weight of muscle; by cunning also, for they had a well-established repertoire of foxy tricks. The lemurs had but one weapon, kindliness; and this in the circumstances was ineffective. Moreover they were by now emotionally refined into such fastidiousness that at the sight of blood they fainted. If one of them was caught and slaughtered by the enemy, his horrified companions would drop like ripe fruit from the trees and break their necks. Within a decade the race was extinct.

With the defeat of the lemurs at the hands of a hardier and a more extravert species, it was written in the book of fate that, sooner or later, a world-situation such as your own must occur, and give rise to an epoch of world wars such as you are now to suffer. Between the downfall of the lemurs and your own age there has been a slow, but in the long run triumphant, advance of practical intelligence. That other application of intelligence, namely to the inner life, has developed but spasmodically, as an accidental consequence of the growth of intelligence in action. And so it has happened that man's motives have remained throughout the career of your species almost invariably primitive. Even in your own day, when primitive impulses are intellectually seen to be inadequate, and you struggle pathetically toward loftier desires, your hearts remain the hearts of apes, and your struggle is vain. From the point of view of cosmical perfection, of course, your struggle is not vain at all. By your gallant effort and by your fated downfall also, you fulfil your part well and truly within the drama of existence. But from the point of view of the advancement of the race your struggle is indeed vain, doomed to failure. The profound reorganization of the human will, which you now see to be necessary, cannot be achieved in time to avert disaster. While the world remained primitive, and man's power over physical nature feeble, this paucity of the inner life, though in itself deplorable, did not imperil the survival of the race. But in your day man has gained considerable power. Not only has he made his world so complex and so explosive that it threatens to break from the control of his practical intelligence but further, and more serious, it is now such that the operation of the old blind motives may destroy it. Nothing could save you but a far more radical exercise of those capacities of self-knowledge which in your species have flowered only in rare circumstances, and in your own feverish epoch are more and more crushed out by the routine of industrial society.

3. PREHISTORIC ORIGINS OF THE WAR

In its earliest phase, then, and throughout its career, your species triumphed by means of pertinacity, quarrelsomeness and practical versatility. Little by little, success has strengthened these qualities. In the early conflict of many intelligent half-simian species, one conquered, the most cunning and courageous of all. The rest vanished. By wit and constancy of purpose the one creature made himself at last the veritable king of beasts, attacking even the great flesh-eating cats, till his very smell became dreadful to them. Thus by extravert intelligence did your ancestors come into their kingdom. For savouring their own experience they had neither need nor inclination. They gulped it down, and then sought more. For probing their own hearts they had no capacity. They could never become clearly aware of themselves. Since then, the aptitude for self-knowledge, which in your stock was never great, has not been fostered, save here and there and in a few periods of your history. There came of course a stage when the mere growth of intelligence made man realize that his heart was an unexplored jungle, and forced him to attack it. But this stage came late, too late. The jungle was by then too dense, too well-established.

Our observers have inspected every one of those great strokes of genius by which man came into his power. We have tasted the surprise and glee of him who first smashed his enemy's face with a stone, the triumph of him who first shaped a flint-edge to his liking, of him who secured fire and used it, of him who improved the floating log into a boat with paddles, and the rolling log into a wheel, of him who wrought the first metal tools, of him who made a sail, and so on. We have seen these inventions attained, forgotten sometimes even by the individual discoverers, re-invented, again and again lost and rediscovered, until at last they became the permanent property of the race. In each case we have entered the mind of the innovator, and felt his sudden ecstasy of achievement, his leap into keener being, like the fanned spark's leap into flame. We have watched him subsequently sink back into the old dream-like routine mentality, forgetful of past insight. Again and again, when a primitive man has stared uncomprehendingly at the very stone with which yesterday he triumphantly cracked the marrow-bones, our observer, being himself but human, has longed to remind the poor fool of his past prowess. As the ages advanced, this intelligence, this power of insight into the potentialities of external objects, evolved from a rare flicker to a constant flame, an established habit of mind. It was formerly intermittent, unreliable. It was like the earliest tools, which were but natural clumsy stones, picked up and used occasionally, and then forgotten. In time it became like the wrought and tempered knife, which is kept ever about the person, used at every turn, used often for mere love of using it, toyed with and applied to all manner of objects which seem at first without any practical significance whatever. Sometimes, indeed, as the ages pass, this keen knife of the mind is even applied to the mind itself. The inventor notices his own inventive activity, and tries to dissect it. The hungry man observes his own hunger, the amorous man his own lust. But the process turns out to be rather bewildering, even painful. Also it distracts one from the actual business of living. In the early stages it is therefore shunned.

Nevertheless, as the epochs unfold, the mind of man becomes more capacious, more unified, more active. It is no longer an ephemeral perception, forgetful of the past, or troubled now and then by a mere gleam of memory. Increasingly it carries the past forward with it, and refers to this stored past for light upon the present and the future. Increasingly every moment of its experience becomes interfused by all the rest of its experience. Today gains meaning from yesterday. Nothing can happen to the mind that does not reverberate, faintly or violently, through its whole nature. Every event is interpreted and valued in relation to other events. The man's mind becomes increasingly one mind, not a host of disconnected stupid little minds, awakening one after the other in response to special stimuli. Or so it tends to become. But in fact, it remains, in spite of all advances, very far from unified.

Along with this growing art of comprehending things together and taking more and more into account, comes an increasing discrimination of the actual differences in the world. Eyes distinguish new delicacies of shape, new shades of colour, ears detect new modulations of sound, fingers touch with increasing percipience, manipulate with increasing skill. Thus, age by age, man's experience of his world becomes richer, more coherent. Beasts, trees, one's fellows, become ever more characteristic, recognizable, reckonable. Space enlarges itself, is measured out in paces, leagues, marches; and time in days, months, seasons, years, generations. There looms a past before the clan was founded, a future for grandchildren's grandchildren. Meanwhile things that were formerly mere 'brute facts', shallow, opaque, barren of significance beyond themselves, reveal unexpected depths of meaning, become luminous, pregnant, charged with mysterious

125

power. The sun and moon, darkness, the storm, the seasons, beasts of the chase and hostile beasts, all gather to themselves out of the past a strange, obscure, potent significance,

Meanwhile also another, very different, class of objects is at length gaining precision and significance. The roving curiosity looks sometimes inward. Intelligence is turned more resolutely than of old upon the anatomy of the mind itself. The hunter, in ambush for his prey, is suddenly confronted with his own being. He beholds that strange thing 'himself', with the surprise and awe which he felt when he encountered for the first time some unfamiliar beast of the forest. But this time he has no clear apprehension of the mysterious quarry, only a most tantalizing glimpse, as of a dark form lurking behind the brushwood. He falls into abstraction. He ruminates his own being. 'I – am waiting for the stag. I – want to kill the stag.' The strain of stalking himself gives him a kind of vertigo. It even frightens him. Suddenly he wakes from his novel experience, to find that the physical quarry that he proposed to ambush has appeared and escaped. He has missed his dinner. He vows he will never again be bemused in this way. But on another occasion something similar happens. He is courting his young love, with the great brown eyes and gentle voice. She is ready to be taken. But suddenly two strange things loom into his inner vision, himself and herself, very near to one another, very closely entwined into one another's minds, yet strange to one another, infinitely remote. Once more he falls into abstraction, fascinated, perplexed. 'I – she. I – she'. As he sinks into this meditation, she sees his face change and fade. She seeks to rouse him by winsome tricks, but he remains for a while abstracted. In sudden fear and resentment she breaks from him and flies.

Thus, little by little, men and women grope toward a certain tentative superficial self-knowledge, and knowledge of one another. And, as they proceed, these strange objects, selves, become charged with ever-greater significance. Individuals come to prize themselves as no less gifted creature could ever do. They are proving that they are mighty selves. And, prizing themselves, they learn at the same time to prize other selves. Woman, whom man once saw merely as a thing to covet and embrace and then to ignore, or at most as a vague 'other', agreeable or irksome, now gathers to herself the significance of all past intercourse, all subtle passages of lust and love and hate, and reveals herself at last as a spirit, mysterious, potent, tender, ruthless. So also the man to the woman. Children, once mere objects to tend, defend, fondle, or, as the mood changed, to spurn, now become beings in their own right, rightly demanding service, even to the death. The group, once a vague swarm of fluctuating, discontinuous phantoms, companionable, quarrelsome, tyrannous, crystallizes at length into a system of persons. Close around oneself there is discovered a nucleus of well-tried friends and enemies, each one unique, incomparable. Over the heads of all, remote, mysterious, the old man of the tribe, or the tribal mother, or later the king of the whole land, embodies in his own person the ancient impersonal presence of the group, and later ascends heavenward as the tribal god, finally to become the one God of all tribes and all existence.

But long before this apotheosis there begin to appear here and there among the tribes beings of an intenser self-consciousness and a more insistent egoism, heroes, violent men for whom nothing is respect-worthy but their own exultant spirits. The word 'I' is ever on their lips and in their deeds. Each one of them is poignantly aware of himself as pitted against a huge, base, reptilian universe; and is confident that he will master it. Each lives for the mere zest of mastery. In his triumphant course each is accompanied by a swarm of jackal followers, not of his own kind, but striving to be of his kind. With them he smites the established powers, changing man's life for good or bad, making his mark upon the world, for very lust of scribbling. At the close of it all he confidently expects translation into some Valhalla. Often as not, all trace of him vanishes in a generation, save his name and legend on the lips of bards. If in any other manner his work lasts, it is more or less an accident. For, though aware of the superficies of his individuality in a manner impossible to his fellows, the hero has neither inclination nor time nor courage to penetrate within it and explore it. He accepts the bright superficies of himself at its face-value, and cares nothing for its deeper potentiality. In this respect he is typical of your kind.

Not only so, but the glamour of the hero has helped to make you what you now are. The ideal of personal prowess, which he set, though at first helpful to man's sluggish spirit, became later the curse of your species. With its facile glory it inveigled your forefathers into accepting outworn values, puerile aims. Throughout the whole career of your species the ideal of heroism has dominated you, for good and bad. In the earliest of all human phases, the almost simian mind of man could not yet conceive any ideal whatever, but the hero ideal was none the less already implicit in his behaviour, though unconscious. The best from which man sprang was already self-regarding, quarrelsome, resolute; and his hands were skilled for battle. Since then, epoch by epoch, the glory of innumerable heroes, the spell of innumerable heroic myths have ground the ideal of heroism into men's hearts so deeply that it has become impossible for you 'modern' men, in spite of your growing perception that heroism by itself is futile, to elicit from your hearts any larger ideal. You pay lip-service to other ideals, to love, and social loyalty, and religious possession; but you cannot feel them reverberate in your hearts, as does the ideal of the splendid all-conquering individual. To this ideal alone your hearts have been tuned by age-long hero-worship. No doubt, throughout your career loyalty has played a part. Your triumph, such as it is, rests upon the work of brilliant individuals cooperating in the group's service. But you have never taken the group to your hearts as you have taken the hero. You cannot. Your hearts are strung for the simpler music. They are but one-stringed instruments, incapable of symphonic harmony. Even your groups, even your modern nations, you must needs personify as heroic individuals, vying with one another, brandishing weapons, trumpeting their glory.

Our observers, wandering through the ages which you call prehistoric, have watched your kind spread in successive waves into every habitable corner of your planet, multiplying itself in a thousand diversities of race, diversities of bodily form, or temperament, of tradition, of culture. We have seen these waves, as they spread over the plains and along the coasts and up the valleys, every now and again crash into one another, obliterate one another, augment one another, traverse one another. We have seen the generations succeed one another as the leaves of an evergreen tree. As the leaves of a young tree differ from the leaves of an old tree, the early generations differ from the later in bodily and mental configuration. Yet they remain within the limits of their specific type. And so, inevitably, do you, spiked leaves of the holly.

We have watched all the stages, gradual or sudden, by which the common ancestor, crouched, hairy, and pot-bellied, has given place to the more erect Pithecanthropus, to the still almost simian Neanderthalian, and at last to the taller and more human progenitor of all your races. We have seen the first bare rippled backs, and the first broad upright brows. We have seen woman's breasts form themselves out of the old simian dugs. We have watched the gradual crystallization of your four great racial beauties, white, yellow, brown and black. We have followed in detail many a minor strand of bodily character, and the many facial types within each race, which blend and part and blend again, generation by generation. Similarly we have traced, generation by generation, the infinitely diverse exfoliation of the simian mind into your four great racial temperaments, and all the subtleties of disposition inborn in the many stocks within each race.

There came at length a stage in the career of your species when, through the operation of intelligence, men began vaguely to feel that there was something wrong with their own nature. They had already, here and there, acquired a superficial self-knowledge and mutual insight. They had begun to distinguish, though haltingly, the lesser and the somewhat greater goods of the spirit. From mere sex, mere parenthood, mere gregariousness, they had passed here and there to a kind of love and a kind of loyalty; but they could not maintain any sure footing on this higher plane. They were for ever slipping into the old bad ways. Increasingly they surmised that the purely animal way of life, even when glorified into heroism, was not the best that men and women could attain. Yet when they anxiously peered into their chaotic hearts to discover what was better, they could see nothing clearly, could find no constant illumination. Our observers, studying your early races, report that for each race there came a phase, early or late, poignant or obscure, in which there spread a vague but profound restlessness, a sense of potentialities not exercised, a sense of an insecure new nature struggling to shape itself, but in the main failing to do more than confuse the old brute nature. It is of this phase of your career that I must now speak.

4. THE HISTORICAL PERIOD

The action of the drama accelerates. With ever-increasing speed the human intelligence masters its world, brings natural forces more and more under control of the still primitive will, and unwittingly prepares a new world, a man-made world, which is destined to become in your day too intricate for the still unfinished intelligence to master, too precariously balanced to withstand the irresponsible vagaries of a will that is still in essence simian, though equipped with dangerous powers. The ape has awakened into a subtler and more potent cunning. He has attained even a vague perception of what it would be like to be truly human in mind and heart. Ineffectually, intermittently, he strives to behave as a true man would behave; and in rare moments he actually achieves thoughts and actions not unworthy of a man. But for the most part he remains throughout the history of your species, and in your own moment of that history, at heart a monkey, though clothed, housed and armed.

Before we look more closely at your 'modern' world, let us glance at the hundred centuries preceding it. At the outset we see tribes of hunters settling down to till the valleys, especially the valleys of the Nile, the Euphrates, the Indus, the Ganges, the Yangtze. Millennia pass. Mud huts proliferate along the riverbanks, condense into cities, are overhung by megalithic tombs, temples, palaces. The tribes coalesce into kingdoms and empires, and produce the first phases of civilization. Traders score the continents with their tracks. Little ships creep around the coasts, and sometimes venture beyond sight of land. Heroes gather armies and perform mighty evanescent conquests. Hardy barbarians invade the plains, dominate the empires, and are absorbed by the conquered. Daily life becomes steadily more secure, amenable, regular, complex. Triumphantly the intelligent beast finds new ways to gratify its ancient cravings for food, shelter, safety, adventure, for self-display, amorousness, and herd-activity. Yet at heart it remains a beast, disturbed but seldom by an obscure discontent with its own nature and with the world that it has fashioned around it.

With the increase of security a few exceptional minds begin to explore their environment intellectually, and even to probe their own nature. Increasingly the more awakened individuals become aware of their own inner chaos, both of understanding and of will. Here and there, where circumstance is peculiarly favourable to the life of the spirit, men are almost persistent in their self-searching. In India, where the physical cravings are insurgent and irresistible as the jungle, they strive through asceticism to establish the spirit over the flesh. In Greece they seek harmonious fulfilment of body and mind. For the sake of this fulfilment they seek the truth. They pass beyond the rule-of-thumb devices of medicine men, astrologers, builders, navigators, to make guesses about the inner nature of things, about the stars, the shape of the earth, the human body and soul, about number, space, time, and the nature of thinking. Meanwhile in Palestine others conceive a divine law; and in obeying it they expect a heaven of eternal bliss.

Then at length appear, here and there along the centuries, here and there among the peoples, a few supremely penetrating minds. Mostly their careers are cut short by indifferent fate, or by the vindictive herd. But three triumph, Gautama, Socrates, Jesus. Seeing with the mind's eye and feeling with the heart more vividly and more precisely than their fellows, they look round them at the world, and within them at their own nature, as none had done before them. It is a strange world that confronts them, a world of beings superficially like themselves, yet different. So uncomprehending are their fellows, so insensitive, so pitifully weak. In rigorous and ceaseless meditation the three great ones strive to formulate their teeming intuitions in a few great principles, a few great precepts. They live out their precepts in their own lives relentlessly. Gautama said: By self-denial, self-oblivion, seek that annihilation of particular being which is the way to universal being. Socrates said: Let us fulfil ourselves to the uttermost by embodying in ourselves, and in the world that is our city, the true and the good. Jesus said: Love one another; love God; God is love.

From these three greatest of your kind, these three vital germs, issue three vast ramifications of spiritual influence, three widespread endemic infections of the minds of men, passing from generation to generation. The tragedy of your species may be said

131

to lie in its complete failure to embody, rather than merely to mimic, the spirit of these three men.

Our observers, as I have already said, have never been able to establish themselves in any of these three. As the single racial mind of the Last Men we do indeed, if the obscure recollection of that experience is to be trusted, savour and even influence them. But to each individual observer they remain impenetrable. We can, however, study them through their contemporaries, and have done so, very minutely. We have seen those great ones face to face, listened to every word that they have spoken, watched every act they have performed in the presence of any spectator. Through dying eyes we have observed Gautama contemplating death. In the mind of the young Plato we have attended to the quiet ironical voice of Socrates and been confronted by his disturbing gaze. We have heard Jesus preaching on the mount, with dark face kindled. We have stood around the cross and heard him cry out on the God whom he had misconceived.

In such experiences three facts invariably impress us, and fill us with a sense of the pathos of your kind. We are amazed both at the unique genius of these men and at the world-imposed limitation of their genius. We are impressed also by the inability of their fellow-men to grasp even that part of their vision which found expression. For neither their immediate fellows nor you, with all your complacent historical knowledge, can ever understand them. How should you? They themselves strove in vain to comprehend their own profound, unique, intuitions, within terms of their world's naïve beliefs. But though the flame burned brightly in their hearts, they could neither understand it not express it. For neither their conception nor their language was adequate to such a task.

But even if they could have expressed their vision, they would have been misunderstood. For each of these three, though sorely cramped and bewildered by his archaic world, was a veritable man; while his fellows, like the rest of you, were but half-human apes. And so, inevitably, these great ones are misinterpreted even by their own chosen followers. Socrates, who is so much more fortunate in Plato than Jesus in his disciples and Gautama in his interpreters, is seen by us, not only to be more profound in intellect than the great Plato, but to have also a vision, an illumination, perplexing to himself and utterly incommunicable to any of his associates. The lemurs might have understood him. The lemurs might have understood Jesus, and Gautama also. But they, too innocent, could not maintain themselves against the muscle and cunning of man's progenitors.

It is clear to our observers that in your three great minds there occurred an identical insight into the nature of man and of the world. But each interpreted his vision differently, and expressed it differently in action. And from each a very different influence was selected by his followers.

We have traced that influence, that spreading ferment in men's minds. The three proliferations are very diverse. But in the early stages of each, during the first and even the second generation, there occurs a new intensity of experience, an increased though still confused self-knowledge, mutual insight and apprehension of the world. There is also a gloriously increased pertinacity of the will to be man rather than ape. Tidal waves of a new enthusiasm now begin to surge across the peoples, lifting up men's hearts, spreading over the continents. And, spreading, they fade. They multiply into a thousand meandering variations. They are deflected hither and thither, traversing one another again and again. They confuse, annihilate or augment one another. In your day there is not a mind anywhere on your planet which does not pulse, however faintly, to the endlessly wandering reverberations of your three true men.

But long before your day the character of the influence is changed. At first it stormfully resounds in the secret places of men's hearts, and even wrenches their poor ape-hearts into something of the human form. But in the end the simian nature triumphs. Those crude instruments, forced for a while to reverberate in response to a music too subtle and too vast for them, presently relapse into the archaic mode.

The ape nature corrupts the new, precarious, divinely human will, turning it into a lofty egoism, a new heroism,

Here, there is heroism of the intellect, loyal only to the truth-seeking self; there, heroism of the heart, determined to embrace all men in indiscriminate brotherliness, through mere loyalty to the love-proud self; there, heroism of the spirit, domineering over the flesh, proclaiming as the supreme affirmation mere negation.

But there remains a memory, a tradition, a legend, an obscure yearning in the hearts of men for a way of life that is too difficult for them. And so there are formed various mighty associations, whose office is to preserve one aspect or another of the fading illumination. The Christian and the Buddhist churches spread far and wide their hierarchies and their monastic orders. Institutions of learning, schools and universities, are precipitated around the Mediterranean coasts and over the European lands. Indians, Chinese, Arabs, Latins, Franks, thus preserve amongst themselves some smouldering embers. But the flame is vanished.

Yet now and again, once in a few generations, now in this land, now in that, the coals break once more into conflagration. There is a spreading revival of the original ecstasy. Once more, but not for long, the ape-hearts resound obscurely with counterfeit echoes of an experience whose true form they cannot support. Once more it seems to them that they are merged in one another and gathered into God in a mystic communion, that they have pierced behind appearances to the eternal truth, that by self-annihilation they have escaped the limitation of the flesh and individual consciousness, to be gathered into the absolute being. But once more, though the few attain some genuine illumination, the many misunderstand, ignore what is essential and mimic what is accidental; or in frank hostility persecute. Once more, as the insight fades, the institution flourishes, and takes up its place in the established order. Once more the ape triumphs over the man.

Our observers have savoured the minds of the First Men in all these wave-crests of the spirit, these religious revivals, protestations, counter-reformations, these fervours of heart-searching, stampedes of soul-saving, these martyrdoms for an inner light so precious and so misperceived. Everywhere we detect an identical fact. Vaguely aware of his own blindness and incoherence, man yearns toward vision and toward harmony; but he yearns in vain. Vision, indeed, he does now and again achieve, fleetingly, misleadingly; but harmony never. Here and there men see obscurely what they should be doing with themselves, but always their conduct, and their vision also, is distorted by preconceptions and predilections forced upon them by their ape nature. They are confused by phantom lures of immortality, of celestial bliss, of abstract righteousness, of divine love.

Nevertheless men do begin, here and there, to feel stirring within them, striving for expression, some strange new life of the spirit. Did they but know, they are in travail for a twin birth. They are troubled with the first movements of a new piety toward fate and a new loyalty toward man. Of the first they know as yet almost nothing, for whenever they experience it, they confuse it with the old complacent love of a loving God. Of the second, they guess only that they must make the best of man, must seek to know ever more truly both the world and the self, must seek to feel ever more delicately, and to will ever more harmoniously. Obscurely they begin to surmise that the whole active duty of men is to live for men; and that man must be made one, a spirit winged perhaps for enterprise unimaginable in their day. But these two conflicting spirits of cosmical piety and human loyalty remain still deeply hidden in their hearts; and men can neither see into their hearts nor bring forth in action what still is hidden. They cannot obey, they cannot even understand, these two seemingly incompatible divine commandments of the future. Blindly they seek vision; but the knowledge that they would have is for power, not piety. And so they are tricked at every turn by their own cravings. Harmony they seek; but neither within the individual nor in the race of individuals can they attain it. Nor can they find harmony with the universe. In each heart there rages the old conflict between the man and the monkey, and also the obscure new conflict between cosmical piety and human loyalty. In the external world, the quarrelsome apes that fought of old for prey, for mates, for kingship, for hunting-grounds, war now for cornlands, mines, trade, for national glory or security, for fantasies of religion. Armies surge hither and thither. Fields and cities are laid waste; and always in a good cause, whether for some royal master, or some burgher caste, or some nation, or for the glory of God.

While all this is afoot, something else which is new is beginning to happen to mankind. The still unrecognized piety toward fate and fact, and toward the actual course of the world, stirs men to observe the daily features of the world with new interest. At the same time loyalty toward man fires them to master the physical world for man's use, and therefore to understand its working. Some few individuals here and there, fretted by a recrudescence of that curiosity by which the ape had triumphed, begin to pry into the behaviour of physical things. They drop weights from towers, seek new descriptions of planetary motions, peer at the heavens through lenses, observe the workings of flesh and blood, put one stuff with another stuff and watch the issue, brood upon the falling apple, and on the jumping lid of a kettle, devise pistons, cog-wheels, gears, wheels within wheels. Suddenly man puts together a mesh of dangerous little fragments of knowledge, and comes into possession of little dangerous powers. Victoriously the human ape assimilates the teeming influx of new facts. Decade by decade he discovers new features of the intricacy and majesty of the physical universe. Imagination strains to cope with the very great, the very little, the very complex, the very swift, the very long-enduring. Little by little, the familiar universe crumbles away, and a new stupendous universe forces itself on man's reluctant fascinated gaze.

Within this new pattern of things man sees himself as among the very little, the very brief, the very impotent, the wholly mechanical. This discovery, which fills him with indignation and despair, should have been a step in his salvation. It should have taught him to value himself no longer as the immortal, precious, unique child of a God whom his own mind had created, but henceforth as a thread in the fair web of the universe, a theme in the great music, and also as one brief sentient focus of cosmical aspects. But, wholly ignorant of his own interior being, he still cherishes the belief that he is something peculiar, distinct from the physical, something uniquely free, vital, spiritual. And so, when he is forced to regard himself as all of a piece with his world, he feels himself degraded. All that he knows of the physical world is shape, movement, resistance, mechanical sequence of changes. These he takes to be no mere superficies, but the very essence of the physical. And these abstractions he now applies to himself, condemning himself as mere 'matter'. If he knew himself as well as he now begins to know his world, the science of the physical would not dismay him about his own nature, nor remain itself a science of mere appearances. But through inveterate self-blindness the First Men are doomed to misconceive themselves in the light of a physical nature, which, also through self-blindness, they must misconceive. Ignorant of their own interior being, they remain ignorant of the interior being of the world whose gorgeous superficies is now stage by stage terrifyingly revealed.

When the First Men have already firmly grounded their science of the physical world, they begin to direct the same objective study upon their own behaviour. Thus they will acquire in due season a vision of themselves even more devastating, because more precise. They will see themselves at last unambiguously as greedy, self absorbed, vindictive, timorous apes, cunning and powerful up to a point, yet also incredibly weak and stupid. This knowledge, could they but pursue it relentlessly and to the bitter end, should lead them at last up to the locked door behind which is true self-knowledge. Once there, they should be able by biological control to produce a generation capable of penetrating that interior stronghold. Thus should the First Men arrive at last where the lemurs started, and should proceed to surpass those wise innocents in every activity of the spirit. But in the book of fate it is written that this shall not happen. While men are taking the first few halting steps in the new venture, while they are still debating the course, the storm breaks upon them. A world situation arises which demands for its control more intelligence and far more integrity of will than their half-formed nature can achieve.

While man is becoming less and less confident of his own spiritual dignity, he acquires more and more power over his physical world, and sinks further and further into obsession with the material. Steam drives ships across the oceans without care for winds, drives trains across the lands, carrying great loads at incredible speeds. Later comes electricity, and with it the flashing of messages around the planet on wires or on the ether. The age-old dream of flying is at last realized by aeroplane and airship. Meanwhile by machinery and chemical synthesis innumerable materials and utensils are manufactured for comfort, luxury or power.

What is the upshot? From its germ in Europe a new world spreads, devouring the old world. Formerly events happening in one region had seldom any appreciable effect elsewhere. But now, increasingly, each event in every part of the world reverberates within all other events. By means of steam and electricity the human world is becoming one system. Its regions become interdependent economically, even in a manner culturally; but not politically, and not socially. The hearts of men are massed against one another in jealous and mistrustful nations. And across this cleavage runs another, the division in all lands between masters and servants, the economically free and the economically enslaved. The new world should have been a happy and glorious world. But it is not. The new powers should have been organized in service of the human spirit, the one right object of loyalty. But they are not. The First Men can do almost nothing, with their powers, but serve the old ape-cravings for private comfort, safety, self-display and tribal glory.

At the moment of the outbreak of the European War the great majority of mankind are extremely ignorant not only of their own essential nature but of the world. They feel no need that man should be made one, and that all men should cooperate in the supreme racial enterprise. They take the nations to be the true objects of loyalty, and the social classes to be natural elements of the nation. But a minority, mostly in the Western lands, have blindly felt this need of human unity. Their leaders have formulated it obscurely in one manner or another, often discrepantly. But few can take it at all seriously, very few can live for it passionately. In most cases, however bravely they can talk about it, they cannot act for it. If ever they are put to the test, they shy away, affirming that nationalism is 'practical', cosmopolitanism but a remote ideal. Though they see it intellectually, their hearts are not capable of responding to it. If ever the nation is in danger, their cosmopolitanism evaporates, and they stand for the nation in the good old style. Yet intellectually they know that in their modern world this way leads to disaster.

The story of your species is indeed a tragic story, for it closes with desolation. Your part in that story is both to strive and to fail in a unique opportunity, and so to set the current of history toward disaster. But think not therefore that your species has occurred in vain, or that your own individual lives are futile. Whatever any of you has achieved of good is an excellence in

138

itself and a bright thread woven into the texture of the cosmos. In spite of your failure it shall be said of you, had they not striven as they did, the Whole would have been less fair. And yet also it shall be said, even had they triumphed and not suffered their disaster, the Whole would have been less fair.

VI *The War*

1. EUROPE BEFORE THE WAR

I MUST now describe from the Neptunian point of view that moment in the career of the First Men which seemed to those who experienced it an eternity of war.

As the summer of 1914 advanced, our observers crowded in ever-greater numbers into your world, seeking out among you suitable minds in which and from which to observe your coming crisis. As a flock of birds, before settling on a tree, hovers for a moment while each individual selects a convenient twig, so we settled upon your race. The tree knows nothing of its living burden; you were wholly ignorant of your Neptunian guests.

Long before this great company began to arrive, those of us who, like myself, are specialists in your epoch had, of course, already been at work among you, wandering from mind to mind and studying the great movements of human history which were to result in your crisis. But in 1914 an immensely greater company gathered to watch in as much detail as possible your reaction to the unprecedented events of the next four years. In spite of this influx of observers, not every one of you could be directly studied. But a considerable proportion of the total European population harboured within themselves Neptunian visitors. We diligently sought out all those who were significant, not only those in prominent positions but very many obscure persons who seemed to afford peculiarly lucid examples of your nature and of the trend of thought and feeling in your day. Such persons would have been astounded had they known that they were singled out for study along with generals and political leaders; but in truth it was in the masses, rather than in their leaders, that the real drama of the war was taking place. For in the leaders the poignancy and subtlety of experience was in most cases reduced by the necessity of pursuing some official policy.

Throughout the summer of 1914, then, a huge anthropological

expedition, organized on Neptune two thousand million years in the future, was invading your minds in its thousands and its hundreds of thousands. Yet also (to repeat) at the very same time, in the Neptunian sense, other and even greater expeditions were at work upon crises of one or other of the sixteen human species which have their historical location between the First Men and the Last Men. Thus some were studying the fall of the noble Second Men in their long struggle with the cloud-like Martian invaders; others watched the heroic colonization of Venus by the Fifth Men, the last Terrestrials; others, most fortunate, wandered among the lyrical minds of the pygmy Flying Men of Venus, the Seventh species; and many more carried out their devoted work in the field of man's age-long and tortured struggle to take root on Neptune; others again studied the later and happier Neptunian races. But these expeditions I must not now describe, for my concern is with yourselves. In our work upon the First Men we have concentrated our main force in your own crucial age.

In every European capital, in every drab provincial town, in every agricultural district, our observers settled. Had you been gifted with Neptunian vision, you might have seen, whenever you walked in the streets of Berlin, Paris, or London, that the crowd was composed of persons of two kinds. Most of them were uncontaminated members of your species; but about one in twenty (at least in these metropolitan areas) would have appeared to you curiously altered. You would have seen in the expression of their eyes, had you peered closely at them, a fitful gleam, a faint surprise, verging on bewilderment, a queer inwardness combined oddly with an increased intensity of observation and interest, in fact an almost haunted look, which the Neptunian has learned to recognize in such of you as have been singled out by one of his colleagues as a convenient observation-point. It is not surprising that you should manifest some outward symptom when you are thus possessed, as it were, by an all-pervading mental parasite, whose filaments reach into every nook and cranny of your minds. Yet so subtle is this unintentional influence of ours, that the hosts themselves are, as a rule, completely unaware of it, and even their most intimate friends do not notice any alteration in them. Only to Neptunians, using the eyes of other individuals of your species is

141

the 'possessed' look apparent. Sometimes, of course, we deliberately make our presence felt by some act of definite influence, and when such influence is frequent, the host himself may have a sense that he is somehow possessed, or going mad. But the more passive presence of a Neptunian produces only a slight increase of the intensity of consciousness, and especially of self-consciousness.

Conceive then that, before war was declared, Neptunian observers were busy making themselves acquainted with their chosen hosts. That we concentrated in greatest number upon the years of the war and the two decades following, is not to be attributed to any special preference for the mentality of your Twentieth over your Nineteenth Century. As between the generations which, through complacent materialism and sentimentality, brought the war into being, and the generation which, through moral timidity and lack of faith in the human nature of the 'enemy', allowed itself to be herded into the trenches, and again the later generations, which, attaining maturity when the war was over, blamed its predecessors or malicious fate for its own supine laziness and lack of vision, – as between these three groups of persons we have no predilection. To us all alike are 'human', in the manner characteristic of a half-human species. Each is the inevitable product of its predecessors and its world, yet each is in part responsible for its own turpitude. This is, I know, a paradox which must remain insoluble upon your plane of understanding. But to us, there is no paradox. All your generations appear equally culpable, equally pitiable. But since, in the war itself and its consequences, the whole drama of your species finds its climax, it is in the war period and the decades following it that our observers chiefly congregate.

Very thoroughly the pioneers had already sifted your populations for significant individuals, so that when the main expedition arrived it was possible to allocate each new-comer to a suitable host. Most often (but not always) we set our women observers to study Terrestrial women. And as far as possible we contrived to arrange matters so that there should be some kind of temperamental similarity between observer and observed; for thus, we find, the work proceeds most smoothly and effectively. Some of us occupied the minds of the politicians on whose decision so much was to depend, seeking to understand and sympathize with their ingrained political convictions, sorting out the obscure tangle of self-interest and public loyalty which was to determine their behaviour, harking back now and then into their youth or child-hood, or even infancy, to discover the submerged sources of their whims, delusions and prejudices. Others of us familiarized them-selves with the astounding mixture of honest heart-searching and intricate self-deception which was the habitual attitude of your religious leaders to all serious problems, and was so soon to find its most striking expression in the futility of your churches in the face of war. Yet others were savouring the insistent itch of military experts to put their huge lethal toy in action, or the mere boyish braggartism, a relic of the heroic age, which infected your more romantic militarists.

In varying degrees of minuteness we have studied your Asquith and your Grey, your Bethmann-Hollweg, your von Bülow and your Treitschke, your Hindenburg, your Foch, your Clémenceau and your Lloyd George. Each of these, though not one of them is intrinsically of serious interest to us, has called for careful study on account of the momentous results of his actions. Your Lenin, however, we have studied in greater detail; many of my colleagues have had occasion to live through all the phases of that remarkable spirit, in whom, as in no other, we find a most instructive blend of that which might have saved your species with that which was bound to destroy it.

Sometimes we have performed curious experiments by intro-ducing into one mind thoughts and valuations derived from another, as in biological research the experimenter may introduce blood or portions of tissue from one organism to another. Thus it has proved instructive to bewilder statesmen at the council table by momentarily forcing upon them ideas disruptive of their policies and their most cherished faiths. For instance, one of my most brilliant young colleagues, fresh from the revolutionary and exiled Lenin, once contrived that Asquith, the legal-minded premier, in the presence of his cabinet, should sink for a moment into horrified abstraction while a blast of revolutionary schemes and cravings fell on him like a whirlwind. It was indeed instructive to observe how, after the attack the ageing statesman soothed himself by dipping into Carlyle's *French Revolution*, and by slightly changing his attitude to the Welsh thorn in his flesh. Of deeper effects we observed none.

To give another example of this transfusion of thought, Lenin himself, that man of stainless steel, that future Almighty, was once, to his own surprise, so flooded with the timid megalomaniac fantasies of the Czar, that he found himself pitying, even pitifully loving that imperial half-wit. On another occasion, while he was in the act of composing a relentless article on the baseness of an archimandrite, my colleague forced upon him a precise apprehension of the old villain's mind. He suddenly realized in imagination that this profligate priest had once yearned toward the supernal beauty, and that even yet his blind spirit carried out by rote the gesture of prostration before the great lover, Jesus. This incident had a strange and significant effect on the revolutionary. Pent-up springs of mercy and piety welled in him. He experienced, as few Christians have ever experienced, the divinity of Love. Sitting in his hired room in Paris, with the indictment of the priest spread out on the table before him, he whom many were yet to call Anti-Christ, received the divine love into his heart. My young colleague who was in charge of the experiment reports that his host accepted the revelation like any Christian saint, and that for an hour he remained in ecstasy. At the close of that period he whispered in his Russian speech, 'I come not to bring peace, but a sword', and so once more took up his pen.

Not only men of action, but leaders of thought, too, our observers inhabited. In many minds of writers and artists they had detected in the 'pre-war' age the first stirrings of that disillusionment and horror which the war climate was later to foster.

Earlier they had seen the English Tennyson, under the influence of science and a friend's death, face the spectre for a moment, only to cover his eyes and comfortably pray. Carlyle they had seen praise action as a drug for doubt. But now, they saw the writings of Thomas Hardy, formerly neglected, gradually compel men's attention more by their gloomy verisimilitude, than by their obscure conviction of cosmical beauty. In each people our observers heard already, in the midst of the complacency of that age, a whisper of uneasiness, rising here and there to despair. Already the old gods were failing, and no new gods appeared to take their place. The universe, it seemed, was a stupendous machine, grinding for no purpose. Man's mind was but a little friction upon a minor axle, a casual outcome of natural law. He dared not even regard himself as the one divine spark in a waste of brute matter; for he himself was just matter, and his behaviour the expression of his brute nature. Moreover, Freud had spoken, and ripples of horror were already spreading across Europe.

But there was Evolution. Our observers watched Bergson and all those whose faith was given to evolution champion their doctrine of a biological deity with something of the fervour of the old church militant. Their gospel touched few hearts. Disillusionment was already in the air. In laboratories our observers watched great scientists conduct their crucial experiments, and weave their theories, so subtle, so wide-sweeping, so devastating, so true on one plane and so meaningless on another. Again and again we have seen the truth missed when it was hidden only by a film. Again and again we have watched promising enterprises run to waste through the influence of some mad whim or prejudice. In many a study and on many a college lawn we have noted the turn of argument wherein acute minds first began to stray down some blind alley, or first tethered themselves to false assumptions.

But the overwhelming majority of our explorers were concerned with humbler persons. Our pioneers had flitted from mind to mind among artisans, factory hands, dock labourers, peasants, private soldiers, in search of those most significant or most subject to Neptunian influence, so that the main company should be able to settle promptly into posts of vantage for their work. If you incline to commiserate with those of us to whom it was allotted to observe simple minds in obscure positions, you are under a misconception. The difference between your mentally richest and your mentally poorest is negligible to us.

We have sat all day on heaps of road metal in country lanes, wielding a hammer, and savouring humble thoughts in minds not barren but not fortune-favoured. In French peasants we have driven sewage carts over our hectares, estimating the unsown crop, and the cost, and the sowing. In Prussian military messes we have drunk to 'der Tag'. In British foc's'les, homeward bound from

Yokohama and Kobe, we have looked back upon Geisha girls, forward to the wife in Canning Town. In provincial suburbs we have pondered the sententious wisdom of scavengers, while they pushed their hand-carts and condescended to speak with tramps. We have been present with trapped miners, while the flooding water crept up legs and bodies, or lungs were invaded by hostile gases. We have listened to doomed men chanting under the roots of mountains. Some of us, in zeal to observe last acts of piety or panic, have been destroyed in the destruction of their hosts. In factories we have spent our Terrestrial years feeding voracious machines and dreaming impossible triumphs or love idylls. On holidays we have been borne by the released flood of our fellow-workers along esplanades and heaths. Over shop-counters in Bond Street and the rue de Rivoli we have fingered camisoles, stockings, dress pieces. We have pondered, tone by tone, cliché by cliché, the intercourse of customers and shop-girls. We have jostled around buses and down subways, and hurried into city offices. In third-class railway carriages we have read innumerable evening papers through the eyes of clerks and typists, devouring the murders and the sex, skimming the politics. In the discreet darkness of picture palaces we have had forbidden tactual intimacies. In jails we have estimated the civilization of Europe through the rage of its outcasts. We have battered impotently on cell doors, counted and recounted the threads of spider-webs, strained to catch sounds of the world's great tide of life, which had left us stranded. We have entered into inmates of lunatic asylums, to gain insight into your mentality by watching its disintegration. We know also what it is to be segregated as mad by a world madder than oneself. In public-houses and Bier Stuben we have escaped for a while from nagging reality through the cheap ecstasy of inebriation. Or, less forlorn, we have found in the applause of our companions false consolation for our defeat in life.

More precisely it was our hosts that had all these experiences, while we, calm scrutinizers, appraised their minds. With the patience of big-game photographers, who endure tropical heat and drought or stand up to the neck in marsh for the sake of one snap of the camera-shutter, we have suffered interminable floods of rhetoric and infantile philosophy, in the hope of confronting one of those rare denizens of the mind's jungle, those most vital and significant mental occurrences, which give insight into the mentality of an alien species.

We have also suffered vicariously the pains, both maternal and filial, of many births. We have watched the clean pages of many infant minds ignorantly scribbled over with indelible fears and loathings. We have experienced in many young things the same hungers and worships that we ourselves have known in our own far-future childhood upon Neptune. But in Terrestrial childhood we find these young healthy lusts and admirations all poisoned, misdirected, blunderingly thwarted or sapped, so that again and again we are reminded that the folly of your generation, as of every generation of your species, is due less to its innate coarseness of fibre than to the disastrous influence of its parents and teachers. Could we but, like your Pied Piper, rescue all your infants from their mothers and fathers, could we but transport them to Neptune, even with their ineradicable simian impulses and their inherited distortions of mind and body, could we but keep them from the contamination of their elders, what a race we could make of them! We could not indeed bring them further than the threshold of true humanity, but within their natural limits they might be made generous, free-minded, zestful, unafraid. Then, if we could but return them to your planet in the first bloom of maturity, how they would remake your world! But instead they must remain unfulfilled, like seeds which, blown into a cave, send forth long pale stems and flaccid leaves, seeking in vain the light.

The many boys and girls whom we have seen, confident at first that life held in store for them some as yet unimaginable treasure or some opportunity of high devotion, already in a few years disillusioned! We have encountered them at first unsullied, equipped by nature to learn prowess of body and mind, to advance from triumph to triumph of skilled and generous living. Then we have seen their bodies hampered, constricted, poisoned by misguided care, and their spirits even more seriously maltreated. Though in physical athletics they have often been patiently trained to habits of free and effective action, in the athletics of the mind and of the spirit they have acquired a cramped style and blind tactics. In the great game of life they never learned to keep their

147

eyes on the ball. For them indeed the ball was invisible. They hit out stiffly or limply at nothing at all, or at hypnotic hallucinations, conjured before them by the exhortations of blind coaches.

Everywhere we have found in the lives of grown men and women a bewildered futility and resentfulness. The men blamed the women for their hobbled lives, the women the men for their servitude. The rich blamed the poor for disloyalty, the poor the rich for tyranny. The young blamed the old for lack of vision, the old the young for rebelliousness. And increasingly, even in that age before the war, men and women, rich and poor, old and young, were beginning to suspect that they were playing their brief game in a madhouse, with no rules and a phantom ball.

No wonder that in our research among the aged of that time we found very prevalent a most tragic condition of the spirit. Innumerable old men and old women, looking back with conscious complacency upon their achievements, and forward with confidence to their reward in heaven, were yet haunted in the recesses of their being with a sense that their lives had been phantasmal, that they had never really lived at all. Most of them were able on the whole to ignore these deep whispers of misgiving, or to drown them with vociferous piety; but many of the more self-conscious old people whom we studied, whether successful business men or members of the 'professions', socially triumphant old ladies or retired matrons of institutions, reviewed their careers with blank dissatisfaction and a nightmare sense that in their moment of living they had missed some great drudgery-redeeming good, simply by looking in the wrong direction. Only those whose lives had been dominated by concrete misfortune or disappointment, or by the demands of some all-absorbing heroic ministration, escaped this universal distaste of all values.

Such was the condition of the First Men as it was revealed to our observers in their survey of the years before the outbreak of the European War. Such were the beings that they studied. On the whole they found themselves forced to be twi-minded about these distressful creatures. From one point of view, as I have said, they could not but regard your species as not yet human; a thing incredibly stupid and insensitive, incredibly distorted and tortured by the fantastic habits, the rudimentary 'culture' which alone distinguished it from the lower beasts; a thing in some ways further removed from true humanity even than ox or tiger, because it had strayed further down the wrong path; a thing incomparably more filthy than the baboon, because, retaining brutality, it had lost innocence and learned to affect righteousness; a thing which was squandering the little powers that it had stumbled upon for ends essentially the same as the ends of monkeys, and in its frantic grabbing, devouring, voiding, had fouled a whole planet.

But from the other point of view our observers were forced to admit, at first reluctantly, that this errant and brutal thing had in it the distinctive essence which is man. Penetrating with difficulty into the minds of tiger and baboon to compare them with your species, they found indeed less brutality, but also less divinity; in fact a greater emptiness. In you they recognized the first blind restlessness of the spirit, which never troubles the mere beast, and wins its beatitude only in the full human estate. In you they found the rudimentary insight of the mind into itself and into others, that insight which lay beyond the reach of all Terrestrial organisms save Homo Sapiens and the Philosophical Lemurs, whose far more brilliant achievement man himself had terminated. In you they found love, though more often hate; in you philosophy though halting and superstitious; in you worship, though for the most part directed on unworthy objects.

All this might have been truly said of your species at any time of its career; but, at the moment which I am now describing, it was balanced on a still finer knife-edge between beast and man. This was due not to any change in its nature but to the pressure of circumstances. Hitherto, though a sensitive minority had been aware that the aims toward which men commonly strove were for the most part puerile, the majority were able to pursue these aims in undisturbed complacency. But in 1914 many forces were combining to shock even minds of average percipience into a sense of the contemptible insufficiency of the extant plan of human life, both individual and social. It is worth while to enumerate these forces. First, then, although the nations and races were still violently opposed to one another in sentiment, the world was already becoming a single economic system. Each section was growing more and more dependent on the healthy life of others.

Secondly, though national and racial cultures were still for the most part mutually unintelligible and repugnant, the seeds of an all-inclusive world culture were already quickening. Third, the battle between doctrinal religion and scientific materialism, in which science had been steadily advancing all along the line, was already beginning to dissolve and crystallize out in a new alignment. For while the old religion was beginning to seem not only intellectually incredible but also spiritually insufficient, the old science was already appearing not only spiritually arid but intellectually naïve. Fourth, man's increasing awareness of his littleness under the stars was combining with his first crude apprehension of the cosmical enterprise of Life to give him a wider horizon, a new humility, and also the first obscure glimpse of a new aim. Unfortunately in 1914 the effect of these forces was nowhere profound; and only in certain regions of the Western Civilization was it at all widespread. It was not strong enough to prevent the outbreak of war. All it produced was a devastating, though mostly unacknowledged, suspicion in all the combatants that human nature had failed.

2. EUROPE CHOOSES WAR

In August 1914 it was said by the more thoughtful among you that a great war in Europe might well cause the 'downfall' of civilization. They expected that the war would lead at once to complete economic and social confusion. In this prophecy they were wrong. They underestimated the recuperative powers of their material civilization. But the war was to cause a disaster more subtle and profound than any which was foreseen in 1914. It was to undermine man's confidence in his own nature. Henceforth your species was to suffer a kind of racial neurosis blended of guilt, horror, inferiority, and hate. Not only civilization was to be undermined, but the integrity of a species.

In the fateful days when ultimatums and declarations of war were being bandied from capital to capital, the population of Europe was wholly unprepared to take the one line which could have saved it. It had neither the courage nor the imagination for a general refusal to fight. On the other hand it could not accept the war innocently, as earlier generations had accepted wars. Hitherto men had fought with a clear conscience, however much they might personally loathe the distresses that war must bring. But, since the last war in Europe, a change had begun to come over men's minds. Though it was not yet possible for the masses to reject war, it was no longer possible for them to accept it without guilt. Few, even of those who suffered no conscious heart-searching, were wholly immune from that unwitting shame and embitterment which was the characteristic mood of your war-tortured populations, and had never occurred at all widely in any earlier war.

It was extremely interesting to observe within minds of various types the different reactions of your species to the novel fact of war. Most were taken completely by surprise. In the manner character-istic of their species they had lived hitherto without serious thought for matters of public concern. The rivalries of national states might indeed rouse in them some sentimental interest, but the life of the race lay almost wholly beyond their grasp. They were fully occupied in keeping themselves and their families afloat in the maelstrom of economic individualism. Inevitably their chief con-cern was private fulfilment, and its essential means, money. National affairs, racial affairs, cosmical events, were of interest to them only in their economic bearing, or at most as occasions of curiosity, wonder or ridicule. They produced and consumed, bought and sold, played ritual games with balls, and transported themselves hither and thither in mechanical vehicles in search of a goal which ever eluded them. They indulged in illicit sexual inter-course; or with public applause they married, propagated, launched their children upon the maelstrom. They put on their best clothes on Sunday, and after church or chapel they walked in the park. Or, with a sense less of moral guilt than of social degrada-tion, they spent their Sundays in old clothes and upon congenial occupations. Almost invariably they applauded the things they had been taught to revile. Or, if they were 'original' and dared to think and feel spontaneously, they found themselves harassed both by their fellows and by their own archaic consciences. They then either recanted or developed into extravagant cranks. But these were few. The overwhelming majority were enslaved by the custom of the herd.

Such were the beings on whom the fate of the Terrestrial spirit now depended. Nowhere was there any clear perception of the issues at stake, nowhere any recognition that the species was faced with the supreme crisis of its career. Scarcely a man or woman in Europe or America, still less in the remote East, realized that the great test of the human animal had come, and come, alas, too soon.

In their reaction to war, Western men and women revealed themselves as falling into a few well-marked types, which nevertheless graded into one another. Indeed, scarcely any individuals could be said to belong wholly to any one type. In almost all there were traces of every kind of war sentiment, and in many there was an almost diurnal fluctuation of mood from one to another. Nevertheless Western Europeans may be significantly classified according to their most characteristic attitude to the war as follows:

First, in every nation there was the incredibly large swarm of persons who, in spite of their vociferous patriotism, were at most times incapable of taking the war seriously in any sense except as a source of possible danger or profit to themselves. Such creatures we found in all classes, from manual labourers to captains of industry and respected statesmen. In the armies also we found many, who had failed to evade their military obligations. They were of all orders of intelligence, from the very stupid to the acute; but even the most brilliant of them lacked the power to see beyond the horizon of private, or at most family, interest. They were nearly always quite unconscious of their own deficiency; yet almost with the unwitting mimicry shown by some insects, they managed to behave, verbally at least, with impeccable correctness. They were seldom suspected of being inhuman. Often have we experimented on these backward animals, striving to introduce into the mind of some munition-profiteer, some popular demagogue, some climbing staff-officer, or some abject shirker in the ranks, glimmers of a self-oblivious view. Most often the experiment has failed completely; but in some cases we have been rewarded by a curious spectacle. The little self, outraged by the incursion of unselfcentred fantasies, has called 'morality' or 'duty' to its assistance. The ambitious general, for instance, troubled for a moment by the sacrifice of life entailed in some brilliant barren attack, has told himself that it is necessary, and could not see that he was caring only for his reputation as a resolute commander.

The second type recorded by our observers was less contemptible, but almost as backward. These were the persons who, though often strong in a kind of social sense, innocently accepted war and the martial code. Their vision was limited to the hero ideal. They saw the war in the good old way as a supreme opportunity of personal courage and devotion. It came, they said, to purge men of the selfishness bred of industrialism and of the softness bred of security. These guiltless champions of the war might personally behave toward it either with cowardice or heroism; but they never questioned it. With complete sincerity they faced it as a god-sent ordeal. For them it was indeed a religious test, an opportunity to enter into communion with some obscurely conceived heroic deity. To speak against it was sacrilege; but a sacrilege so gross and fantastic that it should be regarded as a sign rather of idiocy than of wickedness. Consequently, though they condemned pacifism whole-heartedly, there was no vindictiveness in their condemnation. Again and again our observers, experimenting in these simple minds, have tried to introduce some doubt, some apprehension that there might be another side to the matter. But such doubts as could be introduced appeared to the subject himself as merely an intellectual exercise, not as a live issue. Such images of brutality and disgust as were introduced were accepted simply as tests of fortitude.

Curiously it was among these archaic souls, these happy warriors, that we sometimes came upon a pellucid kind of religious experience. Fortunate innocents, they were exempt from the guilt and torture which wrecked so many of their fellows. For them the issue was a clear issue between self-regard and loyalty to all that they most cherished. And those who had the strength to bear themselves throughout according to their code had the reward of a very sweet and well-deserved beatitude. We attended many a death-agony that was thus redeemed, especially in the earliest phase of the war. Many an old regular thus found his rest. Many a very young subaltern, whose photograph on the parental mantel-piece truthfully commemorated a bright immaculate boy-soldier, found in his last moment that peace which passed his simple under-standing. But many more, to whom death came less suddenly or more brutally, could not attain that bliss. Hundreds, thousands of these luckless beings, betrayed by their god, we have watched slipping down into the gulf of death, clutching, screaming, bewild-ered and indignant, or utterly dehumanized by pain.

More common than the 'happy warriors' was a third type, namely those who, having passed in spirit beyond this knightly innocence, still tried to retain it. These, when the war began, were first shocked and torn asunder by conflicting motives, by loyalty to the old idea of war and by the obscure stirrings of something new which they dared not clearly face. For, in spite of all their regrets and compassion, they very deeply lusted for war. And because this new thing that disturbed them ran counter to this lust and to the familiar code, they strove to ignore it. Or they persuaded themselves that though war was an evil, *this* war was a necessary evil. They elaborated all manner of arguments to convince them-selves that their country's cause was the cause of humanity, or that the war, though tragic, would result in a great moral purgation. They eagerly accepted every slander against the enemy, for it was very urgent for these distraught spirits to believe that the enemy peoples were almost sub-human. Only so could they feel confident that the war was right, and indulge their martial zeal with a clear conscience. The pacifists they condemned even more bitterly than the enemy, for in tormenting the pacifists they seemed to be crush-ing the snake in their own hearts.

The fourth type, though not actually a majority in all lands, had the greatest influence, because in most of the other types the sentiment of this fourth type was present in some considerable degree. These were at the outset little stirred by patriotism, and for them war had but a slight romantic appeal. They thought only of individual lives and happiness, and nearest their hearts were the lives and happiness of their fellow-countrymen. Under the influence of the lying propaganda with which the spirit of each nation was poisoned by its government, they sincerely believed that the enemy government was in the wrong, and was carrying out a base policy by brutal measures. But they preserved their sanity so far as to believe that the enemy peoples were on the whole not very different from themselves. As individuals the enemy were 'just ordinary decent folk' who, through some lack of resolution, had been led into a false policy. Consequently (so it was said) the 'group spirit' of these swarms of harmless enemy individuals was unhealthy. In the mass they were a danger to civilization, and so at all costs they must be beaten.

Such was the attitude of most men and many women in both the opposed groups of peoples. They lacked faith in human nature. And through their lack of faith in it they betrayed it. They might so easily have risen up in their millions in all lands to say, 'This war must stop; we will not fight.' Yet of course, though in a sense so easy, such a refusal was also utterly impossible to them. Because they were without any perception of man's true end, because they accepted the world as it stood and human nature as it seemed, they inevitably missed the great opportunity, and condemned their species to decline. Pitiable beings, they brought upon their own heads, and upon the future, deluges of pain, grief, despair, all through lack of vision, or of courage. They manned a thousand trenches, endured a thousand days and nights of ennui or horror, displayed what in your kind is called superb devotion. All this they did, and all for nothing. They thrust bayonets into one another's entrails, they suffered nightmares of terror, disgust and frantic remorse. They were haunted by bloody and filthy memories, and by prospects of desolation. Those of them who were parents gave up their sons, those who were women gave up their men, and all for nothing; or for a hope that was as impossible, as meaningless, as self-contradictory, as a round square, for the mad hope that war should end war. They believed that from their agony there must spring a new, fair world. But in fact through their lack of faith in one another the whole future of their species was overclouded.

The fifth type that we discovered was actually opposed to the war. There were many kinds of pacifists. A few were those naïve beings who, loyal to the Christian faith both in the spirit and the letter, simply accepted the commandment 'Thou shalt not kill', and thought no further. But the main body of effective pacifists, even of those who gave as their motive 'religious scruples', were of a very different water. One and all, though they knew it not, were ruled by that imperious, but still unformulated impulse which I have already noted in the case of Paul, the impulse of loyalty to the dawning spirit of man. But since the real spring of their conduct was still so obscure, they had to rationalize it in various manners. Many supposed themselves to be moved simply by the Christian faith. But indeed in these, so our observers discovered, it was not Chrstianity that had bred pacifism, but pacifism that had given Christianity a new significance. Strong in the intuitive loyalty to the great adventure of the Terrestrial mind, they interpreted that intuition as loyalty to the Christian God. They strove, so they said, to love their fellows as Jesus had bidden them, but also they strove to love Jesus himself even more. And for them Jesus, though they knew it not, was the divine spirit embodied in their groping species.

Others there were, upon whom the basis of the same intuition constructed other rationalizations. Some, believing that they cared only for the happiness of individuals, declared that the misery of war must far outweigh all its good effects. They cared nothing for national honour, nothing for treaty obligations to defend weak peoples, nothing for the propagation of national culture. These, they said, were mere phantoms, for which not one life should be sacrificed. Better for the weak peoples to have their countries occupied peaceably than turned into a battlefield. Let them be defended not by force but by the pressure of world-opinion. As for culture, it was worth nothing if it depended on bayonets and guns. Nothing whatever mattered, so they affirmed, but the happiness of individuals. Yet all the while these hedonistic pacifists unwittingly drew the fervour which made them face tribunals, prison, and in some cases a firing party, not from their liberal individualism but from that deep and obscure intuition that the human race was no mere swarm of happy-unhappy individuals, but a vessel still unfilled, an instrument still roughly fashioned, and some day to be used for cosmical achievement. For this they went to prison, for this they resisted the taunts of their own herd-consciences. For this they died; and because they felt it in their hearts that the Western peoples must now at last dare to say, each to the other, 'Rather than make war, we will let you overrun our lands, sequester our goods, sleep with our wives, educate our children to your way of living. For we are all equal vessels of the one spirit, we and you.'

Such was the composition of Europe when the war began. There was the great host of those who regarded it almost solely from the personal point of view; the smaller company of martial romantics; the conflict-racked enemy-haters and pacifist-baiters; the swarms of unimaginative loyal folk, who accepted the war as the only way to preserve human happiness, but were sorely perplexed by the savagery that was expected of them; the minute band of those who intuited that war between modern civilized men was utter folly and sacrilege, than which there could be no worse alternative.

Of these last the more resolute and the more pugnacious refused absolutely to have any part in the great madness, and were therefore persecuted, imprisoned, or even shot. But others, like Paul, less heroic, less confident of their own opinion, or more sympathetic to the great public agony, could not bring themselves to stand aside inactive. They chose therefore to help the wounded, to expose themselves so far as was permitted, to accept so far as possible on the one hand the great common agony, and on the other the private loneliness of those who cannot share the deepest passions of their fellows.

To Neptunian observers these perplexed beings were the most significant matter for study, for in them the balance between the archaic and the modern was most delicate. The conflict which in most had been violently solved, in one way or the other, was in these ever present and insoluble.

3. EUROPE AT WAR

Viewed from the moon, and with eyes such as yours, your little Great War would have been invisible, save through a powerful telescope, which would have revealed it as a minute and intermittent smoky stain on the dimly green surface of Europe. To the Martians, those intelligent clouds who in the fullness of time were to invade your planet, it was unnoticeable. With optical organs much more powerful than any terrestrial telescope, their astronomers were already observing the Earth as a promised land seen from Pisgah. But what concerned them was your atmosphere, your plentiful water, your vegetation. They sometimes wondered whether the many smears and stipples of cloud which kept appearing and disappearing in your temperate zones were intelligent organisms like themselves. But they guessed that it was not so. They detected normal clouds of vapour, and, much more rarely, clouds of smoke and dust, which they rightly believed to be of volcanic origin. The minute traces produced by your war were assumed to be of the latter type. It did not occur to the Martians that these were artificial smoke-palls, beneath which the proud denizens of Earth were blundering through a great, though a fantastic agony.

Even to the average Terrestrial, your little Great War was a minor and a remote disturbance. A few miles behind the lines one might often find complete rural peace, marred only by distant muttering. Across the English Channel men sometimes heard with awe the sound of the guns; but the widespread sense that the tragedy in France had somehow changed the spirit of peaceful landscapes in Surrey, Cumberland, or the distant Hebrides, was but a projection of war-haunted minds. The psychological reverberations of the war did indeed spread far afield. Few corners of Europe escaped such serious influences as the removal of their young men, the rationing of their food, the over-work of their remaining inhabitants. Throughout the continent there was a sense, illusory but profound, that war had somehow altered the very constitution of the universe; or that it had laid bare the sinister depths of existence, which hitherto had been concealed by the scum, the multi-coloured film, of Nineteenth-century civilization. But elsewhere, over whole continents the military operations were known only as a distant marvel, romantic, magical, scarcely real. Folk tilled and hunted, copulated and bore children, propitiated the gods of rain and storm, trapped marauding beasts and sometimes listened incredulously to travellers' tales of the White Man's War. In more remote parts of the earth, on the upper reaches of the Amazon, in African jungles, and on the Thibetan plateau, there were isolated folk who never heard rumour of your war until after it had ceased.

But to most Europeans it did indeed seem that when the war began the whole ground-tone of existence was altered. For a few months many clung to the conviction that this profound change of key was for the good, a transition from the sordid, though safe, to the heroic, though tortured. The Germans pressed forward toward Paris, that mythical city of delight. The French and the British 'gallantly contested every inch', and at last 'miraculously' they held their own. Stories of heroism and horror percolated through Europe, stories of the incredible effects of high-explosive shells, of great buildings collapsing like card-houses, of men's bodies blown to pieces or mown down in hundreds by machine-guns. All this was at first accepted as quite in order, quite as it should be, in the new bewildering heroic universe that had come into being. Amiable bank-clerks and shop-keepers began to spend their leisure in learning to be 'frightful' in the sacred cause, learn-ing to give the right sort of lunge with a bayonet, to stick it success-fully into a belly; learning the right twist to release it. Paul in those early days had bought a little red manual of military training, in which he diligently studied the theory of co-operative slaughter. Here at last, he had told himself, was the grim and heroic reality, the thing that had always lain behind this solid-seeming but, in fact, phantasmal 'civilization'. Yet somehow the little book failed to give him any sense of reality at all. It seemed entirely beside the mark. This killing was after all a laborious, useless, imbecile accomplishment, like learning to play the piano with your toes. Yes, it was a new world that had come into being, and one took some time to get the feel of it. Many people seemed to Paul to unearth a new self to cope with it, a simpler, less doubting, more emotional self, a self that concealed under righteous indignation a terrible glee in the breakdown of old taboos. Even while they inveighed against the enemy's rumoured brutality, these beings of the new world seemed to savour it on the mental palate lingeringly, lustfully. They were trapped hopelessly, these vengeful ones, trapped by the spirit of the archaic animal from which the true spirit of man could not free itself. Talking to such persons, Paul glimpsed images of the half-born foal, which, through my influence, had so long haunted him.

Gradually the romantic early phase of your war was succeeded by something very different. It almost seemed that man, in origin arboreal and subsequently terrestrial, was to end his career as the greatest and most noxious of burrowing vermin. The armies dug themselves in. They constructed immensely elongated and complex warrens, and settled down to a subterranean life of tedium punctuated by horrors formerly unimagined. It became evident to the combatants, and gradually to the home populations also, that the war was not going to be what it ought to have been. It was not a gentlemanly war. It was ruthless in a way that made the wars of the history books seem temperate. It was a life-and-death struggle in which rules were all abandoned. And it was mechanized. The spirit of it was indeed a strange blend of the machine, with its regularity and large-scale effectiveness, and the brute at bay. It was an affair of stop-watches, mathematical calculations, weight and frequency of projectiles, mechanical transport, railway co-ordination; but also it was an affair of mud, dust, blood, knives, even teeth. Everything that happened in it had two sides, a mechanical and a brutal, at the one end the exquisite designing, making, emplacing and sighting of the great gun, at the other, the shattering of human bodies, the agony of human minds. At one end the hum of munition factories, at the other the corpse-laden mud of No-man's-land, and the scream of tortured men out on the wire, imploring, inaccessible. Machinery, that creature of human imagination, had seemingly turned upon its creator, and was not only tearing up his body, but reducing his mind to the brute level from which it had emerged. For strange and disturbing things were now happening in civilized Europe. There were still, of course, plentiful stories of heroism; human nature was said to be showing itself capable of unexpected devotion and fortitude. But also there were whispers of something less reputable. The bravest and most trusted, it seemed, might be suddenly converted into panic-stricken cattle, trampling one another under foot. The most level-headed might suddenly run mad. The most generous might suddenly indulge in brutality or meanness. There were stories also of tragic muddle and betrayal of duty, stories of British shells falling in British trenches, of troops sent up to certain destruction through a staff-officer's blunder, of supplies misdirected, of whole forlorn offensives launched for no reason but to satisfy the pride of some general or politician.

There is no need for me to enlarge upon these matters. They have been well enough recorded by your own scribes, and are, on the other hand, of little interest to the Neptunian observers of your great folly. Though more than ordinarily disastrous, they were but typical of the blend of organization and chaos, which is the out-standing character of your whole world-order. The Neptunian, studying that order, is inevitably reminded of the fortuitous, unplanned organization, and the blindly apt, but precarious behaviour of an ant colony. But though your massed stupidity afforded us little interest, we found in the lives of individual soldiers, and in their diverse adjustments to the war, much to arrest our attention.

For the majority, adjustment consisted in acquiring the tech-nique of a new life, in learning to make good use of cover, to contrive some slight animal comfort for oneself even in the trenches, to make the best of minute pleasures, savouring them, drop by drop, to live upon the hope of strawberry jam, or a parcel from home, or a letter in a well-known hand, or a visit to some woman behind the lines; or, failing these ecstasies, to make the best of plum jam, of a rum-ration, or of sex without woman; to 'wangle' small privileges out of the great military machine, to be expert in 'système D'; and at the same time to take deep into one's heart the soldier's morality of faithful obedience to superiors, faithful loyalty to comrades, and complete irresponsibility in respect of all things further afield; to live within the moment and within the visible horizon; to shut the eyes of the spirit against disgust, and stop the ears of the spirit against horror, against self-pity, against doubt.

It is true that to many spiritually undeveloped beings the war-life was a tonic. Many of those who had been nurtured in pros-perity, or at least in ease, who had never faced distress, and never been tortured by compassion, were now roughly awakened. Generously they gave themselves, and in the giving they found themselves. But others of their kind were broken by the ordeal. The awakening came too late, or to natures incapable of generosity.

But it was not in these, either the made or the marred, that our observers were interested. We were concerned rather to watch the adjustments of those in whom there was at work a force alien to the simple soldier ideal. Many such have I myself inhabited. At the outset they have gone forth with a sense that the heavens applauded them, that there was a God whom they were serving, and who would recompense them for their huge sacrifice with the inestimable prize of his approval. But, soon or late, their faith has been destroyed by the ugly facts of war.

Let me tell of one case, unique, yet typical of thousands on both sides of the line. From the Terrestrial point of view, the events which I am about to relate were contemporary with the story of Paul, already partially recounted; and they culminated in 1917, when the war was far advanced, and Paul had already been more than two years in France. But from the Neptunian point of view my exploration of these events took place some time before I had made the acquaintance of Paul. The specimen case that I shall now report is one of my most interesting treasures. Also, it nearly cost me my life.

He was a young German, a native of Neustadt in the Black Forest, and he had been trained for the care of trees. His hands were skilled in tending the baby pines in their crowded nurseries, and in planting them out in the greater world of the forest. When he wielded the axe or the saw, the deed was done with precision, and also with a deep sense of fate. The resinous odour of the forest and of fresh-cut wood, the ever-present vision of towering shafts and swaying branches, the occasional glimpse of a deer, – these things he valued lightly while he was yet with them; but when he was removed from them he longed for them.

Now this young man, whom I will call Hans, had been selected for study because, though he became a good soldier, he was more than a good soldier. During his career as a forester I had found in him a very unusual feeling for individual trees, and for the massed ranks of the forest. He could not help regarding them as each one a unique spirit, living according to the laws of its own being, and striving toward perfection of life. In his capacity of woodman, tender in nurturing, relentless in the final execution, he persuaded himself that, though to the trees themselves the goal seemed to be merely endless enlargement in girth and stature, he, in his lethal ministration, afforded them in spite of themselves a nobler destiny, a fuller achievement. Sometimes when he regarded a score or so of the great felled trunks, laid flank to flank, with the resin still oozing from their clean-sawn wounds, he would say to the standing forest, 'Do not pity them, for they have gloriously attained their destiny.' Then with reverence, almost it seemed with envy of this beatitude, he would lay his hand on the rough and tawny skin of some prone giant, in a last salute. For the great communal being of the forest, reclining so grandly on its many hills, he had a feeling compounded of benevolence and awe. It was for him a spirit, one of God's nobler creatures. When it began to be depleted for the war he was distressed. But even the forest, he admitted, must be sacrificed for that even nobler forest, the Fatherland.

He was a good son of the Fatherland, and also a good Catholic. They told him that the English and the French were servants of Satan, who wanted to harm the Fatherland. He went to the war filled with a sense of glorious adventure in a great cause. He was very proud of his new life. He cared for his rifle as he cared for his axe, and became as deadly a shot as he was precise a sawyer. When he killed his first man, with a bullet through the forehead, he had that sense of fate, and of calm almost loving execution, which he had known in felling the beloved trees in their ripeness. His next man he overcame in savage hand-to-hand struggle in the dark. For the Fatherland and in defence of his own life he did it; but there was no joy in it. Little by little he earned a reputation for coolness and resolution. He volunteered for a number of dangerous tasks and carried them out with distinction. When steel helmets were issued, he was proud to wear one. Its noble curves suggested the mythical heroes of his race. Its weight on his head crowned him.

At first Hans thought of the war in terms of his forest-born philosophy. He and his comrades were trees, who sought one destiny but were to find another, less easeful but more fulfilling to the spirit. But little by little it began to appear to him that this war, nay this world, was no well-tended forest but a terrible primeval jungle in which everything was crippled by everything else, and all things were useless. He strove to put away this thought by drugging

163

himself with war propaganda, or with duties, or with pleasures. But it would not leave him. So greatly did it disturb him that everything began to seem changed and sinister to him. Common objects looked at him meaningfully, tauntingly. Empty tins and trampled cigarette-ends would leer at him like little devils, deriding him for being trapped. His own hands in their ordinary actions seemed somehow to reproach him for putting them to serve the Devil. He had an overwhelming sense of betrayal. But whether it was that he himself was betrayed, or that he had betrayed something else, was never quite clear. Emblems of his religion, encountered in shattered churches or shrines, sometimes reproached him with his irrevocable treason; sometimes on the other hand they confessed themselves mere jests perpetrated by the universal diabolic power which had masqueraded as the God of Love. He began to think about the men he had killed, and to see them again, especially at night, especially a French corporal whose face he had smashed with a hand grenade. His rifle now took on a snake-like coldness in his hands, so that he shuddered. His helmet pressed on his forehead vindictively. Over all things there was a kind of darkness, which was the worse because he knew it was not 'real'. In his ears there began to be a distant wailing as of wind, which when the great guns roared and crashed, was yet heard screaming above them.

In fact, Hans was on the way to breakdown. Now Neptunian observers found amongst you two kinds of breakdown, very different in origin. Both types are of great interest to us, because the more effectively integrated minds of our own species afford the psychologist no such opportunity of study, even under the most severe strain. One type of Terrestrial disorder, the commoner, was due to the conflict between primitive biological impulses of self-preservation and the behaviour imposed by military obligation. The other, which was more interesting to us, sprang from the conflict between military obligation and the still unrecognized impulse of loyalty to the striving Terrestrial spirit. This was the conflict which was most seriously undermining Hans, though the other also was of course adding to his distress. He himself lacked the self-knowledge to understand his trouble. He thought it was simply a trouble of the more primitive kind, and was bitterly ashamed. He determined not to give way, but to pull himself together. Both loyalty and self-pride demanded it.

In the case of Hans and a small minority of his fellow-men this ruinous mental conflict was complicated by another and even less understood division of the mind, namely by the fundamental and insoluble problem of your species, the discord between loyalty to the adventuring spirit of Man and on the other hand the ecstatic admiration of fate even when tragic. Although deep in his heart Hans was coming to realize that to fight for the Fatherland or any nation was treason to Man, and that this war was diabolic, he had also a vivid though unintelligible apprehension of the whole great hideous tumult as somehow an expression of super-human, in-human, beauty. His mind was therefore torn by a three-cornered conflict, between old tribal loyalty, the new loyalty to Man, and the zest of tragic existence.

It was with dreadful satisfaction that Hans found himself involved once more in the centre of a great offensive. I, his indwelling companion, knew that within the next few days he would meet his death; but I did not know precisely when it would occur. I had therefore to prepare myself to leave him by partially reverting my attention to my own world. But at the same time it was necessary to observe him closely, for the moments of his life which would be of supreme interest to me were now at hand. I had also to keep a wary eye upon his circumstances, lest I should be entangled with him in his death.

All this happened at a time when I had been rather too constantly engaged on work in your world, and was so soaked in your mentality that I could not at all easily disengage myself from it. Moreover I found myself extremely reluctant to do so. Not only was I desirous to follow Hans through to his last moment, and if possible to afford his tortured spirit something of the Neptunian serenity, but also I was by now trapped by an overwhelming affection for your tragic world. It was therefore both with difficulty and with a strangely violent regret that I set myself to recapture in imagination the wider horizons and the crystalline titanic edifices of Neptune, the great limbs and eloquent features of my own race. My regret alarmed me; for it was a sure sign that I had stayed in your world much longer than was wholesome. Like one lost in the snow, who has an overwhelming desire to lie down and sleep, but knows that if he does he will never rise again, and never complete his work, so I now realized that a great effort was necessary. I began to goad myself by thinking of all the precious fruits of my exploration, which, if I were to succumb, would never be delivered to my own world.

Meanwhile the hour of the offensive was approaching. From the felt tone of Hans's body, it was evident that he was going sick; but he would not admit it to himself. He developed a distressing colic and diarrhoea, but he clung to his post. He was seized also by a strong premonition of death, an infection from my own awareness that this was indeed his last battle. While he and his comrades were awaiting the order to attack, Hans experienced a sudden increase of mental lucidity. In desperate haste he reviewed his whole life, his whole experience of existence. He was terrified at the contrast, not the physical but the spiritual contrast, between his forest years and the present. Then, there was a bland rightness about everything. Now, everything, even generous and gallant action, was somehow evil, tainted by an all-pervading shame. He said to himself, 'We have simply walked all together into Hell.'

It was almost the moment of attack. I knew that he would survive the storming of the enemy first-line trench; for I had previously learned from a Neptunian colleague, who had already observed this action through the eyes of another individual, that Hans was to be seen alive in the trench. Therefore I felt secure enough to watch my man minutely for a while, and to prepare his mind to meet death with peace, instead of the rage and despair that had hitherto possessed him. While he was still waiting inactive, Hans was very near to breaking-point. It seemed possible that he would not obey the order to advance. But when the word came, he clambered up with the rest; and as he pounded across the tract of shell-torn earth and tangled wire, he suddenly blazed up with maniac hate of the universe and all its denizens. In those moments it mattered not at all to him whether his bayonet should pierce a blue or a grey uniform. Nothing mattered, but that he should void the hate that was in him. I felt a bullet tear one of his ears. He did not notice it. A near shell killed the man on his

166

right, and half-buried Hans himself. He picked himself up and stumbled on.

It now became clear that I was far more dangerously entangled in your world than I had thought; for at this moment, as I watched the desperate plight of this blind half-human spirit, I found myself suddenly undermined by doubt of my own Neptunian vision. Here was a mind blessed neither with the insensitivity of the beast nor with the all-redeeming vision of my own species, a mind deranged by the horror and guilt of three years of war, and now overwhelmingly nauseated by its own being and by the satanic universe which had spawned it only to devour it, a mind which looked forward to nothing but horror and annihilation for itself, and futility for its world. It suddenly appeared to me that a universe in which such torture could occur must be utterly vile, and that the Neptunian complacency was heartless. This apostasy I noted with dismay; but by now I was in no mood to withdraw myself into spiritual safety. More important it seemed to stay with Hans, and afford him at all costs at least an illusory consolation.

While he was covering the last few paces to the enemy trench, I was somewhat anxiously engaged in two very different undertakings. The first was to thrust upon the mind of Hans an image of the forest, which might serve as the starting-point for a spiritual change. The second, which I undertook at first with reluctance, was to prepare myself for a sudden exit from your world. I successfully established in him the vision of lofty trunks and sombre foliage. As he plunged into the trench with his bayonet in the neck of an enemy, this image took possession of the deeper region of his mind. I then began to think more conscientiously of my own safety, and to steady myself in earnest for the leap to Neptune. I pictured my own far future body, lying asleep in my subterranean garden. I dwelt upon the translucent features of the woman called Panther. I reminded myself of the Mad Star and of the supreme disaster which we, the Last Men, await undismayed. Contemplating this the last scene of the tragedy of Man, I began once more to see your little war in its true proportions. Presently the cramped and unwholesome feel of the young German's body began to fade from me. The racket of battle, the tumbled and bleeding human forms, began to seem as a dream when one is all but wakened, a dream of being entangled in the insensate feuds of wild animals.

But now something happened which recalled my attention wholly to your sphere. A savage tussle was taking place in the trench, and the invaders were becoming masters of the situation. Hans, however, was playing no part in the fight. He was standing aside watching it, as though it were a dog-fight. In his mind was a vast confusion, caused by a sudden enlightenment. Not only had the forest-image started a change in him, but also he had been infected by my own reversion to the Neptunian mentality, so that in those moments he too experienced a kind of awakening. Suddenly he flung away his rifle and rushed with a huge laugh into the melée. Seizing one of his countrymen by the collar and the seat of the trousers, he tugged him away, crying, 'No more brawling.' An officer, seeing that Hans was out of his mind and causing trouble, shot him through the head.

Fortunately I had caught sight of the muzzle of the weapon out of the corner of Hans's eye. Desperately, with a wild leap of the mind, I disengaged myself from your world.

I awoke to find myself in bed in my garden. I could not remember what had happened, but I had a violent pain in my head, and several of my colleagues were standing round me. They had heard me scream, they said, and had come running to my assistance. A few minutes later, apparently, I lost consciousness again and fell into convulsions. I remember nothing further till six weeks later, when I awoke to find myself in the tree-girt hospital where shattered explorers are nursed back to health.

4. PAUL IN THE WAR

While I was studying Hans, I was of course also, in the very same span of Terrestrial duration, resident in Paul. Yet from the Neptunian point of view, let me repeat, my operations upon Hans took place before I had even discovered Paul. Consequently while I was in Hans I knew nothing about Paul and my work upon him, but while I was in Paul I remembered my experiences in Hans. This fact, as I shall tell in due season, had in one respect a curious effect on Paul.

Meanwhile I must revert to Paul's career at the point where I first introduced him into this survey. It will be remembered that he was suffering an agony of indecision about the war, that he hurried to a recruiting office, and then fled away from it. We left him slinking through the streets of London.

During the next few days Paul was frequently troubled by his waking nightmare, the mare that was dead, with her strangled foal. Sometimes it seemed to him that he himself was the foal, unable to free himself from the restriction of an outgrown mentality. Sometimes the whole human race was the foal. Sometimes on the other hand, the foal was just his unborn martial self, throttled by his most unmartial past.

A few days later Paul heard of a curious semi-religious ambulance organization, which, while professing pacifism, undertook voluntary succour of the wounded at the front. It was controlled and largely manned by a certain old-established and much-respected religious sect which adhered strictly to the commandment 'Thou shalt not kill', and to its own unique tradition of good works and quietism. Some members of this sect preached a rigorous pacifism which very soon brought them into conflict with authority; but others, who tempered pacifism with a craving to take some part in the great public ordeal, created this anomalous organization, whose spirit was an amazing blend of the religious, the military, the pacific, the purely adventurous, and the cynical. This 'Ambulance Unit' lasted throughout the war. It was formed in the first instance as an outlet for the adventurousness of the younger sectarians, who very naturally chafed at their exclusion from the tremendous adventure and agony of their contemporaries. Throughout its career it contained many such, normal young men eager for ardours and endeavours, who, though they had no very serious pacifist convictions, remained loyal to the tradition of their fathers, and refused to bear arms. Others there were, both within and without the sectarian fold, who, though they profoundly felt that to make war in modern Europe under any circumstances whatever was treason against something more sacred than nationalism, had yet not the heart to wash their hands of the world's distresses.

Such were the pioneers of this strange organization; but as time

169

passed it gathered to itself a very diverse swarm of persons who were driven from their civil occupations either by public opinion or their own consciences, or finally by legal compulsion. A few, very few, were narrow-hearted beings whose chief motive was simply to avoid what they regarded as the spiritual defilement of a soldier's work. There was also a sprinkling of artists and intellectuals whose main concern was neither religion nor pacifism, but the adventures of the mind in novel circumstances. Among those who were admitted into the Unit after conscription had been introduced into England, some were serious pacifists who had been loyal to their civilian duties as long as possible; and a few, whose pacifism was only skin deep, chose the Unit as the line of least resistance, simply because they had no stomach either for the trenches or for prison.

To the military authorities this fantastic organization was a minute and negligible excrescence on the military machine. The dignitaries of the armies, if ever they came across it at all, regarded it at first as something to be kept at arm's length until it had been brought under proper military control. It was a God-sent butt for ridicule. On the other hand it proved to have its uses; and often it earned a kind of incredulous respect, even affection.

To Neptunian observers this uncomfortable medley of cranks and commonplace individuals appeared, surprising as it may seem, as one of the most interesting phenomena of your whole war. It was not the mere pacifism of these beings that concerned us, for at home and later in the prisons there were pacifists more logical and more heroic. What interested us was the heart-searching bewilderment of minds which could not find harmony either with the great mass of their warring fellows or with the more relentless pacifists. We are interested too in the reactions which these unclassified beings aroused in any ordinary persons who happened to come across them. For they were neither fish, flesh, fowl, nor good red herring. They claimed to be pacifists, but obviously they were 'helping to win the war' by releasing others for more arduous military duties. Surely, then, they were either fools or shirkers. Surely, said the martial-minded, they ought all to be in the trenches, or put in prison, or, better still, shot. But others, the majority, gave them a contemptuous toleration.

To Paul it seemed that by joining this body he would be both taking part in the war and registering his protest against it. In fact, as he ruefully admitted, he would both have his cake and eat it. But what else could he do? He was convinced at last that some mysterious thing inside him would always prevent him from enlisting. But if he could not fight, neither must he shirk. That he was moved at all by the will to avoid the extremity of danger and agony he did not admit; for he pictured himself as a stretcher-bearer rescuing the wounded under fire, or as a motor-ambulance driver trundling his car where the fight was hottest. So little did he yet know of 'modern' warfare.

Paul joined the Unit. With surprise and with shame-faced delight, he learned that he must dress as a British officer, though with certain distinguishing signs. On his left arm he must wear a red-cross brassard, stamped with a kind of postage mark. His hat also bore a red cross on a huge white square. Neptunian observers have been much indebted to this uniform. Nothing could have better symbolized the mental discord of Paul and his like. Nothing could have been more nicely calculated to intensify that discord. One side of Paul clung to the delusion that since he was to be dressed as an officer he must be after all, in spirit, a member of that gallant fraternity. The other side of him recognized that this could not be. He became in fact an object of ridicule, sometimes of indignant scorn. Wherever he went, he felt people wondering what on earth he was, and how he dared to caricature his betters. Pacifists, on the other hand, raised their eyebrows at his military colouring. One day while he was still painfully conscious of his uniform, he met Katherine in the street. Her husband was already in the trenches. She gazed at Paul for a moment in amazement, suppressed a smile, was smitten by Paul's distress, and became blunderingly tactful.

In France Paul was less conscious of his uniform. There were others of his kind, and anyhow no one seemed to mind. Moreover he had work to do. Having had some slight acquaintance with a motor-bicycle, he was set to help in the repair of broken-down cars at the headquarters of the Unit. A few weeks later he became an orderly on a motor ambulance. He made innumerable journeys between the advanced stations and the hospitals, working entirely for the French army. For the first time he dealt with the wounded, with sitting-cases mostly cheerful at their release, and stretcher-cases in all phases of distress and weakness. Paul was at first deeply disturbed by compassion for these much-bandaged blue-clad figures, many of whom moaned and lamented at every jerk of the car. He was also bitterly ashamed before them, because he was whole and full of life. Yet there was another part of him which reacted in a less orthodox manner, and one which Paul himself at first regarded as disreputable, even Satanic. It was almost like the glee of the scientist watching a successful experiment, or of the artist apprehending some high, intricate, inevitable form. Paul tried hard not to feel in this way, or not to know that he felt so. But he could not help it; and he was abashed at his own brutality. It was I who caused this feeling in him, I, working upon his own rudimentary impulses. He need not have been ashamed.

In these days the main concern of Paul's life, apart from the overwhelming wounded themselves, was to get to the end of each journey without a mishap, and to escape night work. There was also an increasing sense that, after all, this was not good enough, not the sort of thing he wanted for his conscience' sake. Occasion-ally he saw a shell burst in the sand-dunes, or knock off the corner of a house. But as for stretcher-bearing in the front line, there was not to be anything of the sort. None of the armies were going to let irresponsible volunteers do work which demanded strict military discipline. One day, however, a gay young member of the party was killed by a shell. Paul found himself torn between regret for the dead boy and selfish satisfaction that, after all, this work was not entirely sheltered.

The weeks and months passed, weeks made up of sultry day-driving and pitch-black night-driving, of blood-stained blankets, packs, overcoats, of occasional alarms, of letters written and received, of bathes in the sea, not far from the steel entanglements which crossed the beach at the end of the line. Then there were talks, talks with those who shared the dilemma of Paul himself, and talks with the utterly different beings who accepted the war with a shrug; laborious, joking conversations with innumerable *poilus*, and still more laborious smutty jests, sometimes with Algerians and Moroccans.

Some months after the beginning of his war career, Paul, who had learnt to drive, was put in charge of a motor ambulance on a new convoy, which was to go far away south to a part of the line beyond the British front. His companions, some forty in all, constituted a fair sample of the Unit. There were sons of rich and religious manufacturers, and there were very small traders. There were printer's apprentices, social workers, mechanics, students, clerks, teachers, shop assistants, artists. There were devout sectarians, less devout sectarians, and those who in revulsion from piety were at pains to shock the devout with cynicism and ribaldry. There were careless young Irishmen seeking adventure without military discipline. There were kindly and earnest products of sectarian schools, and others who had emerged from the same schools with a no less earnest, no less kindly, frivolity. There were grizzled men who secretly cared nothing for pacifism, but sought the quickest way of seeing the spectacle of war. Here I may mention, too, the colourless but useful creature whom I have chosen as my mouthpiece for communicating with you. He has served me well in the past for the recounting of events in which he played no part; but now that it is necessary to dwell for a moment on microscopic occurrences of which he himself was a witness, I find him less manageable. It is not always possible to prevent him from dwelling unduly on the insignificant hardships and dangers in which he participated. Such were the companions of Paul, the unique being whom I had so carefully prepared for this experience.

With a sense that at last the test was coming, the Convoy lumbered south. It left behind it all traces of the British Army, which it so envied, respected, and obscurely feared. Presently it found itself established in a town beside an old royal hunting forest. And there for months it stayed, finding much hard work, but none of the ardours which it sought. In time even the work decreased, to a steady routine. In the earliest and more disorderly phase of the war the pioneers of this 'Ambulance Unit' had found ample opportunity to show that pacifism was not incompatible with courage and endurance; and even now, other Convoys of the Unit, it was said, were being of real use, and suffering real danger and hardship. But this Convoy, it seemed, was fated to idleness. There grew up a general restlessness, a tendency to quarrel over nothing, a disposition to walk violently along the geometrically ruled 'allées' of that prim forest. Paul conceived a sentimental passion for the forest. He withdrew as far as possible from his companions, and tried to think of himself as some kind of a fawn trapped into a human way of life. He found a deep satisfaction in sleeping on a stretcher under the stars and branches. I contrived that the forest should increasingly take possession of him, for I wished to perform a minor experiment on him. Reconstructing in my own mind the personality of Hans, who was at this time sniping Frenchmen further down the line, I brought Paul also under the young forester's influence. Paul began to feel toward this neat French forest almost as Hans toward his grander German one. He spent all his spare time in it, laying bare his spirit, so he thought, to the presence of the trees. He began to write verses again, in his own groping technique. Here is one of them.

TIMBER

Stroke of the Axe! The trunk shivers and gapes.
Stroke on stroke! The chips fly.
'Oh year upon year upon year I grew,
since I woke in the seed.'
Stroke of the axe!
Raw, wounded wood, and the heart laid bare.
'Oh sun, and wind, and rain!
Oh leafing, and the fall of leaves!
Oh flower, love, and love's fruit!'
Fierce bite of the axe!
Staggering, crying timber.
Down!
The twigs and the little branches are shattered
on the ground.
The woodman stands,
measuring.

After some months of futility, the Convoy became so restless that its leaders persuaded the army authorities to give it a change. Henceforth it was to be attached permanently to one of the divisions of the French army. Once more the dark-green vehicles, plastered with red and white emblems of mercy, lumbered through

France in search of a dreaded and a longed-for goal. The Convoy joined its Division in 'Lousy Champagne', whose barren hills were now snowclad. This was during the Great Cold. The bread crystallized, the ration wine froze. The radiators of the cars, boiling at the top, froze at the bottom. At night Paul, shivering in his sleeping-bag under a pile of blankets in his canvas-sided car, thought of the trenches and was abashed.

The weeks rolled by. In quiet times Paul and his friends played rugger with the Division, or walked over the down-like hills which were already beginning to stipple themselves with flowers. It grew warm, hot. They bathed in the stream, their white bodies rejoicing in freedom from stiff military clothes. On one of these occasions Paul, dozing naked in the sun before his dip, dreamed about my seaside holiday with the woman, Panther. This dream had an interesting effect on him. He woke with a sense of the shadowy unreality of all Terrestrial events beyond the immediate reach of his senses; but the bright meadow, the willow-shaded stream, the delicious aliveness of his own sun-kindled body, had gained from his dream a more intense reality, an added spiritual significance. He thought of Katherine, whose breasts at least he had known. His flesh stirred. In sudden exasperation at his own futility and the world's perversity, he dived.

Sometimes the young Englishmen went into the little town behind the lines to take wine or coffee, omelettes or *gauffres*; or to talk to the daughter of the *patron*. By the cynics it was maliciously suggested that this grey-eyed Athene had relations other than conventional with certain members of the Convoy. But to the devout this horror was incredible. Paul at least confessed to himself that he would have gladly lain with her, for he was hungry for woman, and she found her way into his dreams. But, however she treated others, to Paul she remained sweetly unapproachable. His failure with her intensified his discontent with the whole life of the Convoy. He wanted to prove himself a man, to have a share in the world's burden, even if the world was a fool to bear it. To the Neptunian it was very interesting to observe in the Convoy this growing obsession with the need to vindicate pacifism by physical courage. At this time some who had hot blood and little care for pacifism went home to join the fighting forces. Others went home

175

not to enlist but to go to prison for their pacifism. New hands came from headquarters to replenish the Convoy. Now that conscription was in force there was no lack of personnel.

Paul himself, whenever he went home on leave, had thoughts of joining the army. But he knew that these thoughts sprang only from his loneliness in a land intent on war, not from conviction of duty. On leave he was always cowed. He felt himself an outcast. He felt the women flaunting their soldiers at him. And the soldiers, though they let him alone, put him to shame. People at home judged him according to their own natures, as an impossible idealist, a fool, or a common shirker. All arguments closed with the same formula, 'But we *must* fight, to keep the Germans out.' When Paul dared to say 'Would it really matter so *very* much if they came?' he was silenced by stories of atrocities which in his heart he could not believe.

Once when he was on leave he met the Archangel, who was now an army chaplain, and had been wounded. They dined together at a railway restaurant among officers and women. Paul, homeward bound, was shabby. His tunic had a torn pocket, mended clumsily by his own hands. Those hands, which he had scrubbed till they seemed unusually clean, now turned out after all to be ingrained with engine oil; and his nails were ragged. He felt as though, for his ungentlemanly conduct in refusing to fight, he had been degraded from his own social class. This sense of loss of caste was intensified by the fact that he was wearing a closed collar; for since conscription had come in, the Unit had been made to give up the secretly cherished open collar of the officer's tunic. The Archangel was friendly, sympathetic even. Yet in his very sympathy, so at least it seemed to Paul, condemnation was implied. Over coffee Paul suddenly asked, not without malice, 'What would Jesus have done?' While the priest was looking at the tablecloth for an answer, Paul, to his own horror, said in a clear loud voice, 'Jesus would have shot the politicians and the war lords and started a European revolution.' There was a silence in the restaurant. The pained Archangel murmured, 'Strange talk from a pacifist, isn't it?' Then at last quite suddenly Paul's pacifism defined itself in his mind, assumed a precise and limiting outline. To the Archangel he said, not too loud, but with conviction, 'To fight for one's nation against other nations in a world insane with nationalism, is an offence against the spirit, like fighting for a religious sect in a world insane with sectarianism. But to fight for revolution and a new world-order *might* become necessary.' Paul was surprised at himself for making this statement. How it would grieve his pacifist friends! Was it true, he wondered. One conviction at least became clear in his mind. Whatever was needed to bring about a right world-order was itself right. But national wars could never do this, and were utterly wrong. Perhaps the only thing that could bring about a right world-order was not violence but a very great change in the hearts of ordinary people. But could that change ever occur? Somehow, it must.

Such were the thoughts that occupied Paul during the pause that followed the Archangel's protest.

It was always with mingled despair and relief that Paul went back from leave. On leave he was haunted by the foal-image. When he was in the war area he felt there was some life in the creature yet; it was struggling though doomed. But at home it seemed already dead, mere horsemeat, never to be the friend of Man.

Life on the familiar sector was in the main too humdrum to be very repugnant. Sometimes for a day or two there would be activity. The roads would be seriously shelled, and the loaded cars would have to run the gauntlet. It was unpleasant, even nerve-racking, but it was soon over. And always one knew that this was but child's play, not the real thing. During one of these minor disturbances, while Paul was returning to the front with an empty car, and shells were dropping close around him, he saw a figure lying at the roadside, its head badly smashed. Obviously the man was dead, so Paul drove on. But the next car stopped to pick him up, and he was still alive. For months Paul was haunted by that incident, going over it again and again in an agony of shame. It became to him the nadir of his existence. It increased his ludicrous obsession over physical courage.

The Division liked its 'Section Sanitaire Anglaise'. It had come to regard these strayed English no longer with suspicion, but with affection tempered by incredulity. It excused their pacifism as one might excuse a Mohammedan for not eating pork. No doubt in both cases there was some equally remote and fantastic historical explanation. To Frenchmen it was apparently inconceivable that anyone should take pacifism seriously unless it happened to be an element of his religious orthodoxy. For Frenchmen themselves, so the Convoy had long ago discovered, the only serious religion was France, the only orthodoxy uncompromising loyalty to France. If any one suggested that some policy beneficial to France might not be acceptable to other peoples, these amiable, lucid, but strangely unimaginative Latin children would no doubt charmingly express regret, but would also point out that if the policy was necessary for France, they must support it. The extermination of wild animals by the march of civilization is to be regretted, but no sane man would suggest that civilization should be restricted in order to save them. As to pacifism, anyhow, it was no more practicable in Europe than in the jungle. Thus talked the considerate and very gallant officers of the Division, so respect-worthy in sky-blue and gold. Thus talked the amiable *poilus*, so devoted to their distant families and the land they should be tilling. And, indeed, all that the troops said about pacifism was true. They and their like *made* it impossible. Once more, the foal.

One Frenchman indeed did show some understanding of these English cranks. He was one of the two priests attached to the Division. His colleague, a red-bearded lover of wine, wore military uniform, and was a hearty friend of the troops; but M. l'Abbé himself wore his black cassock, tramped the whole sector with his finger in a little volume of St. Thomas, and was revered. He would talk long with the English over meals in dug-outs, for he was interested in their sect and their ideas. Of their pacifism he would repeat, 'Ah, mes chers messieurs, si tout le monde pouvait sentir comme vous!' One day he was caught by a shell, which broke his leg. Members of the Convoy visited him in hospital, where his clean body was making a quick recovery. Then, through some muddle over a change of staff, he was neglected, and died. In the commemorative address given by his colleague, the abbot's death was laid to the account of the God-hating enemy. To Paul it seemed to be due to more complex causes.

In most Frenchmen's eyes the pacifism of these English merely gave an added and farcical piquancy to a body that had already

178

earned respect for its efficiency. For these pacifists were extremely conscientious in their work, as is indeed to be expected where consciences suffer from chronic irritation. The Division also admired, and politely ridiculed, the extravagant cleanliness of the Convoy. In quiet times the paintwork of its cars was sleek with paraffin. Lamps, fittings, even crank-cases were kept bright with metal polish. Some of the members grumbled, but all acquiesced. Thus did the Convoy pay tribute to the great British Army, which in spite of antimilitarism it so faithfully admired.

Cleanliness did not interfere with efficiency. What the Convoy undertook to do, it invariably did. On the other hand, from the Division's point of view, the conscientiousness of these English sometimes went too far, as when they flatly refused to transport rifles and ammunition to the front in their red-cross cars. The General was indignant, and threatened to get rid of this pack of lunatics. But an artist member of the Convoy was at that time painting his portrait, so the matter was dropped.

By now this little speck of Englishmen in an ocean of Latins had acquired a strong group-spirit. Though internally it was generally at loggerheads with itself, all its jarring elements were in accord in maintaining the prestige of the Convoy. If any one indulged in some minor lapse, public opinion was emphatically against him. On the other hand, if the officers of the Convoy sought to introduce customs which to the rank and file seemed unnecessary or obnoxious, the cry of 'militarism' was raised; and the long-suffering officers, though they had behind them the whole power of the British and French armies, patiently argued the matter out with the rebels. Punishment was unknown in the Convoy.

This little group of two score persons was ever in a state of internal strain, either between the officers and the rest, or between one clique and another. Thus the earnestly devout would outrage the earnestly frivolous by organizing religious meetings. The frivolous would conscientiously get mildly drunk on ration wine. The earnestly philistine talked sex and sport, motors and war, to maintain their integrity against the earnestly intellectual, who talked art, politics, pacifism, and what they thought was philosophy. Yet all alike, or nearly all, received something from the strange corporate being of the Convoy. All were intensely conscious of their nationality, and of the need to impress these foreigners with British excellence. Yet all were outcasts from their nation, and deeply ashamed; even though also they consciously despised nationalism, and vehemently prophesied cosmopolitanism.

At last the test came. The Division moved to a part of the line beside the Montagne de Rheims. On the way the Convoy was caught up in a continuous stream of traffic making for the front, a stream of troops, guns, limbers, troops, motor-lorries, tanks, troops, ambulance sections. There was indescribable congestion, long waits, snail progress. Ahead a ceaseless roar of guns. On this journey I found in Paul a ludicrous blend of thankfulness and fright. His body was continuously in a state of suppressed tremor. Now and then he fetched a huge sigh, which he carefully turned into a yawn, lest his companion should guess that he was not looking forward to this offensive with the enthusiasm affected by all true members of the Convoy. Paul kept saying to himself, 'This is the real thing, this is reality.' But sometimes what he said was, 'Reality? It's just a bloody farce.'

The Convoy reached its destination and took over its duties. For a few days there was normal work, save that the roads were fairly steadily shelled. One shell Paul had reason to remember. He was in the courtyard that served the Convoy as a parking-ground. A score of blue figures tramped past the gateway singing, exchanging pleasantries with the English. They marched on, and disappeared behind the wall. Then there was a shattering explosion, followed by dead silence. The English rushed out into the road. There lay the twenty blue figures, one of them slowly moving the stump of an arm. Blood trickled down the camber of the road, licking up the dust. It flowed along the gutters. Paul and his mates got stretchers and carried away those who were not dead, shouting instructions to one another, for the shelling continued. During this operation Paul had one of those strange fits of heightened percipience which my influence sometimes brought upon him. Everything seemed to be stamped upon his senses with a novel and exquisite sharpness, the limpness of the unconscious bodies that he lifted, a blood-stained letter protruding from a torn pocket, a steel helmet lying in the road, with a fragment of some one's scalp in it, bloody and lousy. Paul's legs were trembling with fright and nausea, while the compassionate part of him insisted that these unhappy fellow mortals must be succoured. For some might live. That letter might yet after all be answered. It seemed to Paul now imperative that this *poilu* and his *maraine* should communicate once more. Yet at the same time that deep mysterious alien part of him, which he was gradually coming to accept and even value, laughed delicately, laughed as one may laugh with tenderness at the delicious gaucherie of a child.

It seemed to say to the other Paul, and to the stricken men also, 'You dear, stupid children, to hurt yourselves like this, and to be so upset about it! Babes will be babes; and monkeys, monkeys.'

When Paul was off duty he went up into the forest-clad mountains and looked down at the line of dense smoke which marked the front, overhung at regular intervals by the two rows of captive balloons, stretching indefinitely into the south-east. An enemy 'plane, harassed at first by white points of shrapnel, attacked a French balloon, which burst into flame. A scarcely visible parachute sank earthward from it. Paul went further into the forest. Here there was a kind of peace in spite of the roaring guns. Under my influence the spirit of Hans came on him again, so that he had a perplexing sense that, in the presence of his brothers the trees, he was brought mysteriously into touch also with his brothers the enemy.

The offensive began. Henceforth there was continuous work, with rare meals and no sleep. French and German wounded came flooding in. Hundreds who could find no place in the cars had to stagger all the way down to the chateau where the gaily-clad doctors grew more and more flustered. Slowly, uncertainly, these walking wounded swarmed along the road, their blue and their grey clothes sometimes indistinguishable for dust and blood. The roads now began to be impossible with shell-holes, and choked with wreckage. At one time Paul, hurrying along under shell-fire with a full load of sorrowing creatures shaken together in his reeling car, found himself behind a galloping artillery wagon. At the cross-roads, where some one, for reasons unknown, had propped a dead sergeant against the sign-post, a shell fell on the front of the wagon. The two men and one of the rear horses were killed. Its fellow floundered with broken legs, then died. The leaders stampeded. The road was now completely blocked. French and English dragged the dead horses and the limber to the ditch, tugging frantically at harness and splintered wood, while the wounded in the waiting cars, supposing themselves deserted under fire, cried out for help.

At night things were worse. Cars slipped into ditches, plunged into shell-holes. Paul, with a full load of stretcher-cases, almost drove off a broken bridge into the river. All the cars were damaged by shell-fire. Some were put out of action. One, going up empty to the front, suddenly found itself in a covey of bursting shells. The driver and orderly tumbled hurriedly into a ditch, and a shell burst on the driving-seat. The petrol went up in a huge column of flame and soon nothing remained of the car, but scrap iron and pools of aluminium on the road. Later, a line of tanks, going up, met a line of ambulances, coming down, where there was no room to pass. Confusion and altercations. A tank was hit; once more a column of flame, dwarfing the other, afforded a beacon for enemy guns.

Two or three days and nights of this kind of thing severely strained the Convoy. One or two members had already been wounded, and others had been badly shaken. Nerves developed here and there. Some one began to behave oddly, wandering about delivering meaningless messages. He was taken away. Paul himself was in a queer state; for his head was splitting, his mouth foul, his limbs curiously stiff and heavy. His stomach seemed to have collapsed. Worse, his driving was becoming erratic, and he sometimes said things he did not intend to say. He was continuously scared, and also scared of being found out by his calmer colleagues. His bogy, the foal, began to haunt him again. Somehow it was all mixed up with another vision, a blood-stained letter protruding from a torn pocket; and with yet another, a cow so flattened in the mud by the wheels of lorries and the feet of troops that nothing of it remained three-dimensional except its head in the gutter, and one broken horn. The thought that, after all, this ambulance life was mere child's play compared with what was afoot elsewhere, hurt him so badly that inwardly he whined. For if things grew much worse than this he would certainly crack; and yet 'this' was nothing. Superficially he had maintained thus far something like the appearance of calm. He even contrived an occasional stammering joke. But inwardly he was by now going faint with terror. And this welling terror was beginning to spoil his affected calm. People were beginning to look at him anxiously. Paul found himself reviewing his case in this manner once while he was crouching in a ditch waiting for a lull in the shelling, and for a load of wounded. Yes, inwardly he was by now not far from cracking.

Yet more inwardly still, so he remarked to himself, he was quite calm. That was the odd part of it all. His silly body, or animal nature, as he put it, might very well crack, or run away howling, and yet he, Paul, would have no part in it. He, Paul, the rider of this quivering animal, was unperturbed, interested, amused. The beast might run away with him or throw him. It was proving a rather worthless sort of beast, and he had his work cut out to force it to the jumps. He would damned well master it if he could; but if he could not, well, it was all in the game, the extremely interesting game of being a human thing, half god, half beast. He knew quite well it didn't seriously *matter* if he was killed, or even if he was horribly wounded. It didn't *really* matter even if he cracked, though he must hang on if he could. He had a strange conviction, there in the ditch, that whichever *did* happen would be just the right thing; that even if he cracked, it would somehow be part of the 'music of the spheres'. Even the foal unborn was part of the music. Even this war, this bloody awful farce, was part of the music. If you couldn't be anything but a vibrating, a tortured string in the orchestra, you didn't like it. But if you had ears to listen, it was – great. These wounded – if only they could somehow hear, even through their own pain, the music of the spheres! If he himself were to be caught by the next shell, would he still keep hold of the music? Not he! He would be a mere tortured animal. Well, what matter? The music would still be there, even if he could not hear it, even if no man heard it. That was nonsense. Yet profoundly he knew that it was true.

Presently, for no apparent reason, the sector quietened down. The offensive, it seemed, had been a failure. The advance, which was to have swept the Germans out of France, never began. The Division, moreover, was in a state of mutiny, sensing mismanagement, declaring that thousands of lives had been lightly thrown away. It was withdrawn. The Convoy travelled with it into a flowery region far behind the lines. Tin hats were discarded.

Then occurred a little incident very significant to the Neptunian observer. The Convoy, having borne itself well, was cited in the orders of the Corps d'Armée. It was therefore entitled to have the Croix de Guerre painted on its cars. The artists undertook this task. The bronze cross, with its red and green ribbon, was earned also by certain individual members of the Convoy. Should they accept it, should they wear the ribbon? To refuse would be insulting to the French army. But that pacifists should display military decorations was too ridiculous. There was some debate, but the thing was done. Thus did these pacifists, hypnotized for so long by the prestige and glamour of the military, bring themselves to devour the crumbs of glory that fell from the master's table.

There is no need to dwell upon the subsequent adventures of this war-scarred and war-decorated group of pacifists. The being whose brain I use in communicating with you would gladly tell of them in detail, for in his memory they have a false glamour and significance. But already I have allowed him too much rein. The life of his Convoy is indeed significant to the student of your species; but the events on which he seeks to dwell are minute with an even more microscopic minuteness than the Great War, which to the Neptunian observer, searching for your War through past ages, is so easily to be overlooked. The significance of the war itself, lies partly in its fatal results, partly in that it reveals so clearly the limits of a half-developed mind. The importance of the ulto-microscopic events that I have allowed my instrument to enlarge upon in this section, is that they show how, even in the less conventional minds of your race, the archaic impulses caused devastating perplexity.

When the Convoy had rested, it wandered from sector to sector, till at last it found itself once more near the vine-clad and forest-crowned Mountain of Rheims, and once more destined for a great offensive. Once more the din of the troops, guns, lorries. Once more torn-up roads, smashed cars, night-driving in blurred and suffocating gas-masks. Once more the in-flooding wounded, and now and again a member of the little group itself wounded or killed. This time the offensive went on and on. Car after car was put out of action. Half the personnel were laid low, some by gas, some seemingly by bad water.

One day, as Paul was turning his car round before loading, a shell caught his companion, who was directing him from the road. This was a lad with whom Paul had often worked, and often amicably wrangled about art and life, a boy full of promise, and of the will to make his mark. Now, he lay crumpled on the road. Paul and others rushed to him. The lower part of his body had been terribly smashed, but he was still conscious. His eyes turned to Paul, and his lips moved. Paul bent to listen, and seemed to hear a faint gasping reiteration of one phrase, 'Won't die yet.' With difficulty they got the boy on to a stretcher, his face twisted with added pain. As they carried him away, he stirred feebly, then suddenly went limp, his head rolling loosely with the motion of the bearers. An arm slipped off the stretcher, and dangled. They put him down again and bent over him. A French *broncardier*, who was helping, stood up with a shrug and a sigh. 'C'est déjà fini,' he said. Looking down at the smooth face, he added, 'Oui, mon pauvre, c'est fini. Mort pour la patrie! Ah, les sales Boches!'

Paul gazed at the tanned bloodless features, the curiously changed eyes, the sagging mouth. This was the moment for me to undertake an operation which I had long contemplated. Bringing all my strength to bear on Paul I lashed him into a degree of self-consciousness and other-consciousness which I had not hitherto produced in him. With this heightened sensitivity, he was overwhelmed by vivid apprehension of the life that had been cut short, the intricacy and delicate organization of the spirit which he had known so well, and had now seen extinguished, with all its young ambitions, fears, admirations, loves, all its little whims and lusts and laughters. The experience came on him in a flash, so that he let slip a quick sharp scream of surprise and compassion. He stared fascinated at a smear of blood on the cheek, seeing as it were right through the present death-mask into the boy's whole living past, retaining it in one imaginative grasp, as music may be retained in the mind's ear after it has been interrupted; may still be heard, gathering strength, proliferating, and suddenly broken across with the breaking of the instrument. Paul heard, indeed, what the boy himself did not hear, the terrible snap and silence of the end. This was but the first stage of my operation on Paul. I also contrived that, with his hypersensitive vision, he should seem to see, beyond this one dead boy, the countless hosts of the prematurely dead, not the dead of your war only, but of all the ages, the whole massed horror of young and vital spirits snuffed out before their time. Paul's mind reeled and collapsed; but not before he had glimpsed in all this horror a brilliant, and insupportable, an inhuman, beauty. The operation had been completed, and in due season I should observe the results. He fell, and was carried away in one of the ambulances.

In a few days, however, he recovered, and was able to take part in a new phase of the war, the advance of the Allies. It was a swarming advance along unspeakable roads, over pontoon bridges, through burning villages.

During this final advance Paul one day perceived in a field by the road the mare and unborn foal whose image had so long haunted him. The unexpected but all too familiar sight shocked him deeply. Volume by volume it corresponded with his image, but there was an added stench. How came it, he wondered, that for years he had 'remembered' this thing before ever he had seen it?

One symbolical aspect of his foal was still hidden from him. When at last the armistice came, so longed for, so incredible, Paul did not yet know that the peace ensuing on the world's four years' travail was to be the peace, not of accomplished birth but of strangulation.

The following curious poem, which Paul devised shortly before the end of the war, expresses his sense of the futility and pettiness of all human activity.

> If God has not noticed us?
> He is so occupied
> with the crowded cycle of nature.
>
> The sea's breath,
> by drenching the hills
> and descending along the meadow brooklets
> (whose backwaters
> are playgrounds of busy insect populations),

returns seaward
to rise again.
Water-beetles
skating on the stagnant skin of a backwater.
we get rumour of Oceanus,
of storm-driven worlds and island universes.
And we would annex them!
We would dignify the fiery currents of the Cosmos
by spawning in them!
But the minnow, death, he snaps us;
and presently some inconsiderable spate
will scour the cranny clean of us.

Long after man, the stars
will continually evaporate in radiant energy
to recondense as nebulae,
and again stars;
till here and there some new planet
will harbour again
insect populations.

VII *After The War*

1. THE NEW HOPE

YOUR little Great War reached its ignominious end. During the four years of misery and waste, the short-lived combatants felt that the war area, fringed with the remote and insubstantial lands of peace, was the whole of space, and that time itself was but the endless Duration of the War. But to Neptunian observers, ranging over the considerable span occupied by human history, the events of those four years appeared but as an instantaneous flicker of pain in the still embryonic life of Man. The full-grown Spirit of Man, the Race Mind of the Eighteenth Human Species may be said to use the great company of individual Neptunian observers as a kind of psychical and supra-temporal microscope for the study of its own prenatal career. Peering down that strange instrument, it searches upon the slide for the little point of life which is to become in due season Man himself. The thing is discovered. It is seen to reach that stage of its history when for the first time it begins to master its little Terrestrial environment. Then is to be detected by the quick eye of mature Man the faint and instantaneous flicker, your Great War. Henceforth the minute creature slowly retracts its adventuring pseudopodia, enters into itself, shrinks, and lapses into a state of suspended animation, until at last, after some ten million years, it is ripe for its second phase of adventure, wholly forgetful of its first. It becomes, in fact, the Second Human Species.

When your Great War ended, it seemed to the soldiers of all the nations that a new and happier age had dawned. The veterans prepared to take up once more the threads that war had cut; the young prepared for the beginning of real life. All alike looked forward to security, to freedom from military discipline, to the amusements of civilized society, to woman. Those who had been long under restraint found it almost incredible that they would soon be able to go wherever they pleased without seeking permission, that they

188

would be able to lie in bed in the morning, that they might wear civilian clothes, that they would never again be under the eye of a sergeant, or a captain, or some more exalted officer, and never again take part in an offensive.

For the majority these anticipations were enough. If they could but secure a livelihood, capture some charming and adoring woman, keep a family in comfort, enjoy life, or return to some engrossing work, they would be happy. And a grateful country would surely see to it that they were at least thus rewarded for their years of heroism.

But there were many who demanded of the peace something more than personal contentment. They demanded, and indeed confidently looked for, the beginnings of a better world. The universe, which during the war years, had been progressively revealed as more and more diabolical, was now transfused with a new hope, a new or a refurbished divinity. The armies of the Allies had been fighting for justice and for democracy; or so at least they had been told. They had won. Justice and democracy would henceforth flourish everywhere. On the other hand the armies of the Central Powers had believed that they had been fighting for the Fatherland or for Culture. They had been beaten; but after a gallant fight, and because their starved and exhausted peoples could no longer support them. To those hard-pressed peoples the end of war came not indeed as a bright dawn, as to the Allies, but none the less as the end of unspeakable things, and with the promise of a new day. Henceforth there would at least be food. The pinched and ailing children of Central Europe, whom the Allies had so successfully, so heroically stricken by their blockade, might now perhaps be nursed into precarious health. The beaten nations, trusting to the high-sounding protestations of the victors, not only surrendered, but appealed for help in the desperate task of re-establishing society. President Wilson prophesied a new world, a Brotherhood of Nations, and pronounced his Fourteen Points. Henceforth there would be no more wars, because this last and most bitter war had expunged militarism from the hearts of all the peoples; and had made all men feel, as never before, the difference between the things that were essential and the things that were trivial in the life of mankind. What mattered (men now vehemently

189

asserted) was the fellowship of man, Christian charity, the co-operation of all men in the making of a happier world. The war had occurred because the fundamental kindliness of the peoples towards one another had been poisoned by the diplomats. Henceforth the peoples would come into direct contact with one another. The old diplomacy must go.

These sentiments were tactfully applauded by the diplomats of all nations, and were embalmed, suitably trimmed and tempered, in a new charter of human brotherhood, the Peace Treaty of Versailles.

To Neptunian observers, estimating the deepest and most obscure mental reactions of thousands of demobilized soldiers and of the civilian populations that welcomed them, it was clear that the First Human Species had not yet begun to realize the extent of the disaster which it had brought upon itself. All the belligerent peoples were, of course, war-weary. It was natural that after the four years of strain they should experience a serious lassitude, that after responding so magnificently (as was said) to the call for sacrifice, they should be more than usually prone to take the easy course. But our observers, comparing minutely the minds of 1914 with the same minds of 1918, noted a widespread, subtle, and in the main unconscious change. Not a few minds, indeed, had been completely shattered by the experience of those four years, succumbing either to the conflict between personal fear and tribal loyalty or to that rarer conflict between tribal loyalty and the groping loyalty to Man. But also, even in the great mass of men, who had escaped this obvious ruin, there had occurred a general coarsening and softening of the mental fibre, such that they were henceforth poor stuff for the making of a new world.

The slight but gravely significant lassitude which we now observed in all the Western peoples had its roots not merely in fatigue, but in self-distrust and disillusionment. At first obscured by the new hope which peace had gendered, this profound moral disheartenment was destined to increase, not dwindle, as the years advanced. In those early months of peace scarcely any man was aware of it, but to our observers it was evident as a faint odour of corruption in almost every mind. It was the universal though unacknowledged sense of war-guilt, the sense that the high moral and patriotic fervours of 1914 had somehow obscured a deeper and more serious issue. Western Man had blundered into a grave act of treason against the spirit that had but recently and precariously been conceived in him. Few could see that it was so; and yet in almost every mind we found an all-pervading shame, unwitting but most hurtful. Knowing not that they did so, all men blamed themselves and their fellow-men for a treason which they did not know they had committed, against a spirit that was almost completely beyond their ken. Neptunian observers did not blame them. For these unhappy primitives had but acted according to their lights. They could not know that another and a purer light had been eclipsed in them before they could recognize it.

In many thousands of minds we have watched this subtle guilt at work. Sometimes it expressed itself as a touchy conscientiousness in familiar moral issues, combined with a laxity in matters less stereotyped. Sometimes it became a tendency to blame others unduly, or to mortify the self. More often it gave rise to a lazy cynicism, a comfortable contempt of human nature, and disgust with all existence. Its issue was a widespread, slight loosening of responsibility, both toward society and toward particular individuals. Western men were to be henceforth on the whole less trustworthy, less firm with themselves, less workmanlike, less rigorous in abstract thought, less fastidious in all spheres, more avid of pleasure, more prone to heartlessness, to brutality, to murder. And, when, later, it began to be realized that this deterioration had taken place, the realization itself, by suggestion, increased the deterioration.

But the effects of the war were by no means wholly bad. In the great majority of minds observed by Neptunians after the war, there was detected a very interesting conflict between the forces of decay and the forces of rebirth. The hope of a new world was not entirely ungrounded. The war had stripped men of many hampering illusions; and, for those that had eyes to see, it had underlined in blood the things that really mattered. For the most clear-sighted it was henceforth evident that only two things mattered, the daily happiness of individual human beings and the advancement of the human spirit in its gallant cosmical adventure. To the great majority of those who took serious interest in public affairs the happiness of men and women throughout the world became henceforth the one goal of social action. Only a few admitted that the supreme care of all the peoples should be the adventure of the Terrestrial spirit. Because so few recognized this cosmical aspect of human endeavour, even the obvious goal of world-happiness became unrealizable. For if happiness alone is the goal, one man's happiness is as good as another's, and no one will feel obligation to make the supreme sacrifice. But if the true goal is of another order, those who recognize it may gladly die for it.

In the Western World, during the decades that followed the war we encountered far and wide among the hearts of men the beginnings of a true rebirth, an emphatic rejection of the outworn ideals of conduct and of world policy, and a desperate quest for something better, something to fire men's imaginations and command their allegiance even to the death; something above suspicion, above ridicule, above criticism. Far and wide, among many peoples, the new ideal began to stir for birth, but men's spirits had been subtly poisoned by the war. What should have become a world-wide religious experience beside which all earlier revivals would have seemed mere tentative and ineffectual gropings, became only a revolutionary social policy, became in fact the wholly admirable but unfinished ideal of a happy world. The muscles which should have thrust the new creature into the light were flaccid. The birth was checked. The young thing, half-born, struggled for a while, then died, assuming the fixed grin of Paul's nightmare foal.

In Russia alone, and only for a few decades, did there seem to be the possibility of complete rebirth. In that great people of mixed Western and Eastern temperament the poison of war had not worked so disastrously. The great mass of Russians had not regarded the war as *their* war, but as the war of their archaic government. And as the suffering bred of war increased beyond the limit of endurance, they rose and overthrew their government. The revolutionists who heroically accomplished this change were troubled by no war-shame, for the blood which they shed was truly split in the birth throes of a new world. They were indeed fighting for the spirit, though they would have laughed indignantly had they been told so. For to them 'spirit' was but an invention of the oppressors, and 'matter' alone was real. They fought, so they believed, for the free physiological functioning of human animals. They fought, that is, for the fulfilling of whatever capacities those animals might discover in themselves. And in fighting thus they fought unwittingly for the human spirit in its cosmical adventure. When their fight was won, and they had come into power, they began to discipline their people to lead a world-wide crusade. Each man, they said, must regard himself as but an instrument of something greater than himself, must live for that something, and if necessary die for it. This devotion that they preached and practised was indeed the very breath of the spirit within them. Little by little a new hope, a new pride, a new energy, spread among the Russian people. Little by little they fashioned for themselves a new community, such as had never before occurred on the planet. And because they allowed no one to hold power through riches, they became the horror of the Western World.

To the thousands of our observers stationed in Russian minds it was evident even at the outset that this promise of new birth would never be fulfilled. The ardour of revolution and the devotion of community-building could not suffice alone for ever. There must come a time when the revolution was won, the main structure of the new community completed, when the goal of a happy world, though not in fact attained, would no longer fire men, no longer suffice as the 'something' for which they would gladly live or die; when the spirit so obscurely conceived in men would need more nourishment than social loyalty. Then the only hope of the world would be that Russian men and women should look more closely into their hearts, and discover there the cosmical and spiritual significance of human life, which their creed denied. But this could not be. In few of them did we find a capacity for insight strong enough to apprehend what man is, and what the world, and the exquisite relation of them. And being without that vision, they would have nothing to strengthen them against the infection of the decaying Western civilization. Feared and hated by their neighbours, they themselves would succumb to nationalistic fear and hate. Craving material power for their defence, they would betray themselves for power, security, prosperity.

In short, the new hope which the European War had occasioned, especially in Russia, was destined, sooner or later, to be destroyed by the virus which war itself had generated in the guilty Western peoples. While that new hope, still quick and bright, was travelling hither and thither over Asia like a smouldering fire, this dank effluence also was spreading, damping the fibre of men's hearts with disillusionment about human nature and the universe. And so, that which should have become a world-wide spiritual conflagration was doomed never to achieve more than revolutionary propaganda, and smoke.

2. PAUL GATHERS UP THE THREADS

It is my task to show your world in its 'post-war' phase as it seemed to one of your own kind who had been infected with something of the Neptunian mood. First, however, I must recall how Paul faced his own private 'post-war' problems, and emerged at last as a perfected instrument for my purpose.

Crossing the Channel for the last time in uniform, Paul looked behind and forward with mixed feelings. Behind lay the dead, with their thousands upon thousands of wooden crosses; and also (for Paul's imagination) the wounded, grey, blue and khaki, bloody, with splintered bones. Behind, but indelible, lay all that horror, that waste, that idiocy; yet also behind lay, as he was forced to admit to himself, an exquisite, an inhuman, an indefensible, an intolerable beauty. Forward lay life, and a new hope. Yet looking toward the future he felt misgivings both for himself and for the world. For himself he feared, because he had no part in the common emotion of his fellow-countrymen, in the thankfulness that the war had been nobly won. For the world he feared, because of a growing sense that man's circumstances were rapidly passing beyond man's control. They demanded more intelligence and more integrity than he possessed.

Thus Paul on his homeward journey could not conjure in himself the pure thankfulness of his fellows. Yet, looking behind and forward, with the wind chanting in his ears and the salt spray on his lips, he savoured zestfully the bitter and taunting taste of existence. Comparing his present self with the self of his first war-time crossing, he smiled at the poor half-conscious thing that he had been, and said, 'At least, I have come awake.' Then he thought again of those thousands under the crosses, who would not wake ever. He remembered the boy whom he had known so well, and had watched dying; who should have wakened so splendidly. And then once more he savoured that mysterious, indefensible beauty which he had seen emerge in all this horror.

I chose this moment of comparatively deep self-consciousness and world-consciousness to force upon Paul with a new clarity the problem with which I intended henceforth to haunt him. This task was made easier by the circumstances of the voyage. The sea was boisterous. Paul greatly enjoyed a boisterous sea and the plunging of a ship, but his pleasure was complicated by a feeling of sea-sickness. He fought against his nausea and against its depressing influence. He wanted to go on enjoying the wind and the spray and the motion and the white-veined sea, but he could not. Presently, however, he very heartily vomited; and then once more he could enjoy things, and even think about the world. His thinking was coloured both by his nausea and by his zest in the salt air. Resolutely blowing his nose, meditatively wiping his mouth, he continued to lean on the rail and watch the desecrated but all-unsullied waves. He formulated his problem to himself, 'How can things be so wrong, so meaningless, so filthy; and yet also so right, so overwhelmingly significant, so exquisite?' How wrong things were, and how exquisite, neither Paul nor any man had yet fully discovered. But the problem was formulated. I promised myself that I should watch with minute attention the efforts of this specially treated member of your kind to come to terms with the universe.

Paul returned to his native suburb, and was welcomed into the bosom of the home. It was good to be at home. For a while he was content to enjoy the prospect of an endless leave, lazing in flannel trousers and an old tweed coat. At home, where he was not expected to explain himself, he was at peace; but elsewhere, even when he was dressed as others, he felt an alien. He attributed his sense of isolation to his pacifism, not knowing how far opinion had moved since the beginning of the war. This loneliness of his was in fact due much more to my clarifying influence in him, to his having been as it were impregnated with seminal ideas gendered in another species and another world. He found his mind working differently from other minds, yet he could not detect where the difference lay. This distressed him. He hated to be different. He longed to become an indistinguishable member of the herd, of his own social class. He began to take great pains to dress correctly, and to use the slang of the moment. He tried to play bridge, but could never keep awake. He tried to play golf, but his muscles seemed to play tricks on him at the critical moment. The truth was that he did not really want to do these things at all. He wanted to do 'the done thing'.

There was another trouble. He had not been at home more than a fortnight before he realized with distress that his relations with his parents were not what they had been. In the old days he used to say, 'I have been lucky in my choice of parents. Of course they don't really know me very well, but they understand as much as is necessary. They are both endlessly kind, sympathetic, helpful, and they have the sense to leave me alone.' Now, he began to see that in the old days they really had understood him far more than he supposed, but that the thing that he had since become was incomprehensible to them. Even at the beginning of the war they had lost touch with him over his pacifism, accepting it thankfully as a means of saving him from the trenches, but never taking it seriously. Now, they were more out of touch than ever. It seemed to him that they were living in a kind of mental Flat Land, without acquaintance with the third dimension. They were so sensible, so kind, so anxious to be tolerant. He could see eye to eye with them in so many things, in all those respects in which Flat Land was in accord with Solid Land. But every now and then intercourse would break down. They would argue with him patiently for a while in vain; then fall silent, regarding him with an expression in which he seemed to see, blended together, love, pity and horror. He would then shrug his shoulders, and wonder whether in earlier times the gulf between the generations had ever been so wide. They, for their part, sadly told one another that his war experience (or was it his pacifism?) had so twisted his mind that he was 'not quite, not absolutely, sane'.

After a few weeks Paul went back to his old post in the big suburban secondary school. He was surprised that they took him, in spite of his pacifism and his incompetence. Later he discovered that his father knew the Chairman of the Council. Ought he to resign? Probably, but he would not. He was by now well established as one of the less brilliant but not impossible members of the staff; and though the work never came easily to him, it was no longer the torture that it had formerly been. He was older, and less easily flustered. And he must have money. After all, he found, he rather liked boys, so long as he could keep on the right side of them. If you got wrong with them, they were hell; but if you kept right, they were much more tolerable than most adults. The work was respectable useful work. Indeed, it was in a way the most important of all work, if it was done properly. Moreover, it was the only work he could do. And he must have money; not much, but enough to make him independent.

His aim at this time was to live an easy and uneventful life. He told himself that he did want to pull his weight, but he was not prepared to overstrain himself. He must have time to enjoy himself. He proposed to enjoy himself in two ways, and both together. He wanted to win his spurs in the endless tournament of sex; for his virginity filled him with self-doubt, and disturbed his judgements about life. At the same time he promised himself a good deal of what he called 'intellectual sight-seeing' or 'spiritual touring'. Comfortably, if not with a first-class ticket, at least with a second-class one, he would explore all the well-exploited travel-routes of all the continents of the mind. Sometimes he might even venture into the untracked wild, but not dangerously. Never again, if he could help it, would he lose touch with civilization, with the comfortable mental structure of his fellows, as he had done through pacifism. Thus did this war-weary young Terrestrial propose. Much of his plan suited my purpose admirably, but by no means the whole of it.

So Paul settled down to teach history, geography, English and 'scripture'. He taught whatever he was told to teach, and for mere pity's sake, he made the stuff as palatable as he could. On the whole the boys liked him. He seemed to regard the business much as they did themselves, as a tiresome necessary grind, which must

197

be done efficiently but might be alleviated by jokes and stories. Even discipline, formerly such a trouble to Paul, now seemed to work automatically. This was partly because he did not worry about it, having outgrown the notion that he must preserve his 'dignity', and partly because in the critical first days of his new school career I influenced his mood and his bearing so that he gave an impression of friendliness combined with careless firmness. Paul himself was surprised and thankful that the self-discipline of his classes relieved him of a dreadful burden. He used to say to visitors, in front of the class, 'You see, we have not a dictator, but a chairman.' All the same, he secretly took credit for his achievement.

By thus helping Paul to establish himself in a tolerable routine, I enabled him to keep his mind free and sensitive for other matters. The boys themselves knew that there was another side to him. Occasionally in class the lesson would go astray completely, and he would talk astoundingly about things interesting to himself, things outside the curriculum, and sometimes of very doubtful orthodoxy. He would dwell upon the age and number of the stars, the localization of functions in the brain, the abstractness of science and mathematics, the kinds of insanity, the truth about Soviet Russia, the theatre and the cinema, the cellular structure of the body, the supposed electronic structure of the atom, death and old age, cosmopolitanism, sun-bathing, the crawl stroke, Samuel Butler, coitus and the birth of babies. To these floods of language the boys reacted according to their diverse natures. The stupid slipped thankfully into torpor, the industrious revised their home-work. The shrewd masticated whatever in the harangue seemed to have a practical value, and spat out the rest. The intellectually curious listened aloofly. The main mass fluctuated between amusement, enthusiastic support, and boredom. A few sensitive ones took Paul as their prophet. After these outbursts Paul became unusually reticent and cautious. Sometimes he even told the boys they 'had better forget it all' because he was 'a bit mad then'. He was obviously anxious that rumour of his wildness should not go beyond the class-room door. The sense of secrecy appealed to the boys. Whatever their diverse opinions of the stuff, all could enjoy a conspiracy. Paul's own class began to regard itself as something between a band of disciples (or even prophets), a secret revolutionary society, and a pirate crew.

3. PAUL COMES TO TERMS WITH WOMAN

For some months Paul was so busy becoming an efficient school-master that he had little time for those 'other matters' which I required him to undertake. But when he had established his technique and could look around him, he began to ask himself, 'What next?' His intention was to see life safely, to observe all its varieties and nuances, to read it in comfort as one might enjoy a novel of passion and agony without being upset by it. What was the field to be covered? There was woman. Until he had explored that field he could never give his attention to others. There was art, literature, music. There was science. There was the intricate spectacle of the universe, including the little peep-show, man. There were certain philosophical questions which had formed themselves in his mind without producing their answers. There was religion. Was there anything in it at all? But here, as also in the sphere of woman, one must be careful. One might so easily find oneself too deeply entangled. For the post-war Paul, entanglement, becoming part of the drama instead of a spectator, was to be avoided at all costs. But could he avoid it? Could he preserve in all circumstances this new snug aloofness, which had come to him with the end of war's long torment of pity and shame and indignation? He knew very well that there were strange forces in him which might wreck his plans. He must be very careful, but the risk must be taken. His sheer curiosity, and his cold passion for savouring the drama of the world, must be satisfied.

Paul now began to lead a double life. In school-hours he tried to be the correct schoolmaster, and save for his lapses he succeeded. Out of school he inspected the universe. With cold judgement he decided that the first aspect of the universe to be inspected was woman. But how? There was Katherine. She alone, he felt, could be for him the perfect mate. But she was obviously happy with her returned soldier and her two children. He met her now and again. She was gentle with him, and distressingly anxious that he should like her husband. Strangely enough, he did like the man, as a man. He was intellectually unexciting, but he had an interested and open mind, and could readily be enticed out of Flat Land. Paul, however, disliked the sense that Katherine wanted to hold the two of them in one embrace. No, he must look elsewhere for woman, for the woman that was to show him the deep cosmical significance of womanhood.

The girls of his suburb were no good. In his thwarted, virginal state, they often stirred him, but he could not get anywhere with them. He lacked the right touch. Sometimes he would take one of them on the river or to a dance, or to the pictures, but nothing came of it. They found him queer, a little ridiculous, sometimes alarming. When he should have been audacious, he was diffident. His voice went husky and his hand trembled. When he should have been gentle, he was rough. With one of them, indeed, he got so far as to realize that to go further would be disastrous; for though she was a 'dear' she was dull. Moreover, she would expect to be married. And for marriage he had neither means nor inclination.

Of course there were prostitutes. They would sell him something that he wanted. But he wanted much more than they could sell. He wanted, along with full physical union, that depth of intimacy which he had known with Katherine. Once in Paris while he was coming home on leave, a girl in the street had said to him 'Venez faire l'amour avec moi', and he had stopped. But there was something about her, some trace of a repugnance long since outworn, that made his cherished maleness contemptible in his own eyes. He hurried away, telling himself she was too unattractive. Henceforth all prostitutes reminded him of her. They made him dislike himself.

What other hope was there for him? He once found himself alone with a little dusky creature in a railway carriage. She reminded him of a marmoset. Might he smoke, he asked. Certainly. Would she smoke too? Well, yes, since there was no one else there. They talked about the cinema. They arranged to meet again. He took her to a dance, and to picture shows, and for walks. She told him she was unhappy at home. Things advanced to such an extent that one day he put a protecting arm round her, with his hand under her breast; and he kissed her. She began to trust him, rely on him. Suddenly he felt an utter cad, and determined to give her up. But when he said he would never see her again, she wept like a child and clung to him. He told her what a beast he was, and how he had intended merely to get what he wanted from her, and take no responsibility. As for marrying her, he was not the marrying sort. She said she didn't care. She didn't want marriage, she wanted him, just now and again. Yet somehow he couldn't do it. Was it fear of the consequences? No, not fear, shame. She was only a child, after all, and he found himself feeling responsible for her. Damn it, why couldn't he go through with it? It wouldn't hurt her really. It would all be experience. But he couldn't do it. Yet he had not the heart to keep away from her. Hell! Then why not marry her and go through with it that way? No, that would be certain hell for both of them. The affair began to get on his nerves. His teaching was affected; for in class he was haunted by images of the little marmoset, of her great wide black eyes, or of the feel of her hair on his cheek. Obviously he must put an end to it all. He wrote her a strange muddled letter, saying he loved her too much to go on, or too little; that in fact he did not really love her at all, and she must make the best of it; that he was desperately in love with her and would be miserable for ever without her; that the upshot anyhow was that he could never see her again. He kept to his resolve. In spite of a number of beseeching letters, he never saw her or wrote to her again.

Paul thanked his stars he had escaped from that trap. But his problem remained completely unsolved. How was he to come to terms with this huge factor in the universe, woman? For in his present state he could not but regard sex as something fundamental to the universe. He was desperate. He could not keep his mind off woman. Every train of thought brought him to the same dead end, woman, and how he was to cope with her. He spent hours wandering in the streets of the metropolis, watching all the slender figures, the silken ankles, the faces. Even in his present thwarted and obsessed mood, in which every well-formed girl seemed to him desirable, his interest was in part disinterested, impersonal. Behind his personal problem lay the universal problem. What was the cosmical significance of this perennial effloresence of femininity, this host of 'other' beings, ranging from the commonplace to the exquisite? Many of them were just female animals, some so brutish as to stir him little more than a bitch baboon; some though merely animal, were animals of his kind, and they roused in him a frankly animal but none the less divine desire. So at least he told himself. Many, on the other hand, he felt were more than animal, and the worse for it. They were the marred and vulgar products of a vulgar civilization. But many also, so it seemed to him, were divinely human and more than human. They eloquently manifested the woman-spirit, the female mode of the cosmic spirit. They had but to move a hand or turn the head or lean ever so slightly, ever so tenderly toward a lover, and Paul was smitten with a hushed, a religious, wonder. What was the meaning of it all? The man-spirit in himself, he said, demanded communion with one of these divine manifestations. The thing must be done. It was a sacred trust that he must fulfil. But how?

He made the acquaintance of a young actress whom he had often admired from the auditorium. He took her out a good deal. He spent more money on her than he could afford. But this relationship, like the other, came to nothing. It developed into a kind of brother-sister affection, though spiced with a sexual piquancy. Whenever he tried to bring in a more sensual element, she was distressed, and he was torn between resentment and self-reproach.

There were others. But nothing came of any of them, except a ceaseless expenditure on dance tickets, theatre tickets, chocolates, suppers, gifts. There was also a more ruinous and no less barren, expense of spirit, and a perennial sense of frustration. The girls that he really cared for he was afraid of hurting. Of course, he might marry one of them, if he could find one willing. But he felt sure he would be a bad husband, that he would be sick to death of the relationship within a month. And anyhow he could not afford a wife. On the other hand, the girls toward whom he felt no responsibility, he feared for his own sake, lest they should entangle him. Meanwhile he was becoming more and more entangled in his own obsession. The intellectual touring which he had proposed for himself, and was even now, in a desultory manner, undertaking, was becoming a labour instead of a delight, because he could not free his mind from woman. In bed at night he would writhe and mutter self-pityingly, 'God, give me a woman!'

202

At last he decided to go with a prostitute. On the way with her he was like a starved dog ready to eat anything. But when he was alone with her, it suddenly came over him with a flood of shame and self-ridicule, that here was a girl, at bottom a 'good sort' too, who did not want him at all, and yet had to put up with him. It must be like having to make your living by hiring out your tooth-brush to strangers. How she must despise him! His hunger vanished. She tried to rouse him, using well-practised arts. But it was no good. He saw himself through her eyes. He felt his own body as she would feel it, clinging, repugnant. Stammering that he was ill, he put down his money, and fled.

From the point of view of my work with Paul the situation was very unsatisfactory. It was time to free his mind for the wider life that I required of him. I decided that the most thorough cure could be obtained only by means of Katherine, who was by now a superb young wife and mother. I therefore entered her once more, and found that by a careful use of my most delicate arts I might per-suade her to serve my purpose. Five years of exceptionally happy marriage had deepened her spirit and enlarged her outlook. The colt had grown into a noble mare, the anxious young suburban miss into a mature and zestful woman, whose mind was surpris-ingly untrammelled. I found her still comfortably in love with the husband that I had given her, and the constant friend of her children. But also I found, on deeper inspection, a core of peaceful aloofness, of detachment from all the joys and anxieties of her busy life; of detachment, as yet unwitting, even from the moral con-ventions which hitherto she had had no cause to question. I found, too, a lively interest in her renewed acquaintance with Paul. She saw clearly that he was in distress, that he was 'sexually dead-ended'. Such was the phrase she used to describe Paul's condition to her husband. She felt responsible for his trouble. Also, before I began to work on her, she had already recognized in herself a tender echo of her old love for Paul. But without my help she would never have taken the course toward which I now began to lead her. For long she brooded over Paul and his trouble and her own new restlessness. Little by little I made her see that Paul would be for ever thwarted unless she let herself be taken. I also forced her to admit to herself that she wanted him to take her. At first she saw the situation conventionally, and was terrified lest Paul should ruin all her happiness. For a while she shunned him. But Paul himself was being drawn irresistibly under her spell; and when at last she forbade him to come near her, he was so downcast and so acquiescent, that she shed tears for him. He duly kept away, and she increasingly wanted him.

But presently, looking into her own heart with my help, she realized a great and comforting truth about herself, and another truth about Paul. She did not want him for ever, but only for sometimes. For ever, she wanted her husband, with whom she had already woven an intricate and lovely pattern of life, not yet completed, scarcely more than begun. But with Paul also she had begun to weave a pattern long ago; and now she would complete it, not as was first intended, but in another and less intricate style. It would re-vitalize her, enrich her, give her a new bloom and fragrance for her husband's taking. And Paul, she knew, would find new life. With all the art at her command she would be woman for him, and crown his manhood, and set him free from his crippling obsession, free to do all the fine things which in old days he had talked of doing. For this was the truth that she had realized about Paul, that he also had another life to lead, independent of her, that for him, too, their union must be not an end but a refreshment.

But what about her husband? If only he could be made to feel that there was no danger of his losing her, or of his ceasing to be spiritually her husband, he ought surely to see the sanity of her madness. The thought of talking to him about it all made her recognize how mad she really was, how wicked, too. But somehow the recognition did not dismay her, for I kept her plied with clear thoughts and frank desires, which somehow robbed the conventions of their sanctity.

Katherine I had dealt with successfully. But there remained the more difficult task of persuading her husband, Richard. I had at the outset chosen him carefully; but now, when I took up my position in his mind, I was more interested in my experiment than hopeful of its success. It would have been easy to infatuate him with some woman, and so render him indifferent to his wife's conduct. But if tolerance had to rest merely on indifference, this marriage, in which I took some pride, would have been spoiled. I had decided, moreover, that Richard's predicament would afford me the opportunity of a crucial piece of research upon your species. I was curious to know whether it would be possible so to influence him that he should regard the whole matter with Neptunian sanity.

I took some pains to prepare him, leading his mind to ruminate in unfamiliar fields. I did nothing to dim in any way his desire for his wife; on the contrary, I produced in him a very detailed and exquisite apprehension of her. And when at last she found courage to tell him of her plan, I used all my skill to give him full imaginative insight into her love for Paul and her different love for himself. It was very interesting to watch his reaction. For a few minutes he sat gazing at his wife in silence. Then he said that of course she must do what seemed best to her, but he asked her to give him time to think. For a whole day he acted to himself the part of the devoted and discarded husband, biting through a pipe-stem in the course of his tortured meditations. He conceived a dozen plans for preventing the disaster, and dismissed them all. Already on the second day, however, he saw the situation more calmly, even with something like Neptunian detachment; and on the third he recognized with my help that it did not concern him at all in any serious manner how Katherine should spend her holiday, provided that she should come back to him gladly, and with enhanced vitality.

Paul and Katherine took a tent and went off together for three weeks. They pitched beside a little bay on the rocky and seal-haunted coast of Pembroke. In this choice they had been unwittingly influenced by me. Thoughts of my recent (and remotely future) holiday on a Neptunian coast infected them with a desire for rocks and the sea. In this holiday of theirs I myself found real refreshment. Through the primitive mind of Paul I rejoiced in the primitive body and primitive spirit of Katherine.

She was already well practised in the art of love, at least in the unsubtle Terrestrial mode. Paul was a novice. But now he surprised himself, and Katherine also, by the fire, the assurance, the gentleness, the sweet banter of his wooing. Well might he, for I who am not inexperienced even according to Neptunian standards, prompted him at every turn of his dalliance. Not only was I determined, for my work's sake, to afford these two children full enrichment of one another, but also I myself, by now so well adapted to the Terrestrial sphere, was deeply stirred by this 'almost woman', this doe of a half-human species. Her real beauty, interwoven with the reptilian clumsiness of an immature type, smote me with a savage delight of the flesh, and yet also with a vast remoteness which issued in grave tenderness and reverence.

They lay long in the mornings, with the sun pouring in at the open end of the tent. They swam together in the bay, pretending to be seals. They cooked and washed up, and shopped in the neighbouring village. They scrambled over the rocks and the heather. And they made love. In the night, and also naked on the sunlit beach, they drank one another in through eye and ear and tactile flesh. Of many things they spoke together, sitting in the evening in the opening of the tent. One night there was a storm. The tent was blown down, and their bedding was wet. They dressed under the floundering canvas, and having made things secure, for the rest of the night they walked in the rain, reeling with sleep. Next day they repaired the tent, spread out their blankets in the sun, and on the sunny grass they lay down to sleep. Paul murmured, 'We could have been man and wife so well.' But Katherine roused herself to say, 'No, no! Richard has me for keeps, and you for sometimes. I should hate you for a husband, you'd be too tiring, and probably no good with children. Paul, if I have a baby, it will count as Richard's.'

For three weeks Paul basked in intimacy with the bland Katherine. This, then, was woman, this intricacy of lovely volumes and movements, of lovely resistances and yieldings, of play, laughter and quietness. She was just animal made perfect, and as such she was unfathomable spirit at once utterly dependable and utterly incalculable, mysterious. Paul knew, even in his present huge content, that there was much more of woman than was revealed to him, more which could only be known through long intimacy, in fact in the stress and long-suffering and intricate concrescence of marriage. This, Richard had, but he himself had not, perhaps would never have. The thought saddened him; but it did not bite into him poisonously, as his virginity had done. Fundamentally, he was to be henceforth in respect of woman at peace. Her beauties would no longer taunt him and waylay him and tether him. Henceforth he would have strength of her, not weakness.

In these expectations Paul was justified. His retarded spirit, starved hitherto of women, now burgeoned. I could detect in him day by day, almost hour by hour, new buds and growing points of sensitivity, of percipience, hitherto suppressed by the long winter of his frustration. Even during the rapturous holiday itself, when his whole interest was centred on the one being and on his love-play with her, he was at the same time exfoliating into a new and vital cognizance of more remote spheres. On their last day he wrote this poem:

> Last night,
> walking on the heath,
> she and I,
> alive,
> condescended toward the stars.
>
> For then we knew
> quite surely
> that all the pother of the universe
> was but a prelude to that summer night
> and our uniting,
> and all the ages to come
> but a cadence
> after our loving.
>
> Nestled down into the heather,
> we laughed,
> and took joy of one another,
> justifying the cosmic enterprise for ever
> by the moments of our caressing,
> while the simple stars
> watched
> unseeing.
>
> Thus lovers, nations, worlds, nay galaxies,
> conceive themselves the crest of all that is.

4. LONDON AND THE SPIRIT

Paul spent the last fortnight of his summer holiday at home, preparing for the next term, and feeling the influence of Katherine spread deeply into his being. When he returned to work, he found that he looked about him with fresh interest. Walking in the streets of London, he now saw something besides stray flowers of femininity adrift on the stream of mere humanity. He saw the stream itself, to which, after all, the women were not alien but integral. And just as woman had been a challenge to him, so now the great human flood was a challenge to him, something which he must come to terms with, comprehend.

The time had come for me to attempt my most delicate piece of work on Paul, the experiment which was to lead me to a more inward and sympathetic apprehension of your kind than anything that had hitherto been possible; the deep and subtle manipulation which incidentally would give Paul a treasure of experience beyond the normal reach of the first Men. It was my aim to complete in him the propaedeutic influence with which I had occasionally disturbed him in childhood. I therefore set about to induce in him such an awakened state that he should see in all things, and with some constancy, the dazzling intensity of being, the depth beyond depth of significance, which even in childhood he had glimpsed, though rarely. With this heightened percipience he must assess his own mature and deeper self and the far wider and more fearsome world which he now inhabited. Then should I be able to observe how far and with what idiosyncrasies the mentality of your kind, thus aided, could endure the truth and praise it.

It was chiefly in the streets and in the class-room that Paul found his challenge, but also, as had ever been the case with him, under the stars. Their frosty glance had now for him a more cruel, a more wounding significance than formerly, a significance which drew poignancy not only from echoes of the street, and the class-room, and from the sunned flesh of Katherine, but also from the war.

Paul had promised himself that when he had come to terms with woman he would devote his leisure to that intellectual touring in which he had never yet been able seriously to indulge. But even now, it seemed, he was not to carry out his plan, or at least not with the comfort and safety which he desired. What was meant to be a tour of well-marked and well-guided routes of the mind, threatened to become in fact a desperate adventure in lonely altitudes of the spirit. It was as though by some inner compulsion he were enticed to travel not through but above all the mental cities and dominions, not on foot but in the air; as though he who had no skill for flight were to find himself perilously exploring the currents and whirl-pools, the invisible cliffs and chasms, of an element far other than the earth; which, however, now displayed to his miraculous vision a detailed inwardness opaque to the pedestrian observer.

Even in the class-room, expounding to reluctant urchins the structure of sentences, the provisions of Magna Carta, the pro-ducts of South America, Paul constantly struggled for balance in that remote ethereal sphere. Sometimes he would even fall into complete abstraction, gazing with disconcerting intensity at some boy or other, while the particular juvenile spirit took form in his imagination, conjured by my skill. He would begin by probing behind the defensive eyes into the vast tangled order of blood-vessels and nerve fibres. He would seem to watch the drift of blood corpuscles, the very movements of atoms from molecule to molecule. He would narrow his eyes in breathless search for he knew not what. Then suddenly, not out there but somehow in the depth of his own being, the immature somnolent spirit of the child would confront him. He would intimately savour those little lusts and fears, those little joys and unwilling efforts, all those quick eager movements of a life whose very earnestness was but the earnestness of a dream. With the boy's hand in the boy's pocket he would finger pennies and sixpences, or a precious knife or toy. He would look into all the crannies of that mind, noting here a promise to be fulfilled, there a blank insensitivity, here some passion unexpressed and festering. Rapt in this contemplation, he would fall blind to everything but this unique particular being, this featured monad. Or he would hold it up in contrast with him-self, as one might hold for comparison in the palm of the hand two little crystals, or in the field of the telescope a double star. Some-times it would seem to him that the boy and himself were indeed two great spheres of light hugely present to one another, yet held eternally distinct from one another by the movement, the swing, of their diverse individualities. Then, like a memory from some forgotten life, there would come to him the thought, 'This is just Jackson Minor, a boy whom I must teach.' And then, 'Teach what?' And the answer, more apt than explicit, 'Teach to put forth an ever brighter effulgence of the spirit.'

While Paul was thus rapt, some movement would recall the class to him, and he would realize with a kind of eager terror that not only one but many of these huge presences were in the room with him. It was as though by some miracle a company of majestic and angelic beings was crowded upon this pin-point floor. And yet he knew that they were just a bunch of lads, just a collection of young and ephemeral human animals, who almost in the twinkle of a star would become black-coated citizens, parents, grandparents and discreetly laid-out corpses. Between then and now, what would they do? What were they for? They would do geography and scripture, they would make money or fail to make money, they would take young women to the pictures, they would do the done thing, and say the said thing. Then one day they would realize that they were growing old. Some of them would scream that they had not yet begun to live, others would shrug and drift heavily gravewards. So it would be, but why?

In the lunch hour, or when the school day was over, or in the evening when he was waiting to go to some show, he would let himself glide on the street flood to watch the faces, the action, to speculate on the significance of this gesture and that.

Sometimes he would walk unperturbed through street after street, carelessly turning the pages of the great picture book, dwelling lightly for a moment on this or that, on this comicality or elegance, on that figure of defeat or of complacency. Straying up Regent Street, he would amuse himself by sorting out the natives from the provincial visitors, and the foreign nationals from one another. He would surmise whether that painted duchess knew how desolate she looked, or that Lancashire holiday-maker how conscious that he was a stranger here, or whether the sweeper, with slouch hat and broom, felt, as he looked, more real than the rest. Odours would assail him: odour of dust and horse-dung, odour of exhaust fumes, rubber and tar, odour of cosmetics precariously triumphing over female sweat. Sounds would assail him: footsteps, leather-hard and rubber-soft, the hum and roar of motors, the expostulation of their horns; voices also of human animals, some oddly revealing, others a mere mask of sound, a carapace of standard tone, revealing nothing. Above all, forms and colours would assail him with their depths of significance. Well-tailored young women, discreet of glance; others more blowsy, not so discreet. Young men, vacantly correct, or betraying in some movement of the hand or restlessness of the eye an undercurrent of self-doubt. Old men, daughter-attended, tremblingly holding around their withered flesh the toga of seniority, bath-wrap-wise. Women of a past decade, backward leaning for weight of bosom, bullock-eyed, uncomprehending, backward straining under the impending pole-axe. After the smooth drift of Regent Street, he would find himself in the rapids of Oxford Street, buffeted, whirled hither and thither by successive vortices of humanity, of tweed-clad men, and women of artificial silk, of children toffee-smeared, of parents piloting their families, of messenger boys, soldiers, sailors, Indian students, and everywhere the constant flood of indistinguishable humanity, neither rich nor poor, neither beautiful nor ugly, neither happy nor sad, but restless, obscurely anxious, like a dog shivering before a dying fire.

At some point or other of his easeful wandering a change would probably happen to Paul. He would suddenly feel himself oppressed and borne down by the on-coming flood of his fellows. He would realize that he himself was but one indistinguishable drop in this huge continuum; that everything most unique and characteristic in him he had from It; that nothing whatever was himself, not even this craving for discrete existence; that the contours of his body and his mind had no more originality than one ripple in a wave-train. But with a violent movement of self-affirmation he would inwardly cry out, 'I am I, and not another.' Then in a flash he would feel his reality, and believe himself to be a substantial spirit, and eternal. For a moment all these others would seem to him but as moving pictures in the panorama of his own all-embracing self. But almost immediately some passing voice-tone in the crowd, some passing gesture, would stab him, shame him into realization of others. It would be as in the class-room. He would be overwhelmed not by the featureless drops of an ocean, but

211

by a great company of unique and diverse spirits. Behind each on-coming pair of eyes he would glimpse a whole universe, intricate as his own, but different; similar in its basic order, but different in detail, and permeated through and through by a different mood, a different ground-tone or timbre. Each of them was like a ship forging toward him, moving beside him and beyond, and trailing a great spreading wake of past life, past intercourse with the world. He himself, it seemed, was tossed like a cork upon the inter-crossing trains of many past careers. Looking at them one by one as they came upon him, he seemed to see with his miraculous vision the teeming experiences of each mind, as with a telescope one may see on the decks of a passing liner a great company of men and women, suddenly made real and intimate, though inaccessible. The ship's bow rises to the slow waves, and droops, in sad reiteration, as she thrusts her way forward, oxlike, obedient to some will above her but not of her. And so, seemingly, those wayfarers blindly thrust forward on their courses, in hand-to-mouth fulfilment of their mechanism, ignorant of the helms-man's touch, the owner's instructions. Here, bearing down upon him, would appear perhaps a tall woman with nose like a liner's stem, and fo'c'sle brows. Then perhaps an old gentleman with the white wave of his moutache curling under his prow. Then a rakish young girl. Then a bulky freighter. Thus Paul would entertain himself with fantasies, till sooner or later a bleak familiar thought would strike him. Each of these vessels of the spirit (this was the phrase he used) had indeed a helmsman, keeping her to some course or other; had even a master, who worked out the details of navi-gation and set the course; but of owner's instructions he was in most cases completely ignorant. And so these many ships ploughed hither and thither on the high seas vainly, not fulfilling, but for-lornly seeking, instructions. And because the mechanism of these vessels was not of insensitive steel but of desires and loathings, passions and admirations, Paul was filled with a great pity for them, and for himself as one of them, a pity for their half-awakened state between awareness and unawareness.

After such experiences in the heart of the city, Paul, in the train for his southern suburb, would already change his mood. Even while the train crossed the river the alteration would come. He would note, perhaps, the sunset reflected in the water. Though so unfashionable, it was after all alluring. The barges and tugs, jewelled with port and starboard and mast-head lights, the vague and cliffy rank of buildings, the trailing smoke, all these the sunset dignified. Of course it was nothing but a flutter of ether waves and shifting atoms, glorified by sentimental associations. Yet it compelled attention and an irrational worship. Sometimes Paul withdrew himself from it into his evening paper, resentful of this insidious romanticism. Sometimes he yielded to it, excusing himself in the name of Whitehead.

If it was a night-time crossing, with the dim stars beyond the smoke and glow of London, Paul would experience that tremor of recognition, of unreasoning expectation, which through my influence the stars had ever given him, and now gave him again, tinctured with a new dread, a new solemnity.

And when at last he was at home, and, as was his custom, walking for a few minutes on the Down before going to bed, he would feel, if it were a jewelled night, the overwhelming presence of the Cosmos. It was on these occasions that I could most completely master him, and even lift him precariously to the Neptunian plane. First he would have a powerful apprehension of the earth's rotundity, of the continents and oceans spreading beneath him and meeting under his feet. Then would I, using my best skill on the many keyboards of his brain, conjure in him a compelling perception of physical immensity, of the immensity first of the galactic universe, with its intermingling streams of stars, its gulfs of darkness; and then the huger immensity of the whole cosmos. With the eye of imagination he would perceive the scores, the millions, of other universes, drifting outwards in all directions like the fire-spray of a rocket. Then, fastening his attention once more on the stray atom earth, he would seem to see it forging through time, trailing its long wake of aeons, thrusting forward into its vaster, its more tempestuous future. I would let him glimpse that future. I would pour into the overflowing cup of his mind a torrent of visions. He would conceive and sensuously experience (as it were tropical rain descending on his bare head) the age-long but not everlasting downpour of human generations. Strange human-inhuman faces would glimmer before him and vanish.

By a simple device I made these glimpsed beings intimate to him; for I permitted him ever and again to see in them something of Katherine, though mysteriously transposed. And in the strange aspirations, strange fears, strange modes of the spirit that would impose themselves upon his tortured but exultant mind I took care that he should feel the strange intimate remoteness that he knew in Katherine. With my best art I would sometimes thrash the strings of his mind to echoes of man's last, most glorious achievement. And here again I would kindle this high theme with Katherine. Along with all this richness and splendour of human efflorescence I established in him an enduring emotional certainty that in the end is downfall and agony, then silence. This he had felt already as implicit in the nature of his own species, his own movement of the symphony; but now through my influence he knew with an absolute conviction that such must be the end also of all things human.

Often he would cry out against this fate, inwardly screaming like a child dropped from supporting arms. But little by little, as the months and years passed over him, he learned to accept this issue, to accept it at least in the deepest solitude of his own being, but not always to conduct himself in the world according to the final discipline of this acceptance.

At last there came a night when Paul, striding alone through the rough grass of the Down, facing the Pole Star and the far glow of London, wakened to a much clearer insight. One of Katherine's children had recently been knocked over by a car and seriously hurt. Paul saw Katherine for a few moments after the accident. With shock he saw her, for she was changed. Her mouth had withered. Her eyes looked at him like the eyes of some animal drowning in a well. It was upon the evening of that day that Paul took this most memorable of all his walks upon the Down. I plied him, as so often before, with images of cosmical pain and grief, and over all of them he saw the changed face of Katherine. Suddenly the horror, the cruelty of existence burst upon him with a new and insupportable violence, so that he cried out, stumbled, and fell. It seemed to him in his agony of compassion that if only the pain of the world were his own pain it might become endurable; but it was the pain of others, and therefore he could never master it with that strange joy which he knew was sometimes his. If all pain could be made his own only, he could surely grasp it firmly and put it in its place in the exquisite pattern of things. Yet could he? He remembered that mostly he was a coward, that he could not endure pain even as well as others, that it undermined him, and left him abject. But sometimes he had indeed been able to accept its very painfulness with a strange, quiet joy.

He thought of a thing to do. He would have a careful look at this thing, pain. And so, sitting up in the grass, he took out his pocket-knife, opened the big blade, and forced the point through the palm of his left hand. Looking fixedly at the Pole Star, he twisted the blade about, while the warm blood spread over his hand and trickled on to the grass. With the first shock his body had leapt, and now it writhed. The muscles of his face twisted, he set his teeth lest he should scream. His forehead was wet and cold, and faintness surged over him; but still he looked at Polaris, and moved the knife.

Beneath the Star spread the glow of London, a pale glory overarching the many lives. On his moist face, the wind. In his hand, grasped in the palm of his hand, the thing, pain. In his mind's eye the face of Katherine, symbol of all compassion. And, surging through him, induced by my power in him, apprehensions of cosmical austerity.

Then it was that Paul experienced the illumination which was henceforth to rule his life. In a sudden blaze of insight he saw more deeply into his own nature and the world's than had ever before been possible to him. While the vision lasted, he sat quietly on the grass staunching his wounded hand and contemplating in turn the many facets of his new experience. Lest he should afterwards fail to recapture what was now so exquisitely clear, he put his findings into words, which however seemed incapable of expressing more than the surrounding glow of his experience, leaving the bright central truth unspoken.

'This pain in my hand', he said, 'is painful because of the interruption that has been caused in the harmonious living of my flesh. All pain is hateful in that it is an interruption, a discord, an infringement of some theme of living, whether lowly or exalted. This pain in my hand, which is an infringement of my body's

215

lowly living, is not, it so happens, an infringement also of my spirit. No. Entering into my spirit, this pain is a feature of beauty. My spirit? What do I really mean by that? There is first I, the minded body, or the embodied mind; and there is also my spirit. What is it? Surely it is no substantial thing. It is the music rather, which I, the instrument, may produce, and may also appreciate. My glory is, not to preserve myself, but to create upon the strings of myself the music that is spirit, in whatever degree of excellence I may; and to appreciate the music in myself and others, and in the massed splendours of the cosmos, with whatever insight I can muster. Formerly I was dismayed by the knowledge that pain's evil was intrinsic to pain. But now I see clearly that though this is so, though pain's evil to the pain-blinded creature is an absolute fact in the universe, yet the very evil itself may have a place in the music which spirit is. There is no music without the torture of the strings. Even the over-straining, the slow wearing out, the sudden shattering of instruments may be demanded for the full harmony of this dread music. Nay, more. In this high music of the spheres, even the heartless betrayals, the mean insufficiencies of will, common to all human instruments, unwittingly contribute by their very foulness to the intolerable, the inhuman, beauty of the music.'

By now Paul, having bound up his hand, having wiped his knife and put it away, had risen to his feet, and was walking towards home with trembling knees, pursuing his argument.

'To make the music that spirit is, that, I now see, is the end for which all living things exist, from the humblest to the most exalted. In two ways they make it: gloriously, purposefully, in their loyal strivings, but also shamefully, unwittingly, in their betrayals. Without Satan, with God only, how poor a universe, how trite a music! Purposefully to contribute to the music that spirit is, this is the great beatitude. It is permitted only to the elect. But the damned also, even they, contribute, though unwittingly. Purposefully to contribute upon the strings of one's own being, and also to respond with ecstasy to the great cosmic theme inflooding from all other instruments, this is indeed the sum of duty, and of beatitude. Though in my own conduct I were to betray the music which is spirit, and in my own heart dishonour it, yet seemingly it is not in reality sullied; for it dare avail itself alike of Christ and Judas. Yet must I not betray it, not dishonour it. Yet if I do, it will not be sullied. Mystery! Purposefully to make the music that spirit is, and to delight in it! The delighting and suffering of all minded beings are within the music. Even this very profound, very still delight, this ecstasy, with which I now contemplate my hand's pain and Katherine's distress and the long effort and agony of the worlds, this also is a contribution to the music which it contemplates. Why am I thus chosen? I do not know. But it is irrelevant that this instrument rather than that should sound this theme and not another, create this ecstasy and not that agony. What matters is the music, that it should unfold itself through the ages, and be fulfilled in whatever end is fitting, and crowned with admiration, worship. But if it should never be rightly fulfilled, and never meetly crowned? I have indeed a very clear conviction that over the head of time the whole music of the cosmos is all the while a fulfilled perfection, the eternal outcome of the past, the present and the future. But if I am mistaken? Then if it is not perfected, it is at least very excellent. For this much my eyes have seen.'

He was now coming down the slope toward the street lamps and lighted windows. On the other side of the little valley the water-tower of the lunatic asylum rose black against the sky. He stood for a while. At that moment a faint sound came to him from across the valley. Was it a cat? Or had a dog been run over? Or was it a human sound between laughter and horror? To Paul it came as the asylum's comment on his meditation. Or was it the comment of the whole modern age? For a while, he kept silent, then said aloud, 'Yes, you may be right. Perhaps it is I that am mad. But if so this madness is better than sanity. Better, and more sane.'

On the following day Paul wrote a poem. It reveals the blend of intuitive exaltation and metaphysical perplexity in which he now found himself.

> When a man salutes the perfection of reality,
> peace invades him,
> as though upon the completion of some high duty,
> as though his life's task were achieved in this act of loyalty.
> Was the task illusory?
> Is this beatitude but the complacency of self-expansion?
> Or does the real, perfect formally,

217

yet claim for its justification and fulfilment
admiration?
As a man's love transmutes a woman,
kindling her features with an inner radiance,
does mind's worship
transfigure the world?

VIII *The Modern World*

1. PAUL UNDERTAKES HIS TASK

WITH this spiritual achievement solidly accomplished, Paul was ready to observe London and the world with new eyes. In fact he was now well fitted to carry out the main work that I had purposed for him. He himself would have been content simply to carry on his teaching with new vitality and conscientiousness, and for the rest to pursue with deeper understanding his leisurely tour of the countries of the mind. But he was soon to discover that more was demanded of him, and that he who had so lately learned the lesson of quietness, must now embark on a life more active, more resolute, than anything that he had formerly attempted.

His new purpose dawned on him slowly, and as it became clear to him and formidable, he both lusted in it and feared it. His final and precise apprehension of it flashed upon him as he was waiting on the top of a stationary and throbbing motor-omnibus outside the great railway terminus of Cannon Street, watching the streams of bowlered or soft-hatted business men, hurrying to their offices. There surged through him suddenly a violent hunger, or was it a sacred call, to apprehend precisely and with understanding the whole phenomenon of the modern world, to see it in relation to his recent vision, to discover its deeper significance. So insistent was this new craving that he had to restrain himself from descending there and then into the street to ask each of the crowd in turn what he was really doing with his life, and why.

Paul was frightened by the violence of his own desire, and by its quality of freakishness, even of insanity. He pulled himself together and argued against it. It would interfere with his own work, and with his peace of mind. He was not fitted for any such world-study. Moreover, he ought not to give up his life to merely apprehending; he must do, must serve. However well he should understand, the world would be none the better.

As the days passed, however, this new craving took firmer hold of

219

him. He felt it growing into an irresistible, an insane obsession. So violently did he strive to exorcize it, that he was threatened with breakdown. Clearly, if he were forced to pursue my purpose against this desperate reluctance, he would pursue it ill. I therefore decided that, in order to gain his willing co-operation, I must attempt to give him a frank and precise explanation of my relations with him. This would be a difficult undertaking, and one which would have been impossible to carry out on any but a carefully selected and prepared individual.

One night, as Paul was lying in bed, I constructed in his imagination a detailed image of myself as I should have appeared to his eyes. He saw me as a great grey human monolith, snake-eyed. I then spoke to him, through his own imagination. I explained that I was a human being of the remote future, living upon Neptune, and that it was my task to study the Terrestrial ages of Man. For this work, I said, I had chosen him as my instrument. If necessary I could by an inner compulsion force him to work for me, but the work would fare better if he would enter into it willingly. I explained that, by helping me to render something of Terrestrial history into the consciousness of my own species, which, I said, was mentally far more advanced than his own, he would be serving not only me but his own kind. ,

Next morning Paul recalled the night's experience with amazement, but dismissed it as a dream. On succeeding nights I influenced him again, giving him more detail of my world and my power over himself. I referred him, moreover, to two books. One of these, already published, was *An Experiment with Time*, by J. W. Dunne. This work, I told him, though to the Neptunian mind it was philosophically naïve, might help him to understand the incursion of future events into the present. The other book, which would be called *Last and First Men*, had yet to appear.

When Paul encountered the first of these books, he was profoundly disturbed, and still more so when, some months later, he read the other in manuscript. He now became convinced of the reality of my intercourse with him. For a while he was terrified and revolted at the knowledge that another human mind had access to his every thought, and could even induce him to think and desire as it was not in his own nature to think and desire. That his character should be largely the product of another mind seemed to him at first an intolerable violation of his privacy, nay, of his identity. I had therefore to remind him, patiently and night by night, that even apart from my power over him he was an expression of influences other than himself, that whatever was distinctive of him was not truly his at all. 'You forget', I said, 'that your nature is the product of an infinite mesh of causes; of evolution, of the hither-thither turmoil of human history, and finally of your parents, of Katherine, of the war, and of your boys. Will you then rebel because yet another influence, hitherto unsuspected, is discovered to have part in you, an influence, too, which has very greatly increased your spiritual stature? If so, your recent illumination on the Down was less deep than it should have been. You have not realized in your heart that the bare private individuality is a negligible thing, that what is glorious or base is the form which circumstance imposes on it. I myself am in the same case with you. I am the product of a vast web of circumstance, and my mind is probably open to the critical inspection and even the influence of I know not what beings superior to myself. Compared with you I am indeed of a higher order of mentality, but no credit is due to me for this greater richness and significance of my nature. As well might the concluding chord of a symphony take credit for the significance poured into it by all its predecessors. There is of course in both of us, and in all men, and all living things, and all sub-vital beings, the one universal miracle of spontaneous doing, which is the essential life of all existence. Through the aid or the limitation of circumstance some may do much, others little. What matter which of us does which? All the tones of the music are needed for the music's perfection. And it is the music alone that matters, not the glorification of this instrument or that.'

In a few days Paul was reconciled to his fate to such an extent that he began eagerly to debate with himself how he should gratify the new passion which hitherto he had only with difficulty restrained. The fervour with which he embarked on his task combined the lusty hunger of an appetite with the exaltation of a sacred duty.

I further prepared him by making him realize that his recent experience on the Down was the vital spark lacking to all typical modern thought, the missing and all-relevant word without which its jumble of verbiage could never make sense, the still small voice which alone, working in each heart, could ever bring peace to the modern world. Paul knew, of course, that this experience of his was by no means unique. Other ages had more profoundly entered into it. Even in his own age it sometimes occurred. But it had played little part in the common life of the mind; the few who had known it had nearly always withdrawn into their inner fortress. Disengaging themselves from the dross which confuses modern thought, they had at the same time unwittingly rejected a treasure which had never before come within man's reach. Contenting themselves with vain repetitions of old truths, they were deaf to the new truth which was as yet but stammeringly expressing itself in men's minds. They could see very clearly the central error of the modern spirit, namely, the belief that reality is wholly included in the world of sense. Revolting from this folly, they erroneously declared this world a phantom and a snare, and naïvely conceived that in their ecstasy the soul, escaping from illusion, found herself at last untrammelled and immortal. I was at pains to make Paul see unmistakably that, for those who have entered superficially into the life of the spirit, this is the most insidious, the most lethal of all snares.

On the day after his illumination upon the Down, Paul had told himself that he had escaped from the foundering vessel of himself. The swarms of his fellow men and women all over the world could do nothing but labour incessantly from wave to wave of the maelstrom, pausing only now and then on some crest to look around them and realize that they were ploughing a waste of waters; and that one and all must sink. Paul saw them tormented by self-prizing; though also more nobly tortured and exalted by personal love, and by the intensified pain of watching the beloved's pain. This it was, indeed, that chiefly dignified them above the beasts. But this also it was that tethered them to the waste of waters, like foundering may-flies. Their interest was almost wholly personal, either in self-regard, or hate, or love; but increasingly they saw that in the waste of existence there could be no lasting home for personal spirits anywhere, and so no permanency of comfort for any one's beloved. Each of them, and each beloved, must settle heavily down into old age, like leaky vessels. If only they could have sunk in battle array fighting for some great cause! But their sailing orders had not come through to them, or had been so mutilated that they found no clear direction.

Thus Paul had figured things out on the day after his illumination. By some miracle he himself, seemingly, had escaped from the foundering vessel of himself. He had escaped simply by a leap of the imagination, a soaring flight into the upper air; whence, selfless, he could watch the shipwreck of himself and all selves with a strange, still compassion, but without revolt. Yet subsequently, under my continued influence, he saw that this image was false and dangerous. He had not escaped. No self could escape. And now at last he realized that escape was not desirable. For he had seen something of the beauty for which all selves, if they could but see it, would suffer gladly, and gladly be annihilated.

Paul now once more turned his attention to the world that it was his task to observe. Suddenly a truth, which he had long vaguely known, but had never before clearly stated to himself, became both clear and urgent. At last he saw the situation of his species unambiguously from the cosmical point of view. He saw what it was that he and his contemporaries should be doing with their world. Fate had given them an opportunity which had been withheld from every early age. They had stumbled on the power of controlling the destiny of the human race. They had already gained some mastery over physical nature, and a far greater mastery was seemingly in store for them. Already their world had become one world, as it had never been before. Moreover, they must some day learn how to remake human nature itself, for good or for ill. If they could begin to outgrow their limitations of will, if they could feel beyond their self-regard, their tribal jealousies and their constant puerile obsessions, then they could begin not only to construct a Utopia of happy individuals, but to make of their planet a single and most potent instrument of the spirit, capable of music hitherto unconceived.

What humanity should do with itself in the far future, no one could tell; but one conviction now stood out with certainty in Paul's mind, namely, that over all the trivial and inconsistent purposes that kept the tribes of men in conflict with one another, there was one purpose which should be the supreme and inviolate purpose of all men today, namely, to evoke in every extant human being the fullest possible aliveness, and to enable all men to work together harmoniously for the making of a nobler, a more alive human nature.

Some such purpose as this was obscurely dawning in many minds throughout the Western and even the Eastern world. But though they were many, they were a minute proportion of the whole; and their vision was unclear, their will unsure. Opposed to them were many violent powers, and the dead-weight of custom, not only in the world but in themselves also. What chance was there that these few groping minds would wrench the great world into a new way of living? Paul now with eager interest, nay with passion, with awe, with grim zest, took up his task of watching and assessing the intense little drama of your age.

Lest he should lose sight of the wider bearings of that drama, Paul first meditated on the cosmical significance of human endeavour, which now for the first time was beginning to be tentatively apprehended by man himself. The immediate outcome of his meditation was this poem:

Is man a disease
that the blood of a senile star
cannot resist?
And when the constellations regard us,
is it fear, disgust, horror,
(at a plague-stricken brother
derelict from beauty),
that stares yonder
so sharply?

Gas the stars are.
They regard us not,
they judge us not,
they care for nothing.
We are alone in the hollow sky.

Then ours, though out of reach, those trinkets,
withheld,
unspoiled;

ours the sleeping and uncommanded genii
of those old lamps;
ours by right of mentality;
by right of agony,
by right of long heart-searching,
by right of all we must do with them
when our day comes,
when we have outlived our childishness,
when we have outgrown
the recurrent insanity of senility.
Then surely at last man,
and not bickering monkeys,
shall occupy the universe.

2. THE RESEARCH

Paul now devoted all his leisure to his great exploration. He
began tentatively, by reading much modern literature, and talking
politics and philosophy with his friends. Both these occupations
were of course familiar to him; but whereas formerly they had been
pursued in the spirit of the tourist, a rather bewildered tourist, now
they were carried out with passion and an assurance which to Paul
himself seemed miraculous. This beginning led him on to make a
careful study of the mentality of the whole teaching profession,
both in schools and universities; and this in turn developed into a
wide and profound research into all manner of mental types and
occupations from road-menders to cabinet ministers. With my
constant help, and to his own surprise, the silent and retiring young
schoolmaster, who had always been so painfully conscious of the
barrier between himself and his kind, began actively to seek out
whatever contacts promised to be significant for his task. With
amazement he discovered in himself a talent for devising inoffen-
sive methods of making acquaintance with all sorts of persons
whom he needed for his collection. Indeed, he pursued his work
very much in the spirit of a collector in love with his specimens, and
eager to discover by wealth of instances the laws of their being. If
one day he happened to conceive that such and such a well-known
personage or humble neighbour could give him light, he would be

tormented by a violent, almost sexual, craving to meet the chosen one, and would leave no stone unturned until he had achieved his end.

Under my influence he also developed a captivating power of social intercourse, which, however, would only come into action in special circumstances. In the ordinary trivial social occasions he remained as a rule clumsy, diffident and tiresome; but in any situation which was relevant to his task, he seemed to come alive, to be a different person, and one that he thoroughly delighted to be. It was not merely that he discovered a gift of conversation. Sometimes he would say almost nothing. But what he did say would have a startling effect on his hearer, drawing him out, compelling him to get a clear view of his own work and aims, forcing him to unburden himself in a confession, such that at the close of it he would perhaps declare, 'Yes, that is really how I face the world, though till today I hardly thought of it that way.' Sometimes, however, Paul himself would be almost voluble, commenting with a strangely modest assurance on the other's function. Often he would find himself assuming for the occasion an appropriate personality, a mask peculiarly suited to appear intelligent and sympathetic to this particular man or woman. Paul was sometimes shocked at the insincerity of this histrionic behaviour; though he pursued it, for the sake of its extraordinary effectiveness. And indeed it was not really insincere, for it was but the natural result of his new and intense imaginative insight into other minds. Sometimes when he was in the presence of two very different individuals whom he had previously encountered apart, he would be hard put to it to assume for each the right mask without rousing the other's indignation. Thus, to give a rather crude example of this kind of predicament, having on Monday won the confidence of a member of the Communist Party, and on Tuesday the benevolence of a British Patriot, he happened on Wednesday to come upon them both together in violent altercation. Both at first greeted him as an ally, but before he fled he had been reviled by each in turn.

One curious limitation of Paul's talent he found very distressing. Brilliant as he was at evoking in others a clearer consciousness of their own deeper thoughts and desires, he was incapable of impressing them with his own ideas. Strong in his own recent spiritual experiences, and in his increasing grasp of the contemporary world, he yet failed completely to express himself on these subjects. This was but natural, for he was no genius, still less a prophet; and, save in the office in which I needed him and inspired him, he remained inarticulate. This incapacity disturbed him increasingly as the months and years passed. For increasingly he became convinced that the modern world was heading toward a huge disaster, and that nothing could save it but the awakening of the mass of men into a new mood and greater insight. More and more clearly he saw in his own meditations just what this awakening must be. Yet he could never make it clear to others, for as soon as he tried to express himself, he fell stammering or mute. The trouble lay partly in his incompetence, but partly also in the fact that through my help he had seen both sides of a truth which to his fellows was almost never revealed thus in the solid. Paul's interlocutor, therefore, was sure to be blind either to one or to the other aspect of Paul's central conviction; either to his sense of obligation in the heroic and cosmically urgent enterprise of man upon his planet, or to his seemingly inconsistent perception of the finished, the inhuman, beauty of the cosmos.

Most painfully when he was with members of the 'intelligentsia' did his mental paralysis seize him. He made contact with many writers and artists. Each of these brilliant beings he treated at first with doglike respect, believing that at last he had come into the presence of one who had broken into new truth. But somehow he never went very far with any of them. For a while he delighted them, because he stimulated them to apprehend their own vision with a new clarity. But since their visions were not as a rule very profound, they and he soon saw all there was to see in them. At this point Paul's talent invariably disappeared, and henceforth they thought him dull, bourgeois, not worth knowing. He could no longer hold their attention. He had not the necessary flow of personal tittle-tattle to carry him through when deeper interests flagged. On the other hand, if ever he dared to tell them his own views, he merely made a fool of himself, and was treated either with kindly ridicule or with inattention. Thus, though he came to know his way about the intellectual life of London, he was never taken into any circle or school. Most circles had at one time or other tolerated him on their fringes; yet he remained unknown, for no one ever bothered to mention him to any one else. Thus it happened that he was always apart, always able to look on without pledging his faith to any creed, his intellect to any theory. Every creed, every theory, he secretly tested and sooner or later rejected in the light of his own recent illumination. In this manner Paul served my purpose admirably. As a tissue-section, to be studied under the microscope, may be stained to bring out details of structure that would otherwise have remained invisible, so Paul, whom I had treated with a tincture of Neptunian vision, revealed in exquisite detail the primitive organs of his mind, some of which took the stain and others not. Obviously it is impossible to reveal the whole issue of the experiment to readers of this book, since they themselves suffer from Paul's limitations.

Throughout these crowded years Paul still carried on his daily work at the school, though inevitably as his attention became more and more occupied, his teaching suffered. All his free time, all his holidays, he now spent on his task of exploration. It was a strange life, so rich in human intercourse, and yet so lonely; for he dared not tell any one of the real purpose of his activities, of their Neptunian aspect, lest he should be thought insane. To his friends he appeared to have been bitten by some queer bug of curiosity, which, they said, had filled him with a quite aimless mania for inquiry, and was ruining his work.

To aid his project he undertook a number of enterprises, none of which he did well, since at heart he regarded them only as means of the pursuit of his secret purpose. He worked for a political party, lectured to classes organized by the Workers' Educational Association, collaborated in a social survey of a poor district. Also he haunted certain public-houses, attended revivalist meetings, became intimate with burglars, swindlers, and one or two un-caught murderers, who, he found, were extremely thankful for the opportunity of unburdening themselves under the spell of his mysteriously aloof sympathy and understanding. He made contact with many prostitutes and keepers of brothels. He respectfully explored the minds of homosexuals, and others whose hungers did not conform to the lusts of their fellows. He found his way into many chambers of suffering, and was present at many death-beds.

He was welcomed in mining villages, and in slum tenements. He discussed revolution in the homes of artisans. Equally he was received in the houses of bank managers, of ship-owners, of great industrial employers. He conferred with bishops, and also with the dignitaries of science, but no less eagerly with vagabonds; over stolen delicacies, seated behind hedges. Part of one summer he spent as a dock labourer, and part of another as a harvest hand in the West of England. He travelled steerage on an emigrant ship, and worked his passage on a tramp steamer along the Baltic coasts. He made a brief but crowded pilgrimage to Russia, and came home a Communist, with a difference. He tramped and bicycled in Western Europe; and in England he made contact with many visitors from the East. Yet also he found time to keep abreast of contemporary literature, to haunt studios, to discuss epistemology and ethics with bright young Cambridge philosophers.

In all this work he found that he was constantly and sometimes sternly guided by an inner power, which, though I never again openly communicated with him, he knew to spring from me. Thus he was endowed with an infallible gift of selection and of detective inquiry. Through my help he covered in a few years the whole field of modern life, yet he never wasted his strength on vain explorations. With the precision of a hawk he descended upon the significant individual, the significant movement; and with a hawk's assurance he neglected the irrelevant. Sometimes his own impulses would run counter to my guidance. Then he would find himself directed by a mysterious, an inner and hypnotic, impulsion, either to give up what he had planned to do, or to embark on some adventure for which his own nature had no inclination.

Month by month, year by year, there took shape in Paul's mind a new and lucid image of his world, an image at once terrible and exquisite, tragic and farcical. It is difficult to give an idea of this new vision of Paul's, for its power depended largely on the immense intricacy and diversity of his recent experience; on his sense of the hosts of individuals swarming upon the planet, here sparsely scattered, there congested into great clusters and lumps of humanity, here machine-ridden, there ground into the earth from which they sucked their scanty livelihood. Speaking in ten thousand mutually incomprehensible dialects, living in manners reprehensible or ludicrous to one another, thinking by concepts unintelligible to one another, they worshipped in modes repugnant to one another. This new sense of the mere bulk and variety of men was deepened in Paul's mind by his enhanced apprehension of individuality in himself and others, his awed realization that each single unit in all these earth-devastating locust armies carried about with it a whole cognized universe, was the plangent instrument of an intense and self-important theme of mind. For Paul had by now learned very thoroughly to perceive the reality of all human beings and of the world with that penetrating insight which I had first elicited from him in childhood. On the other hand, since he was never wholly forgetful of the stars, the shock between his sense of human littleness in the cosmos and his new sense of man's physical bulk and spiritual intensity increased his wonder. Thus in spite of his perception of the indefeasible reality of everyday things, he had also an overwhelming conviction that the whole fabric of common experience, nay the whole agreed universe of human and biological and astronomical fact, though real, concealed some vaster reality.

It must not be forgotten that throughout his exploration Paul was jealously mindful of my presence within him, and that his sense of an ulterior, a concealed, reality, was derived partly from the knowledge that within himself, or above himself, there was concealed a more exalted being. He knew that I was ever behind his eyes, ever attentive in his ears, ever pondering and sifting the currents of his brain. Yet, save when I swayed him with unaccountable cravings and reluctances, my presence was wholly unperceived.

It must be remembered that I used Paul in two manners, both as a transparent instrument of observation, and as a sample of your mentality. I was interested not only in the external facts which he recorded, but in his reaction to them, in the contrast between his appraisement of them and my own. That contrast I may express by saying that whereas I myself regarded the Terrestrial sphere primarily with detachment, though with detachment which held within itself a passion of imaginative sympathy, Paul regarded all things primarily from the human point of view, though he was able also by a continuous effort to maintain himself upon the loftier plane. For me it was a triumph of imagination that I could enter so fully into your remote and fantastic world. For Paul it was a triumph that in spite of his fervent humanity, his compassion and indignation, he could now regard his world with celestial aloofness. Thus the two of us together were like two different musical instruments playing against one another in two different tempos to produce a single intricacy of rhythm.

To the Neptunian intelligence, however, there was a slightly nauseating pathos even in Paul's most chastened enthusiasm. Only through the secret and ironical influence of my presence within him could he avoid taking the fate of his world too much to heart. The mind that has but lately received a commanding revelation which exalts it above the pettiness of daily life is very prone to a certain extravagance, a certain farcical pomp, in its devotion. The Neptunian mind, on the other hand, born into the faith and needing no sententious conversion, was sometimes impelled by Paul's solemnity to wonder whether even the final tragedy of man on Neptune called most for grief or for laughter.

3. FRUITS OF THE RESEARCH

Paul had already made it clear in his own mind what the human aim should be. Man should be striving into ever-increasing richness of personality. He should be preparing his planet and his many races of persons to embody the great theme of spirit which was as yet so dimly, so reluctantly, conceived. In fact man should be preparing to fulfil his office as a centre in which the cosmos might rejoice in itself, and whence it might exfoliate into ever more brilliant being. Paul found also in his heart a conviction, calm, though humanly reluctant, that in the end must come downfall; and that though man must strive with all his strength and constancy of purpose, he must yet continually create in his heart the peace, the acceptance, the cold bright star of cognizance which if we name it we misname.

In his exploration Paul sought to discover what progress man was making in this twofold venture. He found a world in which, far from perceiving the cosmical aspect of humanity, men were for the most part insensitive even to the purely human aspect, the need to make a world of full-blown and joyful human individuals. Men lived together in close proximity, yet with scarcely more knowledge of one another than jungle trees, which blindly jostle and choke, each striving only to raise its head above its neighbours. Beings with so little perception of their fellows had but a vague apprehension of the human forest as a whole, and almost none of its potentialities. Some confused and dreamlike awareness of man's cosmical function no doubt there was. As a very faint breeze, it spread among the waiting tree-tops. But what was to come of it?

In such a world there was one kind of work which seemed to Paul, not indeed the most important, for many operations were equally important, but the most directly productive work of all, namely, education. Among the teachers, as in all walks of life, Paul found that, though some were indeed pioneers of the new world-order, many were almost entirely blind to the deeper meaning of their task. Even those few who had eyes to see could do but little. Their pupils had at all costs to be fitted for life in a world careless of the spirit, careless of the true ends of living, and thoughtful only for the means. They must be equipped for the economic struggle. They must become good business men, good engineers and chemists, good typists and secretaries, good husband-catchers, even if the process prevented them irrevocably from becoming fully alive human beings. And so the population of the Western world was made up for the most part of strange thwarted creatures, skilled in this or that economic activity, but blind to the hope and the plight of the human race. For them the sum of duty was to play the economic game shrewdly and according to rule, to keep their wives in comfort and respectability, their husbands well fed and contented, to make their offspring into quick and relentless little gladiators for the arena of world-prices. One and all they ignored that the arena was not merely the market or the stock exchange, but the sand-multitudinous waste of stars.

Of the innumerable constructors, the engineers, architects, chemists, many were using their powers merely for gladiatorial victory. Even those who were sincere workers had but the vaguest notion of their function in the world. For them it was enough to serve faithfully some imposing individual, some firm, or at best some national State. They conceived the goal of corporate human endeavour in terms of comfort, efficiency, and power, in terms of manufactures, oil, electricity, sewage disposal, town-planning, aeroplanes and big guns. When they were not at work, they killed time by motor-touring, the cinema, games, domesticity or sexual adventures. Now and then they registered a political vote, without having any serious knowledge of the matters at stake. Yet within the limits of their own work they truly lived; their creative minds were zestfully obedient to the laws of the materials in which they worked, to the strength and elasticity of metals, the forms of cantilevers, the affinities of atoms.

Of much the same mentality, though dealing with a different material, were the doctors and surgeons; for whom men and women were precariously adjusted machines, walking bags of intestines, boxes of telephone nerves, chemical factories liable to go wrong at any minute, fields for exploration and fee-making, possible seats of pain, the great evil, and of death, which, though often preferable, was never to be encouraged. They were familiar equally with death, and birth, conception and contraception, and all the basic agonies and pities. They protected themselves against the intolerable dead-weight of human suffering, sometimes by callousness of imagination, sometimes by drink or sport or private felicity, sometimes by myths of compensation in eternity. A few faced the bleak truth unflinchingly yet also with unquenched compassion. But nearly all, though loyal to the militant life in human bodies, were too hard pressed to be familiar with the uncouth exploratory ventures of human minds. And so, through very loyalty to life, they were for the most part blind to the other, the supernal, beauty.

Even more insulated, those very different servants of human vitality, the agriculturists, whose minds were fashioned to the soil they worked on, lived richly within the limits of their work, yet were but obscurely, delusively, conscious of the world beyond their acres. In the straightness of their furrows, and the fullness of their crops, in their sleek bulls and stallions, they knew the joy of the maker; and they knew beauty. But what else had they? They had to thrust and heave from morning till night. They had to feed their beasts. Brooding over their crops, dreading floods and droughts, they had not time for the world. Yet they enviously despised the town-dwellers. They censured all newfangled ways, they condescended to teach their sons the lore of their grandfathers, and they guarded their daughters as prize heifers. They put on black clothes for chapel, to pray for good weather. They believed themselves the essential roots of the State. They measured national greatness in terms of wheat and yeoman muscle. The younger ones, town-infected with their motor-bicycles, their wireless, their artificial silks, their political views, their new-fangled morals, revolted against enslavement to the soil. Both young and old alike were vaguely unquiet, disorientated, sensing even in their fields the futility of existence.

Most typical of your isolation from one another were the seamen, who, imprisoned nine parts of their lives in a heaving box of steel, looked out complainingly upon a world of oceans and coasts. They despised the landsmen, but they were ever in search of a shore job. Monastic, by turns celibate and polygamous, they were childlike in their unworldly innocence, brutelike in their mental blindness, godlike (to Paul's estimation) in their patience and courage. They loved the flag as no landsman could love it. They were exclusively British (or German or what not) but loyal also to the universal brotherhood of the sea (or disloyal), and faithful to the owners (or unfaithful). Day after day they toiled, shirked, slandered, threatened one another with knives; but in face of the typhoon they could discover amongst themselves a deep, an inviolable communion. They measured all persons by seamanship, crew-discipline, and all things by seaworthiness and ship-shapeliness. They took the stars for signposts and timepieces, and on Sundays for the lamps of angels. Contemptuous of democracy, innocent of communism, careless of evolution, they ignored that the liquid beneath their keels was but a film between the solid earth and the void, but a passing phenomenon between the volcanic confusion of yesterday and the all-gripping ice-fields of tomorrow.

Seemingly very different, yet at bottom the same, was the case of the industrial workers of all occupations and ranks, whose dreams echoed with the roar of machinery. For the mass of them, work was but a slavery, and the height of bliss was to be well paid in idleness. They loudly despised the wealthy, yet in their hearts they desired only to mimic them, to display expensive pleasures, to have powers of swift locomotion. What else could they look for, with their stunted minds? Many were unemployed, and spiritually dying of mere futility. Some, dole-shamed, fought for self-esteem, cursing the world that had no use for them; others, dole-contented, were eager to plunder the society that had outlawed them. But many there were among the industrial workers who waited only to be wrought and disciplined to become the storm troops of a new order. Many there were who earnestly willed to make a new world and not merely to destroy an old one. But what world? Who could seize this half-fashioned instrument, temper it, and use it? Who had both the courage and the cunning to do so? Seemingly only those who had been themselves so tempered and hardened by persecution that they could not conceive any final beatitude for man beyond regimentation in a proletarian or a fascist State.

Certainly the politicians could never seize that weapon. They climbed by their tongues; and when they reached the tree-top, they could do nothing but chatter like squirrels, while the storm cracked the branches, and the roots parted.

The journalists? Was it they who could fertilize the waiting seed of the new world? Little seekers after copy, they made their living by the sale of habit-forming drugs. They had their loyalties, like the rest of men; but they trusted that in preserving the tradition of the Press, or in serving some great journal, they served well enough. They ignored that in the main their journals spread poison, lies, the mentality of society's baser parts. They made sex obscene, war noble, and patriotism the height of virtue. A few there were of another kind, who sought to bring to light what the authorities would keep dark, whose aim it was to make men think by offering them sugared pills of wisdom, spiced problems of state-craft, peepshows of remote lands and lives, glimpses of the whole of things. They were indeed possible trumpeters of a new order, though not world-builders. But they were few and hobbled, for at every turn they must please or go under. And the thought which they so devotedly spread was of necessity over-simplified and vulgarized, to suit the spirit of the times.

The civil servants, could they remake the world? Wrought and tempered to a great tradition of loyalty, they were devoted only to the smooth-running and just-functioning and minor improvement of the social machine.

The social workers, so formidable with eye-witnessed facts, so indignant with the machine, so kindly-firm with 'cases', so loyal to the social gospel, and to the fulfilling of personality, so contemptuous of cosmical irrelevances, and morally outraged by those who, even in a foundering world, have an eye for beauty! They had their part to play, but they were repairers, physicians, not procreators of a new world.

The religious folk, who should have been society's red blood-corpuscles, transfusing their spiritual treasure into all its tissues, had settled down to become a huge proliferating parasite. Mostly of the middle class, they projected their business interests into another world by regular payments of premiums on an eternal-life assurance policy; or they compensated for this world's unkindness by conceiving themselves each as the sole beloved in the arms of Jesus, or at least as a life member in the very select celestial club. But some, teased by a half-seen vision, by a conviction of majesty, of beauty they knew not whereabouts nor of what kind, were persuaded to explain their bewildered ecstasy by ancient myths and fantasies. For the sake of their bright, featureless, guiding star, they believed what was no longer credible and desired what it was now base to desire.

The scientists, so pious toward physical facts, so arch-priestly to their fellow-men, were indeed a noble army of miners after truths; but they were imprisoned in deep galleries, isolated even from each other in their thousand saps. Daily they opened up new veins of the precious metal; and sent the bright ingots aloft, to be mortised into the golden temple of knowledge, with its great thronged halls of physics, astronomy and chemistry, biology and psychology; or to be put to commercial use, whether for the increase of happiness, or for killing, or for spiritual debasement, or to be instrumental in one way or another to the achievement of pure cognizance. Two kinds of scientists Paul found. Some were but eyeless cave-reptiles, or moles who came reluctantly into the upper world, nosing across men's path, concealing their bewilderment under dust-clouds of pronouncements. Some, though innocent of philosophy, ventured to set up metaphysical edifices, in which they repeated all the structural defects of the old systems, or were sent toppling by the dizzying of their own unschooled desires, whether for the supremacy of mind, or for the immortality of the individual. The public, tricked by the same unschooled desires, applauded their acrobatic feats, and was blind to their disaster. Others, more cautious, knew that all scientific knowledge was of numbers only, yet that with the incantation of numbers new worlds might be made. They were preparing to take charge of mankind, to make the planet into a single well-planned estate, and to re-orientate human nature. But what kind of a world would they desire to make, whose knowledge was only of numbers?

But the philosophers themselves were scarcely more helpful. Some still hoped to reach up to reality (which the scientists had missed) by tiptoeing on a precarious scaffold of words. Others, preening their intellectual consciences, abjured all such adventures. They were content merely to melt down and remodel the truth ingots of the scientists, and to build them together upon the high, the ever-unfinished tower of the golden temple. Some were so in love with particularity that they ignored the universal, others so impressed by the unity of all things that they overlooked discreteness. Yet doubtless by exchange of findings and by mutual devastation they were year by year approaching, corporately, irresistibly, but asymptotically, toward a central truth; which lay ever at hand, yet infinitely remote, because eternally beyond the comprehension of half-human minds. For, like their fellows, the philosophers of the species had a blind spot in the centre of the mind's vision, so that what they looked at directly they could never see. Like archaeologists who lovingly study and classify the script of a forgotten language but have found no key to its meaning, the philosophers were wise chiefly in knowing that whoever claims to interpret the rigmarole of half-human experience is either a fool or a charlatan.

There were the artists, despisers of the mere analytical intelligence. What hope lay with them? Microcosmic creators, for whom love and hate and life itself were but the matter of art, in their view the whole meaning of human existence seemed to lie solely in the apprehension of forms intrinsically 'significant', and in the embodiment of visions without irrelevance. Athletes of the spirit, by the very intensity of their single aesthetic achievement they were prone to cut themselves off from the still-living, though desperately imperilled world.

There were others, artists and half-artists, who were leaders of thought in Paul's day, publicists, novelists, playwrights, even poets. Some still preached the Utopia of individuals, the private man's heaven on earth, ignorant that this ideal had lost its spell, that it must be sought not as an end but as a means, that it must borrow fervour from some deeper fire. Some affirmed, pontifically or with the licence of a jester, that all human endeavour expresses unwittingly the urge of some cryptic, evolving, deity, which tries out this and that organic form, this and that human purpose, in pursuit of an end hidden even from itself. Some, ridiculing all superstition, declared existence to be nothing but electrons, protons, ethereal undulations, and superstitiously asserted that cognizance, passion and will are identical with certain electrical disturbances in nerve fibres or muscles. Some, zestfully proclaiming the futility of the cosmos and the impotence of man, cherished their own calm or heroic emotions, and deployed their cloak of fortitude and flowing rhetoric, mannequins even on the steps of the scaffold. Some, whose sole care was to avoid the taunt of credulity, and the taunt of emotionalism, fastidiously, elegantly, shook off from their fingers the dust of belief, the uncleanness of enthusiasm. Some, because reason (jockeyed and overpressed by so many riders) had failed to take her fences, condemned her as a jade fit only for the knackers; and led out in her stead a dark horse, a gift horse whose mouth must not be inspected, a wooden horse, bellyful of trouble. Some, gleefully discovering that the hated righteousness of their fathers drew its fervour from disreputable and unacknowledged cravings, preached therefore that primeval lusts alone directed all human activities. Some, because their puritan mothers dared not receive the revelation of the senses, themselves wallowed in the sacred wine till their minds drowned. Some were so tangled in the love of mother, and the discord of mother and mate, that they received from woman not nourishment, not strength, but a sweet and torturing poison, without which they could not live, by which their minds were corroded. Some, exquisitely discriminating the myriad flavours and perfumes of experience, cared only to refine the palate to the precision of a wine-taster; but registered all their subtle apprehensions with a desolate or with a defiant conviction of futility, a sense of some huge omission in the nature of things or in man's percipience. Some cognized their modern world but as flotsam gyrating on the cosmical flux, a film or ordure in which men and women swam spluttering, among disintegrated cigarette-ends, clattering cans, banana skins, toffee papers, and other disused sheathings. For them filth was the more excruciating by reason of their intuitions of purity violated, of austerity desecrated. Others there were, no less excruciated, who nevertheless by natatory prowess reached the mud-flats of old doctrine, where at last they thankfully reclined, 'wrapped in the old miasmal mist', and surrounded by the rising tide.

What was the upshot of Paul's whole exploration? For me there issued in my own mind the pure, the delighted cognizance, both of Paul's world and of Paul himself, the appraising organ that I had chosen. For Paul the upshot was a sense of horror and of exaltation, a sense that he was participating in a torrent of momentous happenings whose final issue he could but vaguely guess, but whose immediate direction was toward ruin.

He saw clearly that man, the most successful of all Terrestrial animals, who had mastered all rivals and taken the whole planet as his hunting-ground, could not master himself, could not even decide what to do with himself. All over the West man was visibly in decline. The great wave of European energy, which gave him mastery over nature, which carried the European peoples into every continent, which lent them for a while unprecedented intellectual vision and moral sensitivity, now visibly failed. And what had come of it? The Black Country and its counterpart in all Western lands, mechanized life, rival imperialisms, aerial bombardment, poison gas; for the mind, a deep and deadly self-disgust, a numbing and unacknowledged shame, a sense of huge opportunities missed, of a unique trust betrayed, and therewith a vast resentment against earlier generations, against human nature, against fate, against the universe. What more? An attempt to cover up guilt and futility by mechanical triumphs, business hustle, and the sound of a hundred million gramophones and radio-sets.

Paul asked himself, 'How has all this happened?' And he answered, 'Because we cannot look into our minds and see what really affords lasting satisfaction, and what is merely reputed to do so; because our individuality is a dimensionless point, because our personalities are but masks with nothing behind them. But in the East, where they say man is less superficial, what is happening? There, presumably, men have seen truths which the West has missed. But they stared at their truths till they fell into a hypnotic trance which lasted for centuries. They made it an excuse for shunning the world and all its claims, for gratifying themselves in private beatitude. And now, when at the hands of the West the world is forced on them irresistibly, they fall into the very same errors that they condemn in us. And the Russians? Socially they are the hope of the world. But have they as individual beings any more reality, any more percipience, than the rest of us?'

Over this despair, this disgust of human futility, Paul triumphed by taking both a longer and a wider view.

'We shall win through,' he told himself. 'We must. Little by little, year by year, aeon by aeon, and in spite of long dark ages, man will master himself, will gain deeper insight, will make a better world. And if not man, then surely some other will in the end fulfil his office as the cosmical eye and heart and hand. If in our little moment he is in regression, what matter? The great music must not always be triumphant music. There are other songs beside the songs of victory. And all songs must find their singers.'

Shortly after the final meditation in which he summed up the whole issue of his inquiry, Paul wrote a poem in which he made it clear to himself, though with a certain bitterness, that he cared more for the music which is spirit than for the human or any other instrument. In the final couplet there appears the self-conscious disillusionment which is characteristic of your age.

> If man encounter
> on his proud adventure
> other intelligence?

If mind more able,
ranging among the galaxies,
noose this colt and break him
to be a beast of draught and burden
for ends beyond him?
If man's aim and his passion be ludicrous,
and the flight of Pegasus
but a mulish caper?

Dobbin! Pull your weight!
Better be the donkey of the Lord,
whacked on beauty's errand,
than the wild ass of the desert
without destination.

Vision! From star to star the human donkey
transports God's old street organ and his monkey.

4. PAUL SETTLES DOWN

Paul had by now almost fulfilled the task that I had demanded of
him. Not only had he collected for me an immense store of facts
about the crisis of his species, facts the significance of which he
himself often entirely failed to see, but also in his own experience
he had already afforded me a very precise insight into the capacity of
his kind. He had shown me, through years of inner turmoil, the
aspirations and reluctances of a primitive being haunted by
visions from a higher sphere. In particular he had shown me the
limits of your intelligence and of your will. There were innumerable
problems which Paul even with my patient help could never
understand. There were austerities of beauty which even with my
most earnest illumination he could not admire. But one test at least
Paul had triumphantly passed. He had shown that it was possible
for the average mentality of the First Men, under careful tuition, to
apprehend without any doubt whatever the two supreme and
seemingly discordant offices of the individual mind, namely,
loyalty to man and worship of fate. To the Last Men these offices
are displayed as organic to one another; but to the First Men, they
are for ever discrepant. Paul's intellect at least saw this discrepancy,

241

and refused to be put off with false solutions of the problem. For the rest, though he so clearly recognized that all human purposes should be subordinated to these two supreme ends, he himself, like the rest of his kind, was but a frail vessel.

Since I had no further use for Paul as a visual and auditory instrument through which to examine your world, I now ceased to trouble him with the insatiable lust of inquiry which had mastered him since the conclusion of the war. Hitherto he had pursued his task indefatigably, but now his energy began to flag. This was due partly to the withdrawal of my stimulation, partly to the fact that his uncapacious brain was already charged to the full and could bear no more, partly also to the long physical strain of the double life which he had led. For Paul had indeed been wearing himself out. Katherine, with whom he still spent an occasional week, had declared that he was withering before his time, that his arms and legs were sticks and his ribs an old rat-trap. Privately she had noted also that his embraces had lost their vigour. She had urged him to 'take things easy for a while'. And now at last he discovered that he had in fact neither the energy nor the inclination to pursue the old racketing way of life.

I made it clear to him that I required no more work of him, but that I should continue to be with him to observe the movements of his mind during his normal career. For, though I had no further use for him as an exploratory instrument, it was my intention to watch the way in which his Neptunian tincture would influence him in middle age and senility. At this juncture Paul displayed rather interestingly the weakness of his kind by futile rebellion, and an attempt to pursue a heroic career for which he was unsuited. I must not dwell upon this incident, but it may be briefly recorded for the light which it throws upon your nature. He had already, it will be remembered, become convinced that his race was heading for a huge disaster, from which nothing could save it but an impossible change of heart, of native capacity. In spite of the current 'world-economic crisis', he had no serious expectation of a sudden catastrophe; but he had come to believe in a long-drawn-out spiritual decline, masked by a revival of material prosperity. He looked forward to centuries, perhaps millennia, of stagnation, in which the half-awakened mind of man would have sunk back once more into stupor. But he saw this phase as but a momentary episode in the life of the planet. And he saw the little huge tragedy of the modern world as, after all, acceptable, a feature of cosmical beauty. He knew, moreover, not clearly but yet with conviction, that he himself had played some small part in apprehending the drama of his age for the cognizance of the mature and final human mind. He knew also that without my continuous support he had no outstanding ability. Yet, though fundamentally he had accepted all this, and was indeed profoundly at peace, he could not express this acceptance and this peace in conduct. He could not bring himself to participate in the tragedy without making efforts to avert it, efforts which he knew must be futile, because in the first place he himself was not made of the stuff of prophets, and because in the second place the nature of his species was inadequate. Though he knew it was so, an irrational fury of partisanship now seized him. Instead of continuing the work which he could do tolerably well, instead of striving by his school-teaching to elicit in certain young minds an enhanced percipience and delight, he must needs take it upon himself to become the prophet of a new social and spiritual order.

It is no part of my purpose to tell in detail how Paul, after earnestly seeking excuses for a project which he knew to be ridiculous, gave up his post in the school; how he devoted himself to writing and speaking, in fact to preaching the new truth that he supposed himself to possess; how he tried to gather round him a group of collaborators, whom secretly he regarded as disciples; how he made contact once more with his old acquaintance the author of *Last and First Men*, hailed that timid and comfort-loving creature as a fellow-prophet, and was hastily dismissed for a lunatic; how, subsequently, his literary products proved even to himself their inability to find their way into print, and his efforts at vocal prophecy earned him the reputation of a crank and a bore; how he tried to persuade the Communists that he knew their mind better than they did themselves; how he was expelled from the Communist Party as an incorrigible bourgeois; how the communistically inclined editor of a well-known literary journal, who at first hoped to bring Paul within his own circle, was soon very thankful to get rid of him; how after several disorderly scenes in

243

Hyde Park, Paul was eventually marched off by the police, from whose care he finally escaped only to take up his abode in the Lunatic Asylum near his suburban home; how after some months of enforced meditation he was at last released, thoroughly cured of his disease; how, finally, but not until many far-reaching wires had been pulled in his interest, he was re-established in his old school. These facts I record chiefly so that I may also record another. Throughout this fantastic phase of his life, Paul remained inwardly the calm, the compassionately amused spectator of his own madness.

Of his subsequent career I need only say that within a year he had settled himself firmly into harness once more, with the determination never again to see the inside of a lunatic asylum. He became indeed an admirable schoolmaster of the more advanced and sympathetic type, bent upon reform, but cautious. In consequence of my influence during his youth he was now able to earn a reputation for daring ideas, yet also for patience, tact and extreme conscientiousness. In due season he married, begat children, became a head master, and introduced far-reaching novelties into his school, in respect of curriculum, teaching methods, and dress. From the point of view of readers of this book, the tense of this last sentence should have been future, for up to the date of publication, Paul remains a bachelor. Nevertheless I have already observed his future career, and can report that, when the time comes for him to retire, he will look back on his work with thankfulness and modest pride; that, having earlier determined to commit suicide soon after his retirement, he will change his mind and allow himself a year or two to re-assess his life and his world in the mellow light of a peaceful old age; that during this period he will afford me much further knowledge of the senescent phase of your individuality, with its strange blend of wisdom and puerility, its increased potentiality of insight, progressively thwarted by neural decay; that when there is no further reason for him to remain alive, Paul will no longer have the resolution to kill himself, and will be trapped in the quagmire of senility.

IX *On Earth and on Neptune*

1. SUBMERGED SUPERMEN

I HAVE been describing a situation in which, had the intelligence and the integrity of average men and women been slightly more robust, your world might have passed almost at a leap from chaos to organization, from incipient dissolution to a new order of vitality. Many minds were clearly aware that they were puppets in a huge and tragic farce, though none were able to put an end to it. I have now to tell of a different and much less imposing pattern of events, which was enacted in your midst without revealing its significance to any man. In this case disaster was brought about, not by any lack of native intelligence or of native integrity, but by the action of a savage environment on minds too gifted for your world.

While our observers were watching the forlorn efforts of your species to cope with problems beyond its powers, they detected also in many regions of your planet the promise of a new and more human species. The tragic fate of these more brilliant beings is amongst the most remarkable incidents in the whole history of Man. Here it is impossible to do more than outline this amazing story.

Throughout the career of your species, biological forces have now and then thrown up individuals in whom there was some promise of a higher type. Nearly always this promise was frustrated simply by the physiological instability of the new mutation. The new brain forms were associated either with actual distortions of body, or at best with normal structures which were inadequate to bear the novel strain. During the great ferment of industrial revolution in Europe and America, these biological mutations became much more numerous. Thus was afforded a serious possibility of the emergence somewhere or other of a type which should combine superior mentality with a physique capable of supporting the new cerebral organs.

245

When the earliest phase of industrialism was passed and conditions had improved somewhat, it became less difficult for abnormal beings to preserve themselves. The growth of humanitarianism, moreover, tended to foster these crippled supernormals along with the subnormals for whom they were invariably mistaken. Toward the end of the Nineteenth and the beginning of the Twentieth Centuries, we found here and there in the cities and industrial areas of the Western World, and later in industrial Asia, many hundreds of these individuals. They were of diverse biological constitution, but similar in respect of the factors which, with good fortune, should produce supernormal intelligence and supernormal integrity. Many of them, however, were tormented by gross bodily malformation; some, though more or less like their fellows in general anatomy, were no less hampered by biochemical maladjustments; some, though otherwise normal, were crippled by excessive weight of brain. But a few, sprung from stock of exceptionally tough fibre and ample proportions, were able to support and nourish their not excessively large heads without undue strain, at least in favourable conditions.

Now it might have been expected that these individuals, potentially far more brilliant than the most gifted of the normal kind, would have risen very rapidly to positions of power; and that, at the same time, they would have successfully established their type by propagation. Within a few generations, surely, they would have completely dominated the earlier and inferior species. But this was not to be. Even among the very small minority who combined mental superiority with bodily health, circumstance was fatally and ironically hostile. With regard to propagation, to take the simpler matter first, most of these superior beings, even those who were healthy and sexually potent, were strongly repellent to normal members of the opposite sex. They did not conform to any recognized pattern of sexual beauty. They were neither of the classical nor of the negroid nor of the mongolian styles, which alone were favoured by the 'cinema'. Indeed they were definitely grotesque. Their heads, in most cases, looked too big for their bodies, and they were apt to have bull necks. In many of them, moreover, there was a disturbing uncouthness of facial expression, which to the normal eye seemed sometimes insane, sometimes infantile, sometimes diabolic. Consequently it was almost impossible for them to find mates.

More interesting to our observers was the failure of these potentially superior beings to assert themselves in a world of inferiors. Though they were biologically very diverse, springing in fact from entirely independent mutations, these beings were alike in one respect, namely their very prolonged childhood and adolescence. The new and more complex brain organization could not develop successfully unless it was associated with an abnormally slow rate of growth. Therefore such of these beings as were able to survive were always 'backward' not only in appearance, but in some respects, mentally also. Thus a boy of ten years would look like a child of six; and mentally, though in some respects already more developed than his parents, he would seem to them to be hopelessly incompetent. Judged by similar standards, the normal human child would appear hopelessly backward in comparison with the baby ape, although in reality he would be far more intelligent and promising. Similarly, these superior children were invariably considered by their parents and guardians as distressingly inferior.

This backwardness of the new individual was due, not solely to the slowness of physiological growth, but also to the fact that with more delicate percipience he found in the experiences of childhood far more to delight and intrigue him than the normal child could gather. These beings remained so long in the phase of perceptual and motor experimentation, and later so long in the phase of play, partly because for them these fields were so crowded with interest. Similarly, when at length they attained adolescence, the dawn of self-consciousness and other-consciousness was for them so brilliant and overwhelming that they had inevitably to take many years to adjust themselves to it.

So great was this seeming backwardness that they were often regarded by their elders, and by their own generation also, not merely as inferior, but as seriously deficient. Often they were actually treated as insane. Thus in spite of their superiority they grew up with a devastating sense of their own incapacity, which increased as they became increasingly aware of the difference between themselves and others. This illusion of inferiority was aggravated by their slow sexual development; for at twenty they were sexually equivalent to a normal child of thirteen. But, it may be asked, if these beings were really so brilliant, how could they be so deceived about themselves? The answer is given partly by their serious physiological backwardness, but partly also by the overwhelming prestige of the inferior culture into which they were born. At thirty they had still the immaturity of the normal youth of eighteen; and finding a fundamental discrepancy between their own way of thinking and the thought of the whole world, they were forced to conclude that the world was right. It must be remembered, moreover, that they were isolated individuals, that no one of them would be likely ever to come across another of his kind. Further, owing to the precarious balance of their vital economy, they were all short-lived. Hardly any survived beyond forty-five, the age at which they should have been upon the brink of mental maturity.

One characteristic of their childhood was, as I said, a seeming backwardness of interest, which was taken to be a symptom of mental limitation. Now with the passage of years this limitation seemed to become more pronounced. At an age when the normal young man would be dominated by the will to make his mark in the world by eclipsing his fellows, these strange beings seemed quite incapable of 'taking themselves seriously'. At school and college they could never be induced to apply themselves resolutely to matters which concerned only private advancement. While admitting that for the community's sake it was necessary that individuals should 'look after themselves', so as not to be a burden, they could never be made to see the importance of personal triumph over others in the great game of life, the great gladiatorial display of personal prowess, which was ever the main preoccupation of the First Men. Consequently they could never conjure up the necessary forcefulness, the relentlessness, the singleminded pushfulness which alone can advance a man. Their minds, it seemed, were so limited that they could not form a really effective sentiment of self-regard.

There were other respects in which the interest of these beings seemed to be pitiably limited. Even those few who enjoyed physical health and delighted in bodily activity, could never be persuaded to concentrate their attention earnestly upon athletics, still less to give up all their leisure to the pursuit of the ball. To the football-playing and football-watching population these lonely beings seemed almost criminally lax. Further, while enjoying occasionally the spectacle of a horse race, they could raise no interest whatever in betting. Blood sports they heartily loathed, yet without hate of those who practised them; for they had no blood lust secretly at work within themselves. They seemed also to be incapable of appreciating military glory and national prestige. Though in some ways extremely social, they could not pin their loyalty to one particular group rather than another. Moral sensitivity, too, seemed either absent or so distorted as to be unrecognizable. Not only did they break the sabbath without shame, even in districts where sabbatarianism was unquestioned, but also in respect of sex they were a source of grave offence; for they seemed wholly incapable of feeling that sex was unclean. Both in word and act they were shameless. Nothing but their sexual unattractiveness restricted their licentious tendencies. Persuasion was entirely ineffective, calling from them only a spate of arguments which, though of course fantastic, were very difficult to refute. Compulsion alone could restrain them; but unfortunately, though these beings were so lacking in self-pride and personal rivalry, any attempt to prevent them from behaving as seemed good to them was apt to call forth a fanatical resistance, in pursuance of which they would readily suffer even the extremes of agony without flinching. This capacity for diabolic heroism was almost the only character that earned them any respect from their fellows; but since it was generally used in service of ends which their neighbours could not appreciate, respect was outweighed by ridicule or indignation. Only when this heroism was exercised to succour some suffering fellow-mortal could the normal mind fully appreciate it. Sometimes they would perform acts of superb gallantry to rescue people from fire, from drowning, from maltreatment. But on another occasion the very individual who had formerly gone to almost certain death to rescue a fellow-citizen or a child, might refuse even a slight risk when some popular or important personage was in danger. The former hero would scoff at all appeals, merely remarking that he was worth more than the other, and must not risk his life for an inferior being.

249

Though capable of earnest devotion, these god-forsaken creatures were thought to be too deficient to appreciate religion. In church they showed no more percipience than a cat or dog. Attempts by parents and guardians to make them feel the fundamental religious truths merely puzzled or bored them. Yet Neptunian observers, stationed in these sorely perplexed but sensitive young minds, found them often violently disturbed and exalted by the two fundamental religious experiences, namely by militant love of all living things and by the calm fervour of resignation. Far more than the normal species, and in spite of their own racked bodies, they were able to relish the spectacle of human existence.

Most of them, both male and female, showed a very lively curiosity, which in one or two cases was successfully directed towards a scientific training. Generally, however, they made no headway at all in science, because at the outset of their studies they could not see the validity of the assumptions and method of the sciences. One or two of them did, indeed, have the enterprise to go through with their training, acquiring with remarkable ease an immense mass of facts, arguments and theories. But they proved incapable of making use of their knowledge. They seemed to regard all their scientific work as a game that had little to do with reality, a rather childish game of skill in which the arbitrary rules failed to develop the true spirit of the game with rigorous consistency. Moreover, the further they explored the corpus of any science, the more frivolously they regarded it, being apparently unable to appreciate the subtleties of specialized technique and theory. Not only in science, but in all intellectual spheres, they were, in fact, constantly hampered by a lucidity of insight which seemed to the normal mind merely obtuseness. In philosophy, for instance, whither their natural curiosity often led them, they could not make head or tail even of principles agreed upon or unconsciously assumed by all schools alike. Their teachers were invariably forced to condemn them as entirely without metaphysical sense; save in one respect, for it was often noticed that they were capable of remarkable insight into the errors of theories with which their teachers themselves disagreed. The truth was that at the base of every intellectual edifice these beings found assumptions which they could not accept, or in which they could find no clear meaning; while throughout the structure they encountered arguments in which they could not see a logical connexion.

There was one sphere in which several of these beings did earnestly try to make themselves felt, namely in politics and social improvement. But here they were even more ineffective than elsewhere. They could never see the importance of the accepted political aims or the validity of the recognized party maxims. When politicians demonstrated the inevitable results of this policy or that, these unhappy misfits could only deplore their own stupidity in not being able to follow the argument. When they themselves confessed how they would deal with some problem or other, they were either cursed for their lack of true feeling or derided for their childish idealism. In either case they were charged with being ignorant of human nature; and this charge was, in a manner, just, for they had seldom any conception of the gulf between themselves and the members of the older species.

I have been speaking of those few who were educated so far as to be able to take thought for matters of theoretical interest or public concern. But the great majority never attained this level. Those who were born into comfortable circumstances generally came into conflict with the taboos of their society, and were ostracized; so that they sank into the underworld. Those also who were born into poor families were frequently outlawed by their fellows; and being entirely unfit to make their way in the huge dog-fight of industrialism, they nearly always subsided into the humblest occupations. They became dock-labourers, charwomen, agricultural labourers, clerks of the lowest order, very small shop-keepers, and especially vagrants. It was remarkable that they received on the whole more sympathy and understanding in the lower than in the higher reaches of society. This was because in the simpler, less sophisticated, manner of life their native intelligence and integrity did not come into obvious conflict with the proud but crude culture of more 'educated' folk. Indeed, those whose lot fell among the 'lower' classes of society were generally treated by their peers with a strange blend of contempt and respect. Though they were regarded as ineffective cranks or freaks, as children whose development had somehow been arrested, as 'daft', 'fey', 'mental', they were also credited with an odd kind of impracticable wisdom that was too good for this world. Not only so, but even in practical matters their advice was often sought; for they seemed to combine a divine innocence and self-disregard with a shrewdness, a cunning, which, though it was never used for self-advancement, struck the normal mind as diabolic.

The kind of life into which these abortive supermen gravitated most frequently was a life of wandering and contemplation. Often they became tramps, drifting from one big town to another, trekking through agricultural districts, tinkering, sharpening scissors, mending crockery, poaching, stealing, breaking stones, harvesting. A few became postmen, others drivers of motor vans or buses; but though, whatever their occupations, they worked with incredible efficiency, seldom could they remain for long in posts which entailed subordination to members of the normal species. The women were more unfortunate than the men, for vagrancy was less easily practised by women. Some became seam-stresses. A few, protected by sexual unattractiveness, faced the difficulties and dangers of the road. Others, blessed with more or less normal looks, chose prostitution as the least repugnant way of earning a livelihood.

Our observers, whenever they studied these unfulfilled approximations to a new species, found invariably a mental pattern definitely far superior to the normal, but also one which was much less developed than that of the Second Men, whose career was destined to begin some ten million years after your day. These superior contemporaries of yours had indeed, for beings whose heads were not much larger than your own, remarkable intelligence. They were remarkable also in respect of the organization and unity of their minds. Where the normal personality, torn by conflicts of desire and loyalty, would split into two or more incomplete systems imperfectly related to one another, these preserved their integrity, and chose that action which did in fact offer the greatest good possible in the circumstances. They were almost entirely without selfishness, for they had a capacity for self-insight definitely more penetrating than that of the normal species. Like the Second Men, they had also an innate interest in the higher mental activities, a craving for intellectual exercise and aesthetic delight no less imperious than the simple needs for food and drink. But unfortunately, since they were isolated individuals overwhelmed in childhood by a world of inferior calibre, they were unable to satisfy these cravings wholesomely. They were like potential athletes trained from birth to use certain muscles in grotesque and cramping actions, and the rest of their bodies not at all. Thus they never developed their powers, and were haunted by a sense of falsity and futility in all their mental life. They were beings, moreover, in whom we found a vigorous and lucid innate loyalty toward the supreme adventure of the awakening spirit in man, and in the cosmos. They were very ready to regard themselves and others as vessels, instruments of a great corporate endeavour. But, unfortunately, in their terrible spiritual isolation from their neighbours, they could never whole-heartedly give themselves to the communal life. In spite of the contempt with which they were treated, in spite of their own confusion of mind, those of them who survived beyond the age of twenty-five or thirty could not but observe that the minds of their fellow-men were woven upon a different pattern from their own, a pattern at once cruder and more confused, less intricate yet more discrepant. Moreover, they soon found reason to suspect that they themselves alone had the cause of the spirit at heart, and that the rest of the world was frivolous. Each of them was like an isolated human child brought up by apes in the jungle. When at last he had begun to realize the gulf between himself and others, he realized also that he had been damaged past repair by his simian upbringing. In these circumstances he would, as a rule, content himself with a life of personal kindliness and humour, which was ever rooted in the strength of his own unshakable ecstasy of contemplation.

2. PAUL AND HUMPTY

It so happened that one of these rare beings was sent by his parents to the school where Paul was head master. In appearance he was a great lout rather like a grotesque child of eight seen through a magnifying-glass. His thick neck and immense, almost bald head, was very repulsive to the normal eye. Only the hinder part of his head bore hair, which was sparse, wiry, and in colour like grey sand. The bare and lumpy dome of his cranium overhung two pale brown eyes, so large that they seemed to occupy the whole middle region of his face. Beneath an inconspicuous nose was a huge and clear-cut mouth. So small was the lower jaw that the chin, though well moulded, seemed but another nose under the great lips. The head was held erect in the attitude of one supporting a pitcher on his crown. This carriage gave to the face a farcical dignity which the alert and cautious eyes rendered at times malignant. The thick-set body and great restless hands made women shudder.

No wonder that this unfortunate child, who received the nick-name Humpty, was persecuted by his schoolfellows. In class his laziness was relieved now and then by fits of activity, and by un-couth remarks which roused derision among the boys, but which to Paul were sometimes very disturbing. The form master at first reported that Humpty was stupid and incorrigibly indolent; but later it appeared that he was perpetually active either in remote meditations or in observing and criticizing everything save the work in hand. Puzzled by the lad's seeming alternation between stupidity and brilliance, Paul contrived to give the whole class a series of intelligence tests. Humpty's performance defeated analysis. Some of the simplest tests floored him, yet some of those intended for 'superior adults' he solved without hesitation. Inquiring into the failures in the low-grade tests, Paul found that they were always due to some subtle ambiguity in the problem. The psychologists were not intelligent enough to test this unique boy.

Paul tried to win Humpty's confidence. He took him out to tea, and walked with him occasionally at week-ends. Paul had long been in the habit of taking parties of boys into the country and on the river, and in the summer he organized camping holidays and trips on the Continent. At first he had hoped to fit Humpty into this communal activity, but very soon he realized that nothing could be done with the strange creature in the presence of his contemporaries. He therefore devoted some time to treating the boy separately. Humpty was at first hostile, then politely reticent. When he found that Paul (with my aid) realized the gulf that lay between him and his fellows, he became cautiously well-disposed.

Conversation was at first extremely difficult. Paul's old gift of adopting a *persona* suited to his companions was now invaluable, but failed to produce the sudden and easy intimacy which he desired. The trouble was that Humpty did not belong to any known type. It was impossible to get in touch with him on the assumption that he was a normal adolescent; yet in spite of his infantile traits he could not be successfully treated as a child, for in some ways his interests were already those of an adult. On the other hand, Paul's well-tried policy of speaking to his boys 'as man to man' was in this case unsuccessful, because Humpty seemed to be without the normal craving to be a member of the adult fraternity. With patience, however, and with a sense that he was exploring a mentality more remote than anything he had discovered in earlier adventures. Paul plotted out some of the main landmarks of Humpty's nature. Gradually an important principle emerged in this study. In so far as Humpty was infantile, his attention was arrested by aspects of infantile experience which the normal child would miss. Sometimes, for instance, before a swim he would lie naked on the bank twiddling his toes for a solid quarter of an hour, like a baby in its cot, untouched by Paul's bright talk, or his suggestions that it was time to take the plunge. This conduct filled Paul with despair, till he discovered that what fascinated the boy was the difference between his control of his toes and his control of his fingers. Moreover, Paul had reason to suspect that there was some other more recondite aspect of the situation, which either could not be expressed in the English language, or was too subtle for Paul's apprehension.

When Paul first made the acquaintance of Humpty, he found the boy in a state of morbid diffidence punctuated now and then by flashes of contempt for his fellows. But under the influence of Paul's sympathy and insight Humpty began to realize that he was not, after all, merely an inferior being. As his mind developed, and as he came to understand that he was made on a different pattern from his fellows, it was borne in on him that in many ways he was superior, that he was basically more intelligent, more capable of coherent behaviour, less beset by atavistic impulses, and above all that there were certain aspects of his experience (in some cases

255

the most delectable) to which none but the most sensitive of his
fellow human beings had any access whatever.

A year after his first contact with Humpty, Paul began to feel
that the tables had been turned, that he who had formerly played
the part of the superior was being forced step by step to yield
precedence. The change began one day when Paul had been trying
to rouse Humpty to work harder at school by appealing to his
competitive self-regard. When the sermon was over, the boy
looked at him with a wonder tinged with dismay. Then he gave
out a single bark of laughter, and said, 'But why on earth should I
want to beat Johnson Minor and the rest?' This was not a
very remarkable question, but coming from Humpty it seemed
to have a peculiar significance. And Paul felt that somehow
in his error of tactics he had displayed a gross vulgarity of
feeling.

Somewhat later Paul discovered with dismay that he had been
quite seriously asking Humpty's advice about certain matters of
school policy. It was his custom to ask his boys for advice, so as
to give them a sense of responsibility; but this time he was per-
turbed to find that he actually wanted the advice, and intended to
use it. By now Humpty had sized up the mentality of his fellow-
mortals very shrewdly; and in spheres of which he had experience,
such as the school, he displayed a cold and often a cynical
intelligence.

After another year had passed, the indolent Humpty surprised
Paul by settling down to work, and making up for lost ground
so successfully that he soon became the school's most brilliant,
but most difficult, pupil. He gave his teachers the impression that
in all his work he was but playing a game, or that he was learning
the mental tricks of the human race without believing in them or
approving of them. It was impossible to avoid thinking of him
as a naturalist in the jungle studying the mentality of apes. After
six months his fame as a prodigy of scholarship had spread over
the whole country. This change in Humpty gratified Paul, but
there was another change which was both incomprehensible and
distressing. Hitherto he had seemed to Paul to be dangerously
lacking in self-regard. Amongst the boys his generosity over toys,
sweets and money had caused him to be mercilessly plundered,

while in his work it was inveterate carelessness of self (so Paul thought) that had made him so ineffective. But now, along with his fever of work he developed a propensity for sacrificing the pleasure or well-being of others to his own interests. In most respects he retained his normal and unselfish nature though tinged with a contemptuousness that made him cast favours about him as one might fling refuse to the dogs; but in matters in which he felt a serious concern he was now a relentless self-seeker. It took Paul some months to discover the cause of this extraordinary change, and of the boy's increasing reticence and frigidity. At last, however, Humpty, during a walk on Leith Hill, announced that he would take his head master into his confidence, because he must have the help of some intelligent adult. Paul was then given a lengthy account of the boy's conclusions about himself, about the world which he had the misfortune to inhabit, and about his future. Paul had a sense that the tables had indeed been turned with a vengeance, and that the grotesque youth was treating him with the confident superiority with which normally a grown man condescends toward a child; while the head master himself involuntarily adopted the respectfulness of one of his own prefects receiving instructions. Yet according to all sane standards Humpty's plans were preposterous.

After careful psychological and biological inquiry, so Humpty said, he had discovered that he was profoundly different from the normal human being, and indeed very superior in mental calibre. Unfortunately his nature had been seriously distorted by his barbarous upbringing, 'Though', he added, 'you yourself have certainly treated me with sympathy, and with as much comprehension as can be expected of your kind. Indeed it is to you I owe it that I was not completely ruined during my adolescent phase.' Having made this contemptuous acknowledgement, the formidable boy declared that, in spite of Paul's care, he was probably by now too much damaged to win through in the enterprise which he must attempt. However, he would triumph or die fighting. Here Paul unwisely interrupted to say how glad he was that Humpty was at last determined to show his ability, and that undoubtedly he would make a mark in the world whatever career he chose. The boy stood still and faced his head master, gazing at him with a quizzing expression under which Paul found it hard to preserve his self-respect.

Presently Humpty remarked, with all the assurance and quietness of one who says he must buy cigarettes, or change his clothes, 'What I must do is to make a new world. I am not sure yet whether I shall have to destroy it and produce another.' Paul, with immense relief, burst into laughter. But the other said only, 'I thought you had more intelligence. In fact I know you have. Think! I mean what I say.' With dismay Paul realized that Humpty did mean what he said; and with bewilderment he realized further that something in his own mind applauded. However, he reminded himself that this would-be builder of worlds was merely an eccentric boy; and he set himself to persuade Humpty that he was making a fool of himself, that no single individual, no matter how superior, could achieve such a task. The boy replied, 'What you say is sound common sense, the kind of sense by which your species has hitherto triumphed. But an alien mentality such as mine can see very clearly that common sense is also your undoing, and that, as a species, you have neither the intelligence nor the virtue to save yourselves in your present plight. A superior mind may perhaps be able to discipline you, or to afford you a merciful extinction. With regard to myself, you are right that I shall almost certainly fail. Your world is not easy to move, or to destroy; and I have been terribly mutilated by early contact with an insensitive, a brutish, species. But I must make the attempt. And for a few years I shall need your help. Think the matter over for a few weeks, and you will see that I am right, and that unless you would betray your own highest ideals you must henceforth subordinate everything else to my service.'

Once more Paul earnestly protested against this folly; but to humour the lad he listened during the rest of the walk to his amazing plans. First, Humpty declared he would assimilate all the cultures of the human race. He was convinced that this would not take him long; for, having discovered his own superiority, he had also gained unique insight into the weakness and the limited but solid achievement of the best human minds. Having made himself the master of all man's wisdom, he would proceed to correct it by his own finer percipience and intelligence. Much that he would thus produce would be beyond the comprehension of his fellows, but he would publish simplified versions of all his work, based on his thorough knowledge of the inferior mentality. When this preliminary, easy, and purely theoretical, task was completed, he would set about the practical reform of the world. He was confident that by the time he had reached maturity, his superior tact and the unique power of his personality would enable him to deal with normal individuals much as a shepherd deals with his sheep; but he did not disguise from himself the fact that he would have to cope not only with sheep but with wolves, and that very grave difficulties would arise when the time came to break down the great atavistic organizations and vested interests of the world. This task, he admitted, would need all his skill, and would probably defeat him. Meanwhile, however, he would have taken steps to produce other individuals of superior type. Possibly, if his sexual development turned out normally, some of these would be his own offspring. Possibly he would have encountered other unique beings scattered up and down the world. Possibly he would be able to use his finer understanding of biology and physiology to produce superior men and women from normal ova. Anyhow, by one means or another, if the worst came to the worst, and the normal species proved incorrigible, he would found a small colony of supermen in some remote part of the world. This would become the germ of a new human species and a new world-order. Little by little it would gain control of the whole planet, and would either exterminate the inferior species, or more probably domesticate such members of the subhuman hordes as it required for its own uses.

At the close of this announcement of policy Humpty paused, then began again in a voice which betrayed an unexpected hesitation and distress. 'This programme,' he said, 'sounds to you fantastic, but it should be possible to one of my powers in a world of inferiors. I am no paragon. There should some day be minds incomparably finer than mine. Yet even I, if my health can stand the strain, should prove fit for the task, but for the severe mutilation which I have already received at the hands of your species. Till now I have never told you of my most serious trouble. I must bring myself to lay bare my secret, since you must help me to make myself whole for the work which I am to do.'

Humpty now told Paul that his sufferings during childhood had filled him with a violent hate of whatever passed as morality amongst his fellows. Things had come to such a pitch that, whenever any conduct seemed likely to earn general approval, he conceived an irresistible desire to take the opposite course. In his recent burst of hard work, for instance, public commendation had almost forced him to plunge back into indolence. Only by reminding himself that the real aim of his work was to destroy the so-called morality of the inferior species could he keep himself in hand. His increasing contempt for the well-being of others, though it found its excuse in his self-dedication to a great duty, drew its vigour from the sense that he was earning the condemnation of his fellows. There was also a more serious, or at least more dramatic, way in which his revulsion from the stink of moralism threatened to undo him. He was sometimes seized with an ungovernable, an insane, impulse to violate public decency in whatever manner would seem at the time most outrageous. He himself was sexually backward, but the awe and shame with which his elders regarded sex had in early days intimidated him; and when at last he came to realize the folly and abject superstitiousness of his countrymen in this matter, he conceived a violent craving to shock them.

Having forced himself to broach the subject, Humpty was carried away by his passion. He poured out on the bewildered head master a torrent of grotesque and mostly obscene fantasies ranging from schoolboy smut to acts of brutal sexual aggression. Of the most horrible of these gruesome titbits he said, after a hushed, almost it seemed a reverent, laugh, 'That ought to be done on the island in Piccadilly Circus, if you could catch the right woman there, one of those who look like princesses. But could I do it before they got at me?'

Paul felt with relief that leadership had once more come into his hands. He reasoned with the unhappy boy, and promised to help him. Subsequently he took Humpty to a psycho-analyst who had often dealt successfully with difficult cases in the school. But this time the expert was defeated. It was impossible to cure Humpty by bringing to life his unconscious cravings, for in this strange mind everything was fully conscious. Humpty knew himself through and through. Suggestion and hypnotism proved equally impossible. After a few meetings the analyst began to be ill at ease, for Humpty was taking a malicious pleasure in forcing him step by step to a most unflattering self-knowledge. Not only did the un-happy man begin to realize that his skill was mostly blind guess-work, and that his wisdom left out of account far more than it embraced, but also to his horror he discovered that he was dominated by secret desires and loyalties of a religious type which he had never had the courage to recognize. When Humpty appeared for the fifteenth meeting he was told that the analyst was missing. Later it turned out that the distracted man had suffered a religious conversion, and had fled away into solitude to meditate. Like so many of his profession, he was at bottom a simple soul; and when he found in himself needs that could be satisfied by religion but not by the doctrines of Freud, he could discover nothing better to do than to leap from the frying-pan of one orthodoxy into the fire of another. Within a few weeks he had joined a monastic order, and was studying the psychological principles of St Thomas.

The crippled mind of Humpty seemed now to go from bad to worse. The more clearly he realized the damage that had been inflicted on him in childhood, the more he succumbed to hatred, not of his fellow-men, but of their false righteousness.

In sane periods he told himself that his passion was fantastic; that when the mood was on him he lusted merely to violate and smash, and would harm what was precious no less than what was contemptible; that his obsession was ruining his mind, and making him unfit for his great task; that he must not let himself be dragged down to the level of the unhappy and unseeing beasts who surrounded him.

Paul, watching from day to day the desperate struggle of his protégé, was overawed by the sense of a momentous biological tragedy. For he could not but surmise that, if this lonely and potent being had not been mutilated, he might indeed have founded a new mankind. Humpty had already fallen into several minor scrapes, from which Paul had with difficulty extricated him. The head mas-ter now lived in dread of the final catastrophe which would ruin

Humpty and incidentally disgrace the school. But the school was, after all, spared the extreme disaster. One morning Paul received a letter in which Humpty declared that, realizing that he was defeated, and that at any moment he might do grievous harm to some innocent person, he had decided to die. It was his last wish that his body should be given to a certain world-famous neurologist for dissection. Inquiry proved that Humpty had indeed ceased to live, though the cause of his death was never determined. Needless to say, though he had always been the black sheep of his family, his parents secured for him a decent Christian burial.

Thus ended one of Nature's blundering attempts to improve upon her first, experimental, humanity. One other superior and much more fortunate individual was destined almost to succeed in the task that Humpty had merely imagined. Of this other, of the utopian colony which he founded, and of its destruction by a jealous world, I may tell on another occasion.

3. BACK TO NEPTUNE

My task is almost completed. My mind is stored with an immense treasure, which I have gathered, bee-like, in your world, and with which I must now return to the great and fair hive whence I came. The other side of my task also is drawing to a close. I have almost finished this my second message to my own remote ancestors, the First Men.

Very soon I shall be free to leave your world of sorrow and vain hope, of horror and of promise unfulfilled. Presently I shall return to an age long after the destruction of your planet, and not long before the more tragic destruction of my own more delectable world. Only with difficulty and danger can the explorer, after close work in the past, revert once more to his own world. With difficulty and reluctance also, I shall now begin to put off your mental pattern from my mind, as one may put off a mask. As the grown man who has been long with children, living in their games, grieving with them in their childish sorrows, is torn with regret when at last he must leave them, and half-persuades himself that their nature and their ways are better than his own, so I now with reluctance leave your world, with its childish, its so easily to be avoided yet utterly inescapable, its farcical and yet most tragic, disaster. But even as, when at last the grown man is once more at grips with the world of men, his childishness falls from him, so, when I earnestly revert in imagination to my own world, my assumed primitiveness falls from me.

It is time to recall myself to myself. I have been dwelling in your little world, not as one of you, but in order that I might bring to the racial mind of the Last Men matter for delighting cognizance; in order, also, that your world may find its crown of glory, not indeed in the way that was hoped, but in being exquisitely savoured, life by life, event by event, in the racial mind of the Last Men.

I recall myself to myself. The great world to which I am native has long ago outgrown the myths, the toys, the bogies of your infant world. There, one lives without the fear of death and pain, though there one dies and suffers. There, one knows no lust to triumph over other men, no fear of being enslaved. There one loves without craving to possess, worships without thought of salvation, contemplates without pride of spirit. There one is free as none in your world is free, yet obedient as none of you is obedient.

I recall myself to myself. The most lovely community of which I am a member, the most excellently fulfilled Spirit of Man, within which my mind is organic, must very soon be destroyed. The madness of the Sun is already hideously at work upon my world. There lies before my contemporaries an age of incalculable horror and disintegration. From that horror we must not escape by means of the racial suicide which alone could save us; for our two supreme acts of piety are not yet accomplished. We have not yet succeeded in impregnating the remote regions of this galaxy with the seed of a new mankind. We have not yet completed our devoted survey of the past. Therefore we may not yet put an end to ourselves. We must be loyal to the past and to the future.

I recall myself to myself. Presently I shall wake in my Arctic and subterranean garden. Once more I shall see with precision and with full colour through my own eyes, not through the obscuring organs of the First Men. I shall recognize the familiar forms of Neptunian leaves and flowers, swaying in the subterranean breeze. I shall feel the large easefulness of my own body. I shall yawn and stretch and rise. I shall swim luxuriously in my pool. I shall enter my apartment and ring for food. Then, before I see any of my colleagues, I shall begin to review my exploration; I shall record it, and critically edit it. For now at last I shall have recovered full Neptunian mentality. I shall see with new insight not only your world but my own self as I was during my long immersion in your world. Probably I shall smile at my recent earth-infected thoughts and feelings. I shall smile when I remember this book, this strange hybrid sprung from the intercourse of a purely Terrestrial mind and a Neptunian mind, earth-infected. I shall know that, even when I most strained the understanding of my poor collaborator, I was not really giving him the full wisdom of the Last Men, but something far less profound, something that was already earth-dimmed, already three-parts Terrestrial even at its source in my own mind.

With a great thankfulness I shall recognize my own complete reversion to lucidity. With a new awe and zest I shall lay myself open once more to the inflooding richness and subtlety of my well-loved world.

After many weeks of labour I shall have completed my report, and then I shall leave my apartment and meet many of my colleagues, to exchange findings with them.

But, since in the Catacombs telepathic intercourse may not occur, we shall soon travel south to live together for a while in a great crystal pylon where we may pursue our collaboration telepathically. And when we have made of our combined findings a single, living, apprehension of your species, we shall broadcast our great treasure telepathically over the whole world; so that all the million million minds of our fellows may be enriched by it, so that when the time comes for the next awakening of the single mind of the race, that great spirit also, which is not other than each of us fully awakened, may avail itself of our findings, for its meditation and ecstasy.

When all this is done I shall call up telepathically the ever dear companion of my holdiays, with whom, before my last exploration, I played and slept, where the broken mountain lies spread out into the sea. There once more we shall meet and play, watching the populations of the rock pools, and the risings and settings of the Mad Star. There once more we shall wander over the turfy hillocks and swim, seal-like, in the bay, and make for ourselves nests in the long grass, where we may lie together in the night. There perhaps I shall tell her how, in another world, seemingly in another universe, I myself, striving in the numb, the half-human flesh of Paul, lay with the half-human Katherine. There we shall contemplate the strange beauties of the past and of the dread future. There we shall savour lingeringly the present.

When our holiday is over I shall return with her to her place of work, where they prepare for the spreading of the seed. And when she has shown me how the task is progressing, I shall go wandering about the world for a very long time, absorbing its intricate beauty, watching its many and diverse operations, having intercourse with the great population of my intimate friends, playing my part in the life of my marriage group, visiting the Land of the Young, voyaging in ether-ships among the planets, wandering alone in the wild places of the home planet, idling or meditating in my garden or working among my fruit trees, or watching the most distant universes from some great observatory, or studying with the help of astronomers the slow but fatal progress of the sun's disease.

It may be that before it is time for me to go once more into the past, there will occur again a supreme awakening of the racial mind. It may be that after the unique day of the awakening I shall for a long time move about the world entranced like my fellows, rapt in the ineffable experiences of the single Spirit of Man, contemplating perhaps at last the supernal entities which it is man's chief glory to strive to worship. Sooner or later, however, I shall return once more to my work in the past, either to the First Men or to some other primitive species. I shall bring back with me more treasure of living history, and deliver it into the world of the Last Men. And again I shall play, and again I shall participate in the rich life of my world, and again I shall return to the past. And so on for I know not how many times.

But each time, when I leave the present for the past, there will have been a change in my world, a slight deterioration, sometimes perhaps imperceptible. The climate will have grown hotter and more unwholesome. The inescapable rays of the mad sun will have done more harm to eyes and brains. Society will perhaps no longer be perfect, rational conduct no longer invariable, telepathy perhaps already difficult; and very probably the racial mentality will have already become impossible. But also the exploration of the past will be advancing toward completion, though with increasing difficulty; and the dissemination of the seed of life will be at last begun.

The Last Men can look forward without dismay to the inevitable deterioration of all that they cherish most, to the death of their fair community, and to the extinction of the human spirit. We have only one desire, namely that our two tasks may be accomplished; and that happily they may be accomplished before our deterioration is so far advanced as to make us incapable of choosing to put an end to ourselves when at last we are free to do so. For the thought is somewhat repugnant to us that we should slowly sink into barbarism, into the sub-human, into blind and whimpering agony, that the last of Man should be a whine.

This may well happen, but even by such a prospect we are not seriously dismayed. If it does occur, it will doubtless seem intolerable to our degraded spirits. But today, we are fully possessed of ourselves. Even as individuals, even apart from the exaltation of racial mentality, we can accept with resignation, nay with a surprising fervour of appreciation, even the moral downfall of our world. For we have gone far. We have drunk deeply of beauty. And to the spirit that has drunk deeply of the grave beauty of the cosmos, even the ultimate horror is acceptable.

4. EPILOGUE BY THE TERRESTRIAL AUTHOR OF THIS BOOK

Readers of my earlier book, *Last and First Men*, may remember that it closed with an epilogue which my Neptunian controller claimed to have transmitted to me from a date in Neptunian history many thousands of years after the communication of the body of the book. The present book was obviously originated at a Neptunian date shortly after the transmission of the main part of the earlier book, but very long before its epilogue. Now I have reason to believe that at some date long after the communication of that former epilogue itself, my controller attempted to give me an epilogue to the present volume, but that owing to the serious disintegration of the most delicate brain tracts of the Last Men, and the gradual break-up of their world society, the result has been extremely confused and fragmentary.

I shall now attempt to piece together the random thoughts and passions, and occasional definite statements, which have come into my mind seemingly from my Neptunian controller. By supplementing them with a careful use of my own imagination, I shall try to construct a picture of the state of affairs on Neptune when the disaster was already far advanced.

From the vague flood of intimations that has come through to me I gather that the hope of disseminating a seed of life abroad among the stars, before the disaster should have extinguished man's powers, was not fulfilled. The dissemination had indeed actually been begun, when it was discovered that the vital seed was all the while being destroyed in the process of scattering. This trouble, and other unexpected difficulties, which occurred seemingly at some date after the communicating of the earlier epilogue, not merely delayed the enterprise, but even led to its abandonment for some thousands of years. Then some new discovery in psychophysics raised a hope of achieving the Dissemination by an entirely new method. A vast new enterprise was therefore set on foot; but was seriously hampered by the increasingly cruel climate, the steady deterioration of mental calibre, the ceaseless national wars and civil confusion. It would seem, though the inference is by no means certain, that at the date of this final and intermittent communication, the Dissemination had already ceased for ever; whether because it had been successfully accomplished or because it was no longer physically possible, or because the will to pursue it had already been broken, I cannot ascertain. Probably the work was now beyond the powers of a degenerate and disorganized world-community.

The other great task which the doomed population had undertaken to complete before its final downfall, the Exploration of the Human Past, seems to have been in a manner finished, though in less detail than was originally planned. Several communications suggest that such workers as remained able and willing to enter into the past were trying to concentrate their failing powers on certain critical points of Man's career, so as to reconstruct at least these moments in full minuteness. But as the racial mode of mentality had already become impossible, and as the individual explorers had evidently very seriously deteriorated, it seems clear that such data as were still being collected would never be incorporated in the single racial consciousness, in the aesthetic apprehension of the Cosmos by the fully awakened Spirit of Man. In fact the continuation of the work of exploring the past seems to have become as automatic and irrational as the aimless researches of some of our Terrestrial historians.

In the epilogue to the earlier book it was reported that, as the higher and more recent brain-tracts were corroded by the fury of ultra-violet solar radiation, the surviving members of the community suffered a harrowing struggle between their nobler and their baser natures, a struggle which issued inevitably in the defeat of all that was most excellent in them. At the date of the epilogue to the present book, the race seems to have been reduced to a remnant of distraught and almost sub-human beings clustering round the South Pole, which, one may suppose, was the only region of the planet still capable of supporting human existence at all. The life of this remnant must have been completely aimless and abject. It apparently consisted of half-hearted agriculture, occasional hunting expeditions against the wild creatures that had been driven south by the heat, and frequent predatory raids of neighbouring groups to capture one another's food and women.

The population was evidently obsessed by the terror of death, of starvation, and above all of insanity. The death-rate must have been very high, but there was also a huge birthrate. Conception was no longer controlled. Invalid children seem to have composed a large proportion of the population. Parenthood and sex evidently bulked very largely in the popular mind. There were wild sexual orgies, which apparently had acquired some religious significance; and there was a vast ritual of superstitious taboos, most of which seem to have been intended to purify the soul and prepare it for eternal life. Apparently some divinity, referred to as the God of Man, was expected to destroy the world by fire, but to snatch into eternal bliss those who had kept all the taboos. His Younger Brother, it seems, had already appeared on Neptune, but had been killed by his enemies. This legend should, perhaps, be connected in some way or other with the superior being who, in the epilogue to the previous book is referred to as 'this younger brother of ours'.

Not every one succumbed to these superstitions. My controller himself rejected them, and retained a pathetic loyalty to the ancient wisdom, some shreds of which he now and then remembered. But I have reason to believe that very often his memory of them was but a verbal formula, without insight.

Clearly, for those who, like my controller, had kept alive in themselves something of the former purpose of the race, there was now no longer any reason to refrain from racial suicide. The two enterprises for which euthanasia had been postponed could no longer be usefully continued. But the unhappy members of what had once been the noblest of all human communities had no longer the courage or the common sense to destroy themselves. Those who accepted the popular superstitions declared that the God had forbidden men to seek death before their time. Those who rejected the doctrine of salvation persuaded themselves that they refrained from suicide because to flee was cowardly.

At this point I will report a verbal fragment of communication which is typical of most that I have received, and seems to bear out many of the foregoing inferences.

'Vain to live. Yet Life insists. Work insists. Too many thousands of men, of women, of crawling children with eyes festering. Too little food. Blue sun piercing the deep cloud-zone, parching the fields. Child meat in the flesh pots. Eat the mad, who come to grief. The many mad. Mad men with knives. Mad women with smiles, with skull-faces. (And I remember beauty.) Too many labours and fears. Too hot. Hateful proximity of men hot. Love one another? With sweat between! Love best in the water, the cooling water, that makes the body lighter. The pools, the rains, the house-uprooting storms, the everlasting cloud, blinding purple. God will come soon, they say it. To burn the world, to take away his friends. The God-dream. Too good, too cheap. Radiation the one God, all pervading, cruel. To die quickly, to sleep and not wake! But life insists, work insists. Vain work insists. Yet why? The old far days, Godless, beautiful. The glorious world. The fair world of men and women and of the single awareness. Eye of the cosmos. Heart of the cosmos. Cunning hand. Then, we faced all things gaily. Even this corruption, when we foresaw it, we called "a fair end to the brief music that is man". This! The strings all awry, screaming out of tune, a fair end!'

This passage is typical, though more coherent than most. There are others more striking, but so repugnant to the taste of my contemporaries that I dare not repeat them, passages describing the prevailing brutishness of sexual relations in a population that had already so far degenerated that neither sex could interest the other save in the crudest manner. This impoverishment of sexual life was due to the fact that physical health and beauty had been undermined, that apprehension of the more delicate, aesthetic and spiritual aspects of experience had become almost impossible, that the realization of other individuals as living personalities was very uncommon. Nearly all behaviour was the impulsive behaviour of beasts, though of beasts in whose nature were incorporated many tricks derived from a forgotten humanity.

Some men and women there still were who had not permanently sunk to this brutish level. Several communications make it clear that, although the culture and the actual mental capacity of the Last Men were by now so degenerate, some few, a scattered and dwindling aristocracy, were still capable, at least intermittently, of personal love, and even of perplexed loyalty to certain ideals of conduct. The evidence for this lies in such passages as the following, which with its fleeting recovery of the earlier intelligence, and its bewildered groping after a forgotten ecstasy, affords perhaps the right conclusion to this book.

'She lies motionless in the shallow water. The waves, fingering the hot sand, recoil steaming. Her flesh, translucent formerly, now is filmed and grey, blind like her filmed eyes. We have taken of each other very deeply. The heat tricks us sometimes into intolerance each of the other's unyouthful body, unpliant mind; yet each is the other's needed air for breathing. We have ranged in our work very far apart, she into the astronomical spaces, I into the pre-historical times. But now we will remain together until the end. There is nothing more for us to do but to remember, to tolerate, to find strength together, to keep the spirit clear so long as may be.

The many aeons of man! The many million, million selves; ephemeridae, each to itself, the universe's one quick point, the crux of all cosmical endeavour. And all defeated! The single, the very seldom achieved, spirit! We two, now so confused, participated once in man's clearest elucidation. It is forgotten. It leaves only a darkness, deepened by blind recollection of past light. Soon, a greater darkness! Man, a moth sucked into a furnace, vanishes; and then the furnace also, since it is but a spark islanded in the wide, the everlasting darkness. If there is a meaning, it is no human meaning. Yet one thing in all this welter stands apart, unassailable, fair, the blind recollection of past light.'

A CATALOG OF SELECTED DOVER
BOOKS IN ALL FIELDS OF INTEREST

A CATALOG OF SELECTED
DOVER BOOKS
IN ALL FIELDS OF INTEREST

A CATALOG OF SELECTED DOVER
BOOKS IN ALL FIELDS OF INTEREST

100 BEST-LOVED POEMS, Edited by Philip Smith. "The Passionate Shepherd to His Love," "Shall I compare thee to a summer's day?" "Death, be not proud," "The Raven," "The Road Not Taken," plus works by Blake, Wordsworth, Byron, Shelley, Keats, many others. 96pp. 5³⁄₁₆ x 8¼.   0-486-28553-7

100 SMALL HOUSES OF THE THIRTIES, Brown-Blodgett Company. Exterior photographs and floor plans for 100 charming structures. Illustrations of models accompanied by descriptions of interiors, color schemes, closet space, and other amenities. 200 illustrations. 112pp. 8⅜ x 11.   0-486-44131-8

1000 TURN-OF-THE-CENTURY HOUSES: With Illustrations and Floor Plans, Herbert C. Chivers. Reproduced from a rare edition, this showcase of homes ranges from cottages and bungalows to sprawling mansions. Each house is meticulously illustrated and accompanied by complete floor plans. 256pp. 9⅜ x 12¼.
0-486-45596-3

101 GREAT AMERICAN POEMS, Edited by The American Poetry & Literacy Project. Rich treasury of verse from the 19th and 20th centuries includes works by Edgar Allan Poe, Robert Frost, Walt Whitman, Langston Hughes, Emily Dickinson, T. S. Eliot, other notables. 96pp. 5³⁄₁₆ x 8¼.   0-486-40158-8

101 GREAT SAMURAI PRINTS, Utagawa Kuniyoshi. Kuniyoshi was a master of the warrior woodblock print — and these 18th-century illustrations represent the pinnacle of his craft. Full-color portraits of renowned Japanese samurais pulse with movement, passion, and remarkably fine detail. 112pp. 8⅜ x 11.   0-486-46523-3

ABC OF BALLET, Janet Grosser. Clearly worded, abundantly illustrated little guide defines basic ballet-related terms: arabesque, battement, pas de chat, relevé, sissonne, many others. Pronunciation guide included. Excellent primer. 48pp. 4³⁄₁₆ x 5¾.
0-486-40871-X

ACCESSORIES OF DRESS: An Illustrated Encyclopedia, Katherine Lester and Bess Viola Oerke. Illustrations of hats, veils, wigs, cravats, shawls, shoes, gloves, and other accessories enhance an engaging commentary that reveals the humor and charm of the many-sided story of accessorized apparel. 644 figures and 59 plates. 608pp. 6 ⅛ x 9¼.
0-486-43378-1

ADVENTURES OF HUCKLEBERRY FINN, Mark Twain. Join Huck and Jim as their boyhood adventures along the Mississippi River lead them into a world of excitement, danger, and self-discovery. Humorous narrative, lyrical descriptions of the Mississippi valley, and memorable characters. 224pp. 5³⁄₁₆ x 8¼.   0-486-28061-6

ALICE STARMORE'S BOOK OF FAIR ISLE KNITTING, Alice Starmore. A noted designer from the region of Scotland's Fair Isle explores the history and techniques of this distinctive, stranded-color knitting style and provides copious illustrated instructions for 14 original knitwear designs. 208pp. 8⅜ x 10⅞.   0-486-47218-3

ALICE'S ADVENTURES IN WONDERLAND, Lewis Carroll. Beloved classic about a little girl lost in a topsy-turvy land and her encounters with the White Rabbit, March Hare, Mad Hatter, Cheshire Cat, and other delightfully improbable characters. 42 illustrations by Sir John Tenniel. 96pp. 5³⁄₁₆ x 8¼. 0-486-27543-4

AMERICA'S LIGHTHOUSES: An Illustrated History, Francis Ross Holland. Profusely illustrated fact-filled survey of American lighthouses since 1716. Over 200 stations — East, Gulf, and West coasts, Great Lakes, Hawaii, Alaska, Puerto Rico, the Virgin Islands, and the Mississippi and St. Lawrence Rivers. 240pp. 8 x 10¾.
0-486-25576-X

AN ENCYCLOPEDIA OF THE VIOLIN, Alberto Bachmann. Translated by Frederick H. Martens. Introduction by Eugene Ysaye. First published in 1925, this renowned reference remains unsurpassed as a source of essential information, from construction and evolution to repertoire and technique. Includes a glossary and 73 illustrations. 496pp. 6½ x 9¼. 0-486-46618-3

ANIMALS: 1,419 Copyright-Free Illustrations of Mammals, Birds, Fish, Insects, etc., Selected by Jim Harter. Selected for its visual impact and ease of use, this outstanding collection of wood engravings presents over 1,000 species of animals in extremely lifelike poses. Includes mammals, birds, reptiles, amphibians, fish, insects, and other invertebrates. 284pp. 9 x 12. 0-486-23766-4

THE ANNALS, Tacitus. Translated by Alfred John Church and William Jackson Brodribb. This vital chronicle of Imperial Rome, written by the era's great historian, spans A.D. 14-68 and paints incisive psychological portraits of major figures, from Tiberius to Nero. 416pp. 5³⁄₁₆ x 8¼. 0-486-45236-0

ANTIGONE, Sophocles. Filled with passionate speeches and sensitive probing of moral and philosophical issues, this powerful and often-performed Greek drama reveals the grim fate that befalls the children of Oedipus. Footnotes. 64pp. 5³⁄₁₆ x 8 ¼. 0-486-27804-2

ART DECO DECORATIVE PATTERNS IN FULL COLOR, Christian Stoll. Reprinted from a rare 1910 portfolio, 160 sensuous and exotic images depict a breathtaking array of florals, geometrics, and abstracts — all elegant in their stark simplicity. 64pp. 8⅜ x 11. 0-486-44862-2

THE ARTHUR RACKHAM TREASURY: 86 Full-Color Illustrations, Arthur Rackham. Selected and Edited by Jeff A. Menges. A stunning treasury of 86 full-page plates span the famed English artist's career, from *Rip Van Winkle* (1905) to masterworks such as *Undine, A Midsummer Night's Dream,* and *Wind in the Willows* (1939). 96pp. 8⅜ x 11.
0-486-44685-9

THE AUTHENTIC GILBERT & SULLIVAN SONGBOOK, W. S. Gilbert and A. S. Sullivan. The most comprehensive collection available, this songbook includes selections from every one of Gilbert and Sullivan's light operas. Ninety-two numbers are presented uncut and unedited, and in their original keys. 410pp. 9 x 12.
0-486-23482-7

THE AWAKENING, Kate Chopin. First published in 1899, this controversial novel of a New Orleans wife's search for love outside a stifling marriage shocked readers. Today, it remains a first-rate narrative with superb characterization. New introductory Note. 128pp. 5³⁄₁₆ x 8¼. 0-486-27786-0

BASIC DRAWING, Louis Priscilla. Beginning with perspective, this commonsense manual progresses to the figure in movement, light and shade, anatomy, drapery, composition, trees and landscape, and outdoor sketching. Black-and-white illustrations throughout. 128pp. 8⅜ x 11. 0-486-45815-6

THE BATTLES THAT CHANGED HISTORY, Fletcher Pratt. Historian profiles 16 crucial conflicts, ancient to modern, that changed the course of Western civilization. Gripping accounts of battles led by Alexander the Great, Joan of Arc, Ulysses S. Grant, other commanders. 27 maps. 352pp. 5⅜ x 8½. 0-486-41129-X

BEETHOVEN'S LETTERS, Ludwig van Beethoven. Edited by Dr. A. C. Kalischer. Features 457 letters to fellow musicians, friends, greats, patrons, and literary men. Reveals musical thoughts, quirks of personality, insights, and daily events. Includes 15 plates. 410pp. 5⅜ x 8½. 0-486-22769-3

BERNICE BOBS HER HAIR AND OTHER STORIES, F. Scott Fitzgerald. This brilliant anthology includes 6 of Fitzgerald's most popular stories: "The Diamond as Big as the Ritz," the title tale, "The Offshore Pirate," "The Ice Palace," "The Jelly Bean," and "May Day." 176pp. 5⅜ x 8½. 0-486-47049-0

BESLER'S BOOK OF FLOWERS AND PLANTS: 73 Full-Color Plates from Hortus Eystettensis, 1613, Basilius Besler. Here is a selection of magnificent plates from the *Hortus Eystettensis*, which vividly illustrated and identified the plants, flowers, and trees that thrived in the legendary German garden at Eichstätt. 80pp. 8⅜ x 11.
0-486-46005-3

THE BOOK OF KELLS, Edited by Blanche Cirker. Painstakingly reproduced from a rare facsimile edition, this volume contains full-page decorations, portraits, illustrations, plus a sampling of textual leaves with exquisite calligraphy and ornamentation. 32 full-color illustrations. 32pp. 9⅜ x 12¼. 0-486-24345-1

THE BOOK OF THE CROSSBOW: With an Additional Section on Catapults and Other Siege Engines, Ralph Payne-Gallwey. Fascinating study traces history and use of crossbow as military and sporting weapon, from Middle Ages to modern times. Also covers related weapons: balistas, catapults, Turkish bows, more. Over 240 illustrations. 400pp. 7¼ x 10⅝. 0-486-28720-3

THE BUNGALOW BOOK: Floor Plans and Photos of 112 Houses, 1910, Henry L. Wilson. Here are 112 of the most popular and economic blueprints of the early 20th century — plus an illustration or photograph of each completed house. A wonderful time capsule that still offers a wealth of valuable insights. 160pp. 8⅜ x 11.
0-486-45104-6

THE CALL OF THE WILD, Jack London. A classic novel of adventure, drawn from London's own experiences as a Klondike adventurer, relating the story of a heroic dog caught in the brutal life of the Alaska Gold Rush. Note. 64pp. 5³⁄₁₆ x 8¼.
0-486-26472-6

CANDIDE, Voltaire. Edited by Francois-Marie Arouet. One of the world's great satires since its first publication in 1759. Witty, caustic skewering of romance, science, philosophy, religion, government — nearly all human ideals and institutions. 112pp. 5³⁄₁₆ x 8¼. 0-486-26689-3

CELEBRATED IN THEIR TIME: Photographic Portraits from the George Grantham Bain Collection, Edited by Amy Pastan. With an Introduction by Michael Carlebach. Remarkable portrait gallery features 112 rare images of Albert Einstein, Charlie Chaplin, the Wright Brothers, Henry Ford, and other luminaries from the worlds of politics, art, entertainment, and industry. 128pp. 8⅜ x 11. 0-486-46754-6

CHARIOTS FOR APOLLO: The NASA History of Manned Lunar Spacecraft to 1969, Courtney G. Brooks, James M. Grimwood, and Loyd S. Swenson, Jr. This illustrated history by a trio of experts is the definitive reference on the Apollo spacecraft and lunar modules. It traces the vehicles' design, development, and operation in space. More than 100 photographs and illustrations. 576pp. 6¾ x 9¼. 0-486-46756-2

A CHRISTMAS CAROL, Charles Dickens. This engrossing tale relates Ebenezer Scrooge's ghostly journeys through Christmases past, present, and future and his ultimate transformation from a harsh and grasping old miser to a charitable and compassionate human being. 80pp. 5³⁄₁₆ x 8¼.   0-486-26865-9

COMMON SENSE, Thomas Paine. First published in January of 1776, this highly influential landmark document clearly and persuasively argued for American separation from Great Britain and paved the way for the Declaration of Independence. 64pp. 5³⁄₁₆ x 8¼.   0-486-29602-4

THE COMPLETE SHORT STORIES OF OSCAR WILDE, Oscar Wilde. Complete texts of "The Happy Prince and Other Tales," "A House of Pomegranates," "Lord Arthur Savile's Crime and Other Stories," "Poems in Prose," and "The Portrait of Mr. W. H." 208pp. 5³⁄₁₆ x 8¼.   0-486-45216-6

COMPLETE SONNETS, William Shakespeare. Over 150 exquisite poems deal with love, friendship, the tyranny of time, beauty's evanescence, death, and other themes in language of remarkable power, precision, and beauty. Glossary of archaic terms. 80pp. 5³⁄₁₆ x 8¼.   0-486-26686-9

THE COUNT OF MONTE CRISTO: Abridged Edition, Alexandre Dumas. Falsely accused of treason, Edmond Dantès is imprisoned in the bleak Chateau d'If. After a hair-raising escape, he launches an elaborate plot to extract a bitter revenge against those who betrayed him. 448pp. 5³⁄₁₆ x 8¼.   0-486-45643-9

CRAFTSMAN BUNGALOWS: Designs from the Pacific Northwest, Yoho & Merritt. This reprint of a rare catalog, showcasing the charming simplicity and cozy style of Craftsman bungalows, is filled with photos of completed homes, plus floor plans and estimated costs. An indispensable resource for architects, historians, and illustrators. 112pp. 10 x 7.   0-486-46875-5

CRAFTSMAN BUNGALOWS: 59 Homes from "The Craftsman," Edited by Gustav Stickley. Best and most attractive designs from Arts and Crafts Movement publication — 1903–1916 — includes sketches, photographs of homes, floor plans, descriptive text. 128pp. 8¼ x 11.   0-486-25829-7

CRIME AND PUNISHMENT, Fyodor Dostoyevsky. Translated by Constance Garnett. Supreme masterpiece tells the story of Raskolnikov, a student tormented by his own thoughts after he murders an old woman. Overwhelmed by guilt and terror, he confesses and goes to prison. 480pp. 5³⁄₁₆ x 8¼.   0-486-41587-2

THE DECLARATION OF INDEPENDENCE AND OTHER GREAT DOCUMENTS OF AMERICAN HISTORY: 1775-1865, Edited by John Grafton. Thirteen compelling and influential documents: Henry's "Give Me Liberty or Give Me Death," Declaration of Independence, The Constitution, Washington's First Inaugural Address, The Monroe Doctrine, The Emancipation Proclamation, Gettysburg Address, more. 64pp. 5³⁄₁₆ x 8¼.   0-486-41124-9

THE DESERT AND THE SOWN: Travels in Palestine and Syria, Gertrude Bell. "The female Lawrence of Arabia," Gertrude Bell wrote captivating, perceptive accounts of her travels in the Middle East. This intriguing narrative, accompanied by 160 photos, traces her 1905 sojourn in Lebanon, Syria, and Palestine. 368pp. 5⅜ x 8½.   0-486-46876-3

A DOLL'S HOUSE, Henrik Ibsen. Ibsen's best-known play displays his genius for realistic prose drama. An expression of women's rights, the play climaxes when the central character, Nora, rejects a smothering marriage and life in "a doll's house." 80pp. 5³⁄₁₆ x 8¼.   0-486-27062-9

DOOMED SHIPS: Great Ocean Liner Disasters, William H. Miller, Jr. Nearly 200 photographs, many from private collections, highlight tales of some of the vessels whose pleasure cruises ended in catastrophe: the *Morro Castle, Normandie, Andrea Doria, Europa,* and many others. 128pp. 8⅞ x 11¾.   0-486-45366-9

THE DORÉ BIBLE ILLUSTRATIONS, Gustave Doré. Detailed plates from the Bible: the Creation scenes, Adam and Eve, horrifying visions of the Flood, the battle sequences with their monumental crowds, depictions of the life of Jesus, 241 plates in all. 241pp. 9 x 12.   0-486-23004-X

DRAWING DRAPERY FROM HEAD TO TOE, Cliff Young. Expert guidance on how to draw shirts, pants, skirts, gloves, hats, and coats on the human figure, including folds in relation to the body, pull and crush, action folds, creases, more. Over 200 drawings. 48pp. 8¼ x 11.   0-486-45591-2

DUBLINERS, James Joyce. A fine and accessible introduction to the work of one of the 20th century's most influential writers, this collection features 15 tales, including a masterpiece of the short-story genre, "The Dead." 160pp. 5³⁄₁₆ x 8¼.
0-486-26870-5

EASY-TO-MAKE POP-UPS, Joan Irvine. Illustrated by Barbara Reid. Dozens of wonderful ideas for three-dimensional paper fun — from holiday greeting cards with moving parts to a pop-up menagerie. Easy-to-follow, illustrated instructions for more than 30 projects. 299 black-and-white illustrations. 96pp. 8⅞ x 11.
0-486-44622-0

EASY-TO-MAKE STORYBOOK DOLLS: A "Novel" Approach to Cloth Dollmaking, Sherralyn St. Clair. Favorite fictional characters come alive in this unique beginner's dollmaking guide. Includes patterns for Pollyanna, Dorothy from *The Wonderful Wizard of Oz,* Mary of *The Secret Garden,* plus easy-to-follow instructions, 263 black-and-white illustrations, and an 8-page color insert. 112pp. 8¼ x 11.   0-486-47360-0

EINSTEIN'S ESSAYS IN SCIENCE, Albert Einstein. Speeches and essays in accessible, everyday language profile influential physicists such as Niels Bohr and Isaac Newton. They also explore areas of physics to which the author made major contributions. 128pp. 5 x 8.   0-486-47011-3

EL DORADO: Further Adventures of the Scarlet Pimpernel, Baroness Orczy. A popular sequel to *The Scarlet Pimpernel,* this suspenseful story recounts the Pimpernel's attempts to rescue the Dauphin from imprisonment during the French Revolution. An irresistible blend of intrigue, period detail, and vibrant characterizations. 352pp. 5³⁄₁₆ x 8¼.   0-486-44026-5

ELEGANT SMALL HOMES OF THE TWENTIES: 99 Designs from a Competition, Chicago Tribune. Nearly 100 designs for five- and six-room houses feature New England and Southern colonials, Normandy cottages, stately Italianate dwellings, and other fascinating snapshots of American domestic architecture of the 1920s. 112pp. 9 x 12.   0-486-46910-7

THE ELEMENTS OF STYLE: The Original Edition, William Strunk, Jr. This is the book that generations of writers have relied upon for timeless advice on grammar, diction, syntax, and other essentials. In concise terms, it identifies the principal requirements of proper style and common errors. 64pp. 5⅜ x 8¼.   0-486-44798-7

THE ELUSIVE PIMPERNEL, Baroness Orczy. Robespierre's revolutionaries find their wicked schemes thwarted by the heroic Pimpernel — Sir Percival Blakeney. In this thrilling sequel, Chauvelin devises a plot to eliminate the Pimpernel and his wife. 272pp. 5³⁄₁₆ x 8¼.   0-486-45464-9

Browse over 9,000 books at www.doverpublications.com